I0593639

Jean Ingelow

Studies for Stories

Jean Ingelow

Studies for Stories

ISBN/EAN: 9783337006693

Printed in Europe, USA, Canada, Australia, Japan

Cover: Foto ©Andreas Hilbeck / pixelio.de

More available books at **www.hansebooks.com**

STUDIES FOR STORIES.

STUDIES FOR STORIES.

BY

JEAN INGELOW.

BOSTON:
ROBERTS BROTHERS.
1865.

AUTHOR'S EDITION.

Third Thousand.

UNIVERSITY PRESS:
WELCH, BIGELOW, AND COMPANY,
CAMBRIDGE.

CONTENTS.

THE CUMBERERS.

CHAPTER I.

SOME years ago, while staying at the seaside, my parents renewed their acquaintance with some ladies, whom we will call the Misses Perkins. They were the daughters of a clergyman deceased, and had a slender competence, on which they not only kept up a creditable appearance, but were charitable and useful.

It happened that, shortly before returning home, my parents remarked, in presence of these ladies, that they had intended to leave me behind for a time, because my health was delicate, but that some change of plan prevented the family with whom I was to have been domesticated from receiving me.

Hereupon significant looks passed between the sisters, and the next day a note arrived, which set forth, that though the Misses Perkins were not in the habit of receiving boarders, — far from it, — yet on this occasion they should be happy to step out of their usual path, and accommodate the daughter of their old friend.

Accordingly, I was sent to their house, and the ladies — that is, some of them — took care that I should derive all the benefit that care and kindness could secure to me.

The Misses Perkins covenanted to provide me with sea air, and, besides that, they provided me with many specu-

I *

lations on human life ; on the Providence which throws
certain characters together ; the changes they are intended
to work on one another ; the place each is fitted to fill in
this world ; the reason why some are privileged to be almost always helpers, while others are suffered to be uni-
formly hinderers ; and the cause why some, as it seems,
are compelled to exert themselves so much, while others,
it is evident, are determined to do so little.

But did the Misses Perkins intend to teach me all this ?
Certainly not ; they were by no means metaphysical in
their turn of mind and conversation. They were not given
to abstract speculation. They never talked of the object
of life, or of their missions. They had agreed that I
should have sea air, and I had it.

And now I will just describe to you the Misses Perkins,
their characters and occupations ; and you shall see
whether it was not natural that I should have cogitated on
them a little.

The three elder were the daughters of a first marriage,
and appeared to be from forty to forty-five years of age ;
the two younger were the children of a second marriage :
the elder was twenty-five, and the younger twenty-three
years of age.

Miss Perkins was a tall, bony woman, very plain, but
with a pleasant cheerfulness and activity about her. She
kept the house; and half its comfort, and nearly all its
superfluities, certainly arose from this circumstance. Assuredly she was not intellectual, but her love of order,
economy, and regularity made her a very useful person.
And I saw that if she were to die, her sisters, independently of their affection for her, would miss her sorely from
their household.

She was somewhat garrulous, and fond of describing
her day's occupations to me.

"You see, my dear," she would begin, " I always go out

directly after breakfast, because I cannot order dinner till I have been to the fishmonger's and the butcher's. Things vary very much in price, and it behooves me to buy what is both good and cheap. It would never do to send Mary, who is no judge, and just say, 'Buy soles,' or 'Buy whiting'; because just that day those particular fish might be both stale and dear, while cod was plentiful. No; I just look about for myself; and if all is dear, whý, I take none, but go off to the butcher, and get a larger joint of meat, and perhaps make up with a fruit pie. And there again, you know, servants have no discretion. If I were to say, 'Mary, go and buy damsons for a pie,' she would get them, though they were scarce and stale, and never think to tell me that apples were plentiful. No, my dear, depend on it, where the income is as limited as ours is, a great deal depends on seeing after everything one's self. It takes up a good deal of time, but I like to have a good and plentiful table. I don't like any stinting, or to have Amelia complain of the butter or the fruit, or say the tradespeople cheat us."

" Certainly, that would not be pleasant," I would remark.

" Not at all pleasant, my dear," she would reply; "so you see I have plenty to do; for I always make the pie-crust myself, Mary not being much of a cook. Indeed, we could not expect her to be, at the wages we give her. Her crusts are heavy. Well, all that pretty nearly takes up my morning; for, between ourselves, I very often wash the tea-things, shell peas, and do little things of that kind, so that all may go on quietly, and meals be ready at the right time; for I like them to have everything comfortable. And but for this kind of help, I assure you we should not be nearly so comfortable as we are."

I could easily believe this, and Miss Perkins said it as if it was the most natural thing in the world that she

should like these various occupations, as they added to
the happiness of others.

So much for the eldest Miss Perkins. She might perhaps have been called a twaddler in society, but in her
own sphere she was useful and beloved; and moreover,
by her economy and good marketing, she saved enough to
add greatly to the comfort of several poor old women and
sickly children, in whose behoof I often saw very savory-
looking messes carried out, smoking hot, in little tin cans,
with slices of bread laid on the top, by way of lids. Her
name was Robina, and her youngest sister called her
" Bobby."

The second sister, Miss Anne, was a particularly ladylike woman. She had delicate health, and required to be
very much in the open air. She also, as I soon saw, had
a decided line of work. She undertook almost the entire
management of the garden.

It was really a very good-sized garden, and was quite as
full of scarlet geraniums, heliotropes, and all the gayer
kinds of tender plants, as the gardens of the wealthier
neighbors.

Miss Anne, I understood, took great pains to nurse
young plants through the winter, keeping them in sunny
windows and in a dry store-room. And it was surprising
to see how, every day, she conscientiously went out, and
worked among her flower-beds; regularly setting herself
a certain task, and doing it as a duty. She had no help,
excepting that a little boy came once a week to weed the
walks. And I observed that she by no means confined
herself to the care of the flowers, but cultivated beetroot,
lettuces, and all kinds of vegetables.

" You see, my dear," Miss Robina remarked to me, " we
could not afford to keep a man : it would not pay us, but
all that Ann can raise is pure gain ; for we save seeds, and
exchange cuttings with our neighbors. The flower-garden

costs nothing, and besides being a pleasure to us all, it now looks creditable and cheerful; and if Anne did not spend her mornings in it, it would run to waste, for neither Sarah nor I have time to attend to it. And you know it would be very disheartening to us to live in a wilderness; it would affect our spirits. Now I say that Providence fits us beautifully for our several spheres: for Anne is able to sit indoors very little; but, by taking the garden under her care, she provides herself with occupation, and prevents herself from thinking that she is of no use. She keeps us always gay and neat, and besides, without robbing the garden of more flowers than we can well spare, she gives away many every season to a poor orphan girl who sells them, and thus gains money enough to clothe herself. You must have observed Anne's violet-bed, my dear?"

"Yes"; I said I had done so, and noticed how carefully they were watered and weeded.

Miss Robina smiled. "Anne calls them her charity purse," she replied. "Those autumn violets are very much liked by the visitors. Anne found it rather a burden to her, when first we came here, to spend so much time in the garden, but she was determined to go through with it, and now she likes it very much. I don't know what we should do without her, I am sure; for I don't know anything more melancholy than living in a garden full of weeds; and Amelia, who is so subject to low spirits, often complains as it is, when Anne goes out, or is ill, so that the place gets a little disorderly."

So much for the second sister: let me now introduce you to the third.

Of Miss Sarah Perkins it might certainly be affirmed, that neither in person, voice, nor manner was she an attractive individual. Excepting when she took her daily walk, she was almost always seated near a window, at work. She certainly would have thought it a great hardship to go shopping, or tend flower-beds. She was never asked to do so: on the contrary, it seemed to be an understood thing that the pleasantest corner of the window belonged to her, and that there her little table and her great work-basket were to stand. She was to begin to stitch, and no one was to molest her.

I did not, at first, particularly like Miss Sarah. She was blunt, and not so much of a gentlewoman as the other sisters; and sometimes when I went out with Miss Perkins to see her favorite poor people, I used to be surprised at the fervor with which they would inquire after her; and I really could not commend their taste, for I thought her by no means interesting, and perhaps a little snappish sometimes. But Miss Perkins one day put an end to my wonder. "You see, my dear," she began, for every speech of hers had this little exordium; "you see, my dear, it is a very fortunate thing for us that Sarah is willing to devote herself to her needle as she does; for Anne and I have very little time, and Amelia could never bear work, excepting fancy-work. Now, fancy-work, such as crochet and lambs'-wool patterns, are pretty, no doubt, but they are not of much use in a family like ours. However, Amelia considers it not lady-like to sit turning gowns or darning table-cloths in the drawing-room; and as she never sits anywhere else, she does no work but what is fit for that room. So, as I was saying, my dear," she continued, "it is a most fortunate thing that Sarah is so willing to work for us all. She does nearly all our plain work, and as to trimming bonnets, making mantles, turning gowns and cloaks, and everything of that kind, she so entirely undertakes it all, that a dressmaker's bill is almost unknown to us. She has such an eye for a pattern, my dear; and that, you know, is a great advantage. We should often look very shabby, if it was not for her. And then, it is surprising how she can cut down gowns and cloaks, and turn them, and make them look decent and creditable for the poor, and with what a little expense she can make warm quilts and wraps for our poor old rheumatic neighbors. It would be a sad thing for us, and for a good many beside us, if anything were to happen to Sarah."

These were the ladies of the first family.

I now come to the character of her who caused me so many doubts and speculations. My doubts were (among others) what the mission of Miss Amelia Perkins could possibly be in this world, and my speculations were (among others) as to who would be the worse off if she were taken from it, and who would be the better.

Miss Amelia Perkins never did anything.

Let me not, however, be misunderstood. When I say that she never did anything, I mean that she never did anything that she designed to be for the comfort or assistance of others. There were no duties that she habitually performed; there was no place that she occupied; no one looked to her, or depended on her for anything; no one seemed to be the better for her; she seemed to have no more to do with the course of that stream of life on which she floated than the least little piece of weed may have, that, being detached from its stem, goes sailing down its native brook towards the sea.

Miss Amelia Perkins was moderately good-looking, and to strangers had rather a pleasing manner. She thought it unladylike ever to bustle and be in a hurry, as her sisters sometimes were; she often said people could do what they had to do without that. Accordingly, she was never in a bustle; but then, as I said before, she never had anything particular to do.

She felt that it was a painful thing to be in straitened circumstances, and soon confided this pain to me. She said it often weighed on her spirits, and her sisters, being less sensitive, did not so much feel the trial of it. "And it seems so hard," she said, "to have so little to spend on one's clothes; the others, not having much taste in dress, don't mind it. Besides, being so much older, it matters less to them."

"Excepting your sister Bessie," I observed.

"O yes, Bessie," she replied, "Bessie."

"Well," I remarked, "is it not natural that Bessie should like to be well dressed?"

"Oh, Bessie," she repeated: "why, Bessie is so very plain, that it would be absurd in her to expect to be admired, even if she were handsomely dressed."

I replied that I had always heard it said, that the handsomer people were, the less dependent they were on dress.

Miss Amelia did not appear to agree with my remark, and when I went on to say that I thought Bessie a remarkably happy person, and one who seemed particularly contented, she replied that she supposed Bessie was satisfied with her lot; she saw no reason why she should be otherwise; and then she said that all her sisters were very fond of Bessie. "In fact," she continued, "every one must see what an unfair difference they make between us."

I could not but open my eyes at this, and purposely misunderstanding her, I said, "You mean, perhaps, that they always ask Bessie to do the errands, and write the letters, and read the newspaper to Miss Sarah, while she is at work; things which they never think of asking you to do. Yes, that does seem rather unfair."

Miss Amelia, on this, fixed her cold gray eyes on me, and not being quite sure whether I spoke in earnest or in irony, sat down to the piano, and never favored me with any further confidence. Notwithstanding which, we became so thoroughly aware, Miss Amelia and myself, that we mutually disliked each other, that we shortly made it evident to the other ladies of the family; in consequence of which, I received some hints from the excellent Miss Sarah, which I thought it incumbent on me to attend to.

You must know that Miss Bessie Perkins had a great wish to learn sketching, and I offered to teach her; but as she had a good deal to do in helping her sisters, several days passed before she could take a lesson. One very clear afternoon, Bessie announced that she could go with me; and we were ready, and just about to start, when she exclaimed, "Oh, the letter! I quite forgot it. How troublesome!"

"Must it be written to day?" I inquired.

"O yes," she replied; "because it is a business letter to our trustees, and Sarah is going to dictate it to me."

"Then one person can write it as well as another," said I, mischievously; "you had better ask Amelia to do it."

"Amelia is just beginning to practise," said Bessie; and in truth I heard the old cracked piano sounding up stairs.

"I will tell her you want to go out," I exclaimed, "and no doubt she will write it, for she has been out." So I ran up stairs, and delivered my message. Miss Amelia's brow clouded: "It really is a strange thing," said she, "that Bessie cannot do her own business herself. I heard her myself, at breakfast-time, offer to write that letter."

"But she has been helping Miss Sarah all the morning," said I, "and I did not know that the letter was more her business than yours."

"Sarah should have released her sooner," said Amelia, coldly.

Finding me bent on gaining my point, she at last said that perhaps she might do it when she had done practising; but on my reminding her that that would be too late for the post, she began again at the piano, and as I could obtain no satisfactory answer as to whether she would or would not do it, I was obliged to shut the door, and come down stairs again in no very amiable humor, for

B

I was angry that my favorite Bessie was to be debarred of her walk, and that Amelia should be allowed to enjoy the fruits of all her sisters' labors without contributing anything to them.   Bessie had already taken off her bonnet, and was writing at Miss Sarah's dictation.

"Miss Sarah," I· began — "I understand, my dear," she answered, nodding ; "we shall find it less trouble by far to do it ourselves than get it done for us."

She did not speak bitterly, but as if it was a matter of course.

As the affair was no business of mine, it was a pity that I interfered further in it, by saying, "Miss Sarah, whose gown are you mending ? "

She smiled, as if amused at my remark and my heat in the matter, and replied that it was Amelia's.   "I know Amelia means to go out again and see the steamer come in," she said ; "and I don't choose she should do it with her gown in this state."

"But," said I, "if it were not mended, she could not go out, and then she would have time to write the letter."   ·

"Yes, my dear, she could," said Miss Sarah; "and it would be a discredit to us — I 've been ashamed of it some time past — or she could wear her best gown, and that we cannot afford."

This explanation was unanswerable.   "Come, my dear," said Miss Sarah, who just then was in a very good humor, "suppose you help me a little."   So saying, she put a sleeve into my hand, and I took it with a very good grace, for I was ashamed of having interfered.   And I sat down quietly, and proceeded to trim it with fresh gimp.

When the letter was finished, I returned the sleeve, and Miss Sarah asked me if I felt any cooler; she laughed, and I could not forbear saying that there were some things which provoked my temper very much.

"My dear," she answered, and hesitated, but presently

proceeded, with a sigh, "you would find this provocation quite beyond your powers to set right."

"I am sure if I were you," I said, "I should not be so patient."

"Sarah," said Bessie, laughing, "Miss T. says she cannot think what Amelia's mission is, — I told her Amelia had no particular mission."

"Did you, child?" said Miss Sarah. "Well, if Miss T. lived here long, she would find that Amelia had a very decided mission."

"What may it be, Miss Sarah?" I inquired.

"To teach you forbearance and patience, my dear," she answered, "and try your temper; for at present I think you are ignorant what sort of a temper you happen to have. Ah! we none of us know what we are, till we are tried."

"But, Miss Sarah," I replied, "it seems shocking to think that some people should be sent into the world to teach others forbearance, only by being useless or unaccommodating."

"My dear," she answered, "far be it from me to say that the Almighty *designed* any of his creatures for such a purpose; I meant, that if we do not perform the good part that we all have it in our power to take upon us, God will make our evil subservient to the good of others. God will turn our very faults into blessings, for our neighbors. But, my dear, poor Amelia is young, and we have no right to judge her; we hope she may improve, and I feel sorry that I have been betrayed into speaking hastily of her."

So saying, Miss Sarah rose, and folding up the dress, sent Bessie up stairs with it. After which, we went to sketch; and for Miss Amelia's further doings, I must refer you to my next chapter.

CHAPTER II.

WHEN an author has no startling novelty in sentiment, no thrilling incident, no forcible argument
to present to a reader, is it of any use to inform the reader
of·the fact, and occupy time in apologies for the same?
Or shall the reader be left to find it out for himself, as he
assuredly will do?

Much may be said on both sides.

In general I take the second course, for never having
any startling novelties of sentiment, or thrilling incidents,
or forcible arguments to present, I might always be apologizing.

But at the present moment I feel inclined to take the
first course. The history of a Cumberer, dear reader, or
fair reader, or gentle reader, or whatever else that is complimentary, you expect to be called, (according to the deceitful practice of authors, who are too much in the habit
of flattering you with ideas of your superiority to themselves!) the history of a Cumberer can only contain accounts of those duties which the said Cumberer did not
perform, those incidents in which she took no part, those
projects which she hindered, those hours which she wasted,
those talents which she did not improve, those acquaintances who wished her away, and those relations who bore
with her as with a cross appointed for them. Such is this
history, and I apologize; but I will not again address you,
my reader, by any endearing name, or any name which
takes for granted imaginary excellences, since for anything I

know you may be a Cumberer; and since, if I had not felt morally certain that among my readers were some characters like Miss Amelia Perkins, I never would have set my pen to these pages.

But what, after all, did Amelia Perkins do, and what did she leave undone, that she is so severely spoken of? Let me answer the question by an illustration. If you have a piano, one note of which in the treble is mute, not one tune, even of the simplest kind, can be played on it, — no music worth having can be drawn from it, without making this defect manifest; and yet the note is not actively offensive, it merely does not sound. But now suppose your note not mute, but merely out of harmony with the others, would it not spoil your music still?

Now, call the piano a family, and call the Cumberer a faulty note, and you at once see the harm she does; she makes the tune imperfect when it does not sound, and when it does sound, jars.

But to return to my story.

Bessie and I went out to sketch, and, sitting on the warm sea-beach, we talked together about many things, and among those things, about Amelia.

" It surprises me to see you all take this so coolly," I said.

" How can we help it?" answered Bessie. " Sometimes Bobby says she thinks it was at school that Amelia learned to be ashamed of making herself useful in the house."

" But that does not apply to writing letters."

" No; but there are many things that she thinks not proper for a gentlewoman's occupation, and she does not do them."

" She went to school, then?"

" Yes, to be sure. The elder ones thought we ought to have a good education, for the property we live on is principally theirs. It was their mother's, and does not come to

us when they die.   Bobby blames herself for sending us to
such a good school, but then Anne says, if we had gone
to an inferior one we should not have learnt accomplishments so well; and as we may have to live by teaching,
if we survive our sisters, they thought accomplishments
necessary."

So, then, it was through the kindness and self-denial of
her sisters that Miss Amelia had learnt those accomplishments which gave her now, as she thought, a right to despise them !

How many mothers there are who are in the same case !
How many parents have toiled to give their children advantages which they principally use in finding out those
parents' deficiencies !

I went on diligently with the sketching, and said nothing, but, unlike the parrot in the fable, " I thought the
more."

That night, after I was in bed, I heard a great deal of
noise in the street, but it did not hinder me from going to
sleep, though it filled my dreams with impressions of jan-
gling bells, rumbling carts, passing footsteps, and great
confusion.

I woke later than usual, and, to my astonishment, was
told that scarcely a person in the town had slept but myself, for that a village, not two miles off, was discovered at
midnight to be on fire in three places.   The cottages were
thatched and closely built, and by sunrise were almost entirely burnt down.

There was great commotion in the town all that day;
the sufferers were lodged in the public library, a soup
kitchen was opened, committees were formed, and the
ladies of the town set a clothing fund on foot, and, to
make the money go further, agreed to cut out and make
all the garments themselves.

Now it happened that Amelia, during a visit, had made

the acquaintance of a certain Mrs. Blount, — the Honorable Mrs. Blount, of G—— Hall, — and had contrived to please her very much. This lady had just arrived at the place with her family, and Amelia was only waiting till a certain etiquette, peculiar to the place, had been complied with, to call upon her.

Being charitable and influential, this lady was chosen to canvass a portion of the town for the clothing fund, and when Amelia heard it she became extremely anxious that everything in their house and garden should appear to the best advantage during Mrs. Blount's call. She dressed early in her best, and was seated in the drawing-room, occupied with some elegant piece of fancy-work, when Mrs. Blount was announced, with Captain White, her brother.

They sat a few minutes with Amelia, and then the sisters entered, bringing me with them to contribute my mite.

Mrs. Blount unfolded her errand, and Miss Anne said that they heartily approved of the cause, and gave most willingly, though they could give but little.

Mrs. Blount politely remarked, that if all families gave a little, the sufferers would have no reason to complain.

Miss Bobby then produced the purse, and laid some money on the table. I saw Amelia color and look annoyed as her eye dropped on the money.

Mrs. Blount received it graciously. " And will you help us to make up some of the clothing ?" said she, persuasively.

" With pleasure," cried Bobby.

" With all my heart," said Miss Ann.

" I shall be very happy," said Miss Sarah. They all spoke at once, and Bessie and I expressed our wish to join.

" There is nearly a week to do it in," said Mrs. Blount. " On Saturday evening it is to be returned finished; how much may I send ?"

"You are reckoning on my assistance of course, dear Mrs. Blount," said Amelia.

"O yes," said Mrs. Blount, smiling, and laying her hand on Amelia's arm, "*that*, of course, but don't over-fatigue yourself, my dear. Miss Perkins, I hope you don't allow Amelia to do *too* much."

There was an awkward silence for an instant, then Miss Anne came to the rescue of Bobby. "My dear sister is so careful of our comfort," she said kindly, "that no one is overworked here when it depends upon her."

Miss Sarah then named a certain number of garments of different kinds. "We can do so much," she said, "and return them punctually."

"Is that all?" said Amelia. And to do her justice she spoke in ignorance, for she knew very little about plain work.

"O, my dear," said Mrs. Blount, in a low voice, "you must not measure every one's zeal by your own"; then added aloud, "I am sure your sister's offer is most liberal."

"It is not a question of how much we are willing to do," said Miss Sarah, "but how much we *can do in the time*. And the case being urgent, I think if we all help, so much can be done in the time, and no more."

I thought it seemed rather a pity, when Amelia was so anxious to help, that more was not undertaken.

As soon as Mrs. Blount had retired, Amelia gave her opinion very freely. "Such a beggarly subscription!" she exclaimed. "I'm sure Mrs. Blount will think us so mean. Why can't Robina give a little more for once, instead of lowering us in the eyes of such fashionable people?"

"We can but give what we have got," said Anne, calmly.

Amelia turned away muttering, "Then why can't we take more of the work? I'm sure I could do twice as much, and I would, rather than Mrs. Blount should think we care nothing for what she is so zealous about; it looks so mean."

"What I have taken I shall divide into seven shares," said Miss Sarah, "two for myself, and one for each of you, and if we do that we shall all do well. I hope Miss T., my dear, you remembered that it would entail some trouble on you when you offered to join."

"O yes, Miss Sarah; I shall not go out so much till my share is done."

"Excuse me, my dear; you are here on purpose to be out in the air."

"How shall I do the work, then, Miss Sarah?"

"Why, my dear, you spend a good deal of time indoors in reading, and singing, and drying sea-weeds (and very pretty occupations those are for your age, I am sure); I advise you to give up all that for this week, or else there is still time to tell Mrs. Blount not to send so much work."

But no, I did not choose to give in; and as Miss Sarah had spoken to me rather as to a child, I was the more resolved to show that I was quite equal to womanly responsibilities. So I said, rather more decidedly than the occasion called for, that indoors I would touch nothing but a needle till my share was done.

The work then arrived, and Miss Sarah divided it, taking a double quantity to herself.

She had just finished the division when Amelia came in, and considering how anxious she had been that more should be taken, it was surprising how she grumbled at the size of the bundles. She inspected them all, and said they were very unfairly divided, some were far harder than others.

"I don't think so," said Miss Sarah; "but if it is so, the advantage is yours, my dear; you have the first choice."

After tumbling them over for some minutes, Amelia chose a bundle for herself, and then one was given to me.

2

It certainly was large, and perhaps my face betrayed a little dismay, for Miss Sarah presently put a shirt which she had already fixed into my hand, and said, " There, go on with that, child, while I fix some of yours for you."

Right glad was I of this help; she put as much work in train for me as I could possibly do in one day, and then took back her own.

I set to work cheerfully; she had removed all my difficulties; but she had no sooner resumed her own needle, than Amelia remarked on the unfairness of her proceedings.

" There is Miss T., with a much easier bundle than mine, and yet you fix, and fit, and set for her, and expect me to get mine done in the same time. Why, the fixing is more than half the trouble."

" I wonder you are not ashamed to compare yourself to *that child*," whispered Miss Sarah, once more throwing down her own work; " here, give your piece to me."

It makes me smile now to remember the mingled indignation and shame with which I heard the words "that child."

Had I finished my education, and was I a head taller than Miss Sarah, and should I be called a child? I had taken to my heart the comfortable doctrine that a person could but be grown-up, consequently I was as much grown-up as a woman of fifty. Yet the world would persist in making all sorts of allowances for me that I did not thank them for, because of my years; how very hard.

I mention this, as in fairness bound, because it urged me on to redoubled diligence; and no dress-maker working for her bread ever gave her mind more entirely to her work than I did mine for that first evening.

One by one the sisters dropped in, and we were all hard at work and cheerful, excepting Amelia, who occupied a good deal of time in grumbling about her bundle, and arguing with Bessie as to the comparative hardness of linen and calico.

At length she settled down, worked for an hour, and then declared that she had a pain under her left shoulder.

"That is very common," said Miss Sarah, "with people who are not accustomed to sit at the needle."

But Amelia declared she was accustomed to it; and began to argue about that, till she made herself quite cross; and then she said that as things did not seem to go on comfortably, perhaps she had better read aloud, for there was nothing but arguing.

The sisters agreed. I suppose they thought it was a good change, for she was doing very little work, and annoying them by her temper. So Amelia got a book, but it appeared that she had read the first two chapters, and when they said they had *not*, she opened her cold, gray eyes, and asked if they expected her to begin again.

"No," said Bobby, "go on where you are."

So Amelia went on; but the book contained a story, and she read a page or two with several interruptions, such as — "Who is Mrs. Duncan?" "Why, I told you she was the heroine's mother." "Ay, so you did; pass the cotton, Bobby." "And who is this paternal friend?" "O, I told you before I began, that she lived with an old uncle." "Ah, that's him then; just tell Mary to tell the baker we don't want any cottage bread, Bessie; I see him coming up to the door. Well, go on, Amelia."

"O, if you take so little interest, I might as well spare myself the trouble," said Amelia, in her most morose tones. "It's very disheartening to go on and nobody attending."

"I thought you were reading for us, not yourself," said Miss Sarah.

"So I am," answered Amelia, with asperity.

"Then we must stop you when it does n't suit us to listen," replied Sarah.

"We can attend now," said Miss Anne, and the reading went on ; evidently teasing the good ladies very much, for the baker sent in a message, and a whispered answer had to be returned by Mary, and there were half-pence wanted to make up the change for his bill ; this had to be made known by grimaces to the sisters, and one and another produced pence from her pocket, till the amount was sufficient, and then an odd penny rolled under the table, and Bessie stooped to pick it up, while a whisper went round that the black cotton reel was missing, and Bessie diving once more, bumped her head, upon which they all cried out, "Bless me !" This was too much ; Amelia shut the book with a sudden jerk, and exclaimed, "If you 're determined not to hear, I may as well read to myself."

"Do," said Miss Sarah ; accordingly she did, and so ended the first evening, much more pleasantly, I must say, than it had begun.

Not to make a short story long, on Tuesday evening Amelia was very much behindhand. On Wednesday, when walking-time came, she asked me to go and call with her on the Blounts. I could have no objection, and she came up with me to my room, chose what she wished me to wear, and dressed me herself with great attention ; then she arrayed herself in her best, and we paid our call.

I was surprised, and felt rather ashamed of the way in which she spoke of her sisters to Mrs. Blount. I was sure it would give her friend the impression that they were purposely eccentric, dressed shabbily from mere love of singularity, and for the same reason made their own dresses and cakes themselves.

It flashed into my mind that she had superintended my toilet and taken me with her because I was better dressed than her excellent sisters would have been. I was ashamed of myself for suspecting her motive, when I found she was leading me to mention some people of rank in our neighborhood, with whom I happened to have been staying. She did it so cleverly that I was a mere tool in her hands, and I thought she wished to exalt her companion by way of raising herself.

But when we had left the house, it seemed to me that I must have fancied all this, till she took me to pay another call, and there tried to do the same thing; but though I was afraid of her, I had sense enough to thwart her.

"Bless me, my dear, what a pretty dress!" said the simple-hearted Miss Bobby, when I came in.

Miss Sarah asked me to approach her, that she might see how the skirt was trimmed; I obeyed, and while displaying it, Amelia went up stairs, and I discovered to my surprise that the sisters did not know she meant to pay her call that day, and when she did, had fully intended to accompany her.

That evening I again took my walk, and the other ladies being busy at work, Amelia went with me, stipulating that as she was *obliged* to go, some one should work at her bundle in the mean time. I knew as well as her sisters did that she wished to go, though she thus made a merit of it, but neither they nor I supposed that she would remain out till it was dark, that more of her work might be done.

I knew that it was not customary for two young ladies to be walking about in the dusk among crowds of fine folks, but Amelia took me out so far that I was sure it would be very late when we reached home. At last she turned, and we began to walk back quickly, but just in the most public part of the beach she heard a voice that she knew, and ashamed of being seen, she seized my hand and hurried me to an empty bathing-machine; in an instant she had dragged me up the steps. "Come in here," she whispered, "Mrs. Blount is coming, and I would n't have her see me out here at night for a good deal; so very unfashionable!"

I felt heartily ashamed as she pushed me into a corner. The voices and footsteps approached; unfortunately Mrs. Blount and her companion took it into their heads to sit down on the steps, and we were obliged to overhear their conversation.

There was nothing but canvas between us, and the voices were quite distinct. "Her father is Mr. T——, the author of ——; they are a Highland family."

"Poor and proud, no doubt, like the rest of the clan," said another voice.

Something followed that I did not hear; my cheeks were tingling with shame at this enforced listening, and Mrs. Blount's voice went on still speaking of me. "Yes, a tall slip of a girl, very insipid, and no companion for *her*, but a lady, and that's something."

"Ah!" rejoined the manly voice, "I pity that sweet Amelia, condemned to live with those second-rate old quizzes."

Mrs. Blount sighed, "Poor Amelia; I must have her a good deal with me while I'm here"; and then they got up and walked on, saying how late it was, and we sneaked out of the machine and went home; Amelia in a state of the highest elation, and I of the deepest indignation and shame.

There were the *second-rate* sisters hard at work, and Amelia, when asked why she was so late, condescended to scarcely any answer, and took up her candle with an air of easy superiority.

The next day at breakfast a note arrived from Mrs. Blount, asking Amelia to join a yachting party at ten o'clock, and bring her young friend with her.

"O, of course we shall go," cried Amelia.

"Let Miss T. speak for herself," said Bobby.

As Amelia was to be of the party, it was no self-denial to me to decline, which I did, saying, that if I went I could not finish my share of work.

But Amelia was determined; it was cruel, she declared, to deprive her of almost the only friend she cared about, the only person that was congenial to her, or sympathized with her, so little society as she had, so little to vary her existence in that dull place.

At last her sisters were worked upon so far as to ask me to go as a favor to themselves; but the conversation in the bathing-machine was fresh in my mind, and I held back. And none of themselves could go, for unluckily Mrs. Blount had put in a " P. S. — If your young friend cannot come, we shall hope to see you *both* some other day"; thus taking care to exclude those whom she had ignorantly called second-rate people.

Now I knew the work was almost more than we could do, and besides (potent reason!), I had been called a child; I knew the housekeeping and gardening and exercise had to be set aside for it, and had heard discussions as to how late on Saturday it could with propriety be sent in; so I still said I wished to do my work, and proposed to Amelia that we should wait and both go another time.

But she was much my senior, and had made me a little afraid of her; she was determined to go, and after a very disagreeable scene, in which she accused her sisters of persuading a delicate young girl to sit indoors sewing to the injury of her health, moping and toiling, which she was sure her parents never intended, she so far prevailed as to make all the family bent upon my accepting the invitation. I saw they had been touched on a tender point, and were much pained. I declared that I had taken the work to please myself, but was so sorry to see their flushed faces that I gave way, and went up stairs to dress, but in such an ill humor, and so indignant, that I took care to let Amelia know that I was only going to please her sisters, and not to please *her*.

I will not attempt to describe the events of that miserable day. Nicely dressed, and rendered a little more good-tempered by our walk in the fresh air, Amelia and I presented ourselves at the appointed place. We were received with smiling cordiality, and we embarked.

The sun sparkled on the water, but the wind began to freshen, and our cheeks began to fade, till shortly, with two other miserable girls of the party, we were led down stairs, and shut up in the little cabin, and there we dragged out a wretched existence till it was quite dark night. The rest of the company, not being ill, enjoyed themselves; they had music and a splendid collation, and they made a great noise.

It was ten o'clock when the yacht made the pier, and we crawled out, finding Miss Perkins and Sarah waiting for us in some anxiety, for they thought some accident must have happened to make us so late.

But I must defer the remainder of my recollections for a future chapter.

CHAPTER III.

AMELIA OFFERS HER SERVICES.

IT was quite dark, when, exhausted and faint, Amelia and I were led home by Miss Perkins and Sarah. They put us to bed, and gave us dry toast and hot wine and water. Sarah attended to Amelia, and I fell to Miss Bobby's share. I heard the motherly creature lamenting over me ; wishing she had let me stay at home, and declaring that anxiety had made her quite wretched about us both, for she had thought how it would be when the wind began to rise, and (kind-hearted woman !) had been wishing all day that she had been there instead of us, for she could n't bear young people to be disappointed when they went out expecting to enjoy themselves.

Miss Robina was still sitting by my bed, consoling and petting, when I fell into a sound sleep, and happily forgot my troubles.

It is curious how sometimes a little sound heard in sleep will influence and change the current of our dreams. It was natural that I should dream of the yacht, but odd that I should mingle with this the idea of stitching. I dreamed that it was dark night, and that, seated on the deck, Bobby and Sarah were hard at work, mending the torn sail of the yacht. The wind had sunk ; it was a dead calm, and the water so still that I could see the reflection of the stars on its black surface ; some candles were burning beside us, but hard as the sisters worked, the rent seemed to grow under their hands. I was trying to help, and had a miserable certainty that till this sail could be put up, we never could reach the land; therefore I was frightened to find fresh holes every moment, and to hear Bobby say, "How ever this is to be done I don't know." I thought how shocking it would be if we never could reach the land again; but in another instant Sarah said, in such a distinct voice, "Pass the cotton-reel," that I sprang up half-awake, exclaiming that I could not find it.

I saw a candle in my room; Sarah and Robina were sitting hard at work by my table. I heard the sound of their needles just as before in my dream, but it was not a sail they were working on, it was one of those bundles of clothes. Miss Bobby was at my side in an instant. I exclaimed against this sitting up, said I was quite well, and did not require anything. She replied that I was very feverish, and she could not have slept even if she had gone to bed. "Besides, my dear, I thought you would like a cup of tea; the teapot is kept hot for you, and Amelia has just had some."

I could not decline this tempting offer. Miss Perkins presently brought me some tea; and when I expressed my regret at giving this trouble, she declared that she and Sarah had decided to sit up till four o'clock to get on with the work, for they knew that Amelia and I would be fit for very little the next day. "And you see, my dear, when we were up, it was no trouble just to steal down and keep up the kitchen fire. And neither of you was well enough to be left the first part of the night, so it was fortunate that we had this work to do, was n't it? it was something to keep us awake."

Kind, good creature!

She and Miss Sarah shortly retired to bed, leaving me, as I thought, quite well; but on coming down the next morning I found I could do very little, and that Amelia was lying on the sofa in a very feverish state of mind, sure that if she could have some beef tea she should be better,

and then, when Bobby had made her some (Mary not being a good hand at it), discovering that if she could have
had it earlier in the day it would have done her good, but
now she did n't like it. In short, Amelia was very cross ;
and but for seeing how unpleasant she was when she gave
way to her temper, very likely I should have been cross too.

The sisters sat all the morning hard at work. Amelia's
bundle was scarcely begun, mine was one whole day behindhand, yet the work was promised for Saturday, and
must not be late, because the poor families were to appear
at the different places of worship on Sunday, when some
further collections were to be made for them.

Yet though Amelia knew this, she made several de-
mands upon her sisters' time, and never said a word which
seemed to intimate that she was sorry she had been the
cause of all this extra work, hurry, and fatigue, or that she
was sorry she had been so bent upon the yachting party.
As for me, I believe I could have worked if I had been
allowed to do so ; but being under their care, these generous women could not bear that there should be the least
shadow of cause for Amelia's accusation that I was shut
up indoors and induced to work by them ; they therefore
took advantage of their authority and my youth to forbid
my working at all that day.

In the afternoon Mrs. Blount called to inquire how we
were, and took Amelia and myself for a drive in her pony
carriage. I sat behind, Amelia in front, and I scarcely
heard any of the conversation, excepting once when we
stopped at a gardener's ground, that Mrs. Blount might
buy some fine calceolarias. While we were waiting for
them, I heard her say carelessly, as if referring to a matter
of no consequence, " I suppose you were obliged to give
some of the work you took to your servants." I did not
hear Amelia's answer ; but Mrs. Blount's remark was not
without its effect, for when Amelia came in and found her

sisters hard at work in the hot parlor, she remarked on the folly of their giving themselves all the trouble, and asked why they did not give some of the work to Fanny the housemaid.

"She has not time for more work than I always expect of her," said Miss Perkins.

"She might do this instead, for once," proceeded Amelia.

"Then I should have to do hers," said Miss Bobby, "and what would be the good of that?"

But Amelia was not convinced. "Other people's servants contrive to find time," she said. "Mrs Blount tells me that her maid and the nurse have done a great deal of that work this week."

"Humph," said Sarah.

"And then there's Mary," continued Amelia; "really I do n't know what she finds to do."

"You know very little about a cook's work," said Anne, calmly; "your saying so is a proof of it."

Her dispassionate manner seemed to communicate itself to Miss Perkins, who said, more good-humoredly than before, "Mary has a good deal to do this week that I generally undertake myself."

"But there's the evening, at any rate," persisted Amelia, who could not bear to be always proved in the wrong. "When she has washed the dishes, what can she have to do more?"

"Why, if you really want to know," said Bessie, with some heat, "she has to pluck the fowls that we are going to have for dinner to-morrow, and she has an errand to do."

"Moreover," said Bobby, "she is a very poor hand with her needle, and I should be sorry to trust her with the work, even if she had time."

Amelia said it was a very strange thing; and on my remarking, as we walked up stairs to take off our bonnets, that her sisters all looked flushed and tired, she said, "No-

body shall ever make me believe that our servants cannot
work like other people's."

" But only consider," said I, " Mrs. Blount's maid has
nothing to do but to wait on her personally ; and as for the
nurse, there is only that one little girl to attend. She can
sit at work for hours on the beach, while the child plays at
her side."

" A great deal *you* know about these matters, no doubt,"
said Amelia, in a taunting voice. " However, if Robina
and all of them CHOOSE to do the work themselves, I have
spoken my mind about it, and it is no concern of mine.
The servants can do it if they will tell them, and if they
won't, it cannot be helped."

To this speech, not having learned much forbearance
from the example of the ladies down stairs, I returned an
answer more than sufficiently warm, reminding Amelia that
the hurry and trouble we had seen below was solely and
exclusively our doing, for we had each lost two days, and
if we had done our part, there would have been plenty of
time, and taking part with the sisters for their indulgent
forbearance.

It was not to be supposed that the matter would rest
there ; Amelia answered, and we wrangled and quarrelled
for fully half an hour with much ironical civility of speech,
but considerable bitterness of feeling, the ground of dispute
being shortly forgotten, till in the midst of the contest, and
when we were both so much excited that there was danger
lest our temper should show itself in heightened voices, as
it did already in heightened color, I heard a step on the
stairs, and running to my own room, shut and locked myself in, and refreshed myself with a fit of crying, partly
caused by vexation, partly by humiliation. It did me a
great deal of good, and on reflection I felt heartily ashamed
of myself, for I knew that it was not my business to interfere with Amelia, and I knew that I had not done so with

the most distant hope of reforming her, but only for the sake of speaking my mind. And all this while I might have done essential good if I had been working down stairs instead of quarrelling up stairs; but now my eyes were so red that I was ashamed to go down, and I had to spend another half-hour in cooling my face with my fan, and walking up and down my room with the window open.

I went down at last, and gave a little help; but when I retired at night, I felt a secret conviction that unless somebody sat up to do it, the work would not be finished in time.

I lay awake thinking of this till I heard Amelia come up stairs, and Miss Perkins and Sarah follow at their usual time; but the room over mine remained empty, and I lay listening to the striking of the quarters till it only wanted a quarter to three, and then I heard footsteps. It was as I had thought, Anne and Bessie were stealing up to their room, and treading so carefully that the stairs creaked, as they perversely do on those occasions, ten times more than under less guarded feet.

The end of this was that the work was finished, and by three o'clock on Saturday sent in. No one blamed Sarah for having named too large a quantity, though she herself took it as much to heart as if she had miscalculated their powers on purpose. No one cared either to find fault with Amelia; they seemed rather to think that they ought to have known better than to depend on her; and as for me, they made the most indulgent allowance for my deficiencies, which was always their habit while I stayed with them.

On Monday the other sisters were as brisk as usual, but Anne was evidently unwell, and spent the morning on the sofa, unable to go into her garden. Mrs. Blount called and told Amelia and me (who with Anne were in the drawing-room) how all the committee had remarked on the quantity of work that had come from the Misses Perkins. "It shows," said Mrs. Blount, "how much can be done by combined effort." No one spoke. Amelia did not say anything, and I could not. She continued, "It is so pleasant and cheerful when such a large circle is at work at once, and they do it with no trouble to themselves. I often think of that true proverb, 'Many hands make light work.' No doubt it cost you less trouble than the small pieces taken by single people cost them."

I glanced at Amelia when this was said, and while explaining to Mrs. Blount that I had not done nearly the whole of my share, having missed two entire days, and that Miss Perkins and Sarah had sat up to do it for me, I saw such a vivid color rise in Amelia's cheeks, that I knew she was ashamed to appropriate Mrs. Blount's compliments to herself, though she had not the honesty to disavow them.

"And now, my dears, as you are both still looking a little the worse for that wretched yachting affair, suppose you take a drive with me this afternoon?"

We were perfectly well, but I suppose she required some reason for excluding the rest of the family, and I thought she might have noticed how pale Miss Anne looked after the confinement and fatigue of the past week.

Amelia assented with a gentle sweetness of manner, which she never exhibited but to strangers. She said she often felt languid in hot weather, and was always glad of air.

I declined; and at the same time, as Mrs. Blount was really very good-natured, I ventured to glance at her and then at Miss Anne. It seemed to strike her at once that she had not been civil, and she said with a very good grace, "Perhaps *you* are not too much engaged *to-day* to go with us, Miss Perkins," putting such an emphasis on the word *to-day*, as seemed to say, "I should have asked you before if I had not known that you were busy."

Anne looked up surprised, but not displeased ; she admitted that she should like a drive, and the two sisters withdrew together to dress, leaving me alone with Mrs. Blount.

I was extremely glad when they shut the door, for I saw she could scarcely refrain from laughing, and the moment they were out of earshot, she exclaimed, " Now you unconscionable little puss, why have you hampered me with that faded spinster ? Don't you know that she must sit in front in virtue of her seniority, and Amelia behind ? "

" Yes, but she is very interesting, Mrs. Blount."

" When my daughter is seventeen, I shall not expect her to dictate to seven-and-thirty."

" But, Mrs. Blount — " I began.

" Pooh, nonsense ! I tell you I am not angry, I am extremely amused."

I thought if Miss Anne found out how and why she had been invited to take this drive, it would do her no good, so I continued to tell all I could think of in her favor. She seemed interested, and called me a female Quixote, and when Anne and Amelia came in, said, to my great confusion, " Well, good-by, *Mentoria*, remember you are to drive with me to-morrow."

Her affectionate manner, and, perhaps, her taking Anne out, made Amelia tremble for her exclusive possession of this fashionable friend, and she gave me a very black look, which, unfortunately, Mrs. Blount saw, and was thus put into possession of the fact that Amelia would rather her sister had not been invited.

They were out a long time, and when they returned, Anne seemed little refreshed, and Amelia was out of humor. Mrs. Blount had scarcely spoken to her all the time. " In fact," she said, just as Anne was about to leave the room, "it must have been equally dull for us both."

" Remember that I did not ask her to take me," said Anne, looking back before she shut the door.

"No," muttered Amelia, "I have to thank somebody else for that."

I dreaded lest Anne should hear, and when Amelia went on with sarcastic politeness to say how much she was indebted to me for interfering between her and her friend, I had not a word to answer, and was obliged to be very civil all the evening to avert her further remarks.

The next morning Anne was too ill to come down, and Bessie told me that she never could sit indoors for long together without suffering for it afterwards.

This was said before Amelia, who fired up instantly, and said Anne need not have worked unless she had chosen. "I told Robina at the time, that it could be done easily enough if she would give it to the servants as other people did."

Bessie made no answer. She was pouring out tea for the invalid's breakfast, and she presently carried it up stairs. Many times during the day I saw one and another of the sisters running up stairs with the various little things that were wanted for Anne's comfort; but Amelia was never one of them. In the evening the medical man was called in, and his report evidently made Sarah uneasy. Miss Perkins was more cheerful, but I noticed that she sat up with Anne that night, and the next day was tired and dispirited.

I was quite struck then with the position occupied by a Cumberer. Nothing went on well in the household affairs, because the ladies were withdrawn from their usual occupations, and Amelia did not attempt to throw herself into the vacant place. She evidently had no idea how to assist her sisters, even if she had wished ; and it seemed to be a maxim firmly fixed in her mind that people were not overtasked, not anxious, not in want of help, not glad to be helped, *unless they said so*. She remarked to me during the day, that knowing how to nurse and wait on sick peo-

ple was a gift, not a thing to be learned, and that her elder
sisters had it. In truth, I did not wonder that they did not
appeal to her to help them, for I think nothing is so miserable to a sick person as to feel that she has an *unwilling*
nurse, and to be afraid of asking for what she wants.

Yet Amelia did not wish to appear inactive, for when
Sarah came down in a hurry, wanting some arrow-root,
though Amelia did not know how to make it, she said, " It's
a strange thing when I am anxious to help, that you do
not choose to let me."

" Well," said Sarah, as she left the room, " there are the
letters to post. I shall be glad if you 'll do that."

" Post the letters ! " said Amelia, in an injured tone, when
Sarah was gone ; " why, any servant can do 'that ; it must
be evident to the most prejudiced person that they don't
choose to let me help."

Just then Mary came in. " Have you anything particular
to do just now ? " asked Amelia.

The maid said, " No, not now, that Miss Sarah had gone
up with the arrow-root." " Then post these letters," said
Amelia ; and she took them, Amelia saying, that willing as
she was to help, she did not choose to be turned into an
errand girl to please Sarah's caprice.

Mary had been gone a long time, when I suddenly fancied
that a bell, which had been rung several times, had not
been answered, and I ran up to Miss Anne's room to ask
about it.

" No, my dear," said Miss Bobby, " I did not ring."

I came down ; again the bell rang. I now found it was
the door-bell, and answered it myself.

There stood both the servants, Mary and Fanny. " Dear
Miss," said Mary, " I never gave it a thought that Fanny
was out, when I said I had nothing to do. I did not
know it, I 'm sure, and I thought she would be down
directly."

" No," said Fanny, " Missis sent me out for some sal-volatile, and I went in a hurry."

They proceeded to the kitchen, and there was exclaiming and lifting up of hands ; the fire was out.

" Deary me ! " cried Mary, ready to cry, "and Miss Anne's pudding spoilt in the oven ; I know it 'll be as heavy as lead."

While they were scratching out the cinders and lighting the fire, I ran up stairs with the sal-volatile. " My dear," said Miss Perkins, " would you kindly ask whether the pudding is ready ? Anne fancies she could eat some." I was obliged to tell her that I knew it was not ready ; and when at length it came up, Sarah said it looked strange, and the invalid scarcely touched it, and evidently did not relish it at all.

There was another night of sitting up and anxiety, and in the morning Bessie did nothing but cry and sob all breakfast-time, and Amelia looked grave. But when the doctor came and spoke cheerfully, though I observed without giving any opinion as to the termination of the illness, Amelia blamed Bessie for being so nervous, and said she wondered at her weakness.

" You have not been with her as I have," sobbed Bessie. " Robina called me up to help her in the night, and Anne — Anne — talked nonsense."

" Called you up ! O, that accounts for your crying ; you are tired, that's all. I have perfect confidence in Dr. W. Anne is only feverish."

Notwithstanding this philosophical view of the matter, Bessie continued to sob hysterically, till at last I persuaded her to go and lie down, while I went and sat on the stairs to take down messages for Miss Sarah, Robina being gone to bed.

I could not be of much use ; but when I urged Sarah to employ me, she said decidedly, " My dear, I would not do you such an unkindness as to let you be useless and idle if I can help it; we don't know, my dear, how soon such habits may grow. You may take this prescription to the chemist's to be made up."

So I did that, and then took up my station again on the stairs, and was seldom wanted, though Sarah kindly said she liked to know that some one was there in case she did want anything.

This was indeed but a slight service, but I have since thought that Miss Sarah accepted it more for my good than for her own; and I have felt grateful for a consideration that would not repulse the most inefficient assistance.

CHAPTER IV.

THE FLOWER-GIRL LOSES A FRIEND.

MISS Anne continued very unwell, and I was told that her fever increased. About nine o'clock Miss Perkins returned to the sick-room, and Sarah went to bed. She was very tired, and let me help her to undress; then, hearing a ring at the door-bell, she asked me to go and see if it was Anne's medicine. I ran down with an almost childish wish to be important and useful, which no doubt she saw, though I did not suspect it. ◆

It was not the medicine that had arrived, but a note from Mrs. Blount to Amelia, asking her to join a picnic party the next day, and, as usual, to bring me with her.

Amelia, to do her justice, had seen so little of Anne during her illness, that it was no wonder she underrated its importance, and I was too ignorant to undeceive her. Mrs. Blount knew nothing of it, and the invitation had thrown Amelia into a state of great perplexity; she wished to go, and yet she did not wish to be thought unfeeling. She therefore accepted, but said that if Anne were worse the following day, Mrs. Blount must excuse her.

I did not know whether my absence for the day might not be a relief to the sisters, and I went up to Miss Sarah to ascertain what she really wished me to do.

She seemed to understand that I truly wished to do what was most agreeable to them, and after a moment's thought, said that the last party had turned out so badly, that she and Miss Perkins would be anxious about me, as I was delicate and under their care; for that Mrs. Blount, though kind, would not be prudent or careful as regarded our health; and then she kindly added, that perhaps I might be of use to her, and therefore, on the whole, she did not hesitate to say that she wished me to stay at home.

Bessie was kept up that night to help Miss Perkins, and the next morning, when Amelia and I met her on the stairs, she said she did not think Anne was any worse. Amelia, however, thought she had better not go till she had heard her eldest sister's report, and she lingered on the stairs some little time, but Miss Perkins did not come out, and at last she said, "Well, as Dr. W. had not arrived, and Bessie said Anne was certainly no worse, she supposed she ought to go; at any rate she had better go up and dress." So she did, and then Mrs. Blount came and said how strange it would be of Amelia to stay at home because one of her sisters was a little poorly and lying in bed; were there not three at home to take care of her?

"Anne is really ill," began Amelia.

"O, well, my dear, do as you like; but I thought from your note, it was most likely a feverish cold, and I quite expected to find her on the sofa to-day."

Now, either Amelia must have felt secretly convinced that Anne was much worse than she had said, or she had better feelings than we had given her credit for, and felt deeply ashamed to leave her sisters to another day of toil; certainly she had a severe struggle with herself, before she could decide to leave the better part and go out on a party of pleasure. It was not till Mrs. Blount remarked what a united family they were, and how sweetly they sympathized with one another, that Amelia yielded herself to go with a friend whose society and flattery were so delightful to her, and who, I fully believe, had no idea of the extent of Anne's illness.

So Amelia set off, and I sat alone till Sarah came down, and had her breakfast; Miss Perkins joining her, and telling me that she should be very glad if I would order the dinner for her, and cast up the slate. I was also to pay one or two bills. These little things being new to me, occupied my mind during the greater part of the morning; and when I had written to my parents, I was surprised to find that it was two o'clock, the usual dinner-hour. I heard that Dr. W. had paid his visit almost directly after Amelia went away, and as the house was very quiet all the morning, I hoped Anne was asleep. As I had taken some pains in ordering the dinner, I was a good deal disappointed when a message was sent to me, asking me to sit down alone, and the ladies would come when they were able. So I dined, and then waited till everything was cold, and till Fanny proposed that the dishes should be taken to the kitchen-fire till the ladies came down.

I felt very desolate and did not know what to do with myself. Bessie was gone to bed, and Miss Sarah had requested me not to sit on the stairs. At last I took up an amusing book that Amelia had borrowed, and was deep in the story, when I heard a man's step coming down stairs, and Dr. W. came in. I was surprised, and asked him if he had been up to see Miss Anne again.

He answered, " Ma'am, I have ; " and then he sat down and looked at me attentively, till I felt rather confused, more especially as he suddenly broke the silence by saying, sententiously, " Ha! bottled porter ! "

" I am afraid there is none in the house," said I, rising, " but I'll see."

" Pooh ! " said the doctor, " sit down. Yes, bottled porter."

I then understood that he intended to recommend this beverage to me.

" What's the matter with you ? " he next said.

" Nothing," I replied, " but that I have been growing very fast."

"Ah! well; have you any friends here, ma'am?" said the old gentleman.

I answered in the negative.

"Any acquaintances, ma'am?"

"Only one, very recently made, — Mrs. Blount."

"Mrs. Blount. I know her; all right. Suppose you go and spend a day or two with her."

Seeing me look up amazed, he said, "Well, then, suppose you go home."

"My parents are travelling in France."

"What of that, ma'am? They have not taken the house with them, I suppose?"

I could scarcely help laughing, while I answered, No, but that the house was being painted.

"Painted! people are always painting. Never was anything known like the luxury of the present day, — never. Well, ma'am, young people are always in the way at these times, and never of any use."

I was so surprised and perplexed at this speech, that I did not know what to answer.

"Well, ma'am," he continued, after waiting for me to speak, "I'm sorry you don't see the thing in the light I could have wished, and here's my carriage quite at your service to take you to Mrs. Blount. You would really be better away, for I shall be surprised if that poor thing lives through the night."

My astonishment and terror at hearing these words took away my breath, a film rose before my eyes, and I do not know what I should have done if the old gentleman had not suddenly exclaimed, "Heyday, ma'am, what's the meaning of this? We can't have any fainting; come and sit by the window, directly."

He gave me his hand, and threw up the sash, and though confusion and sorrow kept me silent, I felt no more faintness: Amelia's absence, the necessity of my immediately leaving my hostess, the uncertainty where I ought to go, and pity for the poor invalid, crowded on my mind, till when the old gentleman had given me long enough, as he thought, for consideration, he said, "Well, ma'am, here's my carriage. In my opinion, a carpet-bag would take all you require, but ladies" — spreading out his arms, as if to enclose a whole army of boxes — "have such notions of the luggage they must take about with them, for their hats and their flounces, and their pomatums, and their things, that I'm sure I don't know whether you can find room enough — but there's the rumble!"

I replied that a carpet-bag would content me, and I stole up the back-stairs, taking Fanny with me, who was weeping, for she had been informed of Miss Anne's danger.

I was anxious not to keep Dr. W. waiting, for I thought myself very much obliged to him for the considerate way in which he was treating me. There was no one I could go to but Mrs. Blount; but it would have been much more awkward to go of my own accord than to be taken by him.

He was pleased at my prompt return, and as he handed me into his carriage with elaborate care, I saw the open-mouthed astonishment of his footman; and though I was in tears, I could not but speculate as to whether any female foot had ever stepped into it before.

As we went, I told him that Mrs. Blount had gone out for the day, and that Amelia was with her; I then ventured, with a beating heart, to ask whether he thought Miss Anne's illness was owing to her having sat too much indoors lately.

She had long been in a very critical state, he replied, and, perhaps, if she had been a fine lady, might have led a life of less pain, though no circumstance could have prolonged it.

3   D

It was something, then, to think that a useful life had not been shortened by the wilfulness and inefficiency of some so much inferior to her; but oh, how bitterly did I regret that the last week of her life, before this short illness, had been clouded with anxiety, hurry, and toil, instead of being peacefully spent in those quiet pursuits that she took so much delight in.

But I had no time to indulge in these reflections and the tears they gave rise to; we were at Mrs. Blount's door, and the doctor had to explain to the surprised footman that he wanted to see Mrs. Blount's maid. That elegantly dressed personage presently made her appearance, and, evidently in a fright, asked if any accident had happened to her lady.

" No, ma'am," replied the old gentleman, addressing her, and bowing to her exactly as he had done to me, "but a patient of mine in the house where this young lady was staying, or lodging, or something of that sort, is dying, and you'll be so good as to take care of this young lady (I have n't the pleasure of knowing her name) till your lady comes home, when the matter will be explained to her."

The maid, charmed at his ceremonious manner, made a gratified courtesy, and replied that she would take care of the young lady.

The old gentleman, then, walking round me and inspecting me, as if to see that I was delivered over to the keeping of another in a satisfactory state, said slowly, " All right !" and taking me in one hand and my carpet-bag in the other, led me up to the maid, and, bowing, left me, with a look which plainly said to her, " You have received these valuable and perishable articles in good preservation, and you will be expected to give them up, on demand, in the same state."

He then hobbled down the steps to his carriage, and the maid asked me if I would come up stairs to her lady's dressing-room and have some tea. I could not but observe that the old gentleman's ultra care had impressed her greatly with the idea of the responsibility she had undertaken, for she seemed to regard me in the light of a thing that was sure to come to some harm, or receive some injury, if it could possibly find an opportunity.

When I had taken some tea, I lay on a sofa, feeling very unhappy, wondering whether Anne was sensible, and whether her sisters were apprised of her danger.

At length, when it was quite dusk, I heard the sound of carriage-wheels crushing the gravel before the house, and when they stopped, Amelia's voice, in its merriest tones, talking to little Miss Blount.

I heard Mrs. Blount ask Amelia to come in, and, dreading that they would both come up to the room where I was, and Amelia find out the truth too suddenly, I sent down the maid to draw Amelia aside on some pretence, that I might first speak to her friend.

Mrs. Blount came in, started at the sight of me, but I was so agitated that I could not speak. She soon contrived to calm me, and draw from me all that it was needful for her to know.

"Let her come here at once," she exclaimed ; "the mere sight of you will be a preparation."

Amelia came in almost on the instant; in fact, the maid had not been able to detain her long on pretence of brushing her dress. She was in very high spirits, and so far from taking alarm at the sight of me, thought I was come to see her home. She supposed I was quite tired of being moped in that dull house, and appealed to Mrs. Blount whether it was not rather a pity that her sisters should turn the house upside down for every little illness.

Mrs. Blount said not a word ; she evidently shrank from the task she had to do ; and I ventured, by way of opening, to say, " I fear, Amelia, we can hardly call this a little illness, for you know Miss Anne has had two of your sisters to sit up with her for three nights past."

Mrs. Blount, thrown off her guard, exclaimed, " Is it possible?" and I instantly felt, that by thus betraying Amelia's neglect to her friend, I had given her great pain, which I would not have done for the world at such a time. I had only intended to bring her mind to dwell on her sister's illness.

She looked astonished at my speech, and deeply annoyed, then walked up to the window, where I was standing, and began to draw up the blind, at the same time whispering a few words to me which showed high irritation.

I was so shocked at the mistake I had made, that full of pity for her, I burst into tears, and at the same moment Mrs. Blount, taking her hand, said gravely, " My dear Amelia." This action, and the sight of our faces, on which she had thrown light (the room being previously dusk), instantly opened her mind, and she cried out that she was sure Anne was dying. We did not contradict her, but led her down to the carriage, and Mrs. Blount went with her to rejoin her afflicted family.

She was away more than an hour, and when she returned, told me that Amelia went into hysterics directly she entered the house. " I was sorry," she continued, "that she could not command herself, for the sisters ran down instantly, and entreated her to be calm, and not to let Anne hear the noise, for her life hung on a thread, and the first shock would kill her. It made a great confusion," said Mrs. Blount, "and I felt very sorry that I had been the cause of Amelia's being from home at such a time ; but I assured her sisters I had not the slightest idea there was anything more the matter than a feverish cold, or I should never have thought of taking her away, even if she had wished it. They presently went up stairs again. Poor things! how sad and worn-out they looked. I sat with

Amelia as she lay on the sofa, and she showed a degree of shrinking from seeing her sister that surprised me very much. I should have thought affection would have overpowered any weak terrors at being present during painful scenes. She then said she had told the youngest of the sisters that I had come under her care; and altogether the sight of sorrow I found had brought out all the real kindness of her nature, and made her receive me, an almost stranger, with such a welcoming hospitality, that I felt quite comfortable and easy with her, and could even tell her how miserable I had felt under the idea of being palmed off upon her in such a way as almost to oblige her to receive me.

She laughed, and said, " My dear, you don't understand my nature. I love all young things, and like to have them depending on me, and, in fact, I do want something to do; something to occupy me. If I had had a large family, I should have been a different creature."

I could not but feel surprised, and wondered that this elegant and high-born woman should talk thus to a girl like me. Perhaps she perceived this, but instead of checking herself, she explained her meaning further, telling me that her one child was her late husband's heiress, and that he had left so many directions, so many guardians, trustees, etc., that she found herself left with very little power over her child. " And then, between the governess and the nurse," she added, in a plaintive tone, " there never seems to be anything for me to do for my darling but to play with her." I thought I would send away the governess if I were in the mother's place, but of course I did not say so, but went to bed very much relieved to find that Mrs. Blount was delighted to have me under her patronage, and very much pleased with Dr. W. for having placed me there.

After breakfast the next morning we went to inquire for Miss Anne. The shutters were not closed, and a servant told us that she still lived, that Dr. W. had seen her again, and had expressed surprise that she had lasted so long.

It was affecting to see the orphan girl whom Anne had befriended sitting crying on the steps, and bemoaning her benefactress. "I ha'n't time to see after flowers," said Mary, who looked pale and tired; "it's not to be expected."

"No," said Mrs. Blount, "but as the garden is at the back of the house, and not overlooked from the sick-room, I think there would be no harm in our passing through the kitchen and gathering these violets."

The servant assented respectfully, and I could not but admire the kindness of Mrs. Blount; she could easily have given the orphan girl the shilling for which she would have sold these violets, but by this better plan she provided that the dying woman's charity should extend to the last hour of her life.

We found the leaves of these plants already drooping, and the violets hanging their heads, for they require much care and regular watering; but we gathered all, and made them up under the trees; we then came softly back to the house, and we were met by Fanny, who said Miss Amelia would like to see us. We found her languid and miserable, her face disfigured by crying. "They have promised to call me if there is the slightest change," she said; "and my feelings are so acute, that I cannot stand by and see her suffer as they can. I am sure she suffers greatly. One of them is always fanning her, and another holding up her head."

I am sure Amelia was not at all aware that there was any selfishness in this speech; and when Mrs. Blount said gently, "Don't you think, dear, *you* could fan your sister for a while, it may be a pleasure to you afterwards to think you have done something for her?" she said, "You don't know what it is; she — she — gasps so, poor thing, — that it perfectly overcomes me"; and then she covered her face with her hands, and began to weep afresh.

Mrs. Blount did not say a word; and I inquired how her sisters were. "They look ready to drop, ma'am," said Fanny, who just then came in with a note of inquiry, "but they won't leave the room; they 've eaten nothing since last night at supper-time, and then Mary and I carried them up some sandwiches, and begged of them to eat them, and they came out one by one, and ate them on the stairs."

"Surely such great exertion and fatigue cannot be needful," said Mrs. Blount, quite shocked.

"Poor ladies, they 'll soon have rest," whispered Fanny, "and poor Miss Anne needs a wonderful deal of waiting on."

Hearing a step on the stairs, we then hastily withdrew, and as we went home no comment whatever was made by either, on the things we had witnessed; but Mrs. Blount induced me to tell her all I knew of Miss Anne's charities, and said that when she was gone the poor orphan should not want a friend.

In the afternoon we again went to look at the house. The sun was shining full upon it, but not within it, for the shutters were closed.

CHAPTER V.

THE STRANGE CLERGYMAN'S SERMON.

NOW as this is the history of a Cumberer, I shall not stay to dilate on the kindness shown to me by Mrs. Blount, the events that took place, or the cogitation I indulged in, excepting when they had reference to my heroine; I pass on therefore. to say that the day after Miss Anne's funeral, at which more mourners attended than those of her own family, Miss Perkins sent a message to Mrs. Blount, requesting her to come and see her.

She complied immediately, and on her return I felt naturally anxious to know what had been decided about me.

Mrs. Blount did not at first satisfy me, but sitting on an ottoman before the window, continued to look out at the ships passing through the stripes of sunny and shady water, for the sky was streaked with clouds. I saw that she was vexed, and felt relieved when she at last exclaimed, " Well, my dear, Miss Perkins wishes you to return this day week."

" So soon ? " I replied ; " surely I shall be in their way ; may I not now go home ? — the house must be ready."

" My dear, your parents are not here to be consulted, and as far as I am concerned, I should not like to return you to any hands but those from which I received you ; besides, the agreement for you was made for three months ; and when you hear that your going back is of some consequence to Miss Perkins, I believe you will be ready to do so."

" Of consequence," I exclaimed ; " dear Mrs. Blount, of what use can I be to them ? "

"I have discovered," she replied, "that the sum paid for you will be of great consequence — that good, *good* woman (I wish I were as good, she has no pride about her, not an atom, and no affectation) — told me she looked on it as a providence that you should have been placed with them, for thus they could cover the expenses of their dear sister's illness and funeral."

"Are they so poor?" I answered.

"I had no idea of it," she replied; "in fact I have been deceived and led into a great many mistakes. It seems that, now this poor lady is dead, one third of the property they lived upon is withdrawn, and four people have to live on one third less than five did."

I remembered what Bessie had told me, and answered that I knew it was so.

"Then why did n't you tell me?" she answered suddenly and almost sharply, but instantly she seemed to remember that it was not my business to tell her things that had come to my knowledge in another person's house, for she added more softly, "I have been completely and intentionally deceived, and no one has tried to set me right; Amelia made me believe that there was plenty of property in their family, but that her sisters had a natural liking for living in that *pokey* way, and for having no footman."

Poor Amelia, she has lost her friend, and if she finds that out, it will be punishment enough, I thought, but I did not say anything.

Mrs. Blount presently went on, "Of course the elder sister must naturally feel this death far more than the younger; yet that kind woman, Miss Sarah, sat at her work with a sort of patient sadness about her that interested me very much, while Amelia was idling away her time in the drawing-room, looking more discontented than sorrowful; and being alone with her for a few minutes, she told me what a misfortune it was this property being with-

3 *

drawn, for now her sisters would be more *penurious* than ever. When Miss Perkins told me afterwards what they all had to live on, I was quite amazed; I squander almost as much on dress and gewgaws as they maintain their respectable appearance on."

Then looking up and seeing me look grave, she smiled and said, "What are you thinking of, Mentoria?" for she always called me by this name; perhaps because it amused her as being remarkably inappropriate.

I replied that I was thinking of what she had said, that she had been deceived, and no one had tried to set her right.

She laughed (for she was never grave for many minutes together), and said, "You are too tall to be petted, Mentoria, or I might do without Amelia, and take you; sit down by me and give me a kiss. Now, tell me whether I have done my duty by you; have you been happy with me?"

"Very happy indeed."

"I really think you have. Well, you like me, and I think you cannot like Amelia. Why then did you let her deceive me?"

"I thought it would be very wrong in me to deprive her of a friend, and besides, you might not have believed me."

"Just answer me one question, it can do her no harm; are they aware at home of her real character?"

"Yes, I cannot but be sure that they are."

"Well, Mentoria, I would have been her friend, for I really liked her; but now I have seen her as she is. Keep my secret; do not tell her that I have ceased to care for her, and to respect her. I wish she may ever be worthy of those excellent women, whom she affects almost to despise."

So ended this conversation. At the appointed day I returned to my hostesses, who received me very kindly and calmly.

I saw that Miss Anne was a great loss to her affectionate sisters, and tried to prevent their feeling my presence
an intrusion, keeping as much apart as possible, and still
walking out with Mrs. Blount, who kindly came for me
daily.

After the first day Amelia accompanied us, and seemed
to be trying hard to regain her ascendancy over her friend
by that gentle flattery and attention to all she said which
had won it for her at first. She perceived that something
was amiss, though far from attributing the change to its
right cause ; she thought her friend capricious, and fancied she could not please her because she was interested
in me.

Amelia lived for herself, therefore it was not strange
that she was neither useful nor happy. I did not think
that when at home she seemed much to feel the death of
her sister, yet when walking with Mrs. Blount she spoke
affectingly of the sorrow she suffered ; and I am not at all
sure that she was wilfully deceitful, for it is really easier to
deceive one's self than other people.

Bessie took charge of the garden, and went out daily
just as her sister had done, and again the violet bed
bloomed as before, and the orphan girl sat on the steps
waiting for the flowers.

I felt sure that this constant following of her late sister's
footsteps was a trial to her feelings, yet when I sat down
by her and said, " Dear Bessie, I am sure this is too much
for you," she answered hurriedly, " I shall soon be cheerful in the garden, my dear, and mind you do not let Bobby
think I do too much, it would make her uneasy."

I replied, " I should not think of such a thing ; but I
am coming out soon to help."

" You will be horridly tanned if you do," said Amelia ;
" the sun tans more than the sea. *I* was obliged to come
in yesterday when I went out to help in the garden ; by

tea-time I should have been burnt quite red." Amelia had just come in from a walk.

" It is no worse for us than for Bessie," I could not help saying.

" You are quite mistaken," replied Amelia ; " fair skins like yours and mine tan directly, but nothing hurts that kind of *thick* complexion that Bessie has."

" But in spite of being tanned," she proceeded, " I should certainly have thought it right to help in the garden, if Bessie had not particularly given out that she intended to undertake it herself; and as it was not too much for dear Anne, delicate as she was, I suppose Bessie can easily do it."

" I undertook the garden," said Bessie, " because Sarah was unhappy about it, and said it would make her miserable to see it get into disorder, when our dear sister had been so fond of it."

" Well," said Amelia, " but you undertook it of your own accord, quite vehemently, and declared that you should feel it a pleasure. If you are tired of it you had better say so."

" I am not tired of it," said Bessie.

" Then I am sure I don't know what the discussion is about," rejoined Amelia, " nor why you put on that *injured* air. Since Miss T. came here, she is always putting it into your head that you are a martyr. You did not consult me when you chose to undertake the garden ; what fault of mine is it then that you are tired and tanned ? At this moment, happily for us all, there was a knock at the door, and we withdrew to our rooms before it was answered. Perhaps on reflection Amelia felt that she had not behaved amiably to her sister, for as soon as the sun was low, we saw her go into the garden and begin very diligently to weed a little flower-bed. She seemed so much in earnest that I saw Robina looking at her with pleasure, and Sarah declared that it looked as if Amelia meant to turn over a new leaf.

Just as the bed was weeded, and all the stones, weeds, and rubbish were raked on to the walk, Fanny came to call her in to tea, and she entered, remarking that she should go out again when the meal was over, to finish her work. But a book was brought in from the club, and Amelia opened it, was interested, and read on till it was too late for any more gardening. The next day was hot, and the day after that was damp, so the weeds were left till Bessie, who gardened in spite of heat and damp, raked them away; and there, as far as I know, ended Amelia's weeding.

The day after these weeds were raked away was Sunday. A strange clergyman preached, and his sermon was so striking, that I remember parts of it to this time. This sermon was from the parable of the barren fig-tree, and the text was, "Cut it down, why *cumbereth* it the ground?"

We listened to it with unusual seriousness, and talked of it a good deal during the rest of the day, but no one remembered or discussed it so much as Amelia. She remarked that she had felt particularly edified by it, and that she sincerely hoped it would be a warning to her if ever she should be in danger of becoming a *Cumberer*.

The next morning Mrs. Blount walked out with Miss Sarah, Amelia; and myself, and, seated under the shadow of a great cliff, we reverted to the sermon.

"It was very striking," said Mrs. Blount; "but the concluding remarks gave me a thrill that I have hardly recovered to this hour."

The preacher in concluding had said, "But why do I so earnestly entreat you to consider the sin and peril of thus cumbering the Lord's vineyard? Alas! though there should be but five persons present who are guilty of this sin, and it should be known to me that they alone stood in need of applying these words to themselves, I should feel

that though all the rest of my hearers might seriously ex-
amine themselves as to their state, and consider whether
the lot of the cumberer might not be theirs, yet those five,
those fruitless five, easy and unconscious, would pass the
warning by, and be the last to think it needed."

When these words were referred to I repeated them,
adding a striking remark, to the effect that though the tree-
is represented as blamable for being fruitless, yet being
covered with the leaves of a fair profession, it might be
thought that those leaves covered and hid *even from itself*
the barrenness of the boughs ; it is only the husbandman
who acknowledges and bewails its state, and tenderly en-
treats for it a patience that it does not think it needs.
Nothing but the grace of God, the preacher had said, can
open the eyes of those that cumber the ground. ·

"There," said Mrs. Blount, "that will do, my dear ; I
should not like to have a memory like yours ; if I could
recall great pieces of that sermon at will, I should never
have any peace."

"Still it is a blessing to have a good memory," observed
Miss Sarah ; "and I hope you will never try to forget things
because they make you uncomfortable."

I answered somewhat childishly, for it made all my hearers laugh, that I was sure I should never forget that sermon, for that the clergyman had looked at me several times
so pointedly that I could not but think he considered me
likely to be a cumberer ; and that I had been afraid ever
since that I must be one of *those five.*

Amelia laughed with the others, and said quite good-
humoredly, "You felt rather guilty, perhaps, and that was
why you fancied he looked at you."

Sarah answered very kindly, "Well, my dear, fears about
ourselves are never out of place ; as for me, I must own
that I felt much humbled, for what fruit is there in my
life ? — what return have I ever made to the labors of that

gracious Husbandman, as an evidence of my gratitude for his care ? "

To my confusion Mrs. Blount then said to Amelia, " It seems we all applied it to ourselves. What did you think of it, Amelia ? we shall be glad of your confession to add to our own."

I wondered to hear her speak lightly, yet I observed that she felt considerable curiosity as to what would be the answer ; but nothing could exceed Amelia's unconsciousness, for when I ventured to glance at her, I saw that she was quietly playing with the soft, dry sand, and passing her white fingers through it in search of shells.

" Why," she said, " there seems to me a kind of absurdity and false humility in applying things to one's self that really are not applicable. If the man had said, ' My brethren, I hope those of you are penitent who have committed theft, and those who have committed murder,' I should not have felt that perhaps I had committed theft or murder, because *I know* I have not. Well, it 's just the same in this case ; I am willing enough to acknowledge faults that I commit, but not to be morbid and to distress myself about faults that I do not commit. In fact, you know a member of a large family has no power to be useless, even if she wishes it."

" Very true," said Mrs. Blount ; " but certainly some of us are *more* useful than others."

" No doubt," replied Amelia complacently.

" Then do you think it was morbid in us to apply it to ourselves ? "

" I cannot pretend to say," replied Amelia after a pause ; " I should not have thought it necessary."

Here I was so afraid lest Miss Sarah should find out what Mrs. Blount was about in thus drawing out Amelia, that I pinched her hand, and entreated her with my eyes to desist ; but she only laughed and said, " I thought yesterday that in one particular that clergyman was wrong, but now I have come to the conclusion that he was right in all."

" What was that òne point ? " asked Amelia.

" Mentoria knows," she answered.

" I cannot think why you call her Mentoria," exclaimed Amelia ; " but I have noticed that she has looked rather guilty for some time, blushing up to the eyes, I declare. What fearful act of inefficiency, or what remarkable proof of your uselessness, did you give Mrs. Blount during your stay with her, Miss T., that you look so shamefaced ? "

" How do you know that she is blushing for herself ? " asked Mrs. Blount suddenly ; "*perhaps it is for me !*"

I do not justify this remark, but only record it. It seemed to interest Amelia, for she said, with that peculiar gentleness of manner which she often assumed with Mrs. Blount, " I suppose some persons would think me jealous, and I cannot altogether conceal that I have that proof of affection in my feelings towards you ; for I do feel a little pain at finding that Miss T. is so much more in your counsels than I am.   You do not care for me as I do for you."

Such a remark a short time ago would have brought a warm denial and a shower of kisses.   Now it produced no reply ; and after an awkward silence, during which Mrs. Blount was rather out of countenance, she took advantage of a passing cloud to say she thought there was going to be a shower, and that we had better go home ; which we accordingly did, all feeling more or less uncomfortable.

CHAPTER VI.

CONCLUSION.

WHILST penning these records of a few weeks in the life of a Cumberer, I have often thought how much easier it is to write fiction well than reality.

In fiction, poetical justice is always done ; in real life the justice is done, but it is not always apparent.

The guilty suffer secret remorse, the ill-tempered lose the love of their friends, the untruthful are distrusted ; but these punishments, and many such, are not laid bare to the eyes of others. If they were, man would so far take upon himself to be the judge, that he would think himself justified in adding the punishment of his own neglect or contempt more openly. I proceed to the conclusion of my narrative.

The four sisters went out to return the calls of condolence that had been paid them.

I was at home, writing letters, when Mrs. Blount was announced, and on entering, she told me she was come to take leave, for she must go home to receive some friends, who, not being aware of her absence, had written to say that they were coming to stay with her at her house.

She had brought her little daughter with her, and was trying hard to make her say she was sorry not to see me any more, when Amelia and Bessie came in.

She told Amelia of her intended return, and I saw that her manner of so doing gave a great deal of annoyance. Mrs. Blount was warm-hearted, and kind to those whom she loved ; but she was sudden in taking both likes and

E .

dislikes, and she took a liking without sufficient cause, and did not disguise her change of opinion, when she had ceased to care for the object of her preference. Amelia perceived that Mrs. Blount no longer loved her; but she had not been told why, and no doubt set the change down in her mind to mere caprice.

"So, you are not sorry that you are going away from Mentoria," said Mrs. Blount to her child. "O, I'm ashamed of you!—do say you are sorry."

"But I want to see Spot and Die," pleaded the little creature; "and I want to play with Nell's puppies."

"Ah! you are your father's own daughter; dogs and horses are the delight of your heart.. Would you believe it, my dear, Spot and Die are our two old bay carriage-horses?"

"I have n't any pups here," proceeded the child; "I've nothing but crabs to play with, and they pinch my fingers."

"But Mentoria cut you out such pretty things with her scissors; such a number of ducks, and geese, and parrots, with cherries in their beaks, and you don't love her? Oh, fie! I think you had better give her back all those pretty things."

"No, I sha' n't!" said the little creature. "I do love her A LITTLE!"

"Well, kiss her, then, and kiss Amelia, and Miss Bessie Perkins, for mamma must go."

The little one rose with alacrity from the woolly mat on which she had been seated, and presented her rosy face to each of us in turn; then her mamma did the same and departed. Amelia's deep disappointment was evident; there had been no distinguishing preference shown to her, no sorrow at parting, none of the warmth of the first meeting, and no hint that she should hope soon to receive her as a guest.

I could not but wish that it had been otherwise, and as I

sat with a book in my hand, I stole a glance now and then at Amelia, who, flushed and angry, was no doubt wondering what could be the cause of the change, and why Mrs. Blount had not followed up a hint which she had given more than once in my presence, to the effect that she hoped Amelia would soon be well acquainted with her house and neighborhood. Amelia at length took up her parasol, and went up stairs, saying, when Bessie observed that she thought Mrs. Blount had taken rather a cool leaving of her friend, "Oh, no doubt I shall hear from her soon, when she is removed from the influence of the person who has made her dislike me!" I felt my cheeks blush high, though not with the sense of detected guilt; and, though I appeared to be reading with great diligence, not a sentence impressed itself on my mind.

Sarah shortly came in. She and Bessie went up stairs, returned again, and were seated at work, before I could recall myself from the brown study in which I was indulging.

At length Mrs. Blount's name was mentioned, and my attention was instantly arrested. "She took a very cool leave of Amelia," repeated Bessie, "and never hinted at asking her to stay with her, which Amelia always said she meant to do; perhaps she will some other time."

"She *never* will!" said Sarah.

"How do you know?" asked Bessie, surprised.

"I found it out the other day," said Sarah with a·sigh, "when I went out with Amelia, Mrs. Blount and Miss T."

I could not help breaking into the conversation, by saying, —

"And with which of us three were you displeased on the occasion, Miss Sarah?"

Sarah made no answer; and Bessie said, with some resentment, —

"Well, I 'm sorry if Amelia has been deprived of a

friend. And besides, in a family, what is an advantage to one is an advantage to all."

"My dear," said Sarah, "if you think Miss T. had anything to do with it, I believe you are mistaken. My dear Miss T., you asked which of you I was angry with ; I was not angry with any, but I was sorry for all. I was sorry for Mrs. Blount, that she had the bad taste to ridicule Amelia before me, and the want of sense to suppose I did not see what she meant ; and I was sorry for you, because you were so much out of countenance ; and I need hardly say I was sorry for Amelia, for I see, what I never thought before, that other people see her faults as plainly, or more so, than her own family do. I had no right to be angry ; but I own I had hoped that Mrs. Blount would be a friend to her."

At this moment Amelia came in, and the conversation about her ceased. She was not in a good humor, — it was scarcely to be expected that she should be ; and she shortly showed it by speaking very unpleasantly to her elder sister about the crape tucks of her dress.

"I told you," said Sarah, "that you ought not to sit about on the sand in your new mourning. Crape will not stand sea air. You should wear your common gown on the shore."

"And I told *you*," returned Amelia, "that if you would persist in making our common gowns yourself, and making them of that inferior material, we should be obliged to wear our best."

"I am not obliged to wear mine, my dear," said Sarah, with a sigh ; "and my mourning ought to be as deep and as good as yours."

"Mourning ought to be handsome !" proceeded Amelia.

"My dear," said Sarah, "it ought to be such as the mourners can afford to buy."

Amelia was too much out of temper to consider her

sister's feelings ; and she answered, contemptuously, "that the feelings of the mourners could not be very keen, if they could stop to consider every shilling at such a time ; their grief must be very moderate, if they could not leave· such things as that to dress-makers, but must needs be measuring and trimming old bonnets and turning skirts directly that the funeral was over"; and then, being thoroughly excited, she burst into a passion of angry tears, and exclaimed that "if it had been dear Anne that was in mourning for one of them, she was sure *she* would not have considered the expense of every yard of crape," — going on to lament her loss, and declare that *she* was always kind and affectionate, *she* always understood other people's feelings, till I thought I ought to get up and leave the room, which I did, though I could not help-marvelling that Amelia did not remember, in this panegyric, that every word she said was a reproach to herself for being such a contrast to the sister whom she had lost.

In the quiet of my own room, the sermon before spoken of recurred to my mind, with certain salutary fears lest in judging Amelia I should condemn myself. Its peculiarity had been its eminently practical nature, and from it I had first learned the true position, both in the natural world and in the spiritual vineyard, of a Cumberer; from it I had also learned to notice, that it is both natural and inevitable, that those who have no settled occupation themselves, should be those most prone to find fault with the work of others.

But my acquaintance with Miss Amelia Perkins was drawing to its close. On coming down, I found her in high good humor, discussing with her sisters about certain boxes, and about going out to make some purchases. She had received a letter by the afternoon's post, inviting her to go and spend a month with her cousin at York. I heard some regret expressed by the sisters that it should be such an expensive journey; but they agreed that Amelia should go, as the younger sisters had some expectations from this cousin, and as Amelia was bent on a visit; she said she wanted something to recruit her spirits, after the sad scenes she had just gone through.

So the purchases were made, and the boxes were packed, and for two days every one was occupied about Amelia; the servants in getting up and ironing her various possessions, Miss Sarah in working, and Miss Perkins in collecting her things together and supplying deficiencies.

So at length everything was ready, — the boxes packed, the fly at the door, the farewell kisses given. Amelia drove away, and after that — what after that? Why, we were much more at ease than we had been hitherto.

People did their work; they did not find fault with the way in which other people did theirs; no one wished to practise all the time that others were writing letters; in short, that good old English word "comfortable" expressed what we felt that day and the days following. We had not felt comfortable before. It was a delightful help merely *not* to be hindered.

And now I take my leave of Amelia. Her character might perhaps be a warning to others like her, if it were not the most difficult thing in the world to persuade any person, who *really is such*, to consider herself or himself as a Cumberer.

Many a delicate invalid, who overtasks herself, thinks herself, notwithstanding, quite a burden, while she is teaching, by her example, the most improving lessons of patience, gentleness, and resignation; and many an awkward, yet warm-hearted and eager girl, weeping over her various mistakes, blunders, and short-comings, in her anxious attempts to be kind and to help others, and to do a great deal in a little time, has been willing enough to take to herself the appellation, false indeed in her case, of a Cumberer.

But the true Cumberers are not likely, in, the first place, ever to consider this matter at all; and, in the second place, if they do, to admit that they deserve so undesirable a title.

Let, therefore, those who have the care of young people think of it for them. Let those who have the rearing of Cumberers seriously consider what they are about; for Cumberers are not all born such, some are made such.

I remember an anecdote told me by a lady, whom I have the pleasure to know intimately, which so strongly bears on this point, that I will venture to relate it as a warning to those who, from amiable weakness and false kindness, cherish in others that selfishness which is at the root of the Cumberer's character.

Shortly before the old workhouse system was modified, this lady tells me that she went to the workhouse of the small town where she resided, with a present of tea for a good old woman who lived there.

The mistress of the workhouse was busy, and the door was opened by a pauper boy, who showed her into the little parlor belonging to the establishment. Here, to the lady's surprise, she found a sickly-looking girl *in curl-papers*, practising some tunes on a very wretched piano.

The lady having told her errand, perhaps expected this girl, whom she presently recognized as the mistress's daughter, to go and seek her mother; but if she did, she was disappointed. The girl lingered in the room, looking listless and disconsolate. She did not like to take the liberty of going on with her practising, and she seemed to have nothing else to do.

At length the mistress, a pleasant, hearty woman, entered the little parlor, made many apologies for keeping the lady waiting, but said it was washing-day, and she had been giving out the soap required, and also cutting the bread and cheese which the children were to have that day for their dinner.

" Your daughter is probably unwell," said the visitor, "as she does not help you."

" O no, ma'am !" replied the foolish woman ; "but she does n't like going out to walk much, and that makes her look pale ; and since I sent her to boarding-school she can't bear *stirring* about in the house, paring potatoes and ironing, as I do."

Thinking it no business of hers, the lady answered, " Indeed," and then informed the mistress that she had brought some tea for her old pensioner.

" Thank you, ma'am," said the mistress, " I 'll take it up to her soon, for I shall have to go up to give out some things from the linen-press. I have a deal of running up and down stairs."

" Surely your daughter could save you some of the trouble," said the visitor, surprised, and held the packet of tea towards the girl, who rose so slowly and reluctantly to take it that the mother said, " O, ma'am, I 'll engage that old Bet shall have it long before tea time ; I 'll take it up."

" As you please," replied the lady ; and the girl, perhaps, seeing that her conduct was not approved, left the room.

The visitor then said, " Mrs. Green, is it possible that you take all the fatigues of this place on yourself, when you have that daughter quite old enough to help you ?"

" Why, you see, ma'am, the poor thing likes to get away from the pauper women, and now she learns music, she — she — does not like to go and help in the kitchen like a servant," replied the mistress, blushing.

" Not when her own mother does it, and it is her mother's duty to do it ? Surely your daughter does not think herself superior to you ? because if she does, she is very much mistaken," said the visitor.

The mother blushed again for her untidy, vulgar-looking child, and said, " Why, ma'am, when she goes to school she looks as different as can be, almost as neat and nice as if she were a young lady; but I don't wonder she should go slipshod here, *for there's nobody to see her but me.*"

"And who in this world ought she to respect if not her own mother?" asked the visitor. "In whose eyes should she wish to look better?"

"Ah! well," said the mistress with a sigh, "*she will some day*, mayhap; but though she's a good girl enough in some things, I don't deny that she has faults, and it's one of them *not to mind me;* and as to the curl-papers, ma'am, her hair curls so badly, that if she did n't keep it up in them till afternoon, when she goes out of doors, it would be straight."

"If I were her mother," said the lady, "she should never wear curl-papers before *me.* If her hair did not curl, she should wear it plain."

"She would look a deal better if she would," said the weak mother; "and so I often tell her."

"And I hope you will excuse my saying," proceeded the visitor, "that she would also look a great deal better tidily dressed, and cheerfully helping in either kitchen or laundry, than playing here on the piano in such a discreditable state of untidy neglect."

"What you say is very right, ma'am," said the mistress; "but young girls get such notions out of the books they read from those circulating libraries, — they read about fine ladies, and they want to be ladies too, and sit doing nothing."

"If you do not use your authority to prevent her from reading all the trash of a circulating library, I am afraid she is not likely to be any comfort to you," said the guest.

The mistress looked grave, and said she had not read any of those novels herself; but she had heard say that they were not all good for girls to read; though as her daughter was soon going back to school, it did not so much

matter ; and, no doubt, when she was grown up she would
be a very different girl.

"Finding that what I said made no impression," said my
friend, "I then left the workhouse ; but often when in after
years I returned to it to read with or bring some little
comfort to the old women, I saw that weak, but fond, unself-
ish mother toiling up and down stairs, and spending her
strength in the vain attempt to fulfil more duties than could
be properly performed by a single individual, my heart
ached for her, though I could not but feel that she had
encouraged, by indulgence, those faults in her daughter's
character which should have been most strenuously com-
bated."

The girl grew up idle, useless, vain, and selfish ; the
mother worked for both as long as her strength permitted ;
when it failed, she petitioned the poor-law guardians to
give the place to her daughter ; but they declined, on the
ground of her utter incompetence ; and the consequence
was, she had to go to service, while her mother, being respected as a hard-working and honest woman, got a place
in an Alms-house, and then lamented, when too late, that
she had brought up her daughter to cumber, instead of to
cultivate, the ground.

And now I will venture to add a few words to those who
are at present, or who are in danger of becoming, Cumberers ; and as no one will admit that she is of no use, benefit,
or help to any one, and that if she should die, no one would
be the worse off by the value of those household charities,
those domestic duties, or those acts of kindness which
were received from her ; it will be desirable not to judge
so much by *actions* in trying to discover the truth, as by
motives.

How beautiful is that saying of Holy Writ, — " The *desire* of a man is his kindness !" Is it then our habitual
state of mind to be wholly occupied with our own plans,

our own advantages, our own pursuits, or do we constantly
devise plans by which we can add to the comfort of others ?
Is self our *motive*, are we self-seekers, self-sparers, self-
justifiers, or are we considerate and observant for others ?

We must not only consider whether what we do is a
pleasure in some instances, but whether we design it to be
a pleasure to our families.

Thus I once heard a lady, who was a noble instance of
a Cumberer, say, "It is very unjust your saying that I
don't do anything to help in the house, or to amuse the
family; there's my music." "Yes," replied the sister-in-
law, to whom the remark had been addressed, "but though
you do play beautifully, and thus often *happen* to amuse
us, you don't play for *our* benefit or pleasure, but your
own; if it were unpleasant to you to play, you would not
do it, for you very often play when it *is* very unpleasant *to
us*, and at very inconvenient times, and I cannot but think
your happening to be fond of music, and thus happening
to amuse us, does not prove what I said to be incorrect,
that you seldom do anything which you *design* to be useful
or agreeable, and I wish it was otherwise."

And now I will add to this little paper the last news I
heard concerning Amelia. She inherited a handsome fortune from the old relative whom she went to visit, and
she very shortly married, but having quarrelled with her
sisters, and thus lost her best counsellors, she and her husband soon contrived to spend all that portion of the property which was in their own power, and being always in
debt, through carelessness and mismanagement, together
with a selfish dislike to trouble, which she had indulged in
her girlhood, they were at length obliged to apply to their
eldest sister to lend them what assistance might be in her
power. This excellent woman did so, by taking their two
eldest children to live with her for a certain period; while
they let their house, dismissed their servants, and went to

live for a year or two at Boulogne, to retrench, and if possible practise such economy as should enable them to return to their native country.

Here, for want of a more satisfactory termination, must end the records of a Cumberer.

MY GREAT-AUNT'S PICTURE.

CHAPTER I.

THE following papers were lately put into my hands by an anonymous correspondent, with a request that they might be arranged for the press.

At first sight they appeared to be intended for the perusal of some particular person, but, after due consideration, I came to the conclusion, that since it was vain to seek for that person, and not less vain to attempt to discover my unknown correspondent, it would be best to throw them loose upon the world to find themselves an owner; therefore, my reader, I offer them to you, or, in the words of the old proverb, " I present you with this cap, and if it fits, I pray you put it on."

Many confess (thus the manuscript begins) that they are proud; some will even confess that they are vain; some will sigh frankly over their passionate tempers; and others again will admit that they are of careless dispositions. But who tells, who confesses how mean she is, or how sly, or how envious? Who does this, or could hope for sympathy if she did?

Nevertheless, though such confessions are not sanctioned by custom, there is that within me which so longs to express itself, that I must needs forsake the beaten track of easy acknowledgment. I must leave those faults which no one feels much shame in taking to herself, and confess to you how *envious* I am; and though I do not expect much sympathy from you, I shall, at least, have the comfort of being understood, since you also, like a captive taken anciently in war, are marked in the face as the bond-slave of — Envy. By that unmistakable mark I know that we both serve the same hard mistress, and that, like me, you have received pain from those pleasures of others which you are not permitted to share.

Now, it is a curious fact that you do not consider yourself to be an envious person, and you would be angry and hurt if your friends thought it of you. I did not know till lately that I was envious, and, of course, I am very anxious to conceal it from my friends, though with you I am not so particular, because our hearts are so much akin, that though we may disapprove of, we cannot despise one another.

But let me proceed. Know then, my envious kinswoman, that I have two maiden aunts, dear and kindly women, and that they live in a delightful cottage near the sea. There is no house to be seen on either hand, and the shore is lonely and beautiful. The house is settled half-way down in a scoop of the sloping hills, and from the sea it looks like a pure white egg in a green nest of moss and twigs, for the trees rise behind it, and fern lies around it, and in the dingle below there is a tiny singing brook which the sun never catches sight of all the summer long, so thickly is it roofed over by the trees.

Last August I was invited to stay at this place with my aunts, for the first time since my childhood. When I arrived I was much grown and altered, and a great deal of discussion ensued as to whom I most resembled.

"She has the family features, certainly," said my Aunt Mary.

"But she is not so much like any of the present generation," added my aunt Phœbe, "as like the picture of her great-aunt Beatrice which hangs over the mantel-piece."

As she spoke I looked up at the picture, and a momentary sensation of pleased surprise stole into my heart. Had I then those delicate eyebrows, that clear cheek, those large thoughtful eyes? But I had scarce ventured to admit to myself that there was a likeness, when something peculiar in the expression gave me pain. I wondered what it meant. It was not precisely pensive, it was not anxious, it was not penetrating. It might consist of all these feelings, but there was something more besides that I could not fathom.

I looked again. "The expression is yet more like than the features," said my dear aunt Mary, and then they dropped the subject; but I could not dismiss it; and often during the evening while they talked, sitting one on each side of me, asking after my parents, and my sisters, and some old friends of theirs who lived near my native home, I could not help casting furtive glances at the picture, and always felt both pain and pleasure in the likeness to myself. Once when I looked, the sun, just about to set, had covered it with light, which came in through a side-window, and the features, before so quiet and so pale, seemed to flush up with sudden bloom : it did not improve them, for it gave, with the appearance of life that flashed from my kinswoman's eyes into mine, a glance half reproachful, half regretful, which seemed to say, "You have all the notice, and I hang up here unobserved. Oh that I could but step down from my frame, and show those doting old women how much fairer I am, and how far worthier of all this fondness and caressing than you are!"

I thought this was an odd fancy of mine; yet, when the sun had gone down, and the dusk had hidden my kinswoman's picture, I could not but feel glad; and I went on chatting to my aunts till the darkness had covered everything, and the moon had risen, and was hanging like a great lamp over the sea. It was the only lamp we had. My aunts were evidently so much interested to converse

again with the grown-up niece whom they had made so
much of when a child, and I was so well pleased to find
them absorbed in me and my communications, and so delighted to watch the beautiful highway, yellow, and yet wan
of hue, which the moon had laid over the leaden-tinted
waters, that time was allowed to slip away, and I believe
we were all surprised when the maid brought in bedroom
candles, and said it was the hour for retiring.

Then we rose up, — for we had been sitting before the
front windows, — and I, in turning, glanced up again at
my kinswoman's picture ; pale, how very pale, in the moon-
beams which had wandered up the vale.   O, what a look
seemed to meet me as I gazed !   " Yes," I said to myself,
" I know now the true meaning of that expression ; if your
living face had looked at me thus, I should have known,
fair lady, that you were envious of me."

My aunts had told me, before we parted for the night,
that they had sent for my cousin, Rosie Grant, to visit
them whilst I was there ; and that she was coming the next
day.

She was a year younger than myself, and I did not doubt
that she was much my inferior ; for she had enjoyed fewer
advantages, her parents not being able to afford them for
her.   I thought I should find her an untaught little Cock-
ney, prim and womanish in manner, nevertheless ; for one
seldom sees much simplicity among Londoners.   " That
does not matter to me," I thought, "for I would always
rather have a foil than a rival."

The next day this Rosie came ; a round-faced, yellow-
haired creature, with deep dimples, and a head all over
rippling curls ; there was nothing classical or finely drawn
about her features.   I saw at a glance that no likeness was
in her face to our beautiful aunt ; but there was a sunny
radiance in her expression, a simplicity and obedience in
her manner, a something so joyous and artless in the greet-

ing she gave to her aunts, that I was delighted; especially when I found that, though nearly seventeen years old, she treated me with deference and docility, as if she felt that the difference between us was great.

My aunts sat at home and knitted. Rosie and I spent the day on the beach together. I naturally took the lead, and none of my proposals came amiss to•her; she was equally happy anywhere; clambering among the woods which were nestled in on the deep spaces between the cliffs, or picking up shells, or reading under the shadows of the rocks.

That was a delightful day; and when we came home at seven o'clock to tea, we were not sorry to find three gentlemen sitting with my aunts, a father and two sons. Very agreeable young men, these latter were; but I must say that neither of them cared to talk to pretty, simple Rosie; they both seemed to feel that I was more likely to understand them, and I made no effort to have it otherwise.

After tea my aunts asked for music, and Rosie inquired where she should find mine. I told her; she brought it, opened the piano, set the stool for me, and I played several pieces one after the other. I had been well taught, and I believe I played them accurately, though I have no particular talent for music. The guests were pleased, and still asked for more; they said they so seldom heard music, that they hoped I would not leave the piano so soon. So I played one more piece; but I did not quite know it, and after making several blunders, got rather lamely to the end, heartily wishing that I had been contented to stop earlier.

"Now, Rosie, you may play something," said my Aunt Mary.

"My books are not unpacked yet, aunt," said the little girl.

My aunt smiled. "That excuse will scarcely serve you,

Rosie," she said ; "play something without your notes, my dear."

Rosie evidently did not like to play before strangers, and she blushed till her delicate neck and forehead were tinged with crimson. She, however, sat down, and the guests, apparently to relieve her bashfulness, began to talk on indifferent subjects. Under cover of this talk, Rosie presently began to play, and one voice after another became silent. She was not playing anything more difficult than I had attempted ; but, O the difference in feeling! I perceived that I had merely gratified their ears, but that my cousin was touching their hearts. How unlucky, I thought, that I was not aware how well she played ; if I had known, nothing should have induced me to exhibit my own inferiority.

They shortly asked me to play again, but I declined, and held so resolutely back that they soon desisted, and the time passed very unpleasantly to both of us ; for Rosie was obliged to go on playing, shy as she was, and I felt more every piece she performed, that I wished I had known of her proficiency beforehand. I began not to like Rosie so much, and was glad when the guests went away, which they did about nine o'clock ; and then my Aunt Mary drew Rosie's arm through hers, and said, "Come, let us walk on the terrace, in the moonlight, Rosie, and you shall tell us about them all at home ; I have hardly spoken to you yet, child."

My Aunt Phœbe asked me to come with them ; but I said I was afraid of the evening air, so I was left alone, till, happening to lift up my eyes, I became conscious of a strange kind of fancied companionship. There was the picture looking at me with its large pensive eyes. "I know what is the matter with you," it seemed to say ; "you are envious of your Cousin Rosie's music."

I turned away my head, and would not look : but there

was a kind of charm for me in that face, and after a while my eyes were again attracted to it.

"You need not disclaim the bond between us," it seemed to say; "you had better not, for we understand each other. Stay with me; why indeed should you go out (though the night be lovely) and walk silently by while your aunts make much of Rosie; you were everything last night, now you are quite eclipsed by this new star."

"It is ridiculous to suppose that I can be envious of such a silly childlike creature as that," I mentally answered to the face in the frame. And so I sat, more and more pained to see that look in it, and to feel certain that just then it must be visible in my own face, till my aunts came in, and we shortly retired, — Rosie and I sleeping together.

As soon as breakfast was over the next morning, Rosie was impatient to go down to the beach; but I said I wished to write a letter first, so my aunts gave her permission to descend by herself, and walk about till I could join her.

We were standing out in the veranda when Rosie was thus set at large, and she forthwith set off down the slope, half running, half dancing, quickening and quickening her pace as it became steeper till she was obliged to run as fast as she possibly could. She stopped when she had reached the level sands, and looking up, laughed and waved her hands to us, and then ran off to the water-side.

My aunt had said to her that morning, "Rosie, my dear, what a child you are; when do you mean to grow up?" And I felt at the time that my quieter manners impressed them with the idea that I had a better regulated mind, and more ladylike habits. Now, however, they seemed to have forgotten that they had expostulated, and they both laughed heartily. I thought this more like the behavior of a schoolboy than a young lady, and stood looking quietly on. I felt that her careless ease, her joyous youth and spirits, were beautiful in their eyes; and therefore, though it was natural to me to be quieter in my movements, I believe I should have run down like Rosie, if I had known that they would admire her for it.

"How that dear girl enjoys herself!" said one.

"O, she is a sweet, happy creature," said the other. "And why don't you race down in that way? Eh, Millicent?"

I hesitated, and then replied, "that I preferred to enjoy things in moderation."

I saw that my aunt Phœbe felt that there was something in that. "To be sure, my dear," she answered, "moderation is a very good thing."

"And besides," I continued, with still a little hesitation in my manner, as if I did not wish to find fault with my cousin, and with a certain air of reluctance and regret, "I don't know, aunt, that it is altogether ladylike in Rosie to race about in that way the moment she is out of her mother's sight."

"Her mother!" exclaimed my aunt Mary; "nothing would please her mother better than to see her taking this healthy exercise."

"It would be out of place in Hyde Park," said my aunt Phœbe, rather coldly I thought; "but I see no harm in it here, where there are only two old aunts and one young cousin for lookers on."

It certainly is part of the misery of many, to feel keenly the merits and perceive the beauties of others; it is indeed those merits and those beauties which make half our pain. And when my aunts went on as it were, apologizing for Rosie, by telling me anecdotes concerning the sweetness of her temper, her usefulness at home, her obedience, and her pretty natural ways, I felt that I had brought it upon myself, and that every word said for Rosie was said against me; for I was sure that my aunts had thought my insinu-

ations unkind. Presently, the young gentlemen who had
spent the previous evening with us, made their appéar-
ance ; they brought their sister with them, and a message
from their father to the effect, that he should be happy to
take out all the ladies that evening in his yacht.

They sat with us some time. I did not go down to
Rosie, and one of my aunts at length went and fetched
her in. At the open street-door I heard her sweet voice.
"Aunt," she said, "the sea air has made my hair perfectly
straight."

My aunt laughed, and called her long locks "rats-tails";
what a figure she must look, I thought; but I was not
sorry, I felt rather pleased.

I called her as she was going up stairs, and our guests
arose as she appeared at the door, and spoke to her. As
I had been sitting at work so neat and so free from dust
or soil, I had felt what a contrast Rosie would be to me ;
all blown about as she had been with the wind, and so
untidy. That was why I called her.

But when she came and stood within the door, I mentally regretted what I had done ; for as she looked out
between those long falls of nearly straight hair, there was
such a radiant sweetness in her gentle face, and such a
flush of health, as far more than made up for any little disorder of dress ; and though it seems to show such a paltry
state of feeling, I know *you* will understand me, when I
confess that I regretted that I had been the means of her
showing how sweet she could look under any disadvantage. Once more, I felt that where I had been sustaining
my part well, she had come forward and thrown me into
the background; for now she must needs produce her
little apron full of fern leaves, and plovers' eggs, and
shells, and sea-weeds, to show to my aunts ; and every one
looked at her, and talked to her, and turned to her, and
turned away from me.

O, what little things these are to tell, what paltry, ignoble trifles! yet these, and such as these, occupied me every day, and all day long; while hourly my great-aunt over the chimney-piece chastened me with her serious eyes, and seemed to say, "Look up, Millicent, look at me; this is how you are looking now, and every day your likeness to me grows stronger." For several days I would not allow that envy had place in my heart; it was several more ere I could acknowledge that it was always working there, destroying my pleasure, distorting, beginning to show itself to the penetration of others, and making me hateful in my own eyes, and in the eyes of my Maker. Every morning I awoke, and resolved to shake it off; but it was so entwined with my heartstrings, that it seemed as natural to me as the very pulse in my veins.

If Rosie had been ugly, morose, uninteresting, I felt that my visit would have been pleasanter; and yet, every one was kind, polite, attentive to us both. O, why could not I be happy to let her shine as well as myself?

Well, I thought to myself, I have certainly never given way to envy before; but Rosie has some peculiar faculty for arousing it. When I go home and get away from her, my envy will cease. My aunts seemed always to be taking Rosie's part; perhaps because of those very slight insinuations against her, which I could not help sometimes uttering; I could not help sometimes disparaging her. The family that I had before mentioned were particularly pleased with her; they praised her beauty, simplicity, and sweetness, and that to *me*, and expected me to agree with them; in fact, they even seemed to do it in compliment to me, as if being her cousin, I must needs be proud of her.

Once, when they had praised everything else about her, they even praised her name: "Such a pretty name," they said, "and so appropriate." I hastened to inform them that it was not her real name, only a name that she had given herself; her real name was Anne.

"A name that she gave *herself,*" was the reply; " I should not have given her credit for such conceit and self-consciousness as knowing that such a name would suit her." And the speaker showed evident discontent with Rosie.

" My dear," said my aunt Mary, "you should have mentioned that the name was adopted by your cousin before she could speak plainly, or know the significance of it."

" O yes," I said, rather vexed ; "did I not mention that ? "

" O no, my dear," replied my aunt in a low voice, "of course not." We were sitting on the sand, and almost immediately our friends left us, and said they must go home to dinner.

" Aunt," said I, when they had withdrawn, " why did you say, ' Of course not ? ' why is it of course not ? "

" Because it would not have answered your end, my dear," replied my aunt calmly.

I felt my cheeks burn ; what was my purpose.? Did she mean that my purpose was to disparage my cousin ? I really dared not ask her, for though she had not been very explicit, I was quite certain that she had read my inmost thoughts, and I was obliged to begin talking of something else, lest she should explain herself without being asked.

From that hour, my little remaining pleasure in the visit was gone, and I longed to be away from the object of my envy and from the observer of it. Every day I envied, and often was reproved, especially by my great-aunt's picture. At length the day came for my departure ; Rosie had left the day before, and remembering my aunt's fond parting with her, and the great regret expressed by this family of friends on her departure, I was very much hurt to find that the same feelings were not aroused for me, nor the same degree of sorrow felt at losing me. I came down stairs ready equipped for my journey, and my aunts, after kissing me, informed me that they had got a present for me.

"Which we think will be acceptable," said my aunt Mary.

"Because, my dear Millicent," said my aunt Phœbe, "we have noticed that you really cannot keep your eyes off it; you are far more attracted by it than by anything else in our little house."

"What is it, dear aunt?" said I, half frightened.

"My dear," she replied, "it is your great-aunt's picture." I was obliged to accept it.

CHAPTER II.

THE LILY CROWN.

I WAS obliged to accept that picture. I was obliged to carry it home and show it to my parents, who said it was the very image of me, and that they should hang it up in the drawing-room.

Woe worth the day! Such shocking things as it was always telling me about myself no one would believe who had not felt their truth. It told me that I was envious of my own sisters whenever people preferred their manners, their voices, their conversation, their very dress, to mine; that if they were well, I envied their superior bloom; that if they were ill, I envied the care, the anxiety, the attention they excited. I envied the elder her precedence, I envied the younger her sprightliness.

And yet, I do not know that I ought to murmur, or that I have any right to be sorry ; for hard, inconceivably hard as the cure is, I humbly hope the days are beginning to dawn that shall see its completion.

But I must proceed. It was bitter to me to be admonished, day by day, by that beautiful serious face, and to be told that I envied my sisters. I struggled for some time against believing that I was guilty of so odious a fault, but at length I was compelled to admit the fact, and, in so doing, I felt as much ashamed as if all the household had known it as well as myself.

I did not yield willingly and unconsciously to this besetting fault, but the clear dark eyes looking down on me from under their drooping lashes were such a punishment in their constant supervision, that I am ashamed to say it was quite a relief to me when a plan was decided on by which my sisters would be out of my way for the rest of the summer. They were invited by my married brother to make a tour of the Continent with him and his two little daughters, and my parents consented that they should go.

Did I envy them the pleasure they were likely to derive from this tour ? I believe I did feel some pain at heart to think that I had not been included in the invitation, but it was such an inexpressible comfort to be left in quiet with *no one to envy*, as almost made amends for any disappointment. I hoped that by the time my sisters returned envy might have died out for want of fuel to feed the flame, or that I might have argued myself or schooled myself into a better frame of mind. I have heard it said that the envious person, though he is made miserable by his neighbor's prosperity, does nothing to diminish that prosperity, — he is, in short, no one's enemy but his own.

I used at one time to excuse my envy by thinking of this saying, but I soon found out that, though plausible, it is false. The envious person is, in truth, his own enemy, but he is as truly the enemy of every one whom he envies. This passion, like all others, must necessarily seek to display itself in action. They who bitterly envy cannot possibly refrain from showing and acting on it, they *must* be consistent. They *cannot* praise heartily, they *cannot* cordially assist, they *cannot* report fairly, they *cannot* generously make allowance, they *cannot* be just.

But I proceed, —

My sisters went on their tour, and I was left at home. I had no one to envy, and the picture began to lose its influence over me. I no longer dreaded to look at it, for it did not reflect my thoughts, and I could now sit and occupy myself at my little work-table without that constant looking up, which had become quite a habit with me.

One afternoon, after a very quiet morning, I put on my bonnet, and descended the old steps of the terrace which lies against the west side of the house. I went into the garden and wandered about for some time among the flowers, till I came to a favorite border of hollyhocks (which were just then in full bloom) and stood before them, occupied in thinking how short a time had completed their growth in comparison with my own : deep red, primrose colored, and studding the tall stalks with delicate rosettes, or cup-shaped, with a towering little pillar within, how very beautiful I thought them ! I was still gazing at them, and thought I should never be tired of admiring their loveliness, when I felt a hand upon my shoulder, and my father's voice aroused me from my revery.

"What, in a brown study, Millicent, my child ? " said he.

. "No, papa," I answered; "I was only looking at the hollyhocks."

"For want of more lively occupation," he continued. "Ah, it was too bad to leave you moping here by yourself. You were always too quiet, too fond of reflection, Millicent.'

"Is not that a fault on the right side, papa ? "

"I don't know, my dear ; you are so quiet now, that I really quite forget your presence sometimes : I never hear your voice, or your footsteps. This really must be put a stop to, as I was saying yesterday to your mamma."

"How, papa ? " I inquired.

He only smiled, and said, "We shall see."

I assured him that I did not feel dull.

"Young people," he observed, "always want companions, and it is natural and proper that they should have them, as I said to mamma. So, my dear child, I have written to your uncle, told him how the case stands, and asked him to spare your Cousin Rosie to come and spend

a few weeks with you, for as you have met already she
will not feel like a stranger here ; I expect his reply to-
·morrow."

" Thank you, papa," said I ; but O what a pang shot
through my heart at the mention of this most mistaken
kindness !   I could not smile, I could hardly appear glad ;
now, I thought, my rest is over, and I am again to come
under the dominion of envy.

My father told me that he expected an answer the next
day ; till it came, I was in a fever of hope that the invitation would be declined.   But no, my father handed the
note to me : " Here, Millicent," he said, " your uncle says
they cannot very conveniently spare their dear child, she
is so useful at home, but they feel that it will be such an
advantage to her to have your companionship, such an improvement to her, that they mean to send her.   In fact,
Millicent, Rosie has described you in such glowing terms
at home, as so ladylike, so clever, so well-informed, so
charming, that they feel they ought not to deprive her of
the benefit of your society."

My father laughed, but was evidently pleased ; and I
could not help blushing, for I felt that I had taken very
little pains to describe Rosie, with her sweetness, simplicity, and gentleness, in *my* home circle.   These words
in the letter were a reproof to me, also, as reminding me
of what I had observed at my aunt's, namely, that Rosie
had formed a very strong attachment and liking for me.   I
knew she admired me, and she had once or twice expressed a kind of half romantic, half childish fondness for
dressing me, and adorning my hair.

She once said, " She was glad she was my cousin."   I
tell this to show how unenvious she was.

" Why are you glad, Rosie ? " I had inquired.

" Oh," she answered, " because I like to be with you.   I
love you, and I like to see your beauty and elegance.   I
never saw any one like you before."

She said this with such perfect simplicity, that it did not sound like either flattery or affectation.

"Oh, Rosie," I answered, laughing, "you must not pay such compliments."

"Compliments," she answered, lifting up her dimpled face as if surprised. "Why, Millicent, you must know that you are beautiful; every one thinks so, why should not I say it then?"

She had an affectionate sweetness about her that most people would gladly have responded to. I did not, because this sweet manner, and everything else about her that was good and interesting, excited not my love, but my envy.

Rosie arrived by the railway. She was full of joy; and when I went to meet her with the pony-carriage, she expressed the greatest delight at the prospect of paying such a delightful visit in the country, and being, as she artlessly said, with me.

And now, as day by day Rosie and I were together, I felt that, unless I watched narrowly over my actions, envy would again assert her dominion. I did watch; I prayed for assistance, more because I felt the pain of my propensity than the sin of it. I did strive; and so long as I relaxed not these efforts, I believe that I overcame. . . . .

[Here several leaves have been torn from the manuscript; and, though some fragments of paper remain, they only contain a few broken sentences, of which I can make nothing, excepting that they refer to the lapse of several weeks, till the narrative is continued thus.]

Rosie and I were practising together when this note arrived. My mother presently brought it to us, and said, "Here, my dear, is an invitation for you and Rosie to join a picnic in Sir Eliot Morton's wood. They are to boil the kettle under the trees; and the Mortons, and the Blakes, and the Wilsons, are all to be there. Should you like to go?"

"What time is it to be, mamma ? " I inquired.

"Not till five o'clock," she replied ; "and the Mortons hope, if you come, you will bring some butter, some milk, and some fruit, and also music ; for in the evening they mean to adjourn to the house."

Rosie said nothing, but looked as if she would like to go.

"I would send the eatables forward by the stable-boy," said mamma.

"I think we had better accept, then," I answered ; "it is a splendid day, and Rosie would be sure to enjoy it."

"Yes, indeed," said Rosie ; "I should like it of all things."

It was such a beautiful afternoon, that, though the place was three miles off, we decided to walk ; for almost all the way was shaded by elm-trees, and for more than a mile we were to follow a foot-path which led along by the side of a little glassy river. Rosie was ready first ; for just as we were about to set off, my father called me to write a note for him. We were very early, and I thought it a pity that Rosie should be detained ; so I asked her to go forward, and wait for me at a certain stile, under an ash-tree, a very little way from the gate into my father's grounds.

When the note was written, I followed ; and I well remember my sensations as I stepped out into the delicious air and sunshine. I wandered on, and my thoughts naturally recurred to the events of the past week. Self-satisfied and confident, I congratulated myself that my uneasy feelings towards Rosie were nearly overcome ; for I had heard her praised without pain, and had responded with readiness, if not with cordiality.

I went slowly on till a turn in the deep glen, through which our little river ran, brought me to a place where it spread out into a wide, clear pool ; a few small white water-lilies were lying upon it, and it reflected the rich blue of the sky, excepting where a steep gravel-bank, crowned by the beautiful green ash-trees, was seen in it. I looked in as I stood on the opposite side; something white was under the ash-tree : I instantly recognized it as the figure of Rosie. She, too, was standing looking down into the water. She had taken off her bonnet, and every feature of her sweet face, every lock of her yellow hair, and every fold of her flowing muslin gown was distinctly mirrored in that nether world. She had some peculiar ornament on her head, — flowers. I looked again, not at the living girl, but at her clear image, and saw that she had made a coronet of the water-lilies, and set it on her head.

She, as well as myself, was silent and motionless; the small water-lilies, no larger than roses, studded the sunny water; they were all far beyond the reach of her hand; her shawl and bonnet lay at her feet, and her face was radiant with its tenderest expression of peace and tranquillity.

For a minute or two I stood gazing at her, and thinking that a painter would have given something for such a sight. First, I only admired her and her delicate coronet, but then I began to consider that there would soon be others to admire as well as myself; next, to regret that she should possess an ornament so more than commonly beautiful; then to envy her, and wish I had it instead of her.

I could not conceal my vexation ; and when I had walked round to her, and she, turning to me with a smile, put her finger to the flowers, and said, " Are they not pretty, Millicent ? " my annoyance was so great at the idea of meeting all my young friends in my common cottage bonnet, while she presented herself crowned like some lovely princess, and just suiting her crown, that I could not help saying, under the faint hope that she might be induced to discard them, " They are pretty enough as they float on the water, Rosie, but they are queer things to wear on one's head."

" O, I dried their stalks," said Rosie, innocently.

" I see a drop of water twinkling at the yellow tip inside

5   G

one of them now," I continued, regarding them with an air of strong disfavor.

"O, I am so sorry you don't like them," said Rosie; "I thought you would exclaim about their beauty the moment you saw them."

I was so weak and so envious at this moment, that I could not help laughing sarcastically.

"But," said Rosie, "I am glad I did not begin by asking you to wear them. It was an amusement to me to make the coronet, and twine it with ivy-leaves. I thought you would look so well in it."

"What!" I exclaimed, biting my lip with vexation, "did you make it for me?".

"Yes," said Rosie, "but never mind. It was no trouble, you know; on the contrary, a great deal of amusement, getting out the lilies. See, I have gathered every one that was within reach."

How much, while she said this, the folly of my envious spirit stared me in the face!

If I had only expressed the admiration I felt, or even refrained from disparagement, Rosie would have given me the crown which she had made on purpose for me, and would have gone unadorned herself to this rural feast.

As it was, I had completely outwitted myself. I could not accept what I had disapproved of, and I could not ask her to take it off without betraying myself. What base, what evil feelings are these to describe, perhaps the basest that deform our fallen nature! but you know them, you can understand them, you can follow me as I detail their workings.

We sat silent for a few minutes; we were still too early for the picnic. I know not what Rosie was thinking of. My thoughts were made up of shame, envy, and ill-humor; till, suddenly, Rosie exclaimed, "O Millicent! I quite forgot to bring my music."

A sudden thought struck me. "Go back for it, then," I said, "and I will sit here and wait for you; it is only a quarter of a mile, and we shall still be in plenty of time, for it is not like a formal party."

Rosie thanked me, and instantly started off on her errand, wearing the lily crown on her head. Now, I thought, here is a chance for me; I am perfectly determined to get some lilies for a crown while Rosie is away. There will be time to plait them, and I can easily say, when she returns, that I have altered my mind, and think they look very tolerable. I can tie a stick to the end of my parasol, and by that means I shall easily draw them to land.

Accordingly, I procured a stick, and having fastened it, looked about for a favorable place where they grew nearest to the edge of the pool. As I stood on the bank, the reflection of the blue sky was so clear in it, that even the small black images of the little swallows, floating high in the air, were as distinctly visible as the nearest grasses, or the yellow flags that grew thickly by the brink. There was one change in it, however, for a small white cloud had come up, and its image lay down in the pool like a heap of snow.

I saw that, small as it was, it would soon obscure the sun, and for a little while change the hues of the whole landscape; and I have a recollection of thinking at the moment, that it was an apt emblem of misfortune, coming up, when least expected, and bringing instantaneous dimness over the brightest and most sunny scenes.

But I did not think that the emblem had any significance for me; and I took my stick and descended cautiously to the margin of the glassy pool.

CHAPTER III.

THE HAYMAKERS.

A S I said before, I descended that green bank and
stooped over the liquid mirror; but had no sooner
done so, than I started back·with such sudden surprise as
I remember to this day. What had I seen there? It was
only for a moment that I had looked down into these polished deeps, but the face they had presented to me —
which seemed to have come up to meet me — is indelibly
fixed on my memory. My aunt Beatrice seemed to have
met my glance from among the lily leaves; so strongly,
so truly reflecting her picture, that for the moment I could
hardly believe that the face was really my own.

Once again I had seen that peculiar expression which
hovered over it like a shadow. Once again, considering it
as I might have done the face of another person, the
thought was forced upon me, " She is envious of me."

I stood for a moment diverted from my purpose; but
upon consideration, this curious likeness interested me,
and, stooping over the water, I again leaned forward to
meet my own face and look at it well.

Yes, it leaned towards me, in all things a duplicate of
the face in the frame; the dark eyes a little anxious, a little
reflective; the long hair drooping forward to shadow the
cheeks; the lip slightly pouting, as brooding over feelings
not altogether free from pain.

Ah, my Aunt Beatrice, if that had been truly *your* face
looking up at me, with the azure of a reflected sky behind
you, with your white dress gathered about your throat, and

your two hands holding back the hair which nearly touched the water; if that had truly been your face, I, not being blinded by self-love, might have taken warning by its expression, instead of softening its meaning, and trying to explain it away.

It was base and bitter envy that overshadowed it, and this painful image over which it brooded was the image of a young girl in whose heart such shadows were never found, — a girl who loved you, and whom all but you must needs have loved ; but whose remembered sweetness, though you thought on it then, was an example that you would not follow, and a warning that you threw away.

So I arose from my contemplation, and taking my long stick I tried very hard to draw the lilies to land; but one after the other, as I succeeded in drawing it so close as to be almost within reach of my hand, would slip from my hold, dip under the water, and reappear in its old place.

I thought I should be more successful on the other side of the pool, where the water was deeper, so I went round; and I remember seeing some haymakers in a field not far off, and wishing I had one of their rakes ; for so much time had already been wasted in fruitless attempts, that I began to fear Rosie would return before I had secured the flowers ; and, in the plenitude of my folly, I hoped she might delay to come.

Happy indeed it was for me that such wishes are made in vain. But it is needless to anticipate.

I found a place where I thought the lilies grew rather closer to the edge ; but the grass was slippery, and the soil was damp. I came near ; I drew one lily close to land. Another moment and I had cautiously stooped for it; my hand grasped it. I rose again. My feet felt suddenly cold, I cast a hurried glance downward, and found to my indescribable terror, that the tuft of grass on which I was standing had given way, and was sliding down the steep descent with me into the water. Not rapidly. My impression is (perhaps through the vivid distinctness of that fearful instant), that I went down somewhat slowly into the water. I tried to throw myself backwards; but it was too late, and with my feet still on that clump of grass, I went down on the clay, till the water was first over my knees, then over my shoulders, then over my head. Yet, such was the wonderful manner in which this descent, to apparently inevitable death, seemed to sharpen the faculties of life to unnatural power, and lengthen out moments of time, that I distinctly heard the washing and bubbling of the water as it closed me in. I distinctly saw the rocking of the lilies as the watery rings spread over the surface; and I was aware, when I looked at the trees which overshadowed my father's house, that I probably saw them for the last time.

These sensations were vivid and strong; but the instant I was submerged, I ceased to think, and became conscious of an overpowering weight on my head.

I do not know how long this lasted, I know nothing till I was breathing again, up in the air and light, and fighting for life among the rocking lilies. Every breath was a shriek, and in mortal terror, lest I must soon go down again like a stone, I cried out, and struggled vainly to reach the longed-for bank, which I saw almost close at hand, when I beheld a white figure flying towards me. It was close — it had flung itself down on the bank, and grasped with one hand the leaves of some yellow flags, that providentially grew there; with the other it had seized my hair, as I was again going down; and in an instant, perhaps less, my face was above water, and I heard Rosie, who was faint and panting with swift running; I heard her beseeching me not to struggle, and I saw that, as she lay on the brink, a very little thing would drag her in. But I could not obey her. I believe that at first I did not understand her. The water gurgled in my ears, and the trailing water-weeds almost covered my face. I again struggled, and then she cried out, adding her call for help to my distracted voice, and exclaimed in despairing tones, " O my darling, my darling, be still ; there are only these flag-leaves to hold me up, and some of them are breaking away. Millicent, I cannot drag you out ; but I can hold you up till help comes. The haymakers have heard us ; they are coming ; we shall soon be safe, — only be still."

I was still ; sufficient sense had returned to me for that. I held her arm with my cold hands. I heard the cracking rustle of the flag-leaves, as one after the other they gave way. I saw Rosie's white face grow fixed as stone with fear, and just as I became conscious of shouts and encouraging cries near at hand, at that same instant Rosie made a murmur of despair ; I felt her grasp of me tighten ; but the last of the flag-leaves broke away, and two instead of one went down under the rocking lilies.

It has been well said, that " time measures not the tides of soul ; " that which had seemed to me to include cycles of life and suffering must all have been enacted in a very short space indeed. We went down again ; but the time during which she had held me up had saved my life. Perhaps, four or five minutes was all that it comprised, then we went down ; and for what a purpose had I brought both our lives in peril !

I did not think of that : again I felt that weight upon my head, then I became unconscious, and then there was a period, long or short I know not, when I heard dimly ; then was aware of light before my eyes, then could open them and look about me.

I was lying on my back under some green trees ; some of the haymakers, healthy, sunburnt women, were standing about me. I looked up into the sky, and saw swallows flying about, and I saw a white cloud.

" Lord be praised," said one of the women ; " I thought
she was drowned."

" Give her air," said another voice ; "she don't know
where she is yet ; but, bless you, there 's no fear of her
being drowned, she was not a minute, not half a minute,
under water. It was nought but fright made her swoon
off."

I saw another woman approach me, unfasten my hair,
and dry it with her apron.

I knew I was safe ; but where was Rosie ? I tried to
speak, but could not ; and I tried to move, but was unable
to stir, .while all this time the women talked on among
themselves, under the impression that I was not able yet
to understand them.

"Which of them was it that took her out ?" said one.

A laboring man's name was mentioned. " And a lucky
thing for him," said the first speaker ; " as good as a year's
rent, I 'll be bound."

" As good as ten pound," said another ; "let the Squire
alone for that."

" Lie still, my pretty miss," said the woman who was drying my hair ; " Missis and the Squire are sent for ; they 'll be
here directly ; don't be frightened." I made another effort
to rise, and she stooped towards me, lifted me up, and supported me in her strong motherly arms. Then I could see
the pool ; O how eagerly I gazed at it. It was still already as glass, — as still as if nothing had ever disturbed
its serenity ! but O, terrible sight to me, who well knew
what it meant, — in the very centre of it lay floating the
crown of lilies !

O, when I saw it floating, and believed that Rosie's yellow locks lay under it, my despair was too great for my
frame : I fainted, and now I believe that some time did
pass, though I was unconscious of it.

I opened my eyes as from a troubled dream ; my parents

and some of our servants were standing by me ; some people were preparing to lift me up and carry me away ; but I cried out that I would not go, I must see Rosie ; I wanted to know what had become of Rosie.

Gaining strength through the energy of my desire, I released myself from them, and urged my steps towards the water. The lily crown was floating slowly, slowly down the river, but I saw a group of people standing silently, as others had stood about me.

I held out my arms to my father, for strength failed, and he carried me towards them, set me on my feet, and they divided and let me in.

Rosie was lying on the grass ; her face was nearly hidden by her hair. She was crownless now ; one of her arms lay above her head, and her cold white hand still grasped the long green flag-leaves ; drops of water trickled from them, and from her white clothing and disordered hair. I stood, I looked, and in my despair I uttered no lamentation, but I thought of that great multitude above with palms in their hands, and I sunk upon my face on the grass, crying out that Rosie was dead, and that I had been the cause of it.

I do not know all that followed ; reason assures me that the time was short, though memory presents it as long.

Attempts were made to calm me, but I could not attend to entreaties or commands ; my mind was dark, my senses were confused, and delusive phantoms seemed to float before me wherever I turned. My Aunt Beatrice — not a picture, but a living, breathing creation — seemed to rise up out of the water and follow my wandering eyes, and, hanging suspended over Rosie's head, I thought I saw the crown of lilies.

I remember that some people took her up and carried her away, and that they gently tried to draw the leaves from her hand, but could not ; but I remember nothing

5 *

of how I was taken home, nor can I recall anything that happened, till, after a very long sleep, or more probably a stupor brought on by narcotics, I opened my eyes in my own chamber.

For a while I felt tranquil, somewhat confused, and though aware that something unusual had happened, not willing, or perhaps not able, to consider what it was.

I turned on my pillow, and I remember experiencing a sensation of surprise at finding that the person who sat watching me in the dusk was not my mother, but an old servant. She was fanning me. My windows were thrown open, for the night was exceedingly sultry. I looked out and saw the red summer lightning playing between some ragged clouds, and said to the maid, " Mary, has there been a storm ? "

" Yes, ma'am," she answered, " a very awful storm ; " and she continued to fan me.

After a while I was obliged to go to sleep again ; but it was a confused and wretched sleep, and towards the close of it I became conscious that some one was singing. I awoke in a fright, and though day had not yet dawned, I knew that I had been some hours asleep. My windows were closed, and the servant, who still sat by me, had let her hands drop on her knee, and was slumbering. A shaded lamp was burning in one corner. I sat up, and by its light looked about me. On the table lay some work that I had placed there when I came up stairs to dress. I saw it, and in an instant the events of the day rushed back upon my recollection, and all the terrors of that doubt respecting Rosie.

I sprang out of bed, threw on my dressing-gown, and went out into the passage, bent upon entering Rosie's room, and satisfying myself.

It was dark, but I groped my way on to her door, which was shut. I opened it cautiously, no light was burning ;

the window-shutters had never been closed, and sufficient light came in from the shining of the crescent moon to show me that, the curtains were not drawn, and that no one was sleeping in her bed.

I cannot describe what I felt, as, half-fainting with the sickness of hope deferred, I turned from this empty room. I was wandering down the passage, when I heard voices below on the stairs. I went to the landing, and, leaning over the banisters, saw my father standing, and our usual physician with him. My father was leaning in an attitude of despondency against the balustrade. I heard the physician's soothing voice, —

" But it is at least a blessing that there is nothing to fear for your daughter."

My father sighed, and I strained my senses to catch what followed.

" Nothing to fear for my daughter," said he; " but how much to hope for my niece ? "

" She has youth on her side."

Then Rosie lived. There was comfort in that, though these sentences showed that she was in danger. The hall lamp was still burning, and I could distinctly see the anxious expression of my father's face.

" You think, then," he said, " that she may survive ? "

The physician hesitated.

" When fever comes on with such fearful rapidity, we cannot pronounce an opinion," he replied; " there is always great danger."

I stayed to hear no more ; my eyes were blinded with tears ; but as they fell down my cheeks I saw light from under a bedroom door, and I urged my way towards it, opened it and entered.

Ah, my little Rosie, my once envied and now beloved, inexpressibly beloved cousin, shall I ever forget the anguish of that moment ? She was sitting up in bed and singing.

Two people sat beside her. They gently laid her down again; but again she rose. Her cap had been taken off; her long yellow hair streamed over her shoulders, for the delirium of fever gleamed in her blue eyes, and the color was high in her cheeks. First she talked incoherently, then again she sang. Wild, but inexpressibly sweet were those unconscious songs. My mother wept over her; but she took no notice, and the attendants soothed and entreated, but she did not hear them. Still, in the silence of that sultry night, her trembling voice sounded through the desolate house, and went out among the branches of the trees, startling the birds from their slumbers.

CHAPTER IV.

CONCLUSION.

I LISTENED, and my heart died within me, for I perceived that the sudden shock of that perilous morning — though I had been permitted to rise up from it little the worse — had prostrated my gentle and lovely cousin. O, how precious she was to me now! With what anguish of heart I reflected on her generous self-devotion; with what bitter tears of useless regret I lamented the paltry feelings which had cost us both so dear!

I stood till the physician returned to her room, and then I went back to my own, threw myself on my bed, and repented. How heart-sickening are the tears of repentance when they are shed for those hours which are past recall! Anything else but this I thought I could have borne; but there was no hope, or a very faint hope, that I should ever be able even to acknowledge my fault to Rosie, and so relieve my heart of some of this intolerable pressure; much less that I should ever be able to make any reparation, by future kindness, for my past grudging and envious behavior. From the nature of things I could never repay her; she had saved my life, snatched me back at the peril of her own, when I was about to fall a prey to my demon mistress, — Envy.

I lay and wept; a sharp distress will drive many a hard heart to the only sure refuge. As I continued to mourn during that desolate night, I perceived my sin against God far more forcibly than I had done hitherto; yet, though my offence I knew was against Him, to Him I was driven

for refuge. I besought Him to spare the life of my cousin,
and to pardon the sin which had endangered it. At length,
but not till morning dawned, that sweet and broken singing became silent, and exhausted and weak, I fell asleep.

About eight o'clock I was awoke by some one entering
my room : it was my mother. My first cry was an entreaty
that she would tell me of Rosie. She appeared depressed
and utterly fatigued with watching and anxiety; she sat
down, and said she hoped I would be calm, and not give
my parents the distress of seeing us both very ill. Rosie
was much the same, — a little quieter, and I was on no
account to enter her room. She was to be kept nearly in
the dark, and as tranquil as possible.

She presently left me, and returned with the physician,
who, finding me exhausted with weeping, and otherwise
suffering from the effects of the shock, desired that I should
be dressed and taken out into the fresh air, and that a
couch should be set for me under the trees. I felt that
this was done partly that I might not hear Rosie's voice,
but I submitted, knowing how much sorrow there was in
the household, and desiring to add to it no more than I
could help. I sat out of doors under the trees, with the
splendor of the green lawn refreshed by thunder showers
stretching away before me, and all the gay flowers; the tall
hollyhocks, the dahlias, and the rich clustering autumn
roses smiling upon me. I felt my heart strangely out of
unison with the freshness, gayety, and peace of nature ;
but I acknowledged that I did not deserve to be with
Rosie, and I felt the truth of what they had said, that no
one's presence was so likely to excite her as mine.

O what a long day was that, and how very long were
those which followed ; never do I remember days of such
unequalled splendor, such cloudless serenity, and I was
kept out in them from morning to night, with my father or
that old servant for companionship. But from my place

under the trees, though I could hear nothing, I could still watch the house. I could see the evidences, now and then, of hurry and confusion, figures rapidly passing the staircase window, servants lingering in the hall watching for the doctor, that he might not be detained an instant at the door. I knew that the chance for Rosie's life was small, and I believed that a very few more days of such suffering as I was then enduring would prostrate me also. Everything that kindness could suggest or love invent was said to soothe me, everything but the one thing I pined to have, — the assurance that Rosie was better.

But on the third day of this sojourn out of doors, I happened for a time to be left alone, and I could not restrain myself, I must needs go into the house ; and there, as I wandered about restlessly in the lower rooms, I observed a peculiar appearance of suspense in those whom I met. They were so much absorbed that they scarcely noticed my presence, and I asked no questions (for nothing definite was ever told me in reply), but I waited till the physician came to pay his evening visit, and then I sat down on the lowest of the stairs, and waited till he should descend.

I leaned my head against the balusters, for I was weak. It was just about the time of day, as I remembered, that we had both been brought home. What days of misery to me, and suffering to her, had been the three which had followed ! The physician at length came down. He lifted me up, and gave me his arm into the parlor. Then he told me that the fever had left Rosie. " Twenty-four hours more, with a pulse at such a height," he said, " and her case would have been past hope, but now, with extreme care, if there is no relapse, I trust that, weak as she is, she may yet be raised."

I was very thankful, but that thankfulness was chastened by much fear : that there still was danger was not con-

cealed from me, and when I was permitted that night to go
into Rosie's chamber, and look upon her while she slept, I
wondered that anything so frail, so faint, so deathly, could
be recalled to the land of the living; but I had been assured that there was hope, and I endeavored not to de-
spond.

Three days had so completely changed that sweet and
dimpled face, that no one could possibly have recognized
it.   Her hair had been cut away, and the unshaded cheeks
were visible in all their sunken whiteness, and the wasted
hands lay in such a hush of repose, or rather of exhaustion,
that but for the evidence that she breathed I could not have
thought that she was still of this world.   But I looked and
mourned; envy had been killed by love; but oh! amid
what bitter pangs of self-reproach, what anguish of remorse this love had grown!

It was more than a week before I was permitted to see
her in her waking moments, but I cannot describe our
meeting, full as it was on one side with the keenest distress, and on both with the strongest affection.   After that
I was permitted to be constantly with her, nursing and attending on her during her tedious recovery; and then it
was that I solemnly resolved she should not love me, being
in ignorance of my besetting fault, but that I would tell
her of it both for the sake of my peace, and that she might
assist me in my efforts towards a cure, for I had become
more humble now; and fearful as was the lesson that I had
received, I still dreaded a relapse.

Therefore, when Rosie first came down stairs, and lay on
the sofa in the little morning-room, I proceeded to finish
a drawing which had been long on the easel, and on which
I had bestowed more than ordinary thought and pains.
There was a clear pool of water in the middle of my picture, a gravel bank rose from it on one side, and a green
ash-tree overhung it; there was a blue sky above, with

one white cloud rising up out of the west ; there were some yellow flags growing by the margin of the pool, and in the centre of it floated a lily crown. As Rosie lay on the sofa, her eyes were soon attracted to this little land-scape. I saw instantly that she recognized it, and that her regards lingered over it with a kind of tranquil joy.

What a happy scene it was for her to recollect! What a gracious reward had been vouchsafed to her to repay her for her pain, even the rescuing of a human life, — the life of one who was extremely dear to her ! But what a pain-ful scene it was for me ! I intended to copy it for her, that she might continue to derive pleasure from it, and to keep the original that it might be a warning to me. I let her gaze at it, and when she was satisfied, — pleased that I should have made it, but so weak, so touched and troubled at the sight of it that her eyes were dim with tears, — I covered it, and approaching her couch, told her that I had something to say to her. I knew she would still love me, and that she would feel neither resentment nor disbelief, so I knelt by her, and with my arm supporting her, and her cheek leaning against mine, I told her all that I have told to you.

And when I had done, true to the lovely simplicity of her character, she did not attempt to palliate, or even to excuse. She listened with wonder, with pity, with sympa-thizing love. She kissed me many times, but it was evi-dently a mystery to her ; and then she reminded me that God could forgive us all our sins, and she proposed that we should pray for the forgiveness of ours. Sweet, simple Rosie ! she believed that I had been envious because I had told her so ; she knew in theory that envy was a wicked thing, but so little had she ever been tempted to such a sin, that she scarcely knew either the blackness or the misery of it. And when she had paused awhile over my narration, and caressed me with all her own simplicity

H

and tenderness, she said, "Ah, Millicent, if you had told me that you were vain I could easily have believed you, but God has made you so rich, and so beautiful, and so much beloved, that I can scarcely understand what there is for you to envy."

I felt the truth of what she said. God had placed me in the best and happiest part of this his beautiful world. I was young, healthy, cared for, and sometimes, even in my most envious days, I had seriously considered whether there was any person with whom, on the whole, I could change with advantage, and I had decided that I had not yet met with such a person. And yet, notwithstanding this deliberate decision, I had basely envied almost every one with whom I came into contact the brighter part of her less favored lot.

I rose from my cousin's side, feeling lighter at heart for her sincere pity and simple-minded, generous forgiveness. I felt that a great fault could not be eradicated at once, but I believed and knew that of Rosie, at least, I never could be envious again. And why? Because I loved her so heartily, that all her joys, her advantages, her hopes, had become mine. The great commandment offers the only solution of that problem which afflicts the envious. "How shall I be cured?" we ask; it answers, "Thou shalt love thy neighbor *as thyself.*"

But can love be *learned?* Can it be fostered, cultivated, indulged? Can I make myself love my neighbor? Let us ask another question which may help us to the answer of this. Can hatred be *learned?* Can it be encouraged, cherished? Can I make myself hate my neighbor? Yes. How can I do this? I can do it by reflecting on the least agreeable parts of his character to the exclusion of his better qualities; I can impute bad motives to his indifferent actions; I can disparage his virtues and fail to excuse his faults; I can decline, in his case, to admit the strength of temptation; I can treasure up and dwell on imaginary slights or little affronts that he may have shown me, till they exasperate me; I can tell others of his behavior, dwelling always on its darkest side, till it appears all the darker by frequent repetition.

And can I make myself envy my neighbor? Yes, I can. I can do it by constantly comparing him with myself on those points, and those only, where he has the advantage, by considering that those advantages are precisely such as I want in order to make me happy, by exaggerating their importance, and by dwelling so much on the lot of others that I neglect the means of improving my own; and by sitting idle, brooding over my hard case, and mourning because I see no way for making myself useful, beloved, or admired, while others with no better opportunities or talents, are up and doing those very things which, but that I am absorbed in envying them, I could do just as well.

By an opposite course I can foster, cultivate, and encourage affection. This, it is granted, must be difficult at first, too difficult indeed for any but those who seek Divine assistance.

But I must proceed. Rosie stayed with me till she had quite recovered her health, and then went home, carrying with her the blessings and the love of all our household. Shortly afterwards, my sisters returned, and I, knowing what was in my own heart, resolved that by God's help, I would never, while I lived, consider my fault as cured; but watch over it as over a fire subdued, but not extinguished, and which any passing wind will fan once more into a flame. My watch has now been long, and partly lest I should slumber at my post of watcher, and partly that my example may be a warning to you, I have set myself the task of penning these pages.

But, you will naturally ask, how did I discover that you were the bond-slave of envy!

We are so anxious naturally to conceal this fault, and it is one that it would be such an offence to accuse one of, that, though there are few of us to whom it has not been said, or intimated by friends or acquaintances, " You have a high opinion of yourself"; or, " You are exaggerating this story"; or, "You should not be so disdainful of your inferiors"; or, " You are not very industrious"; or, "You are hasty"; or, " You are inconsiderate"; yet, to none .of us, perhaps, has it ever been said, " I perceive that you are envious."

This delicacy is a disadvantage to us ; that which is not *mentioned* we think to be *unknown*. It may certainly be concealed from others for a time, but the essence of envy arises and depends on comparison ; once institute a comparison in the presence of the envious, and unless they are on their guard, it is sure to be betrayed. As when an acquaintance of yours praised Mary's singing in your presence, — Mary, whom you call your friend, — and you replied, " O yes, she sings beautifully, but really it would be a disgrace if she did not."

" How so ? " said your acquaintance.

" O," you answered, " because she is always practising ; indeed, I wonder how she can make it consistent with other duties ; besides, she has been so well and so thoroughly taught ; no pains have been spared with her ;" and you added, in the tone of an injured person, " It would be absurd to expect those who have enjoyed no such advantages to equal her ; it would be quite unfair." Now, why did it give you pain to hear Mary praised, if you really love her, and are not envious of her ? and why was it needful to assure her admirer that she had had such superior advantage ? Did it make your singing any worse to know that hers was better ; and if it was better, why deny that this better singing was any merit of hers ?

I discovered then that you were envious ; but I **was**

confirmed in my discovery the next day, when, as I sat at work with you, a common friend of ours chose to descant oñ the beauty and loveliness of Isabel. You listened for some time uneasily, and with a slightly heightened color. You seemed to assent, and you even smiled, but it was not a cordial smile; and you said gently, "Yes, she is pretty, and has charming spirits; but I think her manner has been a little more subdued since her sister made that run-away match." -

By this remark you made the visitor suddenly silent; the shock of the information that you had conveyed was considerable. You knew him to be ignorant of that fact, yet you took care to convey it as if you were merely referring to something well known to you both, and you presently continued in a quiet tone, " Those charming high spirits have their disadvantages, after all." He slowly answered, " Yes," and then asked if Isabel resembled her sister in person. " O, she is the image of her," you answered good-humoredly; "the sisters are as much alike in face as in manner." (I have never heard any one else advert to this strong likeness, nor can I see it.)

Upon this the visitor, effectually silenced, stooped and picked up his glove; we both thought the information you had conveyed gave him more uneasiness than we should have supposed. He thought it a great disadvantage to Isabel, as you meant he should do; but you had no reward for your information: he could not be interested in the lively conversation which you tried to engage him in; *he liked you none the better because you made him like Isabel less.*

Here the manuscript abruptly terminates. On examination it appears that some concluding pages have been torn away; but I will not draw upon my own invention to supply a conclusion; I prefer to give the story as it stands.

DR. DEANE'S GOVERNESS.

CHAPTER I.

I DO not like this title. It should have been "Dr. Deane's Children's Governess"; but that sounds awkward, and we English are fond of clipping out all words that are not uttered with ease. We never say, Mrs. Richardson's Children's Governess, or Mrs. Chichester's Children's Governess; so let it be Dr. Deane's Governess, it will save trouble.

Dr. Deane's governess, Miss Ann Salter, was quietly seated, about three o'clock on a Wednesday afternoon, by the window of a pleasant little carpeted room, which was evidently used as a school-room. The sun shone in at the window; the light air was blowing in a good many petals of China roses. Four children were playing outside, three girls and a boy, the latter about six years old, and the girls all older.

Miss Ann Salter had a book in her hands; and I can put you in possession of her attitude at once, if you have ever seen a pretty print called "The Governess," by saying that precisely and exactly in the position of "The Governess" sat Miss Ann Salter. If you wish to know whether she had seen the print in question, I am happy to inform you (it being my desire to oblige you with all proper information) that she had.

But if you yourself have not seen this print, I must tell you that it represents a very pretty pensive-looking girl,

6

sitting quite alone, with her feet upon a stool, her hands dropped on her knees, and an open letter in them. Her hair is drawn in a braid from her cheek, and one long curl falls on her neck. She is dressed in deep mourning, and is evidently musing over this letter from home ; perhaps it is from a bereaved mother. There are globes in her, room, and slates and maps, and children's dogs'-eared books ; so there are in the room where Miss Ann Salter sits. But she is not in mourning. She is dressed in a gown of a light-brown color, with three flounces, a stripe of blue at the edge of each, and a very pretty collar and cuffs of her own work. It is always best to be particular in describing these little matters, because it prevents mistakes.

The hands and feet represented in the print are unnaturally small. Miss Ann Salter's, however, were of the usual dimensions ; her hair, dressed exactly like that of " The Governess," was smooth, abundant, and of a somewhat sandy hue. She had very light eyebrows and eyelashes ; and her face, young, healthy, and plump as it was, had no pretensions to beauty, or even to good looks, excepting when she was laughing or looking very animated ; then it was a pleasant young face enough, and as fresh as a milkmaid's.

At the time of which we speak her face was very gently pensive, though it was a half-holiday, though she had a new book on her lap, and though it was quarter-day.

Perhaps she had been seated twenty minutes in this position, when one of her little pupils ran up to the window, and exclaimed, " O, Miss Salter, Johnnie has got papa's great squirt, and he is squirting the roses ! " Thereupon Miss Salter started up, and in a voice a little sharp for such a pensive heroine, exclaimed, looking forth from the window, " Johnnie, you naughty boy, bring that squirt to me immediately " ; and Johnnie reluctantly approached the arbiter of his fate with a large greenhouse syringe under his arm.

"How came you to take that?" asked Miss Salter, with impressive solemnity.

"It was only just inside the greenhouse door," said the chubby little culprit; "and I've only just been squirting some bees that had got into the roses."

"Put it back directly," said Miss Salter.

"May n't I just squirt the rest of the water out first?" asked the boy.

"No," replied the governess, "you may not; and you are not to be always saying, *I only just* did this and that. It is very naughty to make excuses; put back the squirt directly where you found it.

Thereupon the little boy slowly turned away, and carried his stolen plaything across a well-ordered lawn, under some tall fir-trees, and along a gravel walk, till he reached a greenhouse, his governess watching him till she saw him put down the squirt and come out again. She then withdrew her head and shoulders from the canopy of roses, clematis, and passion-flower into which she had been leaning, and at the same moment a respectable elderly servant opened the door behind her, and said, "Master has come in, Miss Salter, and wishes to speak to you, if you please."

O, quarter-day, thought Miss Salter, and answered, "Very well, Andrew, I will come."

As she approached the study door, it was opened, and three female servants issued from it. "How painful it is," she thought, "to be paid my salary just at the same time that they receive their wages. I have no doubt they know why I am summoned just now."

Dr. Deane was going over some accounts with an old lady who superintended his household. He looked up pleasantly, and said, "Sit down, Miss Salter; I thought I should have been ready for you, but you see there are more last words. Well, Mrs. Mills, it certainly does seem a great deal to pay for meat at this time of the year, especially when there is plenty of grass."

"O, it's a shameful price, Doctor, quite shameful! I told Curtis I was sure you would not go on with him," said the old lady, looking quite irate.

"What an interest Mrs. Mills takes in her stupid house-keeping!" thought Miss Salter, sitting down, and falling quite naturally into the attitude of "The Governess." "Really one would have thought it was a matter of life and death to save the Doctor sixpence."

Dr. Deane went on with the accounts, and presently said, "Well, Mrs. Mills, it is as you say, and we had better change our butcher."

"That is exactly what I expected you to say, Doctor," proceeded Mrs. Mills. "I said to Curtis only yesterday, 'You are your own enemy, Curtis; you raise the price of meat till you either lose your customers, or induce them to make up with poultry and fish.' 'Well, ma'am,' said he, 'I hope you will not lose me a good customer by complaining of my prices to the Doctor.' 'Indeed,' said I, 'I shall think it my duty to mention it; I should consider myself unfaithful to my trust if I did not.'"

Thereupon followed a discussion as to what butcher should be employed; it lasted five minutes, and while they pass, and while Miss Salter still sits in the attitude of "The Governess," we will look about us and describe what we see.

We see that the room is a small one, and that its floor is covered with a faded green carpet, which is all the worse for the chemical experiments made by its owner; there are many books, but they are all locked up in glass cases. In glass cases, also, are displayed numerous skeletons of small animals, mice, moles, birds, and cats; and in trays protected by glass lie metallic treasures and specimens of ore from the gold fields. Altogether the room has a cold, shut-up, and glassy effect, not at all home-like, and very much the reverse of comfortable.

But the Doctor himself, whom we also see, looks as if he could make any room comfortable ; he is a fine man with a keen black eye that seems to be always on the lookout for symptoms, a thick black eyebrow, and a thick head of iron-gray hair ; he looks about fifty years of age, has regular features, a delightfully cordial smile, but an abrupt manner, and what the poor call a very out-spoken way with him.

As his old friend, Mrs. Mills, left the room, Dr. Deane turned suddenly to Miss Salter, who straightway changed her position.

" Miss Salter," said he, " you have not looked quite the thing lately. What is it? headache?"

" O no, sir," said the Governess, blushing.

" O no, sir! why, one would think it was a shame to have the headache. By the by, I don't wish the children to drink any more of that beer; Andrew tells me it is quite sour, — the thunder, no doubt. Did you drink any of it at dinner to-day?"

" Yes, a little ; but it is not particularly sour; and I am quite well, sir, indeed," said Miss Salter, blushing more than ever, and perfectly shocked at the notion that, if she did not look "quite the thing," it was in consequence of drinking sour beer.

" Then you really feel perfectly well?" asked Dr. Deane.

" Perfectly well, I assure you, sir."

" Humph," said the Doctor. "Well, Miss Salter, you and I generally have a little conversation on quarter-day; and if you have anything to mention, or to complain of, now is the time. My wish is, as far as I can, to meet your reasonable expectations. Do you find that Johnnie is growing too much of a Turk for you? I know the rogue is always in mischief."

"No; he is pretty good generally, I think, when he is in the school-room; and the little girls are very orderly."

"And your father and all your family are well, I know; I saw them yesterday. Your father seemed in capital spirits, — said the crops were finer than he had known them for years. Well, Miss Salter, have you anything to remark upon?"

Miss Salter considered, and then answered, thoughtfully, "No, sir; there really is nothing particular to mention that I know of."

"Nothing that you wish altered? Then I suppose you wish to retain your situation?"

"If you are satisfied, Dr. Deane."

"I certainly do not wish that we should part. I have found you a conscientious, good girl, and fully clever enough for my dear little dunderheads. You neither neglect them nor overwork them. And besides, having known you ever since you were born, and all your family having been patients of mine so many years, I naturally feel that you are likely to be more comfortable with me than a perfect stranger would be, and also that the highest testimonials would not enable me to trust a stranger as I do you."

An expression of great pleasure came over the face of Miss Ann Salter. "Thank you, sir," she said; "I am satisfied, and much obliged to you for — for —"

"For my good opinion, eh?" said the physician, with a smile. "Well, but now I am going to scold."

Miss Salter looked up rather alarmed, and blushed, with a sort of conscious look, which told plainly that she suspected what was going to be said.

"The fact is," proceeded Dr. Deane, "that I should be very glad if you would try to look as you say you feel. You have told me that the children behave reasonably well, and that you are in good health, and quite comfortable. What I wish is, that you should appear so. When first you came to us, and, indeed, till quite lately, you were as ready for any sort of expedition or amusement as the children themselves ; — such a hand at a nutting ! — in such spirits at hop-picking time ! Now you walk about with your head hanging down, and have the air of appearing to think that it is quite derogatory to smile, and — Well, well, I did not mean to make you uncomfortable ; but I should be glad, Miss Salter, to see you cheerful again, and, in short — contented."

"Contented, sir !" exclaimed Miss Salter, in a tone of astonishment and vexation.

"Well, perhaps I am wrong, — I beg your pardon if I am ; I will change the word, and say, I should be glad to see you less pensive — less depressed."

"One cannot always prevent such feelings," said Miss Salter, with downcast eyes. "Depression is the result of circumstances."

"You are wrong, Miss Salter."

"Sir ? "

"I say you are mistaken. Depression of spirits, when it is real, and when people cannot help it, comes, in ninety-nine cases out of a hundred, from dyspepsia, or from a dis-ordered liver, — in short, from bodily causes."

"Surely, sir, that is looking at it with a physician's eyes !" exclaimed Miss Salter, looking not a little vexed.

"And that is how one must look at it who knows any-thing about it. When people are in perfectly sound health, they may feel acute sorrow, deep anxiety, the keenest dis-tress of mind, the most painful agitation, — they may suffer from disappointment, from remorse, from a thousand other of ' the ills that flesh is heir to,' but not from that lumpish, spiritless feeling, that you and I are talking of by the name of depression, unless they are brooding over something in their lot that displeases them. In short, what I want to say, and what I want you to reflect upon is this ; that as a physician I give it you as my candid opinion, that what we now understand each other to mean by depression is either disease or discontent."

"I am sorry you should have thought me discontented," observed Miss Salter, slowly, though without any appearance of ill temper; "but with such a theory, sir, I do not see how you could have thought otherwise."

"I talk to you with more freedom," was the reply, "than I could do if I merely stood in the position of an employer. I also have the superintendence of your health. Not that it has ever caused me much anxiety; you were always a cheerful, healthy, little romping child, full of life and activity. You came to me, and I think I may say that your natural characteristics have not been unduly restrained; indeed, your excellent spirits and love of out-of-door life have been to me one of your chief recommendations. Well, I was highly pleased with you, and I believed you were just as well pleased with us, till all on a sudden I happened to say to you one day, at the early dinner — (I remember it was the very day after Fanny came to stay with me) — "Will you take some more beef, Miss Salter?" and you turned your face slowly to me, and said, "No, thank you, sir," with such a pensive voice, and with such an air of patient meekness, that I declare I felt for the moment as if I must be a jailer who deprived you of your liberty, or a host that abridged you of your food. Now I have done; and I am sure you will endeavor to alter your manner in this particular. Here is your check; take it with the pleasant reflection that you have earned it well, and that I think so."

Now Miss Salter had an excellent temper, and considerable self-control. Probably she felt annoyed at this plain-speaking; but if she did, she did not show it, but took her check, and perhaps would have said something to the effect that she would give the subject her best attention, if at that moment a knock had not been heard outside the door, which was followed by the entrance of a pretty girl, tall, slender, and yellow-haired. She was elegantly attired in a glossy dress of light-shining silk, a graceful mantle, and a white bonnet, and as she entered, she exclaimed : —

"Uncle, the pony-chaise is coming round. Are you ready?"

"Yes, my dear," said Dr. Deane. "But stop, this is pay-day, Fanny, and I will give you your allowance."

"O, thank you, uncle!" exclaimed Fanny, shaking back her long curls. "I am sure I shall be very thankful for it, I am so poor, — am I not, Annie? Do you know, uncle, I was obliged to borrow a sovereign of Miss Salter, because you insisted on not giving me my money till quarter-day."

"Fanny, Fanny, you are a very extravagant child. Why, even when people earn their money, I never pay them beforehand. And you, you little useless, idle thing, you that are only a consumer, and not a producer, you actually want to coax me to pay you money that you never earned before the time when I agreed to pay it; and because I will not, you little drone, you go and borrow of the industrious bee. I wonder you trusted her, Miss Salter! There; count your money, child, and tell me whether it is right."

"No, uncle; one sovereign too much."

"Then pay your debt with it, like an honest young woman. And now, remember that I never mean to do this again; I am 'principled against it,' as the Americans say." So saying, Dr. Deane bustled out of the room, leaving the two girls together.

"Here is your sovereign, dear," said Fanny to Miss Salter. "Was it not lucky that I chanced to mention having borrowed it? I had not the least notion that uncle would give it me."

"Nor I," remarked Miss Salter; "the Doctor considers

it quite wrong, you know, to exceed one's income. Really, Fanny, I think you should be more careful."

"So I will, dear," said Fanny, stooping to kiss her. Fanny was tall but exceedingly slender ; and though very graceful, had not the agreeable air of health presented by the Governess. "I thought I had been careful till I found my money was all gone," she observed.

"No wonder, if you have three new bonnets in one summer."

"Why, you would not have me wear a dingy bonnet, would you ? "

"No, but I would not have you wear a delicate, gauzy thing like this, in the dusty road, during a drive. A straw-bonnet would look as well and more appropriate to-day. Stoop a little, will you, it is not quite straight." Fanny stooped. Miss Salter adjusted the bonnet to her mind, shook out the folds of her gown, and altered the set of the mantle.

"Have you not been talking some time with my uncle ? " asked Fanny. "I thought when I came in you looked uncomfortable."

"I only looked as I felt then," said Miss Salter, sighing.

"O well, I must say that if my uncle is not pleased that Johnny is so noisy, that I think it is more his fault than yours ; for really, Annie, I am sure he pets him more than he does the little girls. However," said Fanny, re-flecting that this was no business of hers, "my uncle is very kind to all the children, and to me too."

"It was not about Johnnie that he spoke," said Miss Salter, blushing again at the recollection of the lecture she had received ; "he thinks — he intimated that I was — I don't know that I can tell you now ; I will some other time."

As she spoke, an expression of the gentlest pity came over the fair face that was looking down into hers, and its owner said with a sigh, and in a tone of sympathy, "Dear Annie."

" Of course I must expect this kind of thing in my painful position," said Miss Salter.

"Yes," said Fanny, with more sincerity than wisdom or knowledge of what she was talking about; "but it is a great comfort to know that all the trials of the Christian shall 'work together for good.' I am afraid, dear, that you have felt your position more than usual lately. I noticed this morning that you looked particularly depressed." At the mention of this word Miss Salter sighed; but as a loud, cheerful voice was heard in the hall, calling, " Fanny, Fanny ! come, child, I am ready," Fanny hastily ran out, and Miss Salter retired to her room, where she put on her hat, and went into the garden.

" Uncle," said Fanny, when they had driven about a quarter of a mile, " don't you think Miss Salter has looked rather depressed lately ? " She said this partly from a little feeling of womanly curiosity, and partly because, in her kind heart, she had found a place for the Governess.

" Depressed ? " said Dr. Deane ; " yes, my dear, I have been talking to her about it this morning."

" Have you, uncle ? " replied Fanny. She longed to ask another question, but did not dare.

" O Fanny ! Fanny ! mind I never see you pursing up your mouth, and looking as if you were trying hard not to laugh when anything droll is said in your presence. And then if you really cannot help laughing, never let me see you turning away your face to hide it, and heaving up a sigh to show that you are determined not to be amused."

" Does Miss Salter do so ? " asked Fanny, with her natural simplicity. " Yes, I think I have noticed it ; but, however, one naturally makes allowance for her, and it is no wonder she feels pensive. Obliged to descend from her position in society, separated from her family, poor girl, obliged

to work for her living, always seeing those about her who
are in superior circumstances."

"Why, is not Lucy, the dairymaid, separated from her
family, and obliged to work for her living, and to see those
about her who are in superior circumstances ; and does she
look depressed ?"

" O, no ! but she was most likely always brought up to
know that she was to go to service."

" Does that circumstance make service agreeable to
her ? "

" Yes, I suppose so, uncle."

" How do you know that Miss Salter had not the advantage of knowing that she was to be a governess ?   Have
you inquired ? "

" No, uncle ; I took it for granted that she had not."

" And what else have you taken for granted, Fanny? Tell
me ; for I think I see a ray of light breaking through ob-
scurity."

" I don't know what you mean, uncle."

" Never mind that ; give me your views, and tell me
what you have been pleased to take for granted, respecting
governesses in general."

" I have read a good many interesting stories," said Fanny, hesitating, "that had a governess for their heroine.
The last I read was particularly interesting, and it made
me feel that, as a class, they deserved a great deal of consideration, and — I don't exactly know how to say what I
mean, but when I came here I felt that I ought to be particularly polite and friendly to Miss Slater, and to feel ɐ
great deal of pity for her."

" Humph ! now give me a sketch of the story."

" O, the heroine is a tall, dark-eyed, lovely creature,
brought up in the greatest luxury, and accustomed to associate with refined people. Her father loses all his property,
and dies. The story opens with her taking leave of her

bereaved mother. They are so poor that she is obliged to
take her long journey in the depth of winter, on the top of
a coach, and she reaches her first place at night. And the
story goes on to say that the people are very vulgar, and
treat her with the greatest insolence and harshness, particularly the master of the house, who dislikes her from
the first."

" But she, no doubt, is a miracle of patience and discretion ? "

" Yes, uncle, she is very unhappy, but bears all with the
sweetest meekness, though she often retires to her own
room to weep, and think over the happy past ; and then it
goes on to say that she saves one of the children's lives,
and the house is just going to be robbed, but she over-
hears the thieves talking and disclosing their plans behind
a hedge."

" A likely incident ! Well, go on."

" It ends not quite so naturally as it begins. She marries — "

" Of course she does ! The eldest son lives at home.
He is a paragon of elegance and excellence, in spite of his
vulgar bringing up. He is also particularly handsome ;
she marries him."

" Nothing of the sort, uncle."

" Then she marries the curate ; I know she marries the
curate ! and immediately after his rich uncle comes from
India, lives with them, dies blessing them, and leaves them
all his fortune."

" No, she does n't, uncle. She marries a young baronet,
who is struck with the pensive sweetness of her face, as
she takes the children out for a walk."

" Indeed ! "

" But the most interesting part of the story is her journal," proceeded Fanny, " with the description of all her
lonely feelings ; really it is quite harrowing to read it, —

such beautiful resignation, and, at the same time, such melancholy."

"Pray, my dear, have you talked over this story, and especially this journal, with Miss Salter?"

"Yes, uncle."

"O Fanny, Fanny, you exceedingly silly little goose."

CHAPTER II.

" I DO not know why you should call me silly, uncle,"
said Fanny, looking very much disconcerted ; " I am
sure I have always meant to be kind to Miss Salter."

" My dear, your kindness was commendable. What I
complain of is your habit of taking things for granted,
and acting as if things were proved, because you have no
doubt concerning them. But I am going to this farm-
house. Now, be discreet, and do not say anything without
reflection."

" What can it matter what I say here ? " thought Fanny.
" People living in such a place are not likely to be great
observers of manners or of cultivated language, I should
think."

Fanny's face showed her thoughts so plainly, that Dr.
Deane said in answer to it : " Fanny, my child, take my
advice, and think before you speak here. The good woman of the house is no gentlewoman ; but I would not have
you hurt her feelings for a good deal."

Fanny was surprised, but said nothing, though her uncle's warning made her look about her attentively. There
was nothing, as she thought, to reward scrutiny. The
farm-house, instead· of being a delightful old thatched
building, with picturesque gables, and walls covered with
vines, was an ugly red brick house, square, neat, new, and
undecorated by any graceful creepers. There was a barn
in full view, and some turkeys were strutting about before
it ; a stout, red-armed country girl was putting potatoes
into a trough for their meal ; and there was a large duck-

pond near the front parlor window which was well stocked with poultry, whose white feathers were strewed thickly over the grass.

As the pony-chaise stopped before the door of the square red house, a pleasant-looking woman stepped out, and welcomed the doctor with, "You're quite a stranger, sir."

"And very glad to be so," replied Dr. Deane. "You can hardly see too little of the doctor, eh, my good friend?"

The farmer's wife laughed good-humoredly at this little sally. She was short, plump, healthy-looking, and had a tone in her voice and a look in her eyes that seemed familiar to Fanny, she hardly knew why.

"You'll excuse my shaking hands, sir," said she, "and you too, Miss," curtseying to Fanny; "for I've been picking walnuts all the morning, and they make the hands as black as ink. Come in, sir!"

By this time they had alighted, and the Doctor said, presenting Fanny, "This is a great friend of your daughter's; Mrs. Salter, my niece; Fanny, this is Miss Salter's mother."

"I am sure I am much obliged to the young lady for taking notice of my Annie," said Mrs. Salter.

Fanny's surprise, which caused the clear color to flush up all over her face, was far too great to admit of her saying a word; and it was fortunate for her that she was following Mrs. Salter into the parlor, and that the little bustle of setting chairs, and making her visitors comfortable, was occupying that worthy matron's attention till she had in some degree recovered herself. Then Mrs. Salter recurred to the subject, and said, "It must be very pleasant for my Annie to have such a nice young lady to speak to."

"Yes, they are great friends, indeed," replied the Doctor; "young people are generally companionable."

"To be sure, sir," said Mrs. Salter, still keeping her admiring eyes upon Fanny, "young people can run up a friendship in a day. And my Annie has plenty to talk about; dear me, when she gets a holiday, and comes over to see us, her tongue never stops, bless her!"

Fanny was still mute; Miss Salter's home and Miss Salter's mother were so different to anything she had imagined, that she could not find anything to say; but she sufficiently recovered her powers of observation to notice that there was a somewhat strong smell of tobacco in the room.

"Well, sir, and how is my dear girl? quite well, I hope," said the fond mother.

"Very well, indeed, she told me so herself this morning; and would have sent her duty, I am sure, if she had known I was coming here, but she did not; indeed, I did not know it myself; but I found I had a quarter of an hour to spare, so I thought I would bring my niece to see you."

"Thank you, sir, for the visit. I'm always pleased to hear that my Annie is well; being my only girl, I feel more for her than for my great rough boys; and though I know that she has had a rise in life, I sometimes wish I had her with me, for all that."

A pretty white kitten at this moment pushed open the door, and Fanny, having nothing to say, was glad to call it to come and sit on her knee, while silently listening with some shame and a great deal of surprise to the conversation which followed.

"I have sometimes wondered why you spared her to live away from home, as she is your only daughter," observed the Doctor.

"Why, you see, sir," replied the mother, "John and me, we married very young, and we were, I may say, badly off for a good many years, we had such a large family; farming, too, is not what farming used to be, so that altogether, what with bad seasons, and many mouths to

feed, I assure you, though I don't wish to complain, that
few people have known what it is to look at every penny
before they parted with it more than we have. Well, at
last, after my nine boys, Annie was born, and very fond
we all were of her, natural enough we should be ; but my
boys were so rough, that they soon made a complete tom-
boy of her, that they did, bless her ! and I was so taken
up with my dairy and the poultry, that try as I would, I
could not find time to teach her. I managed to teach her
to read, and her eldest brother would set her a sum now
and then, but she almost ran wild ; though she could milk
a cow prettily enough when she was nine years old, and
was mighty fond of picking fruit for market, and cramming
turkeys. I was beginning to wonder how I could ever
manage to get schooling for her, when my husband's mother came to live with us ; she soon saw how things were
going on, and one day she said to me, ' Annie, I know you
have hard work to get on, paying all their own, and giving
the boys their learning. And,' says she, ' the two hundred
and fifty pounds that I have saved, John should have, and
welcome, to lay out on his farm, only that I know better
than to think he would take it of me while I am alive ; and
as for the boys, they will soon be a help to you, and able
to earn their own living ; but this little Annie,' says she,
' that is as bright as the day, it often lies like a weight on
my mind, that if anything should happen to her father,
there is nothing for her but to go to service.' ' Mother,'
said I, ' we must put our trust in God. John here has the
best of health, and I am stout and active for my age, so
I hope for the best ; but I do not deny that I should like
to see my Annie married before I die.' Well, she was a
very short-spoken woman, and when I said that, ' married,' said she, ' husbands that are worth having are not
so easy to come at !' She did, indeed, sir. So says I,
' Grandmother, I am sure John and I would always wish

to take your advice about the dear child, as is no more than our duty, so speak your mind.' However she never said a word; but next market-day, just as I was ready to start off for G—— in the spring-cart, she came down, and says she, 'I am going with you.' I put her down at the Miss Jessops' school, and I took her up again when I had sold my poultry and butter; she never said a word, good or bad, till we got home and supper was over, then she said, 'John and Anne, I've been to the Miss Jessops, who I hear from our vicar keep the best school in the town, and I have made an agreement with them that, if you are willing, they shall have Annie for six years for my money; and then whatever happens she will be independent, and able to get her bread.' Of course, we were agreeable to let her go, and very thankful. Her grandmother had the pleasure of seeing her in your house, and of feeling that she was now independent before she died."

"Ah, I always thought your husband's mother was a sensible woman," observed Dr. Deane.

"Yes, sir, she really was. And the good education she gave Annie has been quite a rise in life for her, as I tell her. And though her grandmother did talk about husbands being hard to get,—my Annie—why, dear me, I know a young man that would—however, I'll say no more about that," continued Mrs. Salter, bridling.

The Doctor smiled, and Mrs. Salter, having already remarked that she should say no more about it, continued in a reflective tone, and with an air of pretending to think lightly of the young man whom she had hinted at: "I must say for him that he has been very well brought up, and does credit to his bringing up, which is more. However, when he comes to me and says, 'Mrs. Salter, I know she'll never care for me,—I don't believe she cares a straw for me,—'Keep up your spirits, William,' I always say, 'you are young yet, and so is she.'"

"O, it is young William Watkins, is it?" asked the Doctor suddenly, for he had a decided tinge of curiosity about him.

"No, sir," replied the hostess, thrown off her guard, "it is young William Dobson at the mill; he is in a capital way of business, and owns such a good house! he is a very fine strapping young fellow, too." ·

"Then you are quite in his interest, Mrs. Salter?"

"I leave it entirely to the child herself," replied the mother coolly; "but that cherry-orchard of his is quite a picture! I really don't know how many sieves of fruit he did n't send up from it this season, though his mother told me. They have a very snug little farm, you know, sir, as well as the mill, and everything prospers with them."

"He is a very fine young fellow, and I can only wish your daughter may reward him for his liking," said the Doctor.

"Well, sir, perhaps she may," replied the mother, laughing; "he was always coming here during her holidays, and sometimes, when she had been a little cool with him, I would go as far as to say, 'Ain't you ashamed of yourself?' and then she would laugh and say, 'I don't want him to make a fuss about me; I can do very well without him, mother.'"

Fanny was listening with great interest and attention; and Mrs. Salter, catching her eye, continued, "But I beg your pardon, miss; when I begin talking about my Annie, I do n't know how to leave off."

"Don't apologize, Mrs. Salter," said the Doctor, rising, "I am sure what you have said has interested my niece very much."

Fanny finding herself thus appealed to, roused herself and said a few civil things to this good mother about her daughter; but she felt so surprised, and so ashamed of herself for the false conclusions which she had so confidently arrived at, that she was very glad to find herself again in the pony-carriage, safe away from the ugly farm-house, which she had still great difficulty in thinking of as Annie Salter's home.

"Well, Fanny," said the Doctor, after a long silence, "what do you think of Mrs. Salter's notions of a rise in life ; and above all, what do you think of her definition of independence ? "

" Of course she is wrong," said Fanny, "in saying that Annie is independent, because she earns her own living ; that is the very thing that prevents her from being independent."

" Prove that, my dear child."

" O, you know, uncle, that servants, and governesses, and people who live in gentlemen's houses, are always called their dependents, — their paid dependents."

" Yes, it is the custom to call them so ; it means that their staying in such houses depends on the owner's pleasure ; but though the ambiguity of language enables us to use this word in two or three senses, we must not forget that we can often, with equal truth, call the same persons both dependent and independent. Which am I, Fanny ? "

" Independent, of course, uncle."

" How can that be ? I am dependent on my own exertions. I am not what is called an independent gentleman, but a professional man, depending on my profession for my bread."

" But you are independent of anyone *else*," said Fanny ; "you only depend on your *own* exertions. I mean, that you are your own master."

" To be sure. Then where is the difference between me and Miss Salter ? "

" O uncle ! she is not her own mistress ; she is under you, and she must work so as to please you for her money."

"So must I work in such a manner as to please others for my money; and Miss Salter is not dependent on my exertions, only on her own."

"I never heard of such a thing," exclaimed Fanny; "surely she is your dependant."

"Call her so if you like, but she is quite independent of me. If I do not please her, she has only to go and leave me; I cannot make her stay, any more than my patients can make me stay if I choose to go. We are both dependent and independent, — independent of other people's exertions, and dependent on our own."

"Then," said Fanny, "why do we use that word so falsely ?"

"Because we have inherited it from the times when servants really were dependent on their masters. Serfs and retainers may not leave their masters at pleasure ; they are dependent. There was no such thing as a governess in those days ; but we have foolishly extended a word to them which is particularly ill-suited to express their condition ; we speak as if they were dependent on *us*, whereas the peculiar difference between them and other young women is that they are dependent on themselves, or what, in all other cases, we call independent."

"I shall certainly tell all this to Miss Salter," said Fanny; "she has often talked with regret about her trying position, and my happier lot."

"Who began first to talk in this way, Fanny ?"

"O, I did, uncle ; I made friends with her from the first, because I felt for her position ; but, uncle, if she is independent, what am I ?"

"Consult your own good sense, my dear ; how do matters stand ? Your dear parents left no property behind them beyond what I spent in your education. I take you to live with me as my duty and my pleasure. I do not choose that you should earn your own bread, because I have plenty. You are therefore dependent upon me ; and all young ladies living at home and doing nothing are in like case, unless they have private fortunes."

" Then," said Fanny, laughing, " I am glad I am in that case. I cannot help feeling, though, that it is not pleasant for Annie to be a governess, in spite of what her mother said about its being a rise in life."

" You think it would be better, then, for her to go and live at home, doing the work of the house and the farm as her mother does, — very hard work it has been for the good woman, — far harder than most servants do for wages, — and her only relaxation is to go in the spring-cart to market, and sell her butter and eggs ; or to sit over the fire while her husband and his friends smoke their pipes, and talk of the turnip crops, or discuss the price of wool."

" Oh ! " exclaimed Fanny, " fancy Annie driving the spring-cart to market ; how ashamed she would be of jogging along in it ! and then selling her butter and eggs herself at a stall, taking up the raw sausages, and exhibiting the plumpness of her ducks and geese, and then sitting with those prosy, coarse farmers under a cloud of tobacco-smoke ! No ; she is far better off as she is."

" So I think, and so her mother thinks ; she is educated and refined ; these are blessings, and it is another that she should be living with people equally well educated, equally refined. Such being the case, I do not see how you can talk of her as being in a painful position without absurdi-ty ; for if it is in itself painful to live among one's superi-ors, then every household in the land contains some mem-bers that are in painful positions ; all the servants may feel how painful it is that they should have to dine in the kitch-en, when Miss Salter dines in the parlor, they waiting upon her. Miss Salter may feel it painful to know that you have no reason to work for your living as she has. You, on the other hand, may feel it hard that you have nothing to call

your own but what is given you by me, notwithstanding
that you admit that it is a pleasure to me to give it. I, in
my turn, may feel how hard it is that I should have to be
always looking after my patient, Sir John W., instead of
having a hereditary estate like him, while all the world
knows that he is fretting his life away because it is so painful to him that his cousin should have made good a title to
the R—— peerage against him, Sir John, and should be
frequently driving past his door with the coronet on his
carriage."

"Well, uncle," said Fanny, gently, " I suppose my mistake has been that I have taken for granted that every
governess has come down in the world ; the books, you
know, almost always represent a governess as lovely and
ill-used, and living among people who are really her inferiors in birth and original position. So when I first saw
Miss Salter, I resolved that I would make a friend of her,
be extremely polite to her, and, in short, pity her position,
and try to make it pleasanter to her."

"But now that you discover that she is not a fit object
for pity, that she is not ill-used, and that she is not of gentle birth, I hope you will be too just, too really considerate,
and too sorry for the mischief you may have done by your
ill-timed pity, to withdraw your companionship from Miss
Salter ; I hope, as she has never deceived you about herself, but has merely accepted your mistaken compassion,
and responded to your spontaneous advances towards
friendship, that while you will leave off condoling, you will
not leave off chatting with her, and sitting with her as
usual."

"O, no," said Fanny ; and added slowly, "Of course
not."

"You will be as friendly as before," proceeded the Doctor, "though the romance of the thing has flown away on
the wings of Mrs. Salter's ducks and geese."

"Yes," said Fanny; but she rather over-calculated her own powers of self-control, for when the pony-carriage reached the Doctor's garden, Miss Salter came up to it, and asked Fanny to walk with her in the shrubbery. Fanny, though she assented, colored and seemed uneasy, and when Miss Salter asked, "Where did you drive, dear?" she hung her head like a culprit, and answered, blushing violently, "We went — that is, my uncle took me — at least — we went to call on your mother." Miss Salter, though Fanny's flattering suppositions that she was a heroine in painful circumstances, and that she had come down in the world, and ought to be treated with all consideration, had been too agreeable to be put away, was notwithstanding too sensible not to feel that by her assumption of pensiveness, and that peculiarly injured air so necessary to a heroine, she had made herself ridiculous in the Doctor's eyes, and now Fanny's excessive confusion and evident reluctance to say where she had been, made her ridiculous in her own eyes. She walked in silence for some time; at length she said : —

"Dr. Deane told me this morning that mother was well." ·

"O yes!" replied Fanny; "we only went for a call; and I thought your mother a very nice person indeed, Annie, and she seems very fond of you."

A sharp pang of shame darted through Ann Salter's mind, as she saw the evident confusion of Fanny, and the shock it had been to her to find everything connected with her friend, the governess, so different from what she had pictured to herself.

She walked beside Fanny in deeply mortified silence. "If I had not suffered her to remain in her self-deception," she thought, "there would have been every likelihood that she would have come to be fond of me for my own sake; but now that she finds I am not what she expected, how can she continue to care for me?"

7   J

As for Fanny, she had begun to walk with her friend, but had not a word to say; she felt herself under some strong constraint, which she could not throw off; and when they reached the end of the shrubbery and turned again, she involuntarily quickened her pace, remarking, "That she had not finished a letter, which ought shortly to be posted, and must go in to write it."

Ann Salter saw how it was; she only detained Fanny to say, "Did you call anywhere else this morning?" and when Fanny answered "No!" the color rushed to her face, as she turned back to the shrubbery. "So then," she thought, "the Doctor must have taken Fanny out on purpose that she might see my family, and the way in which we live. I was sure he meant something more than he said, when he talked about my depression."

CHAPTER III.

THE eldest of Ann Salter's little pupils went to bed at half past eight in the evening, at which time she was expected to make her appearance in the drawing-room, and then she and Fanny generally sang or played ·duets together, till the hour for family prayer. On the evening after her conversation with Fanny in the garden, she was unusually silent, and felt a constraint upon her which made her long for bedtime ; depression had given way to a feeling of ingenuous shame ; she wished she had · not allowed Fanny to talk of her parentage, taking for granted that she was of gentle birth, without informing her of the truth, nor to speak of her position as a sad one, and of her case as one demanding sympathy, without setting her right. " How absurd I have been ! " she thought ; " how could I suppose that ·Fanny would never meet with my father or mother, and how wicked I am now to feel ashamed of them ! " At last she was able to rise and take her candle. " You are early to-night, Miss Salter," said the Doctor. " It has struck ten, sir," said Ann Salter, blushing, " and I was up very early this morning ; I had some writing to do." What the writing had been which she left her chamber to accomplish she did not tell the Doctor, but when she reached her room she took out her journal, and said to herself, " How could I be so silly as to write all this stuff just because Eveline D'Arcy in the novel wrote a journal, and because Fanny seemed to think it so interesting ! " and as she turned over the leaves, she added thoughtfully, " But after all, I am not persecuted, and cer-

tainly I am not in any great affliction; I wish I had not
imitated Eveline D'Arcy's style of journalizing. I wish I
could behave naturally, and not be always wondering what
other people will think of me. How foolish Fanny will
think me now that she has read all this, and now that she
has seen my dear mother! Well I shall not rise early to-
morrow to write down to-day's experience; I am not going
to record how Dr. Deane said he thought I was discontented, and how Fanny was surprised to find my mother
was not a gentlewoman. No! I have had enough of journals for the present. I shall not write again in a hurry."

So saying, she put away the luckless journal. "Fanny.
said I should soon tire of it," she thought. "Fanny declared that I should not write it long, and I *almost* made a
vow that I would persevere; however, I suppose when
next she asks to see it, I shall have to confess that I am
wrong and she is right. I *am* tired of it; I will not write
another word." Having formed this resolution, she went
to sleep. On the next morning before breakfast, observing Johnny hard at work with a slate and pencil, she asked
him what he was doing, and the little urchin replied that
he was writing his journal. Whereupon the Doctor, who
was carving slices of ham for breakfast, looked very much
amused, and said, "Quite right, my boy, you could not do
better. Who taught you to write a journal, eh?"

"Nobody taught me, papa," said the boy; "but Kitty
says she sees Miss Salter writing her journal when she
wakes in the morning; but she says I can't write one, but
I shall, for Kitty does, and so does Emily."

"Pass your plate for a piece of ham," said the Doctor,
"and tell me what you put down in your journal; is it like
this: 'To-day I ate so much pudding that I fell asleep
over my sum'; or, 'To-day I had a bad mark for throwing my ball through the window?'"

"I don't want to write that," said the little boy, sullenly;

"I only want to write about having holidays, and going out to fish for sticklebacks, and having shillings and sixpences given me."

"O, very well then, you had better write no journal at all. Miss Salter does not write down all the pleasant things, and leave out all the unpleasant, I am sure."

"Do you approve of journals, sir?" asked Miss Salter, not wishing to give a direct answer to the Doctor's appeal.

"Approve? yes, Miss Salter, if the journal is one of events, and only sparingly interspersed with records of frames and feelings; nothing is more likely to help us to correct our faults than a *true* description of how we have been overtaken by them. If I am in a passion to-day, and write down all about it when I am cool, it makes me feel ashamed of myself."

"But, sir," interrupted Miss Salter, "one often hears it said that the journals of good people seem to be written on purpose for publication, and that the world may see how deeply they repented of their faults; surely when people write journals, it must be with a view to their being seen."

"My young friend," was the reply, "if a man keep a *true* and impartial record of the events of his life and his behavior under them, he cannot possibly wish it to be seen, even after his death. His graver faults and his deep repentance after them he might be able to give to the world, but his little petty feelings of envy, malice, meanness, or peevishness, he could not bear to expose to his nearest and dearest friend. The *deceitfulness* of his heart he must feel an anxious desire to conceal, though its wickedness, if he represented it vaguely and in general terms, he might not care to keep to himself."

"Well, I must say," observed Miss Salter, "that the faults of those good men whose lives I am fond of reading are always such as I should not mind confessing myself."

"Their faults as represented in their journals. Very
true ; for when people write their real autobiography, they
generally take the utmost care not to let it go out of their
hands in their lifetime ; and they either destroy it on their
death-beds or leave injunctions that it shall not be opened
after their decease."

Now Fanny, having read Ann Salter's journal, would not
for the world have looked at her while the discussion was
going on ; for she could not but remember that the said
journal, over which, by the by, she had shed many sym-
pathetic tears, was not exactly a record of follies or of
faults ; it was rather a reverse picture of what Johnny had
intended to set down in his ; namely, an account of what
Eveline D'Arcy would have called "trying circumstances,"
"slights," and "painful events connected with my unfortunate position." Ann Salter was not less uncomfortable
than Fanny ; but, as she was liable to be swayed by every
one's opinion, she now began to think she ought to continue her journal. "Though if I do," she mentally added,
"I shall take care that no one ever sees it ; in fact, what
would be the use of showing a journal written on the
Doctor's plan ? It would make people dislike one, instead of feeling interested."

"I should think it must be very difficult, sir, to write
such a journal as you describe," she presently said, "because it would be so terrible to think that, in spite of all
one's care, it might be found and read."

"And such being the case, you think the temptation
would be great to be vague and general in one's confessions, and not to write truly."

"But it might be done in a cipher," continued Miss
Salter, thoughtfully ; "I think I know one that I could
write it in."

The Doctor laughed ; he had not expected that his plan
of journalizing would so soon be put to the test ; and he

would have continued the subject, but that the children, having now finished their breakfast, were carried by their punctual little governess to have their faces washed, and find their Bibles, that they might be ready for family prayers. The children did their lessons very well that morning; and Miss Salter never once relapsed into the attitude of " The Governess." She had just dismissed them to have a game at play in the garden, when she heard the Doctor's step. He was advancing rapidly, and she observed that Johnny was teasing him by asking some childish question; for the Doctor answered, hurriedly, " There, go away; papa cannot attend to you; go and play in the hop-garden, you and your sisters, and if you are good you may have a half-holiday." A half-holiday! thought Miss Salter; what can that be for? " Where 's Cousin Fanny?" she heard the Doctor say. " Here, Fanny, I want you." " Cousin Fanny is gone out," said the children, who were now jumping round him for joy. " Tut, tut," cried the Doctor; " where is Miss Salter? Not with her, I hope."

" No, sir, I am here," said Ann Salter, rising and looking out at the window.

" O, you are at home, Miss Salter," said the Doctor, rather gravely; his hurry seemed to subside. " Well," he said, after looking at her for a moment in silence, " I will come in and speak to you."

" I hope I am not going to have another series of remarks on my depression," thought Ann Salter; but she had not time for many reflections; the Doctor entered. " I have just been out in the pony carriage," he observed, with gravity.

" What is that to me, I wonder?" thought Miss Salter; " there is something odd about the Doctor's manner, I am sure."

" Indeed, sir," she replied.

"Yes," he continued slowly and calmly, "I went to the farm, — your father had been stacking hay, — I am not alarmed about him, — but he has met with an accident. There, don't look so frightened, he is not in danger, — sit down."

Ann Salter sat down again, for she had started up. She felt faint and giddy, but the Doctor's next words enabled her to control herself. "And your mother wants you to come over and help her to nurse him; you can be of great use."

"I want to know what the injury is," said the poor girl, shivering.

"What the injury is? — well, I can scarcely tell at present; he was stunned at first, but he soon came to himself, and his arm is broken; that is, I hope, the extent of the mischief."

On his first entrance, the Doctor had rung the bell; it was now answered by a female servant, who was ordered to bring down Miss Salter's bonnet and cloak, "and anything else she will want in a drive," added the Doctor. Confusion and anxiety kept Ann Salter silent a few moments; she felt that she would like to go over and help her mother, but her mind was in a whirl, and when she found that her walking apparel was produced in a great hurry, and that the gig was coming round, she burst into tears, and exclaimed, "Oh! I am afraid I shall find my dear father very ill!"

"I hope not," replied the Doctor; "and one reason why I am in a hurry is, that I want to take some medicine over, and some other things that I require."

"And think what a comfort you will be to your mother, Miss!" observed the maid.

Again the notion that she could be of use enabled her to rally; and she got into the pony-gig, continuing to shed tears, it is true, but perfectly mistress of herself,

and able to listen to all the Doctor's directions and re-
quirements.

"Now, Miss Salter," he said, when he had left her a few
moments for reflection, "I am taking you over partly because your poor mother, sensible woman as she is, was so
completely overpowered when she saw your father's state,
that I feel she is not fit to be with him,.at least for the
present. The person who is with him should be calm,
and not give way to any display of feeling, even if he
should say affecting things. 'Ah, my poor dear,' he said
to your mother when he came to himself, 'I am going to
leave you!' He went on to say that he wished to see
his children and give them his blessing; your poor mother
went into hysterics, and I had to get the servant-man to
take her away, which I was sorry for, because I wanted
help. Now, if your father should talk in that way to you,
do you think you can answer calmly, 'Father, you must
not talk ; the doctor says quiet is necessary, and that if
you can keep quiet you will most likely do well?'"

"I will try, sir."

"Do so, and remember there is to be no kissing and
weeping over him when you first enter. You are to walk in
with me, sit down by him, just watch him, apply the lotions
according to my directions, give him drink, and take no
notice when he talks, excepting to tell him to keep quiet."

"Surely he will think me unfeeling."

"Never mind what he thinks ; do your duty. I have to
tell you what your duty is ; do it even at the risk of being
thought unfeeling by your sick father. His face is a good
deal bruised and disfigured ; but if I tell you that those
bruises are not of the slightest consequence, I suppose you
will not be shocked at seeing them."

"O no, sir, my nerves are strong."

"Yes, I know they are ; well, I am putting you into a
very responsible position. I have told your poor mother

7 *

she must not attempt to go near your father till to-morrow, for she cannot stand it, and he gets excited when he sees her. So now follow your own judgment, and form your own conclusions, venture to be independent. If he is worse, send for me ; if any of his friends come to see him, keep them out of his chamber; if he says he never can recover, tell him quietly that you believe he is mistaken ; and if he wants to see his sons, say he shall see them to-morrow."

"Very well, sir, I will."

"Ah, that tone sounds promising; I am pleased, and I believe I may trust you."

"But if I do all this, I am to have the comfort of hope? I am to believe myself that he will recover?"

" Humanly speaking, I see no reason why he should not get better, with the blessing of God; no reason, indeed, with proper attention to keep him calm and quiet; but every reason for anxiety, if his feelings are worked on, his mind distracted, and his nerves flurried. You will sit up with him to-night."

"O yes, sir, I am not at all afraid, and I shall be so thankful to help mother. If she can rest, she will be quite herself again to-morrow."

"To be sure, and I shall come early to see him, and you may depend on my telling you what I really think of him; as to the children, I shall let them have a holiday to-morrow, and you need not be uneasy about them. I dare say Fanny will hear them say their lessons."

"O, thank you, sir; you are very good."

"And mind your father does not see you looking depressed ; that might discourage him," continued the Doctor, forgetting his late conversation with the governess, who, however, remembered it while she replied, " O no, sir, I should not think of such a thing"; and immediately all her foolish little fancies, and airs, and discontents flashed back upon her recollection, as such things will on the minds of all of us when the pressure of circumstances has suddenly broken off the ordinary thread of our thoughts, and when we think of the feelings and speeches of yesterday, as if they had occurred ten years ago, and could never by any possibility be entertained by us again. What did it matter now to Ann Salter that the servants knew she received a salary for her services ; that she was in what she was pleased to consider a " dependant's position," and that the beloved parent to whom she was going wore a white coat instead of a black one, and was not what is called a gentleman ?

But though Ann Salter felt comforted in the belief that her father's life was not in danger, and that she was going to be of use to both her parents, she felt her heart beat fast, and her limbs shake as they drove up to the door of the farm-house ; and she thought she would have given anything in the world if she might have retired only for five minutes to pray for help from above, and for composure and skill to meet this emergency.

This she could not have ; the Doctor ushered her at once into the kitchen, where sat her poor mother with her arms flung on the dresser, and her face resting upon them. She sobbed and wept afresh at the sight of her daughter, and exclaimed, " Ah, poor thing, she does not know how bad her father is ! Ann, my dear, your poor father was very near being killed this morning."

" Yes, I know, dear mother," said Ann, striving to speak calmly, and distressed to see her mother so helpless.

" She hardly looks as if she did know it, Doctor," observed the poor woman, as if hurt at her daughter's self-command.

" She is come to help you, and to nurse her father," replied the Doctor, addressing both mother and daughter, for he saw that the fortitude of the latter was ready to give

way; "and she can be of no use if she is not calm. Come,
Mrs. Salter, I have brought you a composing draught, and
when your neighbor comes to help you in the house do you
go to bed."

"She is come; she is sitting by my poor husband,"
sobbed the wife.

"Then I will send her down to you. Come with me,
Miss Salter."

Ann Salter only waited to give her mother one kiss, and
then stole up stairs after the Doctor. The door of her
father's chamber was wide open; she saw him lying on
his bed breathing hard. There were no curtains to the
window, but a heavy shawl had been fastened before it to
darken the room, and the brown curtains of the bed were
let down. The window was open, as the slight movement
of the shawl sufficiently proved; but the poor restless
patient was so much in the shadow that at first his daughter could not distinguish his bruised features, and their
troubled expression. A woman was sitting by the bed-
side, fanning him, for it was very hot. Dr. Deane took
the fan from her, and sent her down, putting Ann Salter
in her place. He then gave her some directions, showed
her the medicines, remarked that her father's head was not
now very clear, and that if he did not notice her presence
she need not draw his attention to it. He then shook
hands with her and left her.

What her feelings were as she saw him gradually going
down the stairs, and afterwards when she heard him drive
away, it would be impossible to describe. She was now
left virtually with the whole responsibility of the case on
her own hands: it was not yet one o'clock, and she knew
she should not see Dr. Deane again till the next morning;
his prescriptions had been already made up, and she should
not even have the comfort of seeing the apothecary's boy;
yet when she had sat a quarter of an hour by her father

(who happily for himself and for her was now in a half doze), she felt equal to her task ; she had found the opportunity for prayer that she had so ardently desired, and she knew that her proving equal to her task was of the utmost consequence ; so for more than two hours she sat fanning her father, ready to show him a steady and almost cheerful face the moment he awoke. His rest was broken, he was feverish and evidently in pain ; she sometimes thought he was more stupefied than sleepy, and the weary hours dragged on till she knew by the sounds in the farm-yard that it must be past four o'clock, before there was any change in the patient, or she had any person to relieve her from her watch.

At last the neighbor came up, and beckoned her out of the room, saying that the tea was ready. She ran down, and was very glad of some refreshment, for she had not dined. Two of her brothers were in the kitchen, and from them she learned that her mother was gone to bed and had fallen asleep ; she stayed down but a very few minutes, and as she came up stairs she observed that her father's eyes were open, and that the neighbor was saying, " How do you feel yourself now, Mr. Salter ? " " I feel very bad," was the reply, " and very thirsty ; I could fancy a glass of ale ! "

" I 'll go and draw some," said the neighbor ; " a glass of your own home-brewed can do you no harm."

Upon this Ann Salter was obliged to propose toast-and-water as a substitute, and the neighbor appearing inclined to argue the point, she was terrified to see how rapidly her father's face flushed, how excited he became, and how angrily he discussed the point.

" O, do go, do go," she implored ; " do leave him, and let me try to calm him ! " But it was now too late ; he was thoroughly roused from his previous quietude, his pulse quickened ; he complained of violent headache, and soon

began to ramble in his speech. This was no time for tears
or weak fears with his daughter; she had been told what
to do under any circumstances that were likely to arise,
and the neighbor, now humble and distressed at the mistake she had made, was anxiously bent on giving what
assistance she could.

Leeches were put on; and in ceaseless exertion and
anxiety the next few hours were passed; the long summer
twilight had settled into darkness, and the evening star
was shining through the crevice between the shawl and
the window-frame, before peace and silence were restored
in the sick-chamber, or Ann Salter could sit down by her
father's bed.

And yet the time had been so fully occupied, that though
she was fatigued, she had not felt it to be long; and when
some supper was brought up to her, and she was told that
it was eleven o'clock, she could only think of the past
morning and evening as of a dream. She stole to the top
of the stairs, all the household were in bed, excepting the
brother who had brought her supper. "You had better
go and take a turn outside while I sit with father," said
he; "and there is a box come for you, from Dr. Deane's;
it came some time ago, and the man who brought it said
Miss Fanny Deane had sent it."

Ann Salter could not make up her mind to go and
walk, even under her father's window; but she went to
see what Fanny had sent her, and found a kind little note,
some articles of dress, and two or three interesting books,
that Fanny thought she would be glad of; moreover, her
journal.

She took out a shawl and a hood, for in spite of the heat
she felt the want of warm clothing in her father's room;
and she took out her journal, and not wishing it to lie
about, she brought it up to her father's room, and laid
it on the table. Then she dismissed her brother, and

through the weary night sat patiently watching her father; sometimes he dozed, sometimes he was wakeful and restless; but he always found her calm and steady, attentive and cheerful.

Towards morning, when the early dawn began to wake the birds, fatigue made her head droop, and her eye now and then fill with tears; once she dozed a few moments and began to dream, but starting up, she stole to the window, for she heard a fluttering noise: it was the leaves of her journal, the summer air coming in had lifted the paper cover, and it lay open before her. It had also displaced the folds of the shawl, and one slanting sunbeam lay across the page; mechanically, Ann Salter's tired eyes rested on the illuminated sentence; it ran thus: — "*August 3d.* — The children were idle at their lessons to-day, and Johnnie was troublesome and mischievous. I do not like the new housemaid's manner; it is too familiar, and adds to the discomfort of my position. We know that trials are appointed for all; none are free from them, and we strive to be resigned under them; yet it must be allowed that some of the dispensations of Divine Providence are more difficult to bear than others, and I do sometimes feel a wish that some other than the peculiar trial of dependence, and the slights and annoyances it gives rise to, had been appointed for me. Any other dispensation, I often think, would be easier to bear, and I cannot but feel a wish that the nature of my trial might be changed; but let me not be unduly depressed; let me try to conduct myself with gentleness and resignation."

"If the kitchen fire was alight, I would burn this," thought the weary little nurse.

. "Annie, Annie," moaned the voice from the bed, "my mouth is so dry; give me some drink, child; I want some drink."

CHAPTER IV.

THREE days had passed, days of deep anxiety and much exertion to Ann Salter and her mother. The farmer had received greater injuries than had first appeared; but he was getting on favorably, and though entirely unused to illness, was very patient, excepting when the thought of his farm came into his head, and then he could not help showing the restlessness and harass of mind that oppressed him.

After the first day and night, Mrs. Salter entirely recovered her self-possession, and was unwearied in her care of her husband; but more was required in his sick-room than could be done by one person; and his daughter sometimes found the various duties now devolving on her almost too much for her strength. There was the servant to look after; for, as Mrs. Salter justly said of her, she had no head-piece, and though professing to understand a dairy, would spoil a whole churning of butter if she was not well attended to; then she loved to gossip outside the back-door with the farm-laborers, leaving the household work undone.

"Ann, Ann," Mrs. Salter would call gently down the stairs, "have you seen that Emmy has scalded the milk-pans?" or, "Have you seen that Emmy has fed those turkeys?" or, "Have you looked after Emmy, and made her kill those young cockerels ready for to-morrow's market?" Sometimes the answer would be, "No, mother; but I will see what she is about when I have weighed the butter for to-morrow," or, "When I have plucked the

chickens, — they are nearly finished." Sometimes it would
be, " No, mother ; but I will scald the milk-pans myself,
for the grains are just come, and Emmy is gone with them
to feed the pigs."

Sometimes when Mrs. Salter came down for any little
nicety which Ann had prepared for her father, she would
sink into a chair, look admiringly at her daughter, and exclaim, with tender pride : " Deary me, what a thing it is to
have a daughter ! Here I come down and find everything
done to my hands, and her stirring about as busy as a bee.
Ann, dear, I 'm glad you have n't forgotten how to cook."

" O no, mother ! " would be the cheerful answer ; " no
fear of that."

" Ah ! I wish your dear father and me could afford to
have you at home always. Dick, you 're pleased to have
Ann at home, I know ! "

Dick, a great stupid youth of sixteen, his mother's pet
when her daughter was away, would answer, shaking his
fair hair and heavy head, " I should rather expect so,
mother."

Then Mrs. Salter would proceed to carry the little tray
with its savory contents to her husband, being dutifully followed by Dick, who would bear the salt or sugar, as the
case might be, and who never would go up and see his father unless he had some such pretence for presenting himself ; for he was very shy ; and to walk up to his father's
bed with no other object than to say, " How do you feel
yourself to-day, father ? I hope you 're mending," would
have appeared to him a formidable and affecting cere-
mony.

When they were gone, Ann Salter's face would cloud
with involuntary anxiety, and, busy as she was, a number of
moral reflections would crowd into her mind, — reflections
on being discontented with one's lot, — reflections on the
folly of not knowing when one was well off, and on the

K

happy lot of a governess as compared with the housekeeper and factotum in a farm. It was not that she did not love her parents and her brothers, — not that she did not feel willing to exert herself, both strenuously and cheerfully, in their behalf, — but that she perceived how much more carefully one eats bread in one's father's house, if he is poor, than in another man's house, if he is rich. In the Doctor's house she had none of the cares of providing ; none of the anxieties of possession ; her meal and her salary were assured to her. Here she was anxious about every trifle that passed under her hand. " If I spoil these cream cheeses, there is so much money lost that should have gone towards the rent." " If we cannot sell the poultry this week, how are we to pay the shoe-bill ? "

And then would come another set of reflections, which would run thus : Supposing that father does not get well enough to attend to the farm, and mother has to hire somebody to do it for him, then they will not be able to afford to keep Emmy ; and what if I should be obliged to come home and do the work ? Of all my ten brothers, there is not one that can take father's place. What a sad pity it is that those of every family who have the most energy, and can be worst spared, are those that go away ! There are Tom and James in Australia. Then there are Will and George and Alick in Canada, doing very well, and Edward just gone out to them. Well, here are Sam and Joe at home, only because father could not trust them out of his sight, poor fellows ; and there is Dick, a mere spoilt child. I see nothing for it but for me to give up my situation ; and O, what a misfortune that will be ! I shall soon lose a great deal that I have learned, and, perhaps, become coarse with hard work, and low-spirited for want of sometimes hearing a little intellectual conversation. I hope it will not be my duty to come home ; I cannot bear the thought of it.

"Your servant, Miss Ann," said a man's voice behind her, as she was one day indulging in some such reflections as these. Ann Salter turned suddenly, and encountered the blushing face of William Dobson.

"I just took the liberty to come and inquire after Mr. Salter," said the young man.

"You are very good," replied Ann Salter; "my father is better to-day, but his arm is very painful. Will you sit down?"

William Dobson sat down; they were in the kitchen; Ann Salter had been stirring a pudding, and had one of her mother's aprons tied before her. The consciousness of how different her dress and occupation were from anything he had seen in her before, made her blush with a not unnatural feeling of shame and shyness; but she was relieved when he said, "I need not ask how you are, Miss Ann, for though you must have had a great deal of anxiety, I never saw you looking better: activity seems to suit you."

"I am very well, thank you," she answered; and then thought within herself, "Shall I go on stirring this pudding? or, shall I let it spoil because I am too proud to stir it before him?" Good sense prevailed: she took up the spoon, and there was a long pause. She did not think it her duty to find conversation, but quietly waited till her visitor spoke. At last he said, "I had a long letter from your brother Tom this morning, Miss Ann, and thinking you might not have heard this mail, I thought you would be glad to see it."

Ann Salter was glad. Tom was her favorite brother, and she listened to his letter with delight. "How pleased mother will be to hear it!" she observed.

"He is going to write to her," replied William Dobson. "He says so in the postscript."

"Not on the old subject of our going to Australia, I hope," exclaimed Ann Salter, hastily.

" Why, yes, it is on that subject," said William Dobson ;
"and if you have anything to say against it to your parents, Miss Ann, perhaps I had better read what he says,
and then you will have the start of your brother. He says,
' *P. S.* — I have half written a long letter to my mother,
urging her to come out here ; for I know if she was willing
to leave the old place, my father would be heartily glad to
begin life afresh over here. It is of no use begging you
to come, old fellow ; you are too well off where you are ;
but if my family could come over, it would be the making
of them, and I shall leave no stone unturned to get them
to emigrate.' "

Ann Salter was silent. She saw that her brother had
unconsciously chosen a time for his letter when it was
almost sure to prevail ; and, much as she dreaded the
notion of living at home, and working as she now did, the
thought of going out to Australia was more unwelcome
still.

William Dobson continued : " I do not think your
mother would ever consent to go, Miss Ann, if she could
not take you with her ; " (very true, thought Ann Salter ;)
"and I may say, as I 've said before," continued the young
farmer, smoothing his hat with his sleeve, " I may say,
if I could induce you to stay " — here he hesitated (I have
known him all my life, thought Ann Salter) — " I should
think myself a very lucky fellow " (but then, AS FANNY
SAID, he is not a gentleman, thought Ann Salter) ; "and
my mother would be equally pleased," stammered out Mr.
Dobson. (But, to be sure, if Fanny could see me now,
proceeded Ann Salter, she would not think me much like
a gentlewoman.) But whether she would have thought
proper to make any answer to this speech will never now
be known ; for it was but just brought to a conclusion
when Emmy, that roughest of mortals with the softest of
names, rushed into the kitchen and exclaimed : " O, Mr.

Dobson and Miss Ann, here's Doctor Deane just driving up to the door, and that young lady with a white veil, that he brought once before; and the parlor shutters are not opened, I quite forgot them; and the young brood of chickens that was hatched yesterday was a week have got into the passage, and they are now sitting on the door-mat; and, if you please, am I to show the young lady into the kitchen?"

Ann Salter stood a moment, unable to move. That Fanny should see her with a checked apron tied before her, her sleeves tucked up, and she and Mr. Dobson both inhabiting a kitchen, was too much for her philosophy. The first thing that occurred to her was to snatch up the pudding, and put it into the oven; and that done a loud noise, as of a whole brood of chickens running into the kitchen, and their mother after them, forced her to turn round and encounter Fanny, who was entering in the wake of the poultry, and blushing quite as much as her friend Ann.

" My uncle is gone up stairs," said Fanny, stooping to kiss Ann Salter, " and he told me to come in here; pray excuse the intrusion."

" Pray do not call it one," was the reply; " but sit down here if you have no objection, for I have no other place to ask you into to-day."

Fanny sat down. " Now, why cannot I feel at my ease?" thought poor Ann Salter. " I am doing my duty; why cannot I be independent of other people's opinions?"

Mr. Dobson had made his exit through another door. Ann Salter took off her apron, and washed her hands, while Fanny talked on indifferent subjects, and ended some anecdotes of the children, by saying: " Ah, dear Ann, it is such a trouble keeping the children in order; they do not respect me, you know, because they are aware of my de-ficiencies as compared with you. But," continued Fanny, looking about her, " I know very well, dear, that it will be a sad trial to you to come back again, so I ought not to be in any hurry about it."

"A sad trial," echoed Ann Salter involuntarily. "O, Fanny, how can you think so? If my dear father was only well enough to be left, I. should be so thankful to be with you again."

"Indeed!" said Fanny, with rather a blank face.

"It was extremely good and kind of the Doctor to let me come," proceeded the governess, "and it is my duty and my wish to be here; but, O Fanny, I have changed my mind about a good many things since I left you; I now see how sinful and how discontented I was."

"You were sometimes a good deal depressed, dear," said Fanny, recurring to the old word; "but I think that was not unnatural."

"It was unnatural," persisted Ann Salter, "and it was wicked; but I am punished; for O, Fanny, I am afraid I shall never go back to those happy duties and that pleasant house again." And here, having controlled her feelings as long as she could, the governess burst into a sudden fit of crying, and sobbed as if her heart would break.

Fanny, always affectionate, was doubly so now. She was not very acute nor very observant, but she saw on this occasion what was the real state of the case. She even discovered that Ann Salter was ashamed of herself for some of those fine-lady airs which circumstances had so roughly compelled her to lay aside, and she congratulated herself on her cleverness in this respect. "So you will really be glad to come back, dear `Annie?" she exclaimed. "Well, I am sure I shall be delighted when you can come; and, no doubt, that will be soon, for your father is getting better; and when you come we will keep journals again, and see how cheerful we can possibly be on all occasions, instead of feeling it to be rather a graceful and interesting thing to be depressed."

Ann Salter was very anxious to efface the appearance of redness about her eyes, lest her mother should see it, and ask the cause ; so when she had looked at the pudding in the oven, she asked Fanny to come and walk with her in the garden. There was a smoothly-clipped fruit hedge in this garden and a row of cabbage-roses grew by it. Ann Salter gathered some of their most lovely buds for Fanny, and then the two girls sat down in the alcove, which terminated the hedge, and where the farmer had spent many a pleasant summer evening in smoking his pipe. Fanny thought this a very good opportunity for telling her friend of the conversation that she had held with her uncle on the words *dependent* and *independent*, and to her great joy the governess declared that she was quite of the Doctor's opinion.

The two girls were then deep in conversation, and the governess had just been persuaded to say that she thought it possible her father might be well enough for her to return to her duties in a week, when they saw the Doctor coming along the grass-walk towards them. He looked business-like and thoughtful, and when he reached the arbor, he said, " Sit still, young ladies. Miss Salter, I have something to say to you that I am much more sorry to say than you will be to hear."

" Than I shall be to hear, sir ? " was all Ann Salter could reply.

" Yes, yes, indeed ; I know that very well. The fact is, your father has said to me several times, ' I am ashamed to keep my dear girl away from her duties, and I am afraid it must put you to a good deal of inconvenience.' I have always answered, ' I must wait till she is set at liberty ; we must not quarrel with God's appointments.' Well, Miss Salter, your father, though he has no unfavorable symptoms, will require all your mother's time and attention for at least six weeks to come ; and he yesterday asked me such direct questions that I felt bound to tell him so. I was therefore, I confess, not surprised, when to-day he said to me that he felt his wife must have help, and he saw he must ask to have you set at liberty, for that you were your mother's right hand; and, in short, such a pleasure to your parents, so cheerful, and so evidently happy with them, that they rejoiced in the opportunity of keeping you, though the cause was a painful one. So, Miss Salter, though it is with regret, I feel that I can do no less than give you your liberty; and I am rejoiced to find that you are so well pleased to be at home, for I had scarcely expected it would be so."

"Uncle," said Fanny quietly, "is the matter perfectly decided on?"

"Perfectly, my dear; and I left Mr. and Mrs. Salter in high spirits to think how glad their daughter would be to hear the news."

Fanny, by a glance, directed her uncle's eyes to the face of his late governess. It was pale, and altogether distressed. She was making a great effort to take the news quietly, since it referred to a thing inevitable, and evidently not to be avoided. The Doctor made a movement of impatience, as if he would have said, "There is no understanding people; I always seem to be giving pain where I expected to give pleasure."

Miss Salter presently recovered herself, and said to him, "I am much obliged to you, sir, for so kindly acceding to my father's wishes. I hope you will meet with a superior governess to myself for the children, and I am very sensible of the advantages I had in your house."

But then she looked so pale and shocked that further congratulations were impossible, and, as condolences would have been out of place, Fanny only said, in rising to take leave, "I shall come and see you as soon as I can, dear Annie, and I hope you will spend the day with me when you can; I shall be quite dull without you."

"You are very kind," said the late governess, with a sigh, as she preceded them to the house. Yet when they reached the door, saw the pony-chaise standing there, and Mrs. Salter, with a radiant face, waiting beside it, Fanny admired the self-command and good feeling with which, when the mother said, "Well, Annie dear, have you heard the news?" the daughter instantly replied, with a smile, "Yes, dear mother ; and I hope you will find me a help in the house."

"That I shall," exclaimed Mrs. Salter heartily ; "a help and a pleasure too ; no fear of that."

As Fanny and her uncle drove away, the latter said, " I suppose I never did thoroughly understand Miss Salter, and never shall. Now, who would have supposed she did not wish to stay at home, after hearing her mother's account of her? Besides, she always disliked a state of dependence, as she called it ; at least, I was always given to understand so ; but women are quite incomprehensible. I suppose that is their prerogative."

" I believe she has changed her mind, uncle, on that subject," said Fanny.

"Changed her mind ! Well, that is another of the prerogatives of her sex. I really thought I could do no less than meet the old man's wishes ; and I supposed, from what he said, that it was for the happiness of all parties."

" And so it will be, perhaps, uncle," said Fanny, demurely. "But, uncle, you are now in want of a governess, — are you not ? "

" To be sure I am, child."

" Suppose you try *me*," said Fanny ; "for since you talked to me about my being dependent, and Annie being independent, I have often wanted to be independent too."

The Doctor was so astonished at this speech, that he

8

actually stopped the pony-carriage, and stared at his niece for full a minute in mute surprise. Fanny was put out of countenance by this, but only for the moment, and before the Doctor had recovered himself sufficiently to say a word, she added : —

"It would be a very good thing for me, uncle ; for you know I often feel dreadfully weary for want of something to do ; and then it would keep the situation open for Ann Salter, who, in six months or so, may possibly be able to take it again. And then, supposing such a thing, as that I ever had to earn my living, could I have a better preparation ?"

"All true, perfectly true, Fanny," said the Doctor, laughing ; "but who would have expected to hear it from your lips ?"

"And why not ?" persisted Fanny ; "they did not think me such a silly girl at school."

"Therefore, why should I ? you mean. My dear, I never thought you wanted sense ; what you want is stability and independence of character."

"Then what can be better than for me to become independent ?" asked Fanny.

"My dear, don't play upon words ; this is a serious matter, if you are in earnest about it.".

"Yes, I really am ; for since you made me see that I had done harm to Annie by taking too many things for granted, I have wished very much to do her some kindness to make up for it ; and here seems a way. Besides, you know, uncle, if you could not afford to have a governess, it would be my duty to teach the children ; and I assure you, uncle, I have thought a great deal since Annie left us, and I really think I had better have something to do."

"Well, well," repeated the Doctor, "here is another incomprehensible ! I find your sentiments very wise, Fanny, and I will give them my best attention. You are sure you did not pick them up from a book ? "

" O, no," said Fanny, gravely; " I thought of them entirely myself, uncle."

" I shall have some further conversation with you, then, in the evening," replied the Doctor; " and after that I will decide."

CHAPTER V.

WE left Fanny stepping out of the pony-carriage, just after her uncle's declaration that he would decide in the evening upon the important matter she had brought before him.

"I do not see that it is so very important," thought Fanny; "I think it would cause my uncle a great deal more trouble to advertise or inquire for another governess, than to take me, whom he knows, and who am willing to do my best. To be sure, I always thought it was rather a sad thing for Annie to be a governess, but then there would be no disadvantage in it to me. I should not be among strangers, I should be doing it by my own free choice, I should suffer no loss of position, and then, if anything should happen to make it necessary that I should earn my living, I should have proved that I was capable of it. Besides," thought Fanny, "here is an opportunity to do a real kindness ; Annie longs to come back again, and by this voluntary act of mine I shall keep the situation open for her."

In the evening, when the children were gone to bed, and the Doctor and his niece were left alone, Fanny, who already in imagination had made the sacrifice of her time and pleasures for her friend, had come triumphantly through her difficulties, and seen Annie re-established in her old place, was very impatient for her uncle to begin to talk on this absorbing theme; but as he stood for some time on the rug, with his hands behind him, and his brows knit as if in deep thought, she did not like to speak. At last, seeing his dark eyes intently fixed upon her, and reading in them the expression of an evident doubt, she could keep silence no longer, but exclaimed, " Well, uncle, have you not decided yet ? "

" Yet ! " said Doctor Deane, without removing his scrutinizing gaze. " My dear, the advantage to yourself of some fixed occupation I have decided on ; what remains to decide is, whether the proposed arrangement would be of equal advantage to me."

" To you, uncle ? O, you mean to the children, — I think I know quite as much as Annie does ; I have had an excellent education."

" Certainly, I have given you the best that I could afford ; the question is, not whether you know enough, but whether you can impart what you know ; not whether you are aware how children ought to behave, but whether you can make them do it. I doubt very much, Fanny, whether you have the art of governing. And then, again, how do you think you shall like early rising ? "

" O," interrupted Fanny, " I delight in the morning air, — it is so balmy and healthy."

" In December and January ? "

" I — I forgot the cold weather, uncle ; but it is so extremely warm now that surely I need not think of that."

" You had better think of all the disadvantages beforehand, and while you are not bound to undertake the work ; for remember, that if you do begin it, I shall feel deeply disappointed and grieved if you throw it up. It will be a very important step in your life. It is 'putting your hand to the plough.'"

" I did not think you would look upon it in that solemn light," said Fanny, humbly ; " and I always supposed it was my duty to try to be useful ; and I thought it was my mission to teach the children, as they seemed to be left without a governess, and I was at hand with nothing to do."

"My dear, what you say is very sensible and very true; but I do not know whether the sentiments are your own, or whether you got them — like too many of your sentiments — from a story-book. Now the heroine in a story-book, whatever arduous task she may undertake, and however many failures she may suffer from, is always blessed in the end with success."

Fanny reflected for a few minutes, as if turning over her favorite heroines in her mind, and then she said, thoughtfully, "Very true, uncle;" and with deep blushes she added, "but then she is never supposed to undertake her task in her own strength."

There was something very pretty in Fanny's guileless singleness of heart; it suited very well with her transparent complexion and fragile elegance. Her uncle was silent for a moment, as if giving her further time to speak if she had more to say; but as she added nothing, he presently said, "Your remark, my dear child, fully justifies me in looking on this matter in what you just now called a 'solemn light.' It implies that you have, or that you will seek, divine aid in carrying out your proposed task; that you have looked upon it in a religious point of view, as, indeed, all the duties of a Christian should be looked upon; *everything*, we are told, is to be done 'in the name of the Lord Jesus.' Well, I consent, then, that you shall try what you can do; I hesitated at first, because I thought the feeling required to be brought strongly before you, that, 'better it is that thou shouldest not vow, than that thou shouldest vow and not pay.'"

"I don't wish to deceive you," said Fanny; "my first wish was to keep the situation open for Annie, but I feel now that it is important to consider it in a religious light. So, uncle, perhaps I had better not be too confident, and instead of undertaking the responsibility without a trial, may I try teaching the children for a month?"

"Certainly, you may; and I hereby invest you with authority over them. You must make them obey you," ("if I can," thought Fanny), — "and I will support you in all your proper exercises of school-room discipline."

" O, Johnnie is the only one who will disobey."

"Yes, and as he has, in his own small person, twice the activity, and three times the acuteness, of the elder ones, be specially careful, my dear, not to give him the advantage over you, by getting out of temper, and saying irritating things ; never lay yourself open to a repartee, and do not be tempted to answer one, — some children are remarkably clever at a smart answer. When he is in a very great fidget, and particularly inclined to be active, let your discipline be such as will help to spend his activity. Send him down to the very bottom of the hop-garden to fetch your book out of the arbor, and desire him, with gravity, to be quick ; or, if you have forgotten to leave a book there, send him up to the top of the house for this or that trifle ; for you must remember that, independently of the irksomeness of a task to many children, it is of itself quite a punishment to be obliged to sit still ; and if you can relieve them by suffering them to exercise their muscles a little, they are better able afterwards to give their minds to the book."

"Oh," said Fanny, with open eyes, "then, that is why you make Johnnie do so many errands ? I often remarked that he was almost always sent to fetch something down stairs just before prayers, and I wondered why you had so many of the Bibles kept at the top of the house, when they are wanted every day."·

"Indeed, my dear ; then now you know the reason. I always called the child my errand-boy, and many a whipping these errands have saved him ! But I do· not say this to you because I wish to save my child from any merited punishment, only because I wish him to be punished for his faults, and not for that activity of body which he has not yet strength of will enough to govern. Now, I have no more to say, except that I look forward to great good to yourself, Fanny, as the result of this regular work; for I have often told you that anything which made you exert yourself would have a bracing effect, and the frequent exercise that you must now take with the children will be a great deal better for you than the tonic that I am often obliged to give you."

After this conversation Fanny retired to rest, and her new duties being fresh in her mind, she rose in the morning quite as early as her friend Annie Salter had ever been accustomed to do, and came down stairs looking cheerful and blooming. Her uncle was already in the breakfast-room, and the three children with him; they had evidently been informed that cousin Fanny was going to be their governess, for the two little girls cast glances of inquiry at her, as if they half expected to see some change in her appearance to correspond with this accession of power over them and their destiny. As for Johnnie, he preserved a steady gravity as long as his papa was in the room, but the Doctor going out shortly after, he took the opportunity to throw himself head over heels, and then dance round Fanny, cracking his knuckles, and exclaiming, "O, jolly!"

"It is very nearly prayer time," said Fanny, remembering her uncle's advice; "go and fetch the Bibles, Johnnie."

The young urchin, after two or three more gyrations, shot up stairs like a meteor, making almost as much noise in his course, and was presently heard descending again, with an ecstasy of chuckles. Fanny had intended to meet him at the door, and gravely to reprove him for making so much noise; but, before she could carry out her purpose, he was sprawling before her, having caught his foot in the door-mat and come down, a shower of books falling with him.

He rose rather ruefully, and rubbed his elbows, and Fanny, who in other circumstances was the most likely girl in the world to have kissed and condoled, now contented herself with desiring him to pick up the books, and take some of them up again, remarking, that he had brought down twice as many as were wanted. As if doubting whether this steady gravity could possibly proceed from cousin Fanny, his sometime playmate, occasionally his slave, and generally his confidante, the boy looked at her with an earnest, inquisitive expression, and finding that she did not laugh, he proceeded to pick up the books, and carry them slowly up stairs again.

That day was to Fanny a day of almost unclouded triumph. Her duties being new, she gave her whole mind to them, and consequently performed them well; and the fear of failure being before her eyes, she never relaxed the dignified manner with which she had begun the day. The little girls, almost always good and docile, surpassed themselves; and Johnnie himself forgot to fidget, in the absorbing wonder caused by Fanny's complete change of character. As it was imperative to find some reason for it, he confided to his eldest sister his suspicion that the fairies had changed her in the night; but that little counsellor, remarking·that, if this had been the case, the new Fanny would not have known the place where they left off reading yesterday, he was obliged to give up his theory, and bedtime came before he could think of another.

As Fanny had been in the habit of hearing them read occasionally, and setting them lessons, which they said to her in a desultory way, the change, now that she had been formally declared to be their governess, was the more striking. But even this novelty wore off in the course of three or four days; and just when the little girls had become accustomed to cousin Fanny, and had transferred to her all the deference with which they had formerly

treated Miss Salter, Johnnie had begun to find the new
yoke extremely irksome, and had set on foot some vigorous
efforts towards throwing it off.   If it had not been that his
opposition and restlessness kept her attention alive, Fanny
would by this time have begun to feel the duties so easily
performed a little wearisome.   The excitement was over ;
the interest of the experiment was quenched in its success ; but now there was something to rouse her again,
and, under the stimulus of opposition, she reached the first
day of her second week without acknowledging, even to
herself, that playing the governess was not as amusing and
exciting a game as she had anticipated before she tried it.

But on that memorable morning, the first of the second
week, Fanny took a step which from henceforth raised her
into the place in Johnnie's estimation which Miss Salter
had occupied, and entitled her to the same fitful obedience,
and the same general attempts on his part to be a good
boy and do his duty.   She inflicted a punishment which
had been invented by Miss Salter, and tried with the happiest effect.   She called him by his name.

" If the honorable gentleman does not apologize for his
conduct," said the late Speaker of the House of Commons,
" I shall be obliged to address him by his name ! "   The
terrified member immediately apologized most humbly.   It
is almost certain that Miss Salter had never heard this
anecdote, yet she had tried the same punishment on the
members of her small house with the most successful
results.   Each of the children had a pet name, and was
always addressed by it ; even the servants said Master
Johnnie and Miss Kitty ; but on certain solemn occasions,
when there had been any open rebellion or grave fault,
Miss Salter had been known to say, "John Deane, or
Catharine Deane, come with me ; I feel obliged to tell
your papa of your conduct."   Thereupon torrents of tears
and protestations of amendment would ensue ; and, after

some hesitation, the offending member would occasionally be forgiven, and after a period, longer or shorter according to the flagrance of the offence, be called Johnnie or Kitty again. The youngest little girl, being a very timid, gentle child, had never been even threatened with this alarming punishment; and upon the two stronger-minded children it had been inflicted so seldom as to have lost none of its power by familiarity.

Doctor Deane coming home that day about one o'clock, heard a loud sobbing in the school-room, the door of which he opened, and found Johnnie by himself, sitting with his slate on his knee, and continually blotting out his figures with his tears. The two little girls had gone out for their walk with their governess. "What is the matter, Johnnie?" said the Doctor; "have you been a naughty boy?"

Johnnie, with a chorus of sobs, gave utterance thus to his grievance: "Cousin Fanny called me — called me John Deane — and I had n't done anything par — par — ti — cular."

"Serve you right!" exclaimed his father; "I am sure you would not have been called John Deane if you had done nothing particular."

Hereupon finding that his father did not mean to take his part, the young culprit checked his sobs as well as he could, and addressed himself to his task, which was a very easy one; he therefore soon accomplished it, and when Fanny came in again, he was penitent, and asked her humbly to call him Johnnie again.

Fanny felt that the wild creature was now subdued, and she wrote to Annie Salter that night, describing her triumph, and declaring that she found her task both easy and delightful.

Alas! she had deprived it of all its interest! Johnnie was now a good boy, that is to say, he did not consciously contend with her for the mastery, and in the main he de-

sired to please and obey her. She went on teaching till
the end of the week, experiencing a degree of weariness
and distaste that she could scarcely conceal. She also
dragged herself through the fourth week without openly
showing her deep regret that she had been so urgent to be
allowed to be a governess. On the Sunday following it
she did not feel well, neither did Johnnie. She did not
rise on Monday morning, and when Dr. Deane pronounced
her to be suffering from a very mild attack of scarlatina, of
which the children were all showing symptoms, Fanny was
rather glad than otherwise. "At any rate," she thought,
"there will be no lessons to attend to *this* week"; and as
both she and her pupils had taken the complaint in its
very best form, and, though not allowed to rise, were feeling no pain, and little weakness, she did not alter her
mind while the feverish symptoms lasted, but said to herself several times, "*Anything* is better than that school-
room!"

CHAPTER VI.

CONCLUSION.

WHILE Dr. Deane's governess was ill in bed, just a little ill, and able to appreciate the comforts of being petted, and watched, and waited on; and while her young pupils, with blankets folded on their chairs, were sitting up and eating chicken-broth and other agreeable dainties, Ann Salter stopped at home, and tried hard to be happy there. She felt that it was indeed unnatural to long to be away from her kindred, and that it was base to be ashamed of them and their want of refinement, when her own superior education, the nice dresses she had worn during her girlhood, as well as many a cake· and cream cheese that had been sent her, to make her popular at school, were the result of their self-denial. Many a time had her grandmother gone without a new gown, and many a time had her mother walked home from market, instead of taking the coach, in order that she might have and learn all that was suitable to make her independent, and might not be laughed at or slighted by the other pupils, because her clothes were more homely and old-fashioned than theirs.

Ann Salter felt all this; she blessed the memory of her good old grandmother; and was very thankful to her mother, while, being a girl of real good sense, in spite of some little follies that she had given way to while in her situation as governess, she did not fail continually to keep before her mind, that as by the self-denial of others she had been made more refined and better informed than they were, it would be great ingratitude in her to shrink from their want of refinement and despise their ignorance.

So she endeavored not to blush when she saw her mother making out little bills for poultry, butter, and cream, which had been sent for by the neighboring gentry; and spelling the articles and distributing the capital letters after the manner of the uneducated. Sometimes she would say, "Why not let me make out the bills, mother? you know I learnt accounts at school, and I could cast up the items in a very little time."

"Bless me, child," the answer would be, "I have made out the bills for forty years, and it's very seldom that there's a mistake in them."

"Mother," the daughter once ventured to remark, "you have spelt 'guinea-fowl' without the 'u'; shall I put it in?"

"Why, what does it matter, child? Ay, I see I have; I was always reckoned a very good speller, but I forget sometimes, though, I know."

"And let me mark out this second 't' in 'apricot,' mother; I wish you would let me write the bills, mother, I have nothing particular to do just now."

"No, child, I have so much *stirring* work to do, that I like the quiet of sitting down to my writing; it seems to rest my bones."

This argument was unanswerable; and after hearing it, Ann Salter went up to sit with her father, who, being a little better, had a talking fit upon him, and told her a vast number of somewhat queer stories, such as his own "cronies" would have received with bursts of approving laughter. There was nothing decidedly coarse in sentiment about them, but they were related with such a twang, and richness of provincial dialect, and embellished with so many broad jokes, that his daughter had difficulty in preserving her serenity of countenance, and a proper air of interest under the infliction of her father's wit.

But she was sincerely trying to be useful and contented, therefore it was not wonderful that, without losing her own refinement of mind, she gradually became habituated to the manners and customs of home, and was able to hear her mother's bad grammar with tranquillity, and listen to her father's wit, oft-repeated, and always with loud laughter on his own part, as to a rather agreeable thing which showed that he was merry, and consequently improving in health.

Also, in the course of a few weeks, Mr. Dobson's visits, which at first had been to her a matter of supreme indifference, began to interest her in a certain degree, insomuch, that when her father teased and laughed at her, she could not help blushing and feeling very uncomfortable.

She had long ago made up her mind that she never would marry him, Fanny having mainly contributed to this decision, by remarking concerning him, that "he was not a gentleman," and having followed up the disparaging assertion by adding that he was not particularly good-looking, and had a sheepish air. She remembered this now, and sometimes felt angry with Fanny for having said it, and sometimes felt angry with herself for beginning to think otherwise. But one day — one particularly fine day, a day that she often thought of afterwards — when her father, who could now sit up by the window, was comforting his heart by watching the loaded wains coming in from his harvest-fields, she saw him laughing quietly to himself as he looked out; and when she said, "What amuses you, father?" he replied, to her confusion, "Here's thy young man coming again."

"*My* young man, father? pray don't call him so," she exclaimed involuntarily.

"Well, well," answered the accommodating parent, "maybe he comes to see thy mother!"

Ann Salter now recollected herself, and said with gravity, " To whom are you alluding, father ? "

She said this without intending to amuse her father, far from it; and when he laughed till the tears ran down his face, she felt, at first, rather pettish ; but laughter is infectious, and when the farmer, wiping his eyes, exclaimed, " O child, thy little airs are like to be the death of me," she could not help laughing too. *>* To whom be I alluding ? that's school language, I reckon," he continued, " but don't toss up thy little chin too high, for I'm afraid he is too much of a gentleman for the like of thee."

" Too much of a gentleman ! " the word struck Ann Salter forcibly ; what, did Fanny object to him as not a gentleman, and her father as too much a gentleman ?

" If you please, Miss, Mr. Dobson has stepped in to tea, and it is just upon five o'clock," said Emily, appearing some time after, " and your mother says you are to come down and make tea."

Mr. Dobson made himself very agreeable that evening ; he was intelligent and well-educated, and. though very *gauche* and shy, he could talk extremely well, when encouraged by an appearance of interest in the listener whom he most wished to please. Ann Salter had never condescended to make the least reply to the speech he had stammered through, while she was in the kitchen mixing the pudding, and he had found no opportunity for repeating it. The dreaded letter from Australia had arrived, and Mrs. Salter having said that nothing in the world, not even a *barn* full of gold, should induce her to go over among those jumping kangaroos, he felt as if his hopes had received a great blow, for he had relied on her hesitating, and being only induced to stay if he could persuade her daughter to like him and settle in England.

Now, whatever happened, she would not go ; therefore Mr. Dobson felt low in his mind, as if his chief hold and hope had been taken from him.

"Not if I was to have a barn full of gold," repeated the worthy matron, as they discussed the matter that evening.

"A barn full, mother !" said Ann Salter, "you don't know what you are talking of; do you know I was reading the other day that all the gold that had been brought from the gold diggings since they were first worked, would go into an omnibus — a very small omnibus."

"Sure-ly," said Mrs. Salter, amazed. "Yes," proceeded the daughter, "and in the same book I read, that all the gold now coined and in circulation in the world would go into a room twenty-five feet square."

"Well !" said Mrs. Salter, "I should judge that the man who wrote that book did not know much about gold; for I am sure, I must have had as much money through *my* hands as would fill our great oven."

"Not gold money, mother, surely ?"

"If it was not gold, it was gold's worth," replied Mrs. Salter, warmly; "what does it matter whether it was gold or silver, so long as they give you the same quantity of gold for it, and so long as, whether you have it in gold, or notes, or silver, it is of the same value ? — provided the bank you had the notes from does not break," she added, after a moment's reflection.

"But, mother," Ann Salter began, "that was not exactly what I meant."

"I don't think you exactly seem to know what you mean," interrupted her mother with dignity, "if you want to persuade me that twenty shillings and one sovereign are not the same thing? what do *you* say, Mr. Dobson ?"

Mr. Dobson hesitated and blushed; he did not want to offend the good woman, but her head was in a fog of mis-apprehension and a whirl of confusion; she saw at once that both he and her daughter thought her wrong, and in a somewhat indignant state of mind she said that she was sure her poor dear husband must be wanting her, and she should go and sit with him. Mr. Dobson must excuse her, and Ann might call her down at supper-time.

So at supper-time Ann did call her down, but did not return with her to the parlor, preferring to remain with her father and read a chapter or two to him as he lay somewhat restlessly in his bed. Mrs. Salter had quite recovered her good humor when she descended, and she found Mr. Dobson in very good humor also, inclined to eat a plentiful supper, which was always agreeable to her, as she was naturally of a hospitable turn; and she found him also inclined to sit and listen, or at least silently to gaze at her, while she told some of her longest stories respecting her husband's illness, and her own poultry-yard.

At last he rose; the moon was shining brilliantly in at the open door of the passage, and the white jessamine that was nailed against the door threw in a sweet perfume. Young William Dobson looked up the narrow staircase, perhaps wondering whether Ann would come down, perhaps listening to the distant sound of a voice as it came indistinctly from an upper chamber. He lingered so long at the door, that Mrs. Salter began to tell another story, and he leaned his back against the doorpost and listened, as it seemed contentedly; all the time looking forth into the quiet farm-yard, where a group of cows lay still, chewing the cud, and an old gray horse stood fast asleep by the pond, and a flock of ducks, with their heads under their wings, all huddled together, looked soft and white as patches of show in the moonshine.

"Well, I must be going," he said at last.

"Must you, Mr. William?" replied his hostess; "well, good-night; give my respects to your mother."

And a very pleasant young man he is, thought the matron; attentive to his elders, and sensible too; he knows when he hears a good story, and likes to listen to the end of it, — not interrupt, as some folks do.

The sound of a reader's voice had given place to the sound of a sleeper's snoring, when Mrs. Salter crept softly up stairs, and Ann Salter stole lightly away to her own little room, and having shut the door, walked straight up to a certain box, and after lifting out certain neat ribbons and collars, drew from its depth her once cherished and now neglected journal. She set down her candle on the little dressing-table, put her feet on a small wooden stool, and sat with this journal on her knee for some minutes before she opened it.

"Too much of a gentleman!" she mentally ejaculated; "what could make my father say that? How strange it is that different people should see things in such different lights! Well, perhaps father was right in one respect: William Dobson's father and grandfather were as well off and as respectable in their way as himself; but my grandfather was a laboring man by my mother's side, and my other grandfather could scarcely manage to read a chapter in the Bible, he had so little schooling. Father could not have meant that I was not equal to him in education, for though he was sent to the grammar-school for years, and got on so well that the master wanted to persuade his father to send him to college, I am quite as well instructed as he, though I may not be so clever." A long pause. "Fanny certainly did try to set me against him, and I thought I did not care for him, — certainly at one time I should not have cared if I had never seen him again, — but I really, — I *really* do not see that it is any business of Fanny's! Let me see what it was that she said, — Ah! *'Tuesday, the 1st.* — Went out to walk with the children. What a sweet girl Fanny is! so refined, such a horror of everything *second-rate;* I think, however, she carries it a little too far; she thinks it quite a misfortune to have a low origin.' Nothing about it there. *'Wednesday, the 2d.* — Mr. and Mrs. Greaves, Mrs. Sumners, and Captain Combermere dined here to-day, as well as the visitors staying in the house, — no room for me at the table, — had to dine with the children. Fanny was distressed, and said, " I dare say, dear, that being accustomed to good society, you feel keenly the dulness of your present life"; she was so sympathizing that I could not help shedding a few tears, — I did not say anything.' (Bah ! you little goose, exclaimed the young reader, apostrophizing her former self, accustomed to good society, indeed ! You ! when the only din-- ner company you had ever known was a couple or so of your father's grazier friends, who adjourned to the kitchen to smoke and drink beer, when they had devoured your mother's custards and roast pig.) ' *Thursday, the* 3*d.*' (Ah, here it is.) — ' Took a walk with the children, and Fanny accompanied us to my great joy ; we went down Balcombe Lane to see how the hops were growing, and just as we came near young William Dobson's garden, he passed on horseback, and made a low bow to me. He looked very shy, I thought, and colored a good deal. As soon as he had passed out of hearing, Fanny exclaimed, " Who *could* that man be, Annie ? Why, he actually bowed to you ; how did you get acquainted with him ? He is not a gentleman, surely." I said he was a very respectable farmer and miller ; that I had known him a long time, and that we were then walking among his fields. " But surely," she said, " he ought not to have taken the liberty of bowing, — he cannot be a proper person for *us* to be acquainted with," — and I looked after him, and noticed that he had on top-boots and corduroys, and that he did not look quite like a gentleman, though he rode very well. " I am sure your friends would not approve of such an acquaintance," said Fanny. " I am sure they would not mind," I answered ; and she looked quite surprised ; so it is evident that her notions of what is proper — [here a few words were scratched out] — and my father's differ widely. Just then William Dobson turned his horse, and came up to us again, and spoke to me. I was so vexed on account of Fanny's seeing it, that I hardly knew what he said, or what I answered ; but I believe he asked if we would like to go through the gate of his hop-garden down to Balcombe Bridge. I think he said he had the key of the lower gate in his pocket, but I know I answered shortly and coldly, and he bowed again and went off, soon putting his horse into a gallop. I did not mean to hurt his feelings, but really, he had no right to speak to me, particularly when I had a young lady with me, nor had he any occasion to assume that look of disappointment and misery that he put on. Fanny says she thinks he is a very sheepish-looking young man, and extremely awkward.' "

There this wise and truly feminine record ceased for that day. Ann Salter read it carefully, and then, with great deliberation, tore it out and held it to the flame of the candle, which speedily consumed it. She afterwards searched through the remainder of her journal, and tore out and burnt several pages of similar import ; then, observing that there was a great smell of burning in the room, she cautiously opened the window, and straightway a gust of wind blew the tinder of her manuscript suddenly all about her floor and her snowy counterpane. It occupied nearly half an hour to collect the bits and dispose of them safely ; by this time her candle was nearly out, and she was obliged to undress by the light of the moon ; but was scarcely in bed when a shuffling noise in the passage arrested her attention : her mother was evidently making a progress through the house, trying to find out where the smell of burning came from. She opened the door, saying, "Annie, dear, did you see that the oven fire was well out afore you came to bed ?" Annie, blushing, confessed that the oven was innocent of this smell, and described how it originated. Her mother withdrew. She felt ashamed of herself ; she knew what she had burnt were proofs of her folly, and she felt that burning them at that time of night were proofs of her inconsiderateness. But she was young, she was tired, and she had been up since sunrise; so she shortly fell asleep, and forgot all about her journal, and even forgot the subject of it.

And what, meanwhile, became of Fanny? Why, Fanny got better, and somewhat languidly proposed to resume her duties, but Dr. Deane said neither she nor the children were well enough at present; and Fanny was secretly glad. They were to go to the seaside for a month. On hearing this Fanny's joy was extreme, for school was not to be thought of till their return. She was getting on very well, circumstances having assisted her; by the time they returned Ann Salter would have been at home ten weeks. Fanny had never proposed to keep the situation open for her more than six months. Six months are twenty-five weeks, — fifteen only would remain, — and of those, three would be Christmas holidays. Twelve weeks she could surely drag through; indeed, she should consider it a duty to do so, especially as her uncle had spoken of the matter in a religious light. O yes, both duty and friendship demanded of her that the twelve weeks should be spent in the conscientious discharge of her school duties.

The happy party set off for the seaside. Fanny would have liked to call on Ann Salter beforehand, but the Doctor would not hear of it, as the complaint she had suffered from was infectious. He established his niece and the children in a pretty cottage by the sea, with an elderly servant, and promised to come over and see them whenever time permitted. At first, children and governess were .extremely happy; their appetites were keener than usual, owing as much to recent illness as to sea air, and their meals alone were a source of pleasure. Then there was the bathing, and the gathering of shells, and the climbing of cliffs, and the going out in boats; so that the days did not seem half long enough for all their enjoyments ; but a fortnight passed over, and the weather became extremely cold and very wet, the evenings drew in rapidly, the leaves fell, sometimes it was too cold for them to bathe, and always it was too windy for them to row. They had already found more shells than they could possibly carry home, and they could not go on the cliffs, which were slippery and dangerous. They began to wish they had something to do. Fanny bought them some calico at the one little shop which the place afforded, and cut out some doll's clothes for them to make ; she also bought some twine, that Johnnie might knit a large fishing-net, he having set his heart on catching a whale, in case one should visit the coast. Such a thing having once happened, it might happen again, and it was as well to be prepared !

But this work only kept the children good and contented for one long rainy day, and when they rose the next morning, and looking out, saw a rough sea, yellow with the sand that it was tearing up from the shore, all foaming and raging ; and when they saw a black sky, only diversified by great driving clouds, from which the cold sloppy rain was falling, and splashing in torrents against windows and walls, they were very peevish, and said they would rather be at home learning their lessons in the school-room than stop in-doors there all day, and do nothing. Fanny made breakfast last as long as she could, and then she occupied them some time by choosing for the chapters which they daily read the longest she could find ; then she had some letters written home to their papa, and was very particular about the writing and the spelling, but even these letters, — her last resource, — were finished by eleven o'clock, and now what was to be done for the rest of the day ?

She did not know, and the children did not know. There were no story-books, no toys, no lessons, no paintboxes; nothing wanted putting to rights; there was nothing to do, nothing to make, and nothing even to spoil.

Fanny escaped into her bedroom to consider what she should do with the children for the rest of the day, and while there, she heard unmistakable sounds, which testified that a game at romps was going on below; the children were jumping from the chairs, and rushing about the room, and shouting and laughing with the vehemence which often follows enforced quietude. Fanny listened, and resolved to keep out of the way and ignore the noise; but she had nothing to do herself but to watch the racing drops chase one another over the panes, and the one fishing-boat at anchor rocking and tossing upon the restless foaming waves.

"How dull it is!" thought Fanny. "I declare I shall be glad to exchange this for the school-room. What a noise the children make, — how the floor shakes!" Then Fanny read a few hymns, then she looked out again, and so she spent an hour. At last, — O welcome sound! — she heard the clatter of knives and spoons, and a childish hurrah came up from below. Fanny ventured to descend, and found the children quiet, room somewhat dusty, confidential servant making them put it neat, and beginning to lay the cloth. Confidential servant, being a wise woman, was making a fuss about the untidiness of the room, and declaring that she could not bring in the dinner till the chairs had been dusted. She produced some of those domestic inventions called "dusters," and the children diligently polished, and rubbed, and set in order, till the dinner was ready, when it was brought in with great parade, and for the next three quarters of an hour great contentment reigned in the breasts of governess and pupils. Confidential servant then proposed, that as it was very damp and chilly, and not likely to be any finer, there should be a fire "*laid*" and lighted. Fanny consented with pleasure, and the servant, who pitied her in her heart, made the operations of taking down the colored shavings, clearing away several spiders' webs, and laying down the chips and coals for the fire, last as long as she could. The children, whose little hands were cold and red, were delighted to observe the operation, and sat sometime, when it was lighted, warming themselves, and contented to do nothing while they basked in the heat.. Fanny's head ached after the noise of the morning, and she was very thankful for this respite from tumult; but it did not last long. Shortly the loud lamentations began again, " Nothing to do; nothing to play with ; rains here all day,—scarcely ever rains at home." "Wish we were at home ; don't care about holidays." " Always rains on holidays." " O, you pushed me ! " " I did n't." " You did. Cousin Fanny, Johnnie pushed me." " O you little tell-tale thing ! "—another push, then a burst of angry tears. " Johnnie, how dare you push your sister ? Come here, sir." Johnnie inveighed against his sister as a little coward ; he hardly touched her. " You did ; you pushed me very hard." " I did n't," followed by a chorus of sobs and indignant tears. Then the most junior of the Deanes — always timid and inclined to tears — melted likewise, and wished she had her big doll to play with ; her big doll whose eyes Johnnie poked in on his birthday.

Fanny was almost always in despair, and very much inclined to cry too ; when lo ! her good genius, *alias* the confidential servant, marched in. " If you please, Miss, would you like buttered toast for tea to-night ? "

" Yes, Martin ; anything you please," said Fanny, utterly dispirited.

" Then, may I have the children in the kitchen to help to toast it, ma'am ? " said Martin, coolly ; " the kitchen here is as clean and quiet as the parlor, and they eat so much toast, that I had need of four hands instead of two if I am to toast it all."

9   M

"They may go and help you then, Martin," replied Fanny, smiling; and straightway the lamentations ceased, and the combatants, now good friends again, proceeded to the kitchen, where they amused themselves for more than an hour in toasting bread, and seeing the little culinary operations that Martin was conducting at the same time.

Fanny was most thankful for this quiet hour, and as lessons were the only things she had to look to with hope as a means of passing the rainy days, she wrote home to her uncle, begging that a box of books might be sent, and some slates and maps.

The next day was quite as wet and cheerless; the third day a letter arrived. It informed Fanny that the books were packed, but as the Doctor was coming over himself on Saturday, it was thought best that he should bring them with him. O, weary week! rain, and damp, and idleness shared its mornings, peevishness clouded its evenings. Even the dinner and the tea did not afford the same pleasure as formerly,—want of exercise taking away the keenness of appetite.

Saturday came, however, at last, and was a very fine day; so lovely that all grief and discontent were forgotten, and governess and pupils sallied forth, in excellent temper and light spirits, for a long ramble. The Doctor was not expected till the evening; therefore, as soon as the morning dinner was despatched, they set out on another expedition, and did not arrive at the cottage till so late that the Doctor was there before them. In arranging the specimens of shell and weed that they had brought home, and in hearing the little pieces of news from home, the evening passed very happily away, and it was not until all the children were in bed, that the painful fact was casually mentioned by the Doctor, that he had forgotten the box of books. Fanny was terribly disappointed; but, as the weather was now fine again, she could only hope that it would remain so; and, in that case, she should not want the books. But I do not intend to suspend my narrative for the sake of becoming a weather chronicler; suffice it to tell, that until the happy and much-desired day when Fanny found herself once more on the road home, the weather was sometimes fine and sometimes not fine, generally the latter; and the children and their governess reached it longing more for the school-room than ever they had longed for a holiday. "O the delight of regularity and order!" thought Fanny, "and O what a luxury it is to have something to do!"

Fanny remained nearly in the same mind until the Christmas holidays; perhaps a continuance of somewhat dreary weather had something to do with it; perhaps the absence of visitors, and of exciting incidents, made it more easy for her to work cheerfully. Be that as it may, she felt that her duties were not disagreeable now, principle having done much for her, and habit more.

The first week of her Christmas holidays she greatly enjoyed. The second week, strange to say, she began to feel the old dismal weariness that she had suffered at the seaside. She had lost her former taste for silly story-books, and she was strong enough now not to find it any pleasure to lie half-dreaming on the sofa, with nothing in her hand but a little bit of crochet-edging. The third week she began to acknowledge to herself that she longed for the holidays to be over, and to perceive that she was now keeping school to please herself, and not to benefit her friend, of whom, by the by, she saw unaccountably little; and the third week once over, her heart leaped for joy,—she knew that now she had only one day of idleness left,—three weeks and one day being the length of this recess.

"Fanny, my dear, have you seen Ann Salter lately?" asked the Doctor, as they sat at breakfast on that last morning.

"No, uncle, I have not seen her for a long while," answered Fanny; "and she has not replied to my last letter."

"I will take you over to see her to-day, if you wish it," he continued; "I shall have to pass her father's gate. He is looking better than he has done for years, and is more active than ever, I think."

Fanny felt a pang of regret. "Then, perhaps, Annie would like to come back to her situation now," she presently said; "and perhaps I ought to mention the subject to her, uncle."

"I am very well satisfied to go on as we are," said the Doctor.

"Thank you for saying so, uncle; but I took the situation expressly that it might be kept open for Annie; so it would not be fair to deprive her of it."

"What, are you in a hurry to be free again?"

"O no," said Fanny, almost in tears; "but I do not wish to be ungenerous."

"Well, well!" replied the Doctor; "then tell Miss Salter that I shall be happy to see her here again to-morrow, *if she likes.*"

Fanny had no question in her own mind that Annie would like to come back; and she did not notice the quiet smile with which her uncle spoke.

She rose from table, and spent a few hours in seeing that everything in the school-room was neat and in its place. "It is strange," she thought, with her natural simplicity, "that it is almost impossible to be contented for long together. Every day I pray that I may be free from discontent, for it always seems to me a most unamiable vice; and yet I am constantly wishing things were different. All the early part of the time that I taught the children I was longing for a change, and wishing I had not undertaken the task; then we went to the sea, and great part of that time I was pining and fretting to get home again; then there were a few happy weeks, and after that these three uncomfortable weeks, when I have been wearied with wishing to have school again; and now, just as school is going to begin, Annie is to come back again, and take away my occupation. I wonder whether other people are as discontented as myself. I should think not. They have aspirations, of course, as one may read in so many books, but they do not seem to be ever discontented."

Fanny did not know that SOMETIMES people call their discontent aspiration, as being a prettier word, and meaning a more respectable thing.

After luncheon the pony-carriage came round to the door, and Fanny, well wrapped up, stepped into it. The day had been cold, but still, and though its beauty was now over, the cold was scarcely felt, from the absence of wind. Fanny did not dislike the drive, though, when they were within two miles of the farm, snow began to descend, and that so rapidly, that the ground was quite white in a very short time. Fanny was set down at the door of the farm, and Ann Salter and Mrs. Salter met her, and hospitably conducted her in. There was no fire in the parlor, for, as Mrs. Salter explained, they did not expect visitors in such weather, and her good man liked his meals best in the kitchen at that time of year. "But," said Mrs. Salter, "I shall have it lighted directly, Miss Fanny, and I hope you'll take a cup of tea with Annie; for I know the Doctor will be at least an hour before he returns." In the mean time she made Fanny sit with her feet on the kitchen fender, — and a very bright fender it was; the whole kitchen, indeed, was most clean and comfortable, and from its window you could see the snow coming down, and the church spire gradually getting a white mantle on its weather side.

"I suppose *he'll* come to-night," said Mrs. Salter, returning and addressing her daughter.

Who *he* might be Mrs. Salter did not explain, but she presently bustled out again, leaving the two girls together; whereupon Fanny unfolded her tale, and invited Ann Salter, in her uncle's name, to come back again.

Ann Salter did not say anything, but sat, looking rather foolish, while Fanny expressed her kind hope that the children would be found in good order, and perhaps im-' proved; but when she added, "And my uncle says, he shall be happy to see you as soon as you can return," Ann Salter stammered out, "I should be very happy, dear Fanny, only I am afraid,—at least, I mean, I think Mr. Dobson wishes me to stop at home."

"Mr. Dobson?" repeated Fanny, quietly.

"Yes," said Ann Salter, more bravely; "for, as we are to be married at Easter, he wishes to see as much of me beforehand as he can."

Greatly to Ann Salter's relief, Fanny promptly replied, "Married to Mr. Dobson, Annie? Oh, I am so glad, so extremely glad!"

"Are you, indeed?" exclaimed Ann Salter, greatly relieved. "Well, Fanny, all my friends are glad, and say I have done rightly to accept his offer. It is a great pleasure to my dear parents to have the prospect of my being settled in life — and — and besides, it is a pleasure to me."

Fanny murmured forth some congratulations.

"I was almost afraid you would not like my marrying William Dobson," Annie continued. Fanny blushed violently, and answered, "My uncle has said several times that he would be a very suitable husband for you; and if I ever thought otherwise, it was because I did not know any better." Whereupon the girls both laughed, and each secretly felt that a weight had been removed from her breast; for Ann Salter knew the day must come when Fanny must be told of her engagement; and Fanny knew she had used what influence she possessed against Mr.

Dobson, and had long regretted having done so, for she half suspected that her friend had a preference for this worthy man ; besides, now she could be governess to the children as long as she pleased ! So, in mutual confidence, and with many expressions of affection, the two girls passed the time, till Dr. Deane came back for Fanny, driving up to the door just as William Dobson walked up to it from the other side. Thereupon Fanny was formally introduced to him, and, to Ann Salter's secret satisfaction, held out her hand very cordially to shake that of the "man who was not a gentleman."

It was very cold, and it snowed very hard ; but Fanny and her uncle were exceedingly merry under the great gig umbrella, as they drove home.

" So now I feel really like an independent woman ; for I suppose, uncle, you will let me still be the children's governess ? "

"Yes, my dear, as long as you wish it."

"As long as I wish it, uncle ? O, I shall always wish it. Having once tasted the pleasure of independence, I shall never like to be dependent again."

" I would not be too sure of that. Perhaps, like the majority of your sex, you may promise, on due persuasion, that you will 'honor and obey'; and those little words once said, what becomes of independence then ? "

" I don't know," said Fanny, demurely ; " I suppose it must be left behind for Dr. Deane's next governess."

THE STOLEN TREASURE.

9 *

CHAPTER I.

COMPANIONS AT THE WILLOWS.

I HAD been at school rather more than a year, when my class-fellows Margaret and Juliet left, and were succeeded by Caroline Baker, and after an interval of three months by Christiana Black, a girl of Scottish parentage, who was at first a good deal overlooked, owing to her retiring disposition.

But perhaps another reason why she was overlooked was that the school generally took such a very great interest in Caroline, who presently was in everybody's confidence, and had something so engaging and fascinating about her that all the girls loved her, without precisely knowing why. Caroline had not been among us a week before every one was ambitious to give her anything she took a fancy to, every one wanted to walk with her, the girls offered to change gardens with her if she showed the least preference for their gardens over her own, and the little ones were always persisting, each one, that it was her turn to sit next Miss Baker, or that she had been promised that she should help Miss Baker to put her drawers to rights.

But the nature of the charm which so attracted us is not easy to define ; and its cause, strange as it may seem, partly arose from what every one would acknowledge to be a defect. She was capricious, and very changeable in her moods and fancies. Never two days alike, she kept us constantly surprised; sometimes vehement and full of life, sometimes languid and gentle. One day she was earnest, affectionate, or pensive, inviting confidence, and willing to give it; and the next, perhaps, wearily turning away from the exhibition of the loving interest that she had excited.

She was about sixteen when she came to school, and was rather small and slender for her years. Her appearance, when first presented to us by Madame, is so fresh in my memory, that in describing her I feel as if painting from the life.

She was dressed in white, and wore a crimson shawl over her shoulders, for the weather was chilly, and she was a native of the West Indies. She held her bonnet in her hand, and stood quite still, as we rose and walked up to her to be introduced. She had small features, and was pretty; her shining hair, unusually abundant, and of a light brown color, was a good deal brushed back from her face, in a style that was not common then, but which must have been comfortable in the hot climate she had come from. Her eyes were of the same nut-brown hue as her hair, and had that peculiar clearness which causes one apparently to see far down into them; and the well-formed, narrow, black eyebrow gave a great deal of its expression to her face, being sometimes slightly elevated with an air of amusement or surprise, and sometimes suddenly pulled down, with a look of displeasure and gloom.

I give this circumstantial account of her for the use of the physiognomist, and must add to it that she had a pretty mouth, which was dimpled, and almost infantine in its sweetness. She seemed to fancy herself greatly our superior; but there was something extremely engaging in the shy smile with which she looked at each as Madame named her, standing as she did, with her head a little thrown back, and with her eyelids not quite so far apart as we English-bred girls were accustomed to have them. In two or three days she discovered that her school-fellows were her equals ; and in two or three more she found that, compared with most of them, she knew next to nothing ; but she did not seem to feel this at all a degradation ; and the perfection of her manners, and her native elegance, caused the masters to treat her with as much consideration as they did the eldest pupil in the house.

There was something about Caroline which caused her easily to win her way everywhere ; even Madame was not always proof against her charming manner, and the teachers openly favored her in her lessons, but that did not cause any jealousy, because she was every one's favorite.

In the finest of the harvest weeks Caroline's birthday came, and she electrified the second class by declaring, the night before, that she intended to ask Madame for a holiday. Now when an old colonel from India, coming to see his daughters, or the Bishop of —— passing through, had begged that his little girls might have a holiday to play with their school-fellows, it had always been graciously granted ; but that a pupil should ask such a favor had never entered the mind of the eldest or the most daring. When we assembled in the school-room Caroline went up to Madame's table, and with a pretty gravity of manner informed her of the important fact, and inquired whether the school might have a holiday. Madame was mute with astonishment, and all the classes were breathless through suspense.

" Doubtless you have not been told, Miss Baker," said Madame, recovering herself, " that birthdays are not kept here."

Madame spoke in French ; Caroline made no answer. She had been informed of the fact, but it did not suit her to say so, and she continued to look at Madame, till, finding that the latter expected a reply, she said, in the sweetest tones of her winning voice, and in broken French, that "Madame was so kind—so very kind—and—it was such a fine day."

"Is that all you have to say?" asked Madame, with a smile of amusement.

"Madame," said Caroline, taking to her mother tongue, and speaking with a plaintive sweetness that infinitely became her, "I have looked in my French conversations, and there are no sentences in it that tell how to ask for a holiday."

Madame cast a penetrating glance on Caroline, which seemed to say, Is this simplicity, or the perfection of acting? and she evidently remained in doubt; but Caroline met the glance without blushing, and Madame, a little irritated at being so puzzled, escaped, for the moment, from a direct answer to the request by saying, with some asperity, "I cannot possibly allow English to be spoken before me."

At this point it may be considered that the holiday was all but won, for though Madame was not pleased, she had condescended to parley, and Caroline was too clever to let her advantage slip away. She answered in such broken French as made all the girls smile, bringing in the name of Madame's favorite pupil, and saying that if Madame would be pleased to let Mary l'Estrange ask for the holiday, she was sure Madame would find no faults in her French, and she would leave it to Mary to make an excuse for her if she had done wrong.

Madame looked surprised; but she had allowed the conference to proceed, and did not wish to deny the holiday, having permitted us to hope for it.

"Well," she said more graciously, "let Mary speak, then; but let it be fully understood, young ladies, that I am never to be asked for a holiday on a birthday again."

So Mary l'Estrange did, in respectful language, and in

excellent French, ask for the holiday, and Madame told us we might shut up our books, and do as we pleased for the day.

We all poured out to the lawn, and clustered about Caroline, the heroine of the day. We sat down under the shade of the willow-trees and considered what we should do. It was a sultry day, and the air was filled with tiny black flies like morsels of thread; the deep blue sky was pure and cloudless, and transparent waves appeared to chase one another over the roof of the house. Miss Quain began to explain to us the nature of the phenomenon, but it was a holiday, so we scarcely cared to listen. Caroline had never been so delighted with the weather. It had not been warm enough to please a native of the warm south, and she proposed that we should all take a walk into the harvest-field to see the people gleaning, — a sight she had never seen. We did not think of objecting, but sent Nannette in to ask Madame's permission, which we presently obtained, together with a promise that we should have some fruit to take with us, and some bread and milk.

I was specially excepted from the arrangement, not being thought strong enough to bear the noonday sun; but Madame gave me a little indulgence at home which reconciled me to the privation; and then, having seen pupils and teachers leave the house in high spirits, she took the opportunity to go out herself, telling Massey that she would not be home for some hours.

I had been in the garden for a long time, and in returning to the house was surprised to see a black man walking on the gravel, with a fair English child in his arms. He was dressed in wide white trousers, an ample white muslin turban, and a red calico jacket with a muslin one over it; and, to complete his costume, had a shawl tied about his waist, which formed both a petticoat and a scarf.

/ I had not so far forgotten the scenes of my infancy (for I was born at Madras) as not to know that this was a Hindoo bearer, and that he was drowsily singing the child to sleep with words that I had heard before, —

"Niendee, baba, niendee."
(Sleep, baby, sleep.)

I stood listening to the song, remembering enough of Hindustani to make out that the Eastern nurse was informing his unconscious charge that his father was a *burra Sahib* (great man or lord), and that his mother was a *burra Beebee* (great lady), and that if the *chota Sahib* (little master) would be good enough to go to sleep, he would confer a lasting obligation on his *bunda* (slave). While I still listened, Massey came out and said, " O, Miss West ! what an unfortunate thing it is that Madame should be out, for a lady and gentleman are here who particularly wish to see her. They were not expected till to-morrow ; and will you please to come in, Miss, for they wish to see any of the young ladies that are at home."

I should have mentioned that a travelling-carriage stood at the door, and that servants were busy taking down boxes from it.

I went into the drawing-room, and stood for a minute or two within the door unnoticed, looking at the group before me.

There was an *ayah* (nurse) in the room. She was richly dressed in shawls, silk petticoats, and fine muslin drapery, and wore gold bangles on her ankles and wrists. She was holding some Indian toys in her hands, and looking attentively at a lady who was seated on a sofa near her, with a gentleman standing on one side of her, and a sweet little child on the other.

This lady was tall and fair. I noticed a peculiar quivering and trembling about her lips, as if she had great diffi-

culty in controlling herself from weeping, and the gentleman, as he stood beside her, laid his hand on her shoulder,
and said very gently and compassionately, " Now, dearest,
shall we kiss our little one, and " — I knew that the rest of
the sentence should have been — *" and leave her ";* but he
did not say those words. And the lady, whose lips were
now firmly and steadily set together, did not answer a syl-
lable, but kept gazing at the tiny child, with its white frock
and pretty inquisitive face that looked up to her so shrewd-
ly, and yet with such a wistful air, as if it was quite impossible for her to see or hear anything else.

" Now, dearest," said the gentleman again.

The mother breathed quickly, and I shall never forget
the agony of her brow ; but she neither stirred nor took
her eyes from the face of the child.

" We cannot stay till Madame D. comes home," said the
husband.

" I know it," she replied.

" And we had fully decided to leave our child with her."

" Yes," said the mother, quite firmly.

" We are only called on to do it three days earlier than
we had intended," he proceeded.

" All that," she answered slowly, " I acknowledge and
know."

She appeared to speak like a person in a dream, and the
attentive little child, with hands firmly pressed together,
seemed to regard her with wondering gravity.

The gentleman sighed, as if he infinitely dreaded the
scene that must ensue. Once more he said, " Now, dearest," and at the same moment he beckoned to the ayah,
who, in obedience to some words that he spoke in Hindustani, came forward and took up the little child in her
arms.

Then the mother burst into tears, and begged for a few
moments more, and took the child upon her knees, and be-

N

gan to caress her, and lament over her. Poor little creature, she was far from understanding the real and terrible
loss that she was about to undergo : and when the lady
said, " Does my darling know that poor mamma must go
away ? " she only nodded her little head, and said gravely,
" Yes " ; and then began to occupy herself with her mother's rings.

Just then the gentleman observed my presence, and
came to lead me forward to his wife, asking me if I were
one of the pupils.

I said I was, and the lady held out her hand, and drew
me towards her, asking hysterically whether I would be
kind to her little child, and saying, " I am sorry, so very
sorry, that Carry should be out. I did want to see her, and
beg her to be kind to my little one, and be her school-
mamma."

On this mention of Caroline, the gentleman began to tell
me that he was an intimate friend of Major Baker's, and
had been partly induced to bring his child to the Willows,
in the hope that Carry would love her.

I could not but declare that I thought Caroline would be
extremely good and kind to her. I fully participated in
the feeling of attraction that we all felt towards Caroline,
and I drew such a picture of her delightful qualities, that
the lady was evidently comforted, and, drawing me closer,
made me kneel on a hassock beside her, and, with motherly tenderness, held my head with her hand against her
bosom. The other embraced her child, and through the
glossy folds of her rich silk dress I could feel the troubled
beating of her heart.

But the dreaded moment was come ; the gentleman, who
looked as if he longed above all things to have this scene
over, pulled out his watch, and the movement attracted the
poor mother's notice, for she said something in a broken
voice to the ayah, who, folding her hands submissively,

made a low salaam. I remembered enough of my first language to know that she was promising to be tender and attentive to the child. Her speech was scarcely over when the father lifted up the little girl, and held her face to her mother's for a moment, then he kissed her himself, and put her hastily into the arms of her ayah, who hurried with her out of the room.

The mother, after this last kiss, covered her face with her hands, and sat so still that I thought she was listening to the retreating footsteps of the ayah as she carried her treasure away. When these were no longer audible, she looked up and said, —

" Merton, I wish to go."

Massey then put on her shawl and veil, and when she had picked up a little Indian toy that her child had dropped on the carpet, and put it in her bosom, she gave her hand to her husband, who led her to the carriage. A message of compliment and regret being left for Madame, and an assurance that she should receive a letter that same evening, they drove away, and I ran up stairs to look for the tiny pupil,

CHAPTER II.

MADAME'S NEW PUPIL.

I WAITED only till the sound of the carriage-wheels had died away, and then ran up stairs in search of the little girl. I found her with her ayah, seated on the floor of a spare bedroom, with a number of toys strewed about in all directions.

I understood that she was about four years old, but she was scarcely larger than most children at two. She was rather pale, and excessively fair ; a quantity of flaxen hair curled on her neck ; she wore a white frock of Indian muslin, richly worked ; and a gold chain, with a locket attached to it, encircled her throat. Her toys, which consisted of ivory elephants richly gilded, models of soldiers and sepoys, bullock-carts, palanquins of gaudy colors, and curious carved balls, made her look, by their large size, all the more fairy-like and small. Her pretty face was not infantine in its expression ; and the air of command with which she ordered her ayah to set me a chair would have been more suited to a reigning princess than to a child who was now to be for many years entirely under the dominion of strangers.

I heard the ayah informing her that the "Beebee Sahib" would soon be back again ; and the little creature looked at her with a wistful expression of doubt, as if she suspected that these flattering words were too good to be true. I asked her if she would kiss me, but this she positively refused to do ; and then I asked her if she would come into the garden and have a nosegay, but she was an independent little creature, and when she had risen from the floor, and walked up to me, and examined me from head to foot, she declined this also, and then commanded her ayah to bring her bonnet, and carry her down into the "compound," by which she meant the garden or yard. So I was left alone among her Indian toys till my schoolfellows came in from their walk, with Caroline at their head. Caroline was reading a letter, and looked very much disconcerted; but the other girls were laughing, and questioning her as to where the strange little child had come from that they had seen in the garden, with her foreign nurse.

Miss l'Estrange had taken her up in her arms, but had received a slap in return from the tiny hand, together with peremptory orders to set her down again ; and little Nannette had presented a paper of sugar-plums, but the intractable infant had scattered them over the grass, and thrown away the paper.

What she suspected, or why she was so averse to our companionship, we did not know ; perhaps she felt herself in some manner wronged and deceived by her mother's absence, and had some childish glimmering of the truth, that she was at the mercy of strangers.

Caroline had finished reading her letter. "And so," she exclaimed, giving a slight toss to her graceful head, "and so Mrs. Merton expects me, or at least wishes me, to devote myself to this little female nabob. Here is a long account of how she hopes I will always be a friend to the child. Ridiculous ! Am I to bear with all her whims, because ten years ago our fathers were in the same regiment ? And she shall always be grateful ; — I dare say ! No, I never could bear children at such an early age. If this had been a girl as old as myself, it might have been a different matter ; but a spoilt baby like this; I wonder how she could be so absurd ; and actually it seems that

the child is sent here principally on papa's recommendation, and because I am here. How tiresome! here she
comes."

Here she came, indeed, in her ayah's arms, and Belle
ran up to her, as girls will do to little children, and begged
a kiss.

" Do kiss me," said Belle. The child shook her head.

" Why not ? " asked Belle.

" Because I don't like you," said the little creature, in a
sweet treble voice.

" Not like me! why not ? "

"" Because, because," looking at her to find a reason,
" because you 've got an ugly bonnet on."

" Well, kiss me, then," said Caroline, a little tartly;
" look, I have no bonnet at all."

" No, I don't like you."

" Why not ? "

Another pause for reflection, and then in a pettish tone,
" Because you are a cross lady."

" There ! " exclaimed Caroline triumphantly, " did ever
any one see such a capricious little thing ? Oh! very well;
I don't at all want to kiss you. Yes! the idea of my de-
voting myself to that child, and being her school-mamma.
I shall not think of it ; any one who chooses may take her
in hand."

" O Carry," said Belle, " it would be very little trouble
indeed to be her school-mamma ; she has this nurse of her
own to attend to all her whims, and in school-hours she
would be in a different class from yours."

" And she would go to bed long before you," added Miss
Ward.

" That does not signify," said Caroline ; " I do not consider that her mamma had any right to expect me to be
more interested in her than I am in any of you. I like to
do kindness spontaneously ; but to have it represented that

I *ought* to do it, takes away all the pleasure of it ; makes it something that one is to be blamed for if one does not perform, but *not* to be praised for if one does ! So, Mrs. · Merton, you must look somewhere else for your monthly accounts of the health and progress of this little spoilt pet, — though to be sure it will be no great trouble just to write the letters. I will do that, and I think it is enough for a person whom I have never seen."

" I cannot understand how you got this letter," said Miss Ward ; "it seems to have followed the visit with marvellous rapidity."

" O, it was written here," replied Caroline ; "when Mrs. Merton found that I was out, Massey says she sat down directly and wrote this, and said it was to be given to me on my return."

" Well, Carry," said Belle, " it is very flattering that she should consider your patronage of so much consequence for the child ; don't you think so, Sophia ? "

" So flattering," I replied, " that I only wish some one would flatter me in the same way ; I think it would make me quite devote myself to the little creature, though she may be rather spoilt at present."

" The fairy wishes to patronize another fairy ! " exclaimed Caroline.

Upon this the elder girls laughed, and Miss l'Estrange snatched me up in her arms, and in spite of my resistance persisted in carrying me about, caressing me, and pretending to sing me to sleep, as nurses do to babies.

I was very angry, though I could not help laughing ; and when I had contrived to struggle down again, I informed my friend and patroness that now I was fourteen years and eight months old, — eight months, mind, — so that I should soon be fifteen, and I did not choose to be carried about any longer. My offended dignity might have induced me to march out of the room, if I had not been arrested by the sound of fits of infantine laughter, and, behold! the little stranger was pointing to us with her finger, and laughing till her pretty face and neck were tinged with carnation. She evidently thought this little scene was got up for her special diversion, and cried out, " Do it again, do it again, great tall lady."

It would no doubt have been repeated, in spite of my resistance, if a clear voice within the room had not arrested our attention.

"Vhat do I see, ladies? for vhat do you teaze Miss Sophia?" said Madame.

Her neat figure is still before me, the pale green ribbons and feather which adorned her tasteful bonnet, and which so many of her nation are fond of placing next to their rich brown skins and dark eyes; the delicate light shawl of mulberry color, which she held so elegantly, and her rustling lilac silk dress.

" *Comment*, what noise do I hear?" she exclaimed.

Madame never attempted to speak English, excepting on a holiday, when she so far relaxed from her ordinary manner as even to joke with us.

" So, *La petite* does not like to pass for a *Fée*," she exclaimed ; "for what should she not? *Les fées* — the fairies — are very pretty little things."

"Yes, Madame," said Miss l'Estrange, "much prettier than the Amazons."

Madame smiled, and looking up at the stately height of her pupil, replied with a French proverb which intimates that though little things are pretty, great things are sublime. At this moment the group of girls parted, and showed, seated among her toys, the new arrival, and her submissive ayah. The latter arose and made a graceful salaam, as if perceiving at once that this was the mistress of the house.

Madame did not seem so much surprised as might have

been expected ; the fact was, she had met the travelling-carriage on its way to the railway, and had spent a short time with the child's parents at the station.

" And for what are they shown into this dull apartment ? " asked Madame.

Dull it certainly was, for the upper shutters of the room were closed, and the blinds drawn down ; the bed was pinned up in brown holland covers, and the carpets were rolled back into a corner.

Madame desired us to open the shutters, and when the sunshine was let in, she sat down, and said, " Come to me, little one."

The child arose and stood at her knees, answering several simple questions with that respect which Madame scarcely ever failed to inspire. When she had done talking to her, she lifted her up and said, " Kiss me." She was obeyed, and the little creature being set down again, looked at her attentively, and as if to inform her that the kiss had been given under protest, lisped out in the sweetest of silvery tones, " But I don't love you."

" Do you know who I am ? " said Madame, very gravely.

" No," said the child, hesitating.

Madame told her, and added, " Little girls never say that to me ; little girls must be good in my house."

" Yes," said the child, whose hands were clasped behind her.

" You are going to be good ? "

" Yes."

" Then you may take hold of my hand, and come with me to see your pretty bed."

The little creature, in the most docile manner, did as she was bidden, only looking rather wistfully at her toys. Madame, seeing this, made a sign to the ayah to bring them, and at the same time said, " The ladies of the second class may follow also."

So we followed to our own large bedroom, beyond which was another wide room, hitherto unoccupied. The door of this room, to which ours was a thoroughfare, was now open. Massey was in it, and we found that it was fitted up like a nursery, indeed it had formerly been used as such ; and it now contained a rocking-horse, some children's chairs, and two beds, one of which was adorned with muslin curtains, tied back by pink ribbons.

Madame's French taste was very evident in all the decorations of this airy room ; she now looked at it with much approval ; so apparently did the child.

" Is that a pretty bed ? " asked Madame.

" Yes," said the little creature, with a delighted smile.

" I told you to come up, ladies," said Madame, turning towards us, " to inform you that you have free leave from me to come in here and play with this dear little girl, so long as she is good, and you do not abuse the privilege."

She said this in French, but repeated something like it in English, for the benefit of the child. I remember being struck at the time with the truth of what I had heard the elder girls say, namely, that in cases where Madame could secure obedience she was firmly determined to be obeyed ; but that in cases where she could not, she would grant permission to do things that she would rather not have allowed, simply that none of the pupils might find themselves able to elude her vigilance or thwart her with impunity.

I have said there was no entrance to this room but through ours, and as the ayah could not speak English, Madame perhaps thought we should have been induced, by the facilities offered, to come and play with the child.

We were to go in whenever we pleased ; so accordingly, that same night, as we were undressing, we were pleased to open the door softly and peep in. There lay the little creature fast asleep in her embroidered night-dress, and there lay her ayah fast asleep also, not in the bed that had been prepared for her, but on the carpet at the foot of the child's bed, and rolled up in the checked table-cloth of red and blue that she had taken from its place.

"I am glad Madame has said nothing to me about taking any particular notice of the child," said Caroline; "and I am sure when every one else is so much interested there can be no need for my exerting myself."

I thought Caroline said this as if she felt somewhat injured by the notice taken of the little creature, and at first I remember feeling ashamed of myself and reproaching myself for the notice I had taken, as if it were a kind of treason to one in whom I had professed such an absorbing interest myself. But afterwards I began to reflect that it would be unamiable in Caroline to have such feelings as I had imputed to her; consequently, as she was so very charming and so amiable, I decided that she had them not.

So this matter passed. I think it was on the 2d of August that the little pupil came to us, and for three weeks from that day she received every morning a short lesson from the English teacher, her ayah standing beside her. She was perfectly good and docile in the school-room, but during play-hours she behaved just as she had done at first, declining to be caressed or played with by the elder girls, though she would sometimes amuse herself with Madame's two little girls, provided her ayah stood beside her the whole time.

I could sometimes hear her talking to this devoted woman about her mamma: "Would she soon come back?"

"O yes, very soon."

"Would she come to-day?"

"No, not to-day."

"Would she come to-morrow?"

"Perhaps."

Alas! the poor Hindoo knew not the fault she was committing, and had not acquired enough English to be told of it.

" I don't believe you," said the little creature, when this happy to-morrow had been promised a great many times: and using her Oriental imagery, she exclaimed, "You have no straight words, you 've got a *whole country full* of words in your heart, but they 're all crooked ones!"

The ayah smiled, and shaking up a pillow invited Missy Baba to go to sleep. She was unwearied in her attendance and devoted in her love to the child; but about the beginning of September we all observed that one day she looked extremely heavy, and muttered and rocked herself as she sat on the ground. Her eyes followed the child's movements with an air of unutterable regret, and Massey discovering that she was ill tried to make her go to bed; but she preferred to sit on the floor, and though she sighed often she did not complain.

Very soon finding that she could neither move nor eat, Madame sent for a physician. It was a piteous sight to see her sitting on the floor with her little nursling beside her, not able to make the physician understand the nature of her suffering, and quietly refusing to take his medicines.

I was called to ask her what ailed her, but she did not answer, though she spoke to her pretty nursling when she babbled in her native tongue.

Poor ayah, she was very patient, and the child, who refused to leave her, was carried away in her sleep to another room, but this was not till the poor woman was too ill to observe her absence. Two days of gloom and anxiety followed, the child being hardly pacified and kept away from her ayah, by assurances that the least noise would make her worse.

On the third morning Madame sent for me early to her own room, and on the way thither Massey told me that the ayah was dead. Madame was then telling the poor desolate child of her loss, and wished me to be there because I could understand her when she spoke in her Oriental tongue.

CHAPTER III.

MAY MERTON FINDS A FRIEND.

I ENTERED Madame's room with no little trepidation, and saw my poor little schoolfellow sitting on a
stool. She did not exhibit any violent grief, but there was
a painfully forlorn expression about her always wistful face ;
and though she did not cry, she would neither eat nor take
any notice of our caresses.

· When the school-bell rang, Madame sent me down, for I
was of no use. The teachers inquired after the poor child,
and one of them said, that though she was very sorry for
the poor ayah, she thought her removal was by no means
to be regretted on the child's account ; because as long as
that foreign woman was about her, she would never have
thoroughly settled at school, nor attached herself to those
who had the responsibility of her teaching. I could not
tell how this might be, but I thought that, even to a child,
it must be a terrible thing to lose the only person whom
she deeply loved, and with whom she was thoroughly at
home. I hoped she would now begin to attach herself to
us, and soon get over the loss of her ayah.

But from day to day, when I saw her, she was still
pining and fretting, sometimes moping on her little stool,
sometimes crying in Massey's arms, and constantly becoming thinner and paler, losing her appetite, and refusing to
do as she was bid,

At first Madame hoped she would soon forget her grief,
but when three or four weeks had passed away, and still
the tiny face grew thin, and the little sorrowful voice was

heard wailing in the night, she became seriously unhappy about the child; for- she was too young to be reasoned with, too ill to be punished, and too far away from her parents to be sent home. Sometimes they would take her out for a drive, or think to amuse her by bringing her down into the garden, but after taking a few steps she would put her wasted hand to her side, and say in a piteous voice, "It hurts here; it always hurts here," and beg to be taken in again. Her medical attendant said it was extremely bad for her to fret and cry. He assured Madame he could do nothing for her unless she was kept calm and cheerful; an easy thing to say, but difficult to accomplish, for every dose of medicine cost a contention and a passion of tears that almost exhausted her feeble frame; and though she was tempted with many dainties, she could hardly eat enough to sustain life.

Madame was accustomed to be implicitly obeyed, and scarcely knew how to deal with this poor infant, who set her authority utterly at naught, and was not to be flattered or caressed into submission. She had not been well brought up, and though when in health she had yielded to an influence that kept the boldest spirits in order, she now ceased to care for praise or blame, and all her original wilfulness came back again.

Madame was evidently quite wretched, and was losing confidence in herself altogether. She caused each teacher in turn to try her powers with the child, then she called in the elder girls, and encouraged them to exert themselves to make the little sufferer take her medicine. But all was of no avail; low fever came on, and life seemed actually to depend on a docility that it was quite hopeless to expect from her.

Yet the wilfulness of a little child does not alienate affection. There was still something sweet in the baby resentment that blamed "all the cruel ladies" for taking away her mamma and her nurse. The little voice, in all its sorrow, was still silvery and touching, and the wistful features were still pretty, though marred by tears and illness.

It was about this time that Miss Black came among us, but, as I have said before, her coming attracted little attention ; our thoughts, when not occupied with the child, were all given to Caroline. Miss Black always inquired with great interest about the poor little creature, but Madame never thought of asking her to come and see her, because she was a stranger.

One night, when we were all quite unhappy about our little schoolfellow, I was called in to see if I could make her take her food by talking Hindustani to her. I did not succeed, but as Madame did not desire me to withdraw, I sat by the bed thinking how mournful all this was, and wishing there was something more useful for me to do than snuffing the candle which stood on a small table beside her.

Poor little child ! I remember her wailing voice as she sat half-upright in her bed, peevishly refusing either to take her supper or to lie down and sleep, when the door into our bedroom was softly pushed open, and Miss Black came in, with a long white dressing-gown on.

I thought she came to see what she could do to help us, but apparently it was not the case. Miss Black did not look at us, but at something soft that lay upon her arm, and she swept close up to the bed without saying a word. Madame, utterly dispirited, was weeping behind the curtain. The child paused in her low cry, arrested by the sight of the stranger, and said, "Who's that, with her best frock on ?"

"I've got something so pretty here," said Miss Black, still looking down upon her arm ; "I don't know whether I shall show it to anybody." She seemed to consider, and in the meantime the child regarded her with fixed and wondering attention.

"If I knew of any *very* good child, perhaps I should show these little things to her," said Miss Black, pretending to talk to herself.

"Wee, wee, wee!" cried the things on her arm.

"But I dare say nobody wants to see them," she continued.

"I want to see them," said the child, checking a long sob.

"Ah!" said Miss Black, "they seem very hungry, poor little things!"

"Wee — wee — wee!"

"O! do show them to me," sobbed the child; and when Miss Black took up two tiny kittens by the neck, set them on the bed, and let them creep towards her, she was so delighted that she began to laugh, and try to feed them with some of the bread and milk which she had been vainly implored to eat for her supper.

"O! they cannot eat bread," said Miss Black, quietly, "they are too young; but when we have emptied the saucer, they shall have some milk in it."

She sat by the child and supported her feeble frame. "Now, then," she said, "let us eat this," and she held the spoon to the child's mouth, which was opened half unconsciously; for Miss Black had begun to relate a wonderful story about four white kittens who lived in a hay-loft. The child listened with rapt attention till the supper was eaten, when the tale came to a sudden conclusion; then some milk was poured into the saucer, and the real kittens were fed.

When they had lapped every drop of the milk, Miss Black produced a little basket and a piece of flannel, in which she let the child help to place these playthings that had appeared so opportunely.

"Now, then," she said, "let us put them on the table, and you shall sit on my knee, and peep at them, while

Miss West shakes up the pillow, and makes the bed all smooth and comfortable."

No objection was made to this arrangement, but the little wasted arms were held out, and the child, almost too weak now to rise, tried to creep away from the pillows to her new friend, suffering herself to be nursed and fondled till she could be placed comfortably in her bed again. Then, indeed, her face changed, and she said in a piteous tone, "But I don't want you to go away. I want you to get into my bed. Will you?"

Miss Black darted a glance at Madame, who nodded assent. "O yes," she said. "I should like to sleep in your pretty bed very much."

"And I may see the kittens to-morrow?"   ·

"O yes!" repeated Miss Black, lying down beside the child, whose chest still heaved every now and then with a deep sob, but who was so completely wearied and faint for want of sleep, and the comfort-cherishing that children so much require, that now she was with some one who could manage her, she fell at once into a deep sleep, and her little wayward face began to look calm and almost happy.

Madame had kept completely in the background from the moment of Miss Black's entrance, and when she saw that the child would soon be asleep, she made a sign to me to remain perfectly still. She looked so happy, when at length she came up to the bed, and shading the candle with her hand, drew back the curtain, and saw her poor little pupil fast asleep.

"Ah! this has been a terrible anxiety to me," she murmured, and then she stooped and kissed Miss Black, — a thing I had never seen her do to any pupils but the little ones. "I am greatly indebted to you, my dear," I heard her say; "you have relieved me from great dread for this desolate child."

Miss Black cautiously turned her face upon the pillow,

10*   O

—the child's long curls were spread somewhat forlornly across her forehead, she parted them with her soft hand; the little creature was in a most healing slumber, and she said, "I would take the greatest care of her, Madame, if you would take some rest. Will you trust me?"

Madame could not make up her mind to leave the room, but she dismissed me to mine, and took possession of the other bed in the nursery. She was soon asleep, and the door being left ajar, I could see distinctly the little child and her new nurse, and I wondered what it was that had given Miss Black such ascendency. I do not think anything more transpired than what I have narrated, and all her art seemed to have consisted in first surprising and then amusing.

But at fifteen one does not reason much, nor spend the precious midnight hours in any abstract speculations. I fell asleep, and did not wake till we were called, when I found the door shut between us, and was not told anything about the child till after breakfast, when Belle waylaid a maid-servant as she came down stairs, and heard from her that the physician had already paid his visit; that he thought the child better, though extremely weak, and had as usual requested that she might be kept as cheerful as possible.

But about ten minutes before the first school-bell rang, Miss Quain desired me to carry Miss Black's exercise-book and some ink into the nursery, as Madame had given her leave to write her exercise there. I went up and saw the little patient lying in bed, looking decidedly better, and listening to a story, — a story, namely, concerning a young cock-sparrow, of rebellious turn of mind, who would insist upon hopping under a hand-glass, which a gardener had propped up with a piece of wood. His mother, in forcible and affecting language, had entreated him not to enter that dangerous place; but this deluded bird, when she was not looking, went in. The gardener came and shut the glass, and the sparrow was obliged to sit inside, peeping through the glass and flapping his wings, with nothing to eat, while his good, obedient brothers and sisters had some little ants and some juicy caterpillars for their dinner.

This story, though it does not sound probable, nor of very absorbing interest, was precisely suited to the infantile listener, who remarked concerning the sparrow, that if he would not do as he was bid, it served him quite right to be shut in there ; and then, while I was assisting Miss Black with her toilette, she tried to make further acquaintance with her new friend by asking what her name was.

"O, I have such a long name," said Miss Black, "that I don't think such a little girl as you could say it ; my name is Christiana Frances."

"Say it again," asked the child.

The name was repeated, and, after pondering it silently for a while, the child said distinctly, in her sweet treble voice, "Miss Christiana Frances, will you say my little name now ? May Merton is my name."

"Little May Merton, I love you very much," said Miss Black.

"And will you sleep in my bed to-night, Miss Christiana Frances ? " pleaded the little creature.

"O yes, if you are good," replied Miss Black, who well knew that Madame would be too happy to permit it.

"I am good," said the child, glancing towards an empty medicine-glass ; "and you said you would tell me another story." But this other story, my readers, I regret that I cannot lay before you, though it was doubtless of surpassing interest ; for the bell rang, and I left little May to the companionship of her benefactress.

I feel that I have passed over the first appearance of Miss Black among us, as if it had been a matter of very small importance.

It seemed to be so in the first instance ; for, though she could easily make her way among children, she was particularly reserved — intentionally reserved — among us ; but as she is to play a somewhat important part in the little scenes which I am about to describe, I will try to give a sketch of her appearance and manner.

She was rather older than most school-girls, being nearly seventeen years of age. She had only come into the house for the sake of learning accomplishments, and was treated more like a parlor boarder than a mere pupil, though she slept in our room, and took her music and German lessons with us. Her appearance was elegant and agreeable, perhaps somewhat pretty. I speak of her as I saw her at first ; for afterwards affection clothed her deservedly with many charms. She was very womanly in manner and character, and looked quite grown up, though she had a slender, girlish figure. The hair and complexion were extremely fair ; yet she had black eyebrows, which met, and gave her sometimes, when she was deep in thought, a severe expression. There was a certain self-possession and calm about her which was not altogether free from pride, and which made us, from the first, fond of contrasting her character with that of Caroline, who was so winning and engaging, and who could refuse a kindness in a manner more flattering than the simple gravity with which Miss Black would grant it.

Caroline seemed often bent on pleasing and winning all suffrages for herself. Miss Black was never trying to please, though she was often trying to do good. Moreover, she was deeply affectionate. It seemed to be as essential to her happiness to find people on whom she could lavish her care and attentive love, as it was to Caroline to excite and receive the affection of others.

Caroline was clever, Miss Black was intellectual, and by far the most gifted pupil that Madame had ever received ;

but in spite of the difference in their age, she was not equal to Caroline in that peculiar tact, and that superior knowledge of character, by which this singular young creature obtained for herself so much power. Caroline always chose the most acceptable species of flattery to bestow on each schoolfellow whom she wished to influence, and found the readiest way to their hearts, without yielding in return one-half of the affection that she received.

"O, what a name!" exclaimed Caroline, when I told her Miss Black's Christian name; for we, school-girl like, had tried to find it out, but had not hitherto succeeded.

"Christiana reminds me of the Pilgrim's Progress. I shall always feel inclined to address her in antiquated fashion. Prithee, good Christiana, lend me thy French Dictionary."

"But Frances is a pretty name," I observed; "and she says that is the name she is called by."

"I shall always call her by both," said Caroline; "Christiana is a moral name, and Frances is an intellectual name. She is a perfect mass of morality and cleverness, far too much so for my taste,—'stuffed with honorable parts,' as that old gentleman says."

"You don't mean Shakespeare," I exclaimed.

"I mean the man whose scenes and things we read sometimes, and whose picture has a turn-down collar,—yes, Shakespeare, to be sure; I thought at first it was Chaucer, but now I remember it is n't. Well, if the said Christiana Frances likes to sit up in the nursery with May, telling stories of cock-robins, instead of cultivating the acquaintance of her equals, I have nothing to say against it, I am sure."

"No," I remarked; "you always said, that as far as you were concerned, any one might patronize May who was willing."

CHAPTER IV.

MISS BLACK.

I N looking back on those days which followed the illness of little May, I can scarcely recall her image
without that of Miss Black; "My Miss Christiana Frances,"
as May always called her.

Madame, at Miss Black's own request, permitted her to
take up her abode in the nursery, as her bedroom; and
shortly afterwards my bed also was moved there, and a
friendship gradually grew between us, which enabled me
to appreciate and love her character.

Those were happy days for May and me. My old
friends, with the exception of Belle, had all left The Willows; and some of the new-comers often made me extremely uncomfortable, by quizzing me, and laughing at
me, if ever they found me indulging my love of reading,
or secretly studying any subject, by myself. Frances, on
the contrary, used to encourage and help me; and when I
complained of the teazing I endured, she used to sympa-
thize with me, though it evidently surprised her that I
should care for it. When she saw me hardly beset by
Caroline and the elder girls, she would sometimes enter
the lists with me, and turn the tables upon my tormentors;
for she had considerable wit, and used to adopt the quaint
language which Caroline had sometimes addressed her in,
because of her name, and use it much more drolly than
any of her companions.

About this time four of the girls, myself among them,
formed a club, which we called, "The Mental Improve-

ment Club," — a childish thing, no doubt, but well meant, and for which we used to write original articles in prose and poetry. When Caroline discovered this club, she was very merciless upon us, partly, no doubt, pretty dunce, because she could not write well enough (as we were pleased to think) to be worthy of a place in it.

The club sometimes met in the coach-house, sometimes in a bedroom, in short, anywhere that seemed to offer a safe asylum from the ridicule of those who were not members. But I am bound, as a faithful historian, to say that the "mental improvers," as Caroline called us, were so made game of, and, metaphorically speaking, so hunted down by her, that they were on the point of dissolving, when one day a certain picture was discovered pinned to the head of Caroline's bed. This picture was duly headed, in old English letters, "Third Meeting of the Mental Improvers, with Miss C. B., as Aquarius, pouring cold water on the concern." In the centre of the picture were four girls huddled together, and reading from a paper. The unknown artist had expended a great deal of trouble in making the figures extremely sweet and pretty. Standing over them, with a huge watering-pot, was a ludicrous and hideous caricature of Aquarius, with a face so like Caroline's, that it was impossible to mistake it. A certain air of malice was imparted to the features of Aquarius, as the streams of water came pouring down, which by no means impaired the likeness.

Poor Caroline was deeply disgusted at the highly unflattering likeness of herself; perhaps she was still more annoyed at the beauty of the four girls seated on the ground. Their dress and hair were represented as by no means disordered by the shower (for artists will take liberties with nature and possibility); on the contrary, the general air of Aquarius reminded one of the most dirty and common-looking of little maids-of-all-work. Underneath were these words : —

" C. B. returns thanks to her friends and the public for their distinguished patronage, and hopes, by unwearied efforts to merit its continuance. *N. B.* Shower-baths gratis every Wednesday afternoon."

Wednesday afternoon was the time when we met. We all thought in our inmost hearts that there was but one person in the house who was artist enough to have made this really clever drawing. No one said who she thought it was ; and when she whom we suspected knocked at the door and came through the bedroom of the second class with May in her arms, and a countenance of settled gravity, we were a little puzzled. However, we never asked for any explanation ; for the members of the club would have felt it something like vanity, to take for granted that those lovely young creatures on the ground were meant for them ; and as for Caroline, she was much too politic openly to betray any anger ; that would have been to admit that she acknowledged the likeness and the character.

It was soon evident to all the school that Caroline considered Miss Black in the light of a rival, though, as the latter was remarkably independent, and scarcely ever interfered with others, there was for a long time very little opportunity for showing it.

In the mean time little May got quite well, and grew plump and rosy, though she was still so extremely small, that the girls used to say they thought all her growth went into her hair ; rather an unscientific way, perhaps, of accounting for her infantine proportions. Her hair was of very unusual length and beauty, and I well remember that when we used to pass our fingers through the loose curls and straighten them, they would reach to the hem of her frock.

Pretty little May, she was always a pet amongst us, and so light that it required no great strength to carry her about. Frances spent many an hour that winter in carrying her out in the garden, when the sun shone. Though .cheerful and well now, she was very tender, and easily fatigued ; but endowed with a spirit and a will strong enough for a creature five times her size.

Her improvement, under the care of Frances, was surprising, and there was something extremely pretty and almost touching, in the confiding way in which she gave her whole heart to her. Her devotion was fully repaid, for we all felt that Frances loved this morsel of a child more than all the rest of the household put together. She was certainly an engaging and desirable little plaything, and we all, including Caroline, liked to amuse ourselves with her now and then, when she was well and good-tempered ; but we always gave her back to Frances when we were tired of her, as the person to whom she naturally belonged, and whose duty it was to attend to her. Her kindness to May was soon looked upon even by Madame as a kind of duty. Yet I must do her the justice to say that she did not tire of it. All the trouble she took in teaching, cherishing, dressing, playing with, and telling stories to " her child," seemed to cost her very little effort. She was systematically good to little May, not only when she was droll and tractable, but when she was naughty, troublesome, and cross, as all children are at times.

Some of the girls used to wonder how Frances could bestow so much trouble on the child : I never did. I used to think of a speech made to me a few months before, by a little cousin of mine. " I think," said this child, with grave contempt, — " I think I shall dig a hole and bury my doll."

" Poor thing ! " said I, " what has she done ? "

" Why," replied the child, in a sharp tone of injured feeling, " she 's no use at all. I 'm always saying, ' How do you do ? ' to her, and she, — she *never* says, ' Very well, thank you.' "

Now little May was a doll that could say, "Very well, thank you." She was by no means a passive plaything.

If Frances left the door open, she invariably ran out, and had to be brought back laughing and shrieking. If Frances left her ink in an accessible place, May would dip a pen into it; and if a drawing was at hand, May would put some finishing touches to it; if not, she would wipe the pen on her pinafore. If she saw Frances at work, she would seat herself beside her, on her *mora* (stool), and quietly taking a needle and a long thread from the cushion, would lift up some small article, such as a lace collar or a pinafore, and begin to stitch through and through it, drawing up the thread till the whole was one shapeless mass of crumples and tangles, like a particularly bad ball; then she would proudly hand it up to the unconscious Frances, exclaiming, "There, I've mended *him*, I want another to do."

Frances obtained for herself the privilege, as she considered it, of always being allowed to put May to bed; and before carrying her up stairs, she used to take off her shoes and socks, and warm the child's tiny feet in her hands by the school-room fire. O, the brushing and smoothing that those long, silky curls required; no one but Frances would have found any pleasure in such a task; and then, when she had tucked up her little charge and kissed her, she always told her a story out of the Bible before she went away. It was astonishing how much of Scriptural incident and character the child soon acquired in this way, and how many hymns and texts she learned almost spontaneously. Indeed, it was not wonderful that Frances should have taught her best that in which she took the deepest interest, religion. She had none of that false shame which prevents so many school-girls from daring to profess any interest in this most important of all subjects, even when they feel it strongly, and are unhappy at their own want of courage which leads them to conceal it. The girls became aware that Frances thought a good deal on matters that concerned the soul, just as easily and quickly as they did that Frances wished to be a good German scholar; for though neither fact was announced, both were evident to any one with the slightest observation.

Little May reaped the benefit of this openness, which had a most salutary effect in the school, and the more so, as it was not inconsistent with that natural reserve which Frances seldom laid aside. She quietly admitted her religious impressions, but she never enlarged upon them.

Many a delightful evening in the spring-time, when I have entered our bedroom, I have seen little May lying in her pretty bed, and Frances reclining beside her, with her cheek on the same pillow, telling those evening stories till the child gradually closed her eyes and fell asleep in the broad daylight.

May had been at school about eight months, when one morning Caroline received a letter by the Indian mail from Mrs. Merton. She gave a message to little May from her mamma, but it amounted to little more than her best love, and that of the child's father. Caroline, however, read the letter with deep interest and a heightened color, which gave us the impression that there was something more than usual in it. School-time was at hand, so we could hear nothing about it then; but we did not doubt that Caroline, who was eminently sociable in disposition, and completely unable to keep a secret, would tell us the contents of the letter when she had an opportunity.

It was as we had expected. After school, Caroline was walking in the orchard, conning her letter, when she met little Nannette coming out of the hop-garden with an armful of cow-parsley for her rabbits; and she sent her to us, to ask if we would join her. There were six of us together, and we forthwith went and found Caroline under a great apple-tree, seated upon the moss, reading her letter. The tree was thick with pink flowers, the sky was very blue above, and the orchard was full of bees that had come out to rifle the blossoms.

The day, though remarkably clear and sunny, was somewhat cold. We were all clad in the large shepherd's-plaid shawls, which were our garden wear during the cold months; and as we wished to hear the letter comfortably, we began when we arrived to make a kind of tent for ourselves, taking off three of these scarf-shawls, and tying one end of each to a long hop-pole, which we then stuck into the ground, making the whole safe and warm by laying stones to steady the ends which were on the ground. Having thus erected a shelter of the most desirable kind, with its back to the wind, its opening to the sun, a beautiful tree overhead, and a pretty view of the hop-plantation before us, we collected a quantity of dry leaves, and carefully packed ourselves among them like birds in a nest, covering up the whole community with the other four shawls. Caroline then began her communication in these words: " Sir Aimias Merton is dead."

" Dead! That old bachelor dead, of whom we had heard such strange things. Who lived all his days in his own lodge, hoarding his money. Who made his housekeeper give him half of what she got by showing the house. Who refused his young brother money enough to buy his commission; and who had been known to make only one present, — a present of an old mourning-ring to the said brother's bride, muttering that he hoped there would not be a large family, to eat him out of house and home ! "

" Yes," Caroline said, " he was dead, and his brother had come into the estate, and the whole of his princely fortune. Sir Aimias had heard that living was remarkably cheap at Smyrna, and he had actually set out and walked the greater part of the way to that somewhat outlandish city, and no doubt done the remainder of the journey with due regard to economy. He had lived there very comfortably, because very cheaply, for some months, till he was taken ill of a fever, and so died."

" But does Mrs. Merton tell you all this ? " asked one of the party.

" Not exactly in the words I have used, my dear," said Caroline, laughing. " She says : 'Our brother took a pedestrian tour across Europe, and then made his way down to Smyrna ;' that is a respectful way of saying that he *tramped*, as the policemen called it, part of the way, and begged perhaps (who knows ?), the remainder."

" What a change for Mrs. Merton ! "

" And what a change for the Baronet ! Mrs. Merton says they are both coming back directly, and she hopes they shall reach England by the beginning of the midsummer holidays." Here Caroline paused.

" And they will go to live in that beautiful house," said one of us ; " that house which poor Sir Aimias kept in such fine order, but never occupied himself."

" Yes," said Caroline, "and Mrs. Merton says she shall have May and me to spend the holidays there with her."

" May and me ! " — it sounded rather odd ; I thought, not a customary combination.

" I wonder whether they will let May return to school," remarked Belle l'Estrange.

" Not likely," said another ; "and what a grief that will be to Frances ! "

" O, Frances is going to leave soon herself," interrupted Caroline, hastily ; "she will only stay till Christmas."

" Does Mrs. Merton say anything about inviting Frances also to stay with her ? " I inquired.

" How should she," replied Caroline, incautiously, "when she never heard her name ? "

" Never heard her name ! " I exclaimed ; "why, I thought you wrote often to Mrs. Merton, Caroline."

Caroline turned her head till her bright eyes rested upon me. There was something deliberate in the action ; and she conveyed a good deal of tranquil surprise into her survey, which was perhaps intended to punish me for my audacity ; and certainly abashed me greatly, and made me blush up to the roots of my hair, and feel that I had not a word to say for myself.

"I used to write occasionally, just to tell Mrs. Merton that May was well," said she, speaking slowly, and with an air of distaste and languor. "It was a trouble, of course, but I did it ; sometimes I put in the names of her primers, and the pot-hooks she was doing ; but I have not much time for writing, and no talent for it, as you *mental improvers* have ; and of course I cannot give sketches of scenes, and occupations, and characters here, as Sophia can ; and besides, I had no reason to think they would be interesting if I could."

It was pretty evident, then, that Caroline, in writing to Mrs. Merton, had never even mentioned the name of Frances ; and though we were always inclined to take the very best view we possibly could of everything that Caroline did, there was an awkward silence now, which Belle at length broke, by charitably remarking, "Of course, Carry, dear, you could not have known how soon Mrs. Merton was coming home."

Caroline gladly caught at this straw, and cleverly turned it to her advantage.

"Of course not," she said gaily, and with her own fascinating smile ; "but Sophia seems to expect people to have prescience. Ah ! my little presidentess of the 'mental improvers,' you show a marvellous partisanship ; you are quite in the interest of the female pilgrim. You think I ought to have given the exact pedigree and description of Frances, in person, mind, and manners, *just as I should have done, if I had known* that she was so soon to meet Mrs. Merton."

She looked under my hat as she said it, and I do not know how it was, but I certainly felt as if I had done something foolish; and when she laughed and kissed me, I was so much ashamed that I could not help turning away my face.

I turned it towards the entrance of our little tent, and there I saw in the distance Frances walking between the hop-poles, carrying little May. She also was enveloped in her scarf of shepherd's plaid, and she had wound it gypsy-like about herself and the child, so that only the merry little face peeped out over her shoulder, for she was carrying her pickapack; and I shall not soon forget how pretty they looked as they came towards us, through the lengthening perspective of the hop-poles.

May had the sweetest little voice possible; Frances had taught her to sing several simple songs, and used to sing second to her; now her high childish notes, so clear and pretty, sounded like fairy bells in the air, while the deep tones of Frances's contralto voice, though fine, were not so audible at that distance.

"Pretty little May," said Caroline, in a regretful tone; "how seldom one has an opportunity of getting her to play with! I think Frances really does usurp her rather too much."

I cannot describe how much this speech grated upon my feelings. Frances had never refused to give up the child when any of the girls had wished to play with her; but seldom had Caroline wished for her, for she was not naturally fond of children.

"I could not think where you all were," exclaimed Frances, stopping before the opening of our tent.

"No," said May, repeating her words; "we could not *tink* where you all were."

"Comical little parrot," said Caroline; "just put her down, Frances, and let her come in here."

"Yes; I want to get into that funny little house," said May. Accordingly Frances began to unwind herself and the child, and finally set her down in the very midst of us, all warm and rosy after her ride.

"Take care of her," said Frances, addressing us generally, "and mind she does not get her feet damp in coming home."

"I'll carry her in," said Caroline.

"Very well, if you will undertake her, I shall go," remarked Frances; "for I am rather behindhand with my German."

So Frances nodded, and went her way; little May was left with us, and very droll and amusing she was, till she began to grow tired of the tent, and then she said she wanted to go in, — she wanted to find her Miss Christiana Frances.

"What do you want with her?" said Caroline; "look at me, — am not I quite as pretty as Frances?"

May laughed scornfully, as if quite amused at the notion that any one could be so pretty as Frances. "No," she said, "you 're not *half* such a pretty lady. I want to go."

Though she was a mere baby, Caroline was evidently annoyed at this uncomplimentary speech.

"I hope a certain individual does not try to set this little thing against me," she said, in a doubtful tone.

"The idea!" I exclaimed, almost as scornfully as little May had done; "how can you lend your mind to such a wild fancy, Caroline? Why should she try to set her against any one; she is quite above it; and besides, the child *of course* prefers her so infinitely to any of us, that I am sure she never has the slightest cause for any feeling of jealousy."

"You are warm, my little Sophia," said Caroline; but this time I did not feel ashamed.

" Besides, Caroline," observed one of our schoolfellows, · who was by no means aware of the dangerous ground she was treading on, " why, above all people, should she try to set her against *you*, — you, who never interfere with her by any chance, never want to have the child, and scarcely ever take any notice of her ? "

" Pooh ! " said Caroline, impatiently.

" I want to go," repeated May, who was now patting Caroline's cheek, by way of attracting her attention.

" What for ? "

" I want my Miss Christiana Frances ; and she said she would open the drawer to-day, and let me look in it."

" What drawer ? " inquired Caroline.

Upon this I explained that May had often asked to see her ayah's gowns, bangles, etc., but that Madame had not permitted this hitherto ; now her leave had been obtained, and Frances was going to show them to her.

" Oh," said Caroline, whose natural disinclination to trouble herself with children was still strong within her, though she evidently wished just now, for obvious reasons, to stand well with little May. " Well, I suppose I must take this child in, as I promised ; " and she rose half reluctantly, saying, with a half-smile, " What little plagues children are ! " •

" And so is ladies great plagues," exclaimed May ; and then, delighted with her repartee, she repeated it with fits of baby laughter ; and was carried off by Caroline, vociferating that ladies were great plagues.

I do not know that she was more droll and shrewd than many children of her age, but as she certainly was not much more than half their size, she seemed incomparably more so ; and to hear such a little atom bandy jokes with us, as she often did, was one of the most comical things possible.

CHAPTER V.

CAROLINE'S WILFULNESS.

SO little May was carried off by Caroline, and we stayed awhile longer in our tent, the day being a half-holiday. I remember that we discussed the motives and conduct of Caroline in having avoided the mention of Frances as a friend to May, in writing to the child's mother ; and that most of us excused her, or attempted to show that it was purely accidental this silence. After a while we dispersed, the others to their birds in the coach-house, and I to my room, still called the nursery ; on entering I found Caroline and little May there, and to my surprise saw that the chest of drawers, which contained the ayah's possessions, had been opened, and that the contents were some of them scattered on the chairs, the floor, and the beds. May, with a wistful expression, which I had not seen on her face for a long time, was gazing earnestly into an open drawer, and Caroline was curiously examining the different articles.

" How did you get these drawers opened ? " I exclaimed.

" O, they are quite common locks," said Caroline. " I took a key from one of the drawers of the other chest and put it in, and it opened without any difficulty."

" But will Frances like your showing the things while she is away ? " I inquired. " I know that Madame gave her the key, with many directions about showing the things very cautiously, for fear of exciting the child."

Caroline looked a little alarmed, but answered, " Then if Frances expects to be present when they are shown, she should not keep the poor child waiting so long. Madame gave her the key as soon as morning lessons were over, and she has left the child, and does not come to open the drawers; so as the little creature said she wished to see them — I — I undertook to show them to her."

I replied that Frances was in the school-room, doing a German exercise, and probably did not know that May was come in; and I wondered that Caroline should not have called Frances, rather than have at once obeyed the caprice of the child, who was, I observed, though saying nothing, in the highest state of excitement, the very state that Madame was solicitous by all possible means to avoid.

"I cannot get these things over my hands," said Caroline, who had taken up the silver bangles that the ayah had worn; what small hands and wrists that woman must have had!"

I drew near and looked at the white muslin banyans, or jackets, the wide paunjammahs, which form part of the dress of her order, and are sometimes made, as they were in this instance, of rich Benares silk, the curious tortoise-shell combs, which she had worn in her hair, and the long scarfs or veils of muslin which she used to throw over her head and shoulders.. I saw also the Soam pebbles, the small silver paun-box that she had used; for she was very, very fond of chewing paun, the rosare, or fringed cotton quilt, on which she had sat while engaged in shampooing her little beebee, a purse full of rupees, many strings of cowries, a small six-sided box, made of straw, and ornamented at the top with a representation of the cheel, or Brahminee kite, beautifully wrought on it, also in straw; this box was filled with strange little pieces of metal, of various shapes and sizes, and I supposed them to be charms.

Besides all these things, and many more which I have forgotten, there were lying on the beds some beautiful jin-dilly muslins, gauzes, pieces of striped Benares silk, small Indian scarfs, grass handkerchiefs, Delhi shawls, pieces of kinquab (a superb kind of Indian silk), a Trichinopoly chain, a Bombay work-box, chains, bracelets, agates, and gold and coral ornaments, which had doubtless been given into the care of the faithful ayah, for the child's use as she grew older.

I know not what visions of infancy, or what distinct recollections of the dead ayah and her distant parents, the sight of these things may have awakened in the breast of little May, but she continued to gaze at them like one fascinated, till Caroline happened to say, "What a curious smell there is about everything that comes from the East! it is not sandal-wood. What is it?"

"I do not know," I replied ; "but I noticed it about all May's clothes at first, and the ayah seemed always to waft it as she walked. It must be some kind of spice."

Caroline had put on a Benares silk slip of widely striped silk, she had drawn round her one of the Indian shawls, — it looked very well on her slender form, — and she was just completing her costume, by fastening a muslin veil on her head, when the child, attracted by our voices, turned round, and starting at the sight of her, laughed at first, and held out her arms, but in another moment she was evidently frightened, and began to scream most violently.

Caroline, who did not know how thoroughly the child was excited, hoped to quiet her with a few kisses, and when these failed, she first scolded, then entreated, but all to no purpose ; then being afraid of being seen by Madame, whose approval of what she had done was doubtful, she ran to the drawers, flung them open, and began to throw in the costly articles which she had so unceremoniously taken from their concealment ; but her purpose was not wholly accomplished when Frances, attracted by the screams of her nursling, flew into the room, and breathlessly demanded to know what was the matter.

Caroline, discovered dressed in this strange costume, in another person's room, and proving herself so unfit for the office she had taken upon herself, was so angry, and so ashamed of her ridiculous position, that she would not say a word, and I was obliged to explain the matter as well as I could in the interval of little May's piercing screams.

"I did not know you had brought May in," said Frances, rather coldly, and at the same time drawing the key from her pocket. Caroline neither looked at her nor made any answer. "I was perfectly ready to show these drawers to her," she continued ; and then added firmly, "May, if you are not quiet I shall be exceedingly angry."

"Poor little thing!" exclaimed Caroline, indignantly ; "how can you speak so crossly to her? — don't you see that she cannot help sobbing? she has no power to prevent it."

"Yes, she has," said Frances, addressing herself more to the child than to Caroline, and speaking steadily, but not unkindly. "May can stop, and she must ; she will be extremely ill if she goes on screaming in this way. May, do you hear me?"

The child, awed by the unusual manner and expression of Frances, tried to do as she was bid, and would no doubt have succeeded, being assisted by her surprise, if Caroline had not murmured some excuses, remarking, most injudiciously, "She may stop for a moment, but she is sure to begin again. I know she will."

Of course, upon this the child did begin again ; and Frances instantly took her up, carried her out of the room, and shut the door behind her.

There was both indignation and dignity in her manner as she did this ; and if Caroline felt herself reproved, it was probably no more than Frances intended.

"Insolence!" exclaimed Caroline, "insolence! What right has she to assume those miserable airs of superiority

over me, carrying off May as if my presence was improper
for her, and treating me like an ignorant child? Insolence!—but I will have her yet; I 'll have her back
again, even if I have to appeal to Madame. Frances,
indeed; what is she that she is to thwart me, and get the
upper hand in everything? I will enter the lists with her,
and we shall soon see who will win. May shall be my
child again before she is a fortnight older." And, to my
great surprise, she burst into a passion of tears, and hurried to little May's bed, laying her head down on the
pillow, sobbing, and covering her beautiful eyes with the
ayah's muslin veil.

I did not at all suppose that she was serious when she
spoke of appealing to Madame, and of having the little
May back again; for she was too indolent, I thought, to
desire seriously a charge that was sure to be so troublesome. I therefore looked on her speech as an outbreak
of mingled indignation, mortification, and passion. And
when she threw herself on the bed, I could not help feeling amused; for I thought it childish in her to have a fit
of crying, and show her temper so openly, because she
had been vexed. Most of the girls, I thought, would have
been too proud for such an exhibition; and I looked on
very composedly, wondering what would be done next,
till presently the pretty way in which she bemoaned herself—wishing she had never come to this place, this sorrowful place, where it was never really warm, and where
the people were as cold as the weather,—where no one
understood her, and no one really loved her,—declaring
that she was the most unhappy person possible, and that
no half-holiday had ever before been so sorrowful—worked
on my feelings to such a degree, that, before I knew what
I was about, I was at her side, begging her to be comforted, and was caressing her, quite forgetting whether she
was right or wrong, and was lifting up her face, and en-
treating her to be comforted.

"You used to love me before Frances came," sobbed Caroline ; "but now, — now you always take part with her."

I was so completely beguiled, that I thought of nothing but how to comfort her, and only answered that I loved both very much, and hoped she would forget this little scene, and be friendly towards Frances.

Caroline laid her head on my bosom, and, after a great deal more comforting, caressing, and petting, was induced to rise, dry her eyes, and smile again. She stood up, and with my help divested herself of the rich silken petticoat, the Indian shawl, and the ayah's veil, which she had fastened on with some long silver pins, probably intended for that purpose. Then she walked to the glass to arrange her hair, still looking very pensive ; but her first remark, on seeing herself therein reflected, struck me as so very irrelevant, and so completely beneath the dignity of such a heroine in distress as she had just been enacting, that I could not help bursting into a sudden laugh.

" Well, I don't look much worse for my crying fit," was the remark in question ; " but if I were Frances, I would never cry at all, — it really swells up her eyelids, and makes her nose so red, that she looks quite ugly after it. What can you be laughing at, Sophia ? "

" I cannot help it."

" You are not laughing at me, surely? — you are, I believe ! What is the reason ? — tell me, this instant, you little quiz."

" Because as people are not supposed to cry if they can help it, or unless they are really in sorrow, it seemed so droll to suppose that they consider whether it will be unbecoming or not, and act accordingly."

" Ah ! one ought to be more cautious what one says to you, presidentess ; such a straightforward, simple person as myself cannot get on with you at all ; you are always weighing and criticising. This glass hangs in a very bad light ! "

"Caroline, I want to say something to you."

"Well, say it, then."

"You think I observe my friends too closely. I must tell you something that I have observed about you."

"If it is an agreeable thing, you may."

"But it is not an agreeable thing altogether, yet as it concerns me as well as yourself, I must tell you, because not telling it sometimes makes me feel as if I were deceitful."

"Does it make you feel as if you were blushing violent-ly?—because you are."

"Well, I do not care ; I shall tell you notwithstanding."

"I agree with you that you are deceitful, presidentess ; for you say you don't care, and you do. You sha'n't tell me." So saying, Caroline walked up to me, and laying her hands on my shoulders, looked into my eyes and laughed, repeating, "You shall not tell me ; I dare you to it."

"You have a habit," I began ; but Caroline quickly stopped my mouth by clapping her hand upon it, exclaim-ing, "O, you tiresome girl, I cannot bear your scruples, and your principles, and your things ; you must have caught them of Frances ; you were such a charming little creature before she came."

She would not remove her hand till I ceased to make attempts at speaking, and then she pathetically begged me to help her in putting away the Indian articles, which I accordingly began to do, and they supplied us with con-versation till the last shawl was folded, and the last jewel carefully put away. Then Caroline sat down on the side of the bed with an air of the deepest consideration, and said to me, "After all, presidentess, I think I have a curi-osity to hear what you meant to tell me."

" Perhaps it was that you are, in my opinion, a very capricious creature."

" Perhaps it was no such thing ; come, tell me, for I like you to talk confidentially to me, as you used to do before *that* Frances came. I think there is no one in the house that I feel so fond of as I do of you."

" O, but you said that to Belle yesterday, that very same thing ; for she repeated it to me in great triumph."

Caroline laughed, and answered, not a whit abashed : " Well, I dare say I felt very fond of her when I said it ; but now I want to hear this ; tell me, only mind it is not to be anything disagreeable."

" In that case, I am to invent something to tell you, I suppose ; for I told you what I did mean to say was disagreeable."

" It really is very provoking of you to tease me in this way," said Caroline, earnestly, " when you know that I never can sleep at night if anything puzzles me."

I saw she was determined to be told, but my courage failed me ; for I felt more strongly than I had ever done before that Caroline would never forgive me if I really let her see what grave faults I had perceived in her character ; strange to say, I also felt more than ever those nameless attractions which had drawn me to her from the first.

" Come, begin," she exclaimed, drawing me towards her, and making me sit by her on the little bed. " I know it is something agreeable after all ; and if it is not, I shall be in such a passion."

She spoke in joke, but did not think how soon it would be true in earnest.

" I did not like to tell you," I began, " because we have been so affectionate and friendly just now ; it was only this, that you have a habit of making out, at least you seem to take for granted, whenever we show you how much we love you — you have a habit, you —"

11 *

"Well, come to the point," said Caroline, laughing, "and don't blush."

"Why, you seem to take for granted," I exclaimed, with a mighty effort, " that if people love others, they must needs think them perfect ; you think when we are affectionate, at least when I am, that I entirely approve of what you may have been doing, — that I think you quite in the·right."

" If you *do* love me, you must think me right," said Caroline. You must take my part in your mind. No one can love me, and yet see faults in me."

" Do you see no faults in *me ?* " I ventured to inquire.

"O yes ! " was the frank rejoinder, "but then *that's different.* I see faults sometimes, no doubt."

" But I, loving you more than you love me, ought not to see any in you ; is that it ? " I asked.

Caroline laughed again ; but I had, perhaps, come so near to what she had meant, when she made that incautious speech, that she felt embarrassed, and only repeated that she had always been accustomed to have people like her, and not see her faults ; and she was sure if I loved her I could not see them.

" But," I said, " I beg your pardon, I often see them, and yet sometimes for want of courage, and sometimes because you appear to expect it, and often remark that a *friend* is always short-sighted to defects, — I have let you think I considered you quite right when I have blamed you in my heart ; and you are often so affectionate to me that I am sure you do not know what I sometimes think."

" If I understand you aright," said Caroline, " I suppose this is your way of telling me that you do not care for me as much as you have often pretended to do."

" If you think so," I replied, " you do not understand me at all."

It was one of Caroline's peculiarities to be remarkably sensitive to blame ; she could not bear to be found fault with in the most trivial matter. She now looked surprised, and even colored, — a thing that rarely occurred with her. "I don't know what you mean," she said, "unless you give me an instance."

I answered, in some trepidation, "I thought it wrong in you to express a determination to get May away from Frances, yet I tried to comfort you when you were so vexed, and you thought, I believe, that I approved."

Caroline had pushed me slightly from her, and withdrew her arm as I began to speak ; and the moment I was done, — "Express a determination !" she repeated, passionately. "Yes, I do express a determination ; I will strive with Frances, by all means, open and underhand ; she shall not treat me as she has done for nothing. May I will have. Frances may do without her as well as she can."

The point in discussion was already lost sight of between us, and the old grievance recurred to. "Then you will be very wrong, and very unkind," I exclaimed, in great heat. "You will be more than unkind, you will be wicked."

"Wicked !" cried Caroline, starting up with sparkling eyes. "What do you dare to say? What do you mean? How unkind? How wicked?"

"It would be wicked," I repeated, "because it would be *stealing.*" I said this word in a very low tone.

Caroline caught it up sarcastically, and repeated it with a bitter laugh. "Stealing ! as if that tiresome, plain, uninteresting child was worth stealing."

"The more unkind, then," I exclaimed, "if you think so, to steal her from Frances, to whom she is so lovely, so interesting, and so precious. I say it will be stealing, and if you do it intentionally, as you say you mean to do, it will be quite as wicked, and quite as mean, as it would be to steal one of those Indian shawls, or to steal May's diamond locket that her papa left for her."

"Insolent girl ! Insolent creature !" cried Caroline,

drawing herself up to her full height, and looking down on me as I sat nervously on the side of the bed. "And so, I suppose, — indeed, I can have no doubt," she added, with ineffable scorn, "that this conversation, — this pleasing and affectionate conversation, will be repeated to Frances, — Frances, whom you can esteem, — no doubt of it at all. I hope you will not forget to mention that you yourself confessed to being deceitful, and if you will also say that I quite agree with you, it will add to the obligation."

"I shall not mention a word of it," I replied, swelling with pride and mortification; "it has been strictly confidential, and I can only wish now, very sincerely, that it might have ended differently."

Caroline was walking about the room in such a passion as I had never seen her in, though she was naturally of a very excitable disposition; — her eyes sparkled, her cheeks were suffused with crimson, her whole figure seemed to dilate; and she replied, in a tone of the bitterest contempt, that, for her part, she wondered how such a conversation could end otherwise than by a cessation of all friendliness on the part of the *injured party;* that she was thankful for this *dénouement,* and for the avowal of my sentiments; adding, in a very galling manner, that she had quite long enough nourished a serpent in her bosom; "and as to this strictly confidential conversation," she repeated, "if may be kept to yourself for a time; but I mistake you and your sincerity very much if Frances does not know the whole of it within a week."

"I shall not repeat a word of it to her, either now or at any future time," I repeated, passionately.

"As you please," Caroline began, and paused suddenly in her excited pacing of the chamber; presently adding, more calmly, though still in an angry tone, "I never asked you to make such a *solemn* and *deliberate* promise; but since you have thought proper to do so, of your own accord, I suppose you have some reason for it."

As she went on with this sentence, she spoke more slowly, and with unusual emphasis, as if she wished fully to impress on my mind that I had made this promise, and also as if its importance to herself unfolded itself more and more. I was forcibly struck by this change and this sudden coolness, where there had been so much passion. I perceived that now she had this promise she was quite at her ease, and it pained me inexpressibly to perceive that no part of her excitement and agitation had arisen from her quarrel with me, and this unceremonious breaking up of our friendship, but only from the fear of my repeating her words; and I was so vexed and so heart-sore at the utter loss of her affection, that though I could now esteem her less than ever, I could not help shedding some very bitter tears when I saw her take up a fan, and walk about near the windows to cool herself, then go to the glass, smooth her hair, and arrange her ribbons with elaborate care, and finally walk out of the room without deigning to bestow on me one look or one word.

Many sorrowful feelings combined to make me glad to remain alone for a while after Caroline had left me; I reproached myself for the clumsy way in which I had managed my part in the conversation, and wept with wounded affection, and perhaps also injured pride, and, like Caroline, I thought this was the most miserable half-holiday I had ever passed. At length, when the redness that Caroline had spoken of was faded from my features, I stole down stairs, and perceiving, through the staircase-window, that most of the girls were still in the garden, I took my way to the school-room, that I might be alone, and there I saw — what? Why, Caroline and Frances sitting together, doing a piece of bead-work, and talking in the most amicable manner possible!

Remarkable sight! I was too bashful to come close, but sat down at the first desk. Caroline had perhaps made some kind of apology to Frances; for the latter looked pleased, and little May sat at her feet, quite happy again, and trying to thread some very large beads, but continually scattering them, and scrambling under the table to pick them up. At last, taking advantage of a pause in the discourse, she leaned against Frances's knee, and exclaimed, without any preface, "But when is she to come?—she is such a long time coming."

"I told you," said Frances, "that she should come whenever you could count a hundred, without making a mistake."

"Will she have blue eyes?" proceeded May; "will she have blue eyes, Miss Chris-tiana Frances?"

"Blue eyes and flaxen hair," replied Frances, "and two little pink shoes that will take on and off."

"O! I do want her so much."

"What is the child talking of?" asked Caroline.

"Of a wax doll that I have promised her when she can count a hundred, for she has been very idle lately; and when she has learned this one thing, not before, I shall give her the doll for a reward."

"Not before," sighed little May; "and her frock is to be a white frock, Miss Chris-tiana Frances? O! I wish she would come to-night."

Frances smiled. "Well, begin then," she said, "one, two, three, and if you go on properly to a hundred she shall come to-night." By this she convinced me that the doll was already in her possession, and ready to be given at a moment's notice. I am very much mistaken if the same idea did not strike Caroline, for she also smiled and said "*I* never should have patience to keep back anything that I was teased for." This she said in French, and Frances answered, "I have passed my word."

May began to count,—Frances took her up on her knees; the little creature laid her head on her bosom as on a place of tried security, — and when she reached sixteen she stopped, and had to be prompted, and then Frances discovered that her feet were cold, and took off her shoes to warm them, and a great deal of kissing and caressing went on between them ; upon seeing which, a cloud passed over Caroline's brow.

" Let me warm them for you," she presently said.

" O, no, thank you ! " said Frances ; " I could not think of troubling you." She spoke exactly as she might have done if May had been her sister, her natural charge. " Now, May, go on."

" Shall she come, then, when I can count up to *trenty* ? " pleaded the child.

Frances shook her head.

" But may n't she come, if I kiss you a great many times ? " said May, suddenly, as if a bright idea had struck her.

" She may come when you can count a hundred," repeated Frances.

" Then I *will* do it right, Miss Chris-tiana Frances," exclaimed May, with a mighty sigh, and she immediately counted up to nineteen without once stopping even to take breath.

All the remainder of that evening Caroline was particularly friendly to Frances. The next day, Madame, having occasion to drive into the town, invited Caroline and another of the pupils to accompany her. I happened to hear Madame ask them whether they wished her to buy anything ; for, when this was the case, she always chose to know it beforehand.

I was standing close to Madame at the time, holding her gloves, and therefore I could not fail to hear the answers ; one I have forgotten, the other struck me forcibly, it was Caroline's, and given in a particularly low voice : " She wished to buy a doll," she said.

CHAPTER VI.

CAROLINE'S INTERFERENCE.

I REMARKED, at the conclusion of my last chapter, that Madame drove away in the pony-chaise with Caroline, and I soon forgot my speculations about the doll, which the latter had expressed a wish to purchase. How did I contrive so easily to forget a thing in its nature so interesting? Why, my dear readers, I think at this distance of time I can venture to confide to you, that having then reached the ripe age of fifteen, I was deeply engaged in the writing of a grand epic poem, upon which I worked on all holidays and half-holidays.

Some of my schoolfellows gave me their select opinions upon it, when I afterwards read it to them in the hayloft, over the place where our caged birds were kept; they said they thought it very fine; they also said they did not exactly understand it; I am happy to say that I had the strength of mind to burn it shortly after leaving school.

On this half-holiday, as the pony-chaise disappeared, I crept into the said hayloft, and then taking out my pocket inkglass and my little folio, began to write; and was deep in the distressing scenes of the death of my hero, whom I was causing to die in the most affecting manner, weeping abundantly myself over the cruelty of his enemies, and quite sobbing at the noble courage and resignation that I was making him display, when I thought I heard the least possible creaking behind me, and the least possible *soupçon* of a gentle titter.

Perched as I was upon the square-cut blocks of hay,

crying piteously, so that the tears blotted my page, my bonnet lying beside me, and the whole loft radiant with dusty sunbeams, could anything be more ridiculous than my position, or, unfortunately, more conspicuous, if any of the girls were watching me from the top of the ladder-like stairs? To say that I blushed till the very back of my neck was rosy, would but half describe my glowing shame.

I did not dare to turn round, and was almost wishing that my noble hero had never been invented, when suddenly, "All hands pass pocket-handkerchiefs!" cried a voice that I knew, "to dry the Muse's tears."

We were reading just then in class the history of the last naval war, and used to adopt its sea phrases as well as we could.

Instantly a pocket-handkerchief, rolled up like a ball, struck me on the back; another flew over my head; more, more; there were eight of them flying about me; and after this shower the owners rushed in pell-mell, and flung themselves on the hay in convulsions of laughter: some had their shoes in their hands, having taken them off below that they might ascend more gently; some kissed and apologized; some with mock gravity wiped my cheeks, and then tried to read the blotted manuscript, adroitly substituting pieces of the Italian grammar where it baffled their efforts at deciphering.

They were all in ecstasies at my discovered absurdity; and as for me, when the first moments of shame were over, I laughed more than any of them, and was extremely anxious to disavow my poetic fervor, and to make humble apologies for having deserted those gifted spirits, my schoolfellows, for the sake of writing verses in a hayloft.

We went into the garden and amused ourselves in various ways, till the afternoon suddenly clouding, we betook ourselves to the house; the elder girls withdrew to the

Q

dining-parlor; the little ones to the school-room, and I only of the upper class went with them, for I was helping them to make a tiny grotto, which was to be presented to Madame on her birthday, and the shells for which we sorted on the window-sills of this long room.

We were all kneeling on the floor, sedulously intent on our sorting, with the exception of little May, whom Frances had just sent in, and who was playing about the room, jumping over the hassocks, when the pony-chaise drove up, and immediately after Caroline came in, with a large silver-paper parcel in her hand.

Now I have before adverted to the fact that I was at that time remarkably small for my years; consequently, when Caroline glanced round, I can scarcely doubt that she overlooked my individual presence, only thinking that all the little ones were there at their play, for I have since believed that if she had seen me she would have used more caution in what she said.

She was blooming with air and exercise, and her lovely hazel eyes sparkled as if she were excited. " Where is May ? " she inquired.

Several fingers pointed under the table, and presently out crept May, shaking back her extremely long curls, and bearing a hassock in her arms. The little creature was flushed with the effort. Caroline smiled pleasantly on her, and said, "Where do you think I have been, you tiny thing ? "

May answered, in a matter-of-fact way, that she knew.

" O, then you don't want to hear anything about it ? " observed Caroline, "nor to be told what I have got in this parcel ? "

May, upon this, put down the hassock, and came close to where Caroline had seated herself on a form.

"You cannot guess what is inside there ? " asked Caroline, laying her hand upon the softly rustling paper.

"I can guess," cried an eager looker-on from the window-seat. "And I am sure I know," exclaimed another. The folded toy was as lovely a doll as ever enriched the eyes of a little mortal.

"Look at it," said Caroline; "I will just undo a piece of the paper." She did so, and displayed a flaxen-haired beauty, with smiling red lips, and gay blue eyes.

"A doll!" said May, gravely laying one finger on its face, in her own peculiarly infantile manner.

"She is nearly as tall as you are," said Caroline; "I wonder who she is for?"

"I wonder who she is for?" repeated the fascinated child, looking down on the doll's face.

"Well, I will tell you," replied Caroline; "here, take her, she is for you."

May looked at her, and then putting her hands behind her, said wistfully, "My doll's not coming to-day, because I did n't count a hundred; perhaps she 's coming to-morrow."

"This is your doll," persisted Caroline, laughing; "is she not a beauty?"

"But I only did it right up to eighty-one," said the child; "and my Miss Chris-tiana Frances said my doll might not come till to-morrow."

"You silly little thing!" said Caroline, coloring and laughing; "look, this is a doll that *I* am going to give you; it is a present from *me*. When you can count a hundred, Miss Christiana Frances can give you another doll, if she likes; but this is yours now. Here, I bought it for you; kiss me and take it."

May seemed now to understand, and, with a rapturous laugh, she sprung to Caroline, and threw her arms about her neck, and kissed her. Caroline took her up, and gave her the great doll, and praised it, pointing out its beauty and its good qualities. The child blushed for joy. "Are you sure she is my doll ? " she exclaimed; "and what will Miss Chris-tiana Frances say ? "

Caroline made an impatient gesture, and replied : " Miss Black can give you a doll when she likes, May, and I can give you one when *I* like ; it does not at all matter to me what other people do ; and look, here is something more for you." So saying, she produced a paper of sugared almonds. " There," she continued, " these are for you, all for you, because you are the youngest little girl in the school, and you are my little pet. Kiss me."

May readily did as she was desired, and forthwith opened the tempting paper, and began to eat an almond.

" Nannette has a pocket in her best frock," she observed to her new friend.

" Would you like to have one in your frock to keep your almonds in ? " asked Caroline.

" O yes ! " replied May, confidingly ; " and I shall ask my Miss Chris-tiana Frances to make me a little pocket, and perhaps she will, if I 'm good."

" If you 're good ! — poor little thing," said Caroline, with ill-timed pity. " Well, May, I will make you a pocket, for little girls cannot always be good."

" No," said May, simply; " I was n't good when I sucked the paints."

" What paints ? " asked Caroline.

" Those little paints in my Miss Chris-tiana's box ; I thought they were chocolates, and I bit them."

" Yes, and she made her lips all blue," said Nannette, breaking into the conversation ; " and when Massey washed her, the soap got into her mouth."

This cheering conclusion to the affair being brought forward, May observed, in a deeply reflective tone, " I shall not suck the paints any more."

Caroline laughed. " Well, May," she said, " you may go and fetch my work-box, and I will make you a pocket now."

May's delight was very great. She ran for the box, and a little pocket was set in hand instantly; Caroline talking pleasantly while at work about the doll, and how she would make a frock and a hat for her, while May prattled in a confiding way that she had not shown her before.

" There," she said, when the pocket was sewed in, " now, whenever you want anything, little one, you may come to me, and I dare say I shall be able to do it for you."

" Yes," said May, " when my Miss Chris-tiana Frances has n't time : " and then, indicating the kind of thing she generally wanted doing, she said, " Can you play at Loto, and draw cats and two little kittens, Miss Baker ; and can you draw pigs with curly tails ? "

" O, I can do a great many things for little girls who love me," said Caroline.

" I love you," responded May.

" Are you sure you do ? " asked Caroline.

" O yes, I love you very much indeed to-day," replied the frank little creature, and added, " I did n't love you any of the other days."

" Do you love me as much as Miss Christiana Frances ? " asked Caroline.

May laughed as if she considered the question absurd, but presently said, in a consoling tone, " I can't yet, but perhaps I will soon."

" You small oddity ! " said Caroline, " do you remember seeing that pretty little locket that I wear sometimes ? "

" O yes," answered the child. " You mean that one that I opened when I saw it in your box, and you slapped me, and said I was n't to touch it."

This was rather an awkward recollection, but Caroline passed it on, and said, " If I thought you really did love me, I would put a little piece of *your* hair in it; would you like that ? "

May replied that she should, qualifying the admission
though by stipulating that she was to cut off the lock of
hair herself, and she was to see it put behind the little bit
of glass !   To this Caroline assented, taking out whatever
may have been in the locket before, and tying the shining
morsel of May's wavy hair with a piece of gold thread.

I felt a good deal of indignation throughout this scene,
and it never occurred to me that Caroline was unconscious
of my presence, till one of the little ones happening to appeal
to me by name about a shell, she uttered an exclamation
of astonishment and annoyance, and instantly started up
and left the room.   She had not been gone two minutes,
when Frances entered, and May rushing up to her, with
one hand in her new pocket, and her great doll under the
other arm, burst forth into a confused speech, with no
stops, and very little sense in it, but full of delight and ex-
ultation.

"What is it, my little darling ?" said Frances, looking
down on the small face which was quite suffused with
blushes of delight and pride.

" I did n't count a hundred," said May, in a great hurry,
"but Miss Baker gave me my doll, and she said I was to
keep it, and she said it was mine, and I 've got a pocket
that Miss Baker made, and please will you have one of my
sugared almonds, Miss Chris-tiana Frances ? "

Frances took the doll, and I have seldom seen a face
change more than hers did, when the truth dawned upon
her.   She was very keen-sighted and quick-witted, and it
seemed (if I am not mistaken) to strike her at once that
Caroline was trying to supplant her in the affections of her
little favorite.   She colored exceedingly, — her surprise
and pain were evident, — but little May, who, in the midst
of her delighted excitement, seemed to have preserved a
kind of suspicion that this doll might possibly be forfeited
to the higher powers, and that she had not come quite

honestly by it after all, sobbed out in a half-crying tone : " I did n't ask for her ; Miss Baker said I might keep her ; she said she bought her for me." Then Frances controlled herself, and giving back the doll to May. who was stretching up her arms for it, said, " Yes, she is your doll, and you are to keep her, if Miss Baker gave her to you, my little May."

" And will you kiss me, and may I sit on your knee ? " said the child, still aware that something was wrong.

" My little treasure ! " said Frances, with a sigh of inexpressible regret ; but she sat down and took up the child and her doll, sitting silent and deep in thought, while May descanted on the many perfections of her present, and while she related how Miss Baker had shut up a bit of her hair in that funny little box, and she had looked at it behind the glass.

Frances was evidently pained and hurt. She made no reply to the child's prattlings ; but when the girls came in, as they shortly did, to tea, Frances turned to Caroline, and said to her in French, " I thought you were quite aware, Miss Baker, that I had got a doll ready for May ; indeed, I believe I had told you so." She spoke coldly, and with some hauteur. Caroline answered with no less, " No, I was never told so." ·

" But the subject was alluded to, and half-explained in your presence," I could not help saying ; " and you remarked that if you had had such a toy in your possession, you could not have kept it back from a child."

" We all know, Sophia, that you have a most excellent memory," said Caroline, and she said it in such a way as to imply a reproach, — as if I had been in the habit of using my memory against my schoolfellows. She continued : " If Frances is really so much attached to the child as she professes to be, I cannot understand why she is otherwise than pleased at her having a toy given her.

It seems to me selfish to wish that no one but herself should give her anything."

" I have no such wish," said Frances, with some heat. The other girls looked on surprised.

" It is not only that I think you might have chosen a present which would not have made mine valueless," said Frances, " but that part of my influence is overthrown by it, and my reward made nothing worth trying for. Besides," she continued, " it is difficult for me to think that your present was *accidentally* the same as my own."

" Indeed," replied Caroline, with provoking calm ; " well, I hope the poor child at least will be pleased with her doll, for it is evident that other people are not pleased ; and, as Madame has given you such unbounded authority over May, you had better mention to her that my being fond of the child endangers your exclusive right, and ask her to forbid my speaking to May, or even looking at her : no doubt she will."

" Caroline ! " exclaimed Frances, surprised at this strange speech. " Come to me, my pet," said Caroline to May, who, during this French conversation, had been leaning against Frances ; " did they let her stand all this time, and take no notice of her ? " May readily held out her arms, and seeing the locket hanging round Caroline's neck, began to play with it, and to relate to all whom it might concern, how this was her hair, and how Miss Baker said she should always wear it, even when she was grown up to be a lady.

There was a way in which these little things were said and done that seemed greatly to pain Frances. Caroline patronized May as if she was the most friendless little creature possible, with no toys to play with, and no one to take pity on her ; but the teachers presently coming in to preside at the tea-table, put an end to the conversation ; and when I heard Caroline privately whispering to May that she was to sit next her, I slipped into the place by Frances, for I saw that May would not occupy it, and I hoped Frances would not observe Caroline's acts, or at least that I should spare her feelings, by preventing a discussion ; but my intention was frustrated by the little creature herself, who, running up to Frances, said, in a supplicatory tone, " Please may I sit next Miss Baker to-night ? She did ask me ; she said I should not be any trouble."

" You may sit wherever you please, my dear," said Frances, gently. So little May ran round delighted, saying aloud, " I may, I may, Miss Baker ; Miss Chris-tiana Frances says I may sit by you to-night."

She was a privileged person, this little May, and allowed to take many liberties of locomotion not permitted to her elders ; but I thought the triumph of having her was a little damped for Caroline by the occasional reproofs of the English teacher, a personage who by no means relished change and innovation. " Miss Baker, I will thank you to cut that crust, it is too hard for Miss Merton's teeth." " Miss Baker, Miss Merton is spilling her milk." " Pray, Miss Baker, why is Miss Merton without her pinafore ? " and so on.

Poor little May, I must needs pity her, when I remember the siege that was laid to her baby heart, and the deterioration which from day to day ensued in her behavior, from Caroline's unwise and capricious indulgence ; for this day proved only a sample of many days that were to follow, and Caroline seemed to take positive delight in doing all she could to destroy the influence of Frances, to thwart her plans, and steal her cherished treasure.

In all things that gave trouble, May was still left to Frances, and though she did not seem absolutely to fail in her allegiance to her first friend, she was naturally attracted by the presents, caresses, and petting of Caroline ; and

12

really it seemed as if Frances herself was less kind than formerly, for if May became tiresome and naughty from over-indulgence, Caroline would have no more to do with her; so that Frances had the reproving of her faults and childish ill-humors, and Caroline the rewarding of her good behavior.

Yet it was obvious to the least acute observer, that Caroline was doing this for an object, — not for the love of the child; for she was sometimes evidently fretted by the very presence and caresses that she had courted. But Frances, who so deeply loved the child, was pained to the heart for the slack hold that she now had over her, and which was easily being withdrawn from her, — not for May's own good, or even for the good of the withdrawer.

To Frances might have been applied the words of one of our most celebrated modern writers: "I was robbed for no one's enrichment, but for the greater desolation of this world."

CHAPTER VII.

HOLIDAYS AT THE SEASIDE.

IT was very evident to us all how much Frances felt the interference of Caroline with the affection of her little favorite. The more so this was felt, no doubt, because its motives were not understood by her, though she knew that Mrs. Merton was coming home, and that she was a friend of Caroline's friends. She had not been present at the conversation in which Caroline had shown very plainly (as I thought) that her neglect of the little child might have unpleasant consequences; and that Mrs. Merton, instead of supposing that she had shown any neglect, imagined that she had devoted herself to May with more than necessary kindness.

But Caroline was now steadily advancing in little May's good graces, and a coolness had gradually come on between Frances and herself, which she was far from wishing to ascribe to the real cause; on the contrary, she affected to believe that she felt a natural resentment against Frances for having made a caricature of her, in which she had represented her as an old bathing woman; and for having encouraged little May to call her Miss 'Quarius, which she sometimes did still, that being her version of "Aquarius." Now there was no question that it was the "mental improver" who had taught little May this refined piece of wit; and as they always laughed at her when she said it, the child naturally thought herself very clever, and often applied it to Caroline, laughing exceedingly at the same time, as if she had understood her joke, which unquestionably she did not. But it happened occasionally that little May, when she was in a saucy humor, would apply this name to Frances; and once when she did so, Frances looked annoyed, and said to us, "I wish you would not teach the child these nicknames; I don't think you have any right to make her apply them to me; I never 'throw cold water' on your pleasures."

"Why, Frances," said one of us, whom I will not name, *for a reason I have* (as an Irishman would say), "that name was never meant for you; how can you affect to think it was?"

"For whom, then, was it meant?" asked Frances, composedly.

"For Caroline, of course," was the surprised reply; "But we thought that you, of all persons, knew for whom it was meant; we always thought that you made that caricature."

"I!" exclaimed Frances, amazed; "so far from making it, I did not even see it. You never showed it to me, and as there seemed to be always some laughing and whispering about it whenever I asked any questions, I always thought it must be a caricature of me."

Here was a new light thrown on the subject. "I was always surprised when I considered that you had done it," I observed, "because it seemed so unlike you: but who did it, then? No one in the house besides can draw so well as that face of Caroline is done; and indeed no one else in the house can make likenesses."

"Let me look at it," said Frances. The drawing was produced; and Frances, after looking at it attentively, said, with evident surprise: "This head of Caroline is unquestionably my doing. I remember now she was sitting at her French exercise when I drew it, and I missed it, for I had intended to add the figure; but when I looked over my folio the next day it was not there." Here, then, was a deepening of the mystery ; and what school-girl does not love a mystery ? " The remainder of the drawing," continued Frances, " has been added by another hand, — a person who draws in a better and bolder style than I do, and who has used quite a different kind of pencil."

" But none of us can draw in a better and bolder style than you do," observed one of our number ; " and besides, here are the four other likenesses."

" I can hardly call them likenesses," said Frances ; " they are drawings of four extremely pretty girls, about the ages of you four, and one of them is smaller than the others, and has very large dark eyes ; that one is meant for Sophia." She went on with her examination : " One of them has long curly hair, and wears a watch ; that one is meant to indicate Belle ; but the features bear no resemblance to her whatever."

Belle looked disappointed ; we had flattered ourselves that these faces did bear some resemblance to us, and it was mortifying that a judge of drawing should pronounce otherwise.

" I do not believe this drawing was made in the house at all," proceeded Frances ; " there is no one here who could do it, excepting one of the masters, and that is not to be thought of."

" Where was it done, then ? " said Belle.

" Indeed, I cannot say," replied Frances ; " but it has evidently been folded, just as it might have been if it had been sent somewhere in a letter : some people in the house write a great many letters."

Now there was no one in the room but ourselves and Miss Ward ; and she was sitting with her back to us, writing a letter. She was the most impassive and tranquil of mortals ; she was going to leave us in a fortnight ; and she seldom mixed in any of our amusements or conversations. She now, however, was heard to laugh ; and when Frances

said, "Some people write a great many letters," she replied, "Some people have married sisters."

"Yes, I know," said Frances, laughing, and thinking she
was only accounting for the number of letters she wrote.
But when she added, "Some people have brothers-in-law,
who can draw in a better and bolder style than Miss Black
does," we all looked at one another surprised.

"It would be a very great satisfaction to us to know
something about this said drawing," observed Belle. "It
would, particularly to Frances, because Caroline makes her
supposed authorship of it an excuse for quarrelling with
her ; at least, she resents it."

"Yes, I am sorry to hear that," replied Miss Ward, who
was still writing ; "I thought that drawing had been quite
forgotten, not having heard it mentioned for weeks till to-
day."

"Well, as I said before," continued Frances, "it would
be a great satisfaction to know something about it."

Miss Ward laid down her pen and wiped it, and put it
in its place, and composedly shut her desk, and then she
turned half round on her chair, and said, "So it would be,
no doubt, Frances ; but only think what a pretty little mystery it would spoil, — utterly spoil, — a mystery that has
amused and excited these girls for a quarter of a year at
least."

She laughed, and her usually pale face had a slight glow,
as she continued, "I have been treated with great neglect
in the affair. Not one of you even asked me if I had anything to do with it ; I was the only girl in the house that
you passed over."

"How could we possibly guess that you knew anything
of it?" exclaimed Belle.

Miss Ward laughed again, and said, "Very complimentary that speech ; however, you will admit that the caricature has accomplished its mission ; you have endured

scarcely any petty persecution since *I pinned that paper on Caroline's curtain.*" And while we all stood looking at her in breathless surprise, she continued; " Now hear your mystery pulled to pieces ; I found that drawing of Caroline's head on the floor, and thinking it was thrown there as rubbish to be swept away, I adopted it. I write a good many letters, as you have said, and I often amuse my sister with accounts of what goes on here. One day I wrote a particular description of your amusing, and I must say, absurd society ; and Tom, my brother-in-law, asked me what Caroline was like, as I described her as the chief persecutor. So I sent him the drawing, and a few days after came that caricature, which he only sent as a joke, and which I pinned on Caroline's curtain. But now I find it is doing harm ; so I shall certainly tell Caroline the whole affair the first opportunity." She had scarcely done speaking when Caroline came in, and Miss Ward, turning to her, said, " I understand, Carry, that you do not feel friendly with Frances, because you believe she made this drawing."

Caroline colored, and said, " No; she could not but think it was not kind of Frances to have done it, and in consequence of that she never could love her."

" You have no other reason for not being friendly with her ? " asked Miss Ward, composedly.

" None whatever," replied Caroline, incautiously.

" Then," said Miss Ward, " I hope to see you reconciled. Frances did not make that drawing, — my brother Tom did, and I pinned it on your curtain ; so please to transfer your resentment to me, Carry."

Now Miss Ward was taking the matter so very coolly, that it seemed no use to quarrel with her, and the very angry color that mounted to Caroline's temples, and the mortification expressed in every line of her speaking features, seemed less to result from the discovery that Miss

Ward was the guilty person, than that Frances was not; for when' the girls exclaimed that after this striking *dé-nouement*, it was quite essential that there should be a scene, and that the parties ought to fall into one another's arms and be reconciled, weeping and vowing eternal friend-ship, — and when they seized upon Caroline, and pushed her towards Frances, the latter made a step or two forward, evidently intending to kiss her; but Caroline attempted to disengage herself, and reddening with confusion and annoyance, said there had never been any quarrel between her and Frances, and, therefore, there could be no need of a reconciliation, especially a public one. Upon this, Frances hastily drew back; she seemed to feel it almost an insult that Caroline should show such evident dislike to the simple kiss she proffered; and when Miss Ward, coming up to her, said, " I hope you will kiss me instead, Frances, for I have unintentionally caused you a great deal of discomfort," she did as requested, and then, turn-ing hastily, went out of the school-room, and ran up stairs in a great hurry.

Miss Ward, who, with all her matter-of-fact quietude, was by no means destitute of knowledge of character, looked unutterable things as she observed Caroline walk-ing about the room fanning herself, and trying to be cool, and to subdue the outward expression of her annoyance; but the younger pupils coming in, and beginning to set out the drawings and easels in preparation for our draw-ing-master, she did not say anything.

" Frances has not finished her drawing," said one of them, as she put out the folio which contained Miss Black's beautiful heads : " May, go up and tell Miss Christiana that it only wants ten minutes to Mr. W.'s time, and ask her if she remembers that she is not ready."

Little May had just entered the school-room when this was said, and she shook her head, and laying a doll's apron upon the floor, began carefully to fold it up, saying, as she did so, " My Miss Chris-tiana Frances sent me down, and said she did not wish to be *disturved.*" When the small garment was neatly pressed into a very tight little square between May's hands, she looked up and said, simply, " I sha'n't ask my Miss Chris-tiana Frances to cut me out my doll's cap now,—I shall ask Massey, because my Miss Chris-tiana Frances is crying."

"But she must come down in ten minutes," said Miss Ward ; " do run to her, Sophia ; remind her of the lesson, and take her my rose-water for her eyes." I accordingly ran up and knocked at Frances's door ; she certainly was shedding tears, and how much I regretted my promise to Caroline that I would not mention anything that had passed between us on the day of our quarrel, when Frances said to me : " If I could understand Caroline, I should not be so much vexed. I had, of course, observed her feelings towards me, and her trying to deprive me of little May ; and now that I seem to have arrived at a motive for this dislike, and she is shown that it is utterly unjust, she shrinks from me with absolute repugnance ; it is evident that her thinking me the contriver of that drawing is not the real reason of her dislike to me ; I often think she must consider me a kind of rival ; but I certainly have no wish to rival her in anything."

I could only answer to all this : " Talk to Miss Ward, dearest Frances ; I think she understands Caroline better than any of us " ; and then the lesson-bell ringing, we both went down into the school-room.

It then wanted about a fortnight to the holidays, but I was not looking forward to them with so much pleasure as usual, because my parents being abroad, I was to be left with Madame. So many of my schoolfellows were in the same case, that there would be no want of companionship, and, on the whole, we expected to enjoy ourselves very

12 *   R

well, for Madame, with her family, was going to stay at the seaside, and we, of course, were to accompany her. We, therefore, did not make a grief of the necessity of thus remaining away from home, though, as I said before, we looked forward to the holidays with less enthusiasm than usual.

Those of us who were to remain with Madame were Miss l'Estrange and Belle, Caroline, Frances, little May, myself, and the schoolfellow whom I before mentioned, without divulging her name; also Madame's two little girls, and two little French girls, cousins of theirs.

I have often thought, since leaving school, when reflecting on the many excellent qualities of Madame, that she was the most superior woman, on the whole, that I have ever been privileged to meet with. It was not only her remarkable uprightness and openness in little things that made us so comfortable with her, — it was not only her wonderful insight into character that was such a safeguard to us, making us so sure that in the long run she would certainly understand us and do us justice, — but she was so completely above those little arts which some of her craft condescend to. She had such a genial disposition, and so sincerely loved to make her young people happy, that we trusted to her more implicitly and felt more at ease (when we had nothing to conceal) under her scrutinizing eyes, than we could have done with many a person with a more tender heart, and who would have ruled us with a slacker hand. She never, in the least, shrank from her position as a schoolmistress, and would often say, "This is my *school*, and you are my scholars; you are at school, ladies, and you are not to respect me merely as a gentlewoman, but as your mistress." I need not say that this was a strikingly different speech to what many ladies in her position would have uttered. "I have been so many years at school," we were taught to say, instead of, "I have been

so many years at Madame's," or "so many years at the
Willows."

But Madame had another quality for which we were all
grateful; a parent or friend of certain pupils sometimes
came to stay a few days; and when this was the case,
those particular pupils were never extolled at the expense
of the others, nor made out to be particularly interesting
to Madame, nor at all more kindly treated than usual. No
new-comer had to complain, that after her mother or guar-
dian was gone, Madame did not make so much of her, or
allow her so much liberty as at first. The consequence
was, that we all thoroughly respected our "Mistress";
and when she said to us at the commencement of the holidays, "Now, young ladies, you who remain with me may
consider yourselves not as my pupils, but during the next
six weeks as my guests," we so thoroughly believed her at
her word, that we felt like guests, and could talk to her
with a freedom that at other times we never should have
ventured to assume for a moment.

The holidays came; we saw the other girls drive away,
and were a little sorry at first; but then there was the seaside to look forward to, and there were the stories of Miss
l'Estrange and Belle to listen to respecting bygone holidays, for they had spent many at school, and declared that
they had been delightful.

We got up the morning after the other pupils had left,
with a curious sense of freedom. In Madame's own parlor the breakfast cloth was spread, and there being no
teachers, Madame herself made tea, and after breakfast
she asked if some of us would like to go over to the town
in the pony carriage, and make some purchases for her.
Of course some of us did like, and she requested the others to come into the greenhouse and help her there; so we
had a very sociable and delightful morning, Madame telling us amusing stories of French society, and the school
she had herself attended when a little girl.

Dear, good woman, how kind she was to us! and how we did enjoy ourselves during the packing, at which we all assisted; and then set off in two post-chaises for the sea-side, enjoying the thoughts of this change the more because we had been told that the place we were going to was not a town, nor even a village, but a solitary hotel, standing alone by the sea, with no other house within half a mile; so that we could dress as we liked, and delight in the rustic country round with a freedom that one cannot feel at a fashionable watering-place.

The chaise in which I travelled contained Madame's little girls in the rumble, and Caroline, Frances, and little May inside. I should have liked the journey very much but for Caroline's unfriendly conduct to Frances; for to the latter Madame had specially intrusted May; and Caroline, seeming to be jealous, appeared determined to tempt and incite the child to such behavior as should do no credit to Frances's utmost care. Now she would offer her fruit, and when Frances reminded her that it was a forbidden luxury, she argued that a little would not hurt her; and when the child, seeing it all the time, naturally begged for it, Caroline seemed to yield, and said, " Yes, she should have it, if Frances would let her." Frances said no, and the child having been allowed to see it, and hope for it, not unnaturally began to cry. Caroline, upon this, ought to have abstained from it herself, that the little creature might not see it; on the contrary, she not only ate the apricots that she had brought with her, but, at the first market-town we came to, bought some tempting green-gages, and again renewed the subject by asking if a few ripe plums could " possibly hurt the poor child."

The *poor child*, upon thus hearing her claims so patheti-cally set forth, listened with eager interest to a second dia-logue between Frances and Caroline as to the propriety of her having any; and when it was decided against her, she

was very cross, cried again, and said Frances was a cross
lady, and she would not sit on her knee. Thereupon Caroline took her ; and of course Frances could not be pleased,
particularly as by her injudicious comforting and condoling
she made the child extremely troublesome, and entirely
took away the pleasure of our drive.

It was six o'clock in the evening when we first caught
sight of the sea ; we were coming towards it through a
perfectly level pastoral country ; the rich fields were filled
with white flocks and herds, with spreading and particularly formidable-looking horns. There were few hedges ;
the land being very damp, was drained by deep ditches,
which served to enclose the wide open pastures, and thus we
had two vast plains within our view, — that of the land and
that of the water, — the one diversified here and there by
a white sail, the other by a brown steeple. Now this prospect does not sound beautiful, yet it certainly possessed a
solemn and peculiar grandeur of its own : over sea and
land alike we could see the shadows of the clouds chasing
each other, and the desert greenness of the latter was here
and there enlivened and spotted by flocks, just as the uni-
form purple of the other was by whirling sea-birds. A
bank, about ten feet high, divided the two elements ; the
landward side was riddled with rabbit-holes, and gay with
heather and bloom ; against the seaward side shoals of
shells had been flung by the waves, and a reach of soft
sand stretched out to the edges of the curling water.

We stopped at the door of the large solitary house, and
forgot our discomforts for the moment. Madame ordered
tea, and we were all too hungry not to wish to enjoy it.
We stood at the bay window of the upper parlor, where
we were to take this meal, delighting in the view of the
sea ; and I remember, though I did not pay much attention to it at the time, that I heard a conversation going on
between the civil landlady and Madame, by which it ap-

peared that for that night the house was so extremely full that we could not have the bedrooms ordered for us ; and in fact, as we had come a day earlier than we were expected, this was no real hardship.   Madame said she supposed they would accommodate us as well as possible, and the landlady withdrew, with many curtseys.   We then drank tea.   Massey came in, and said that unless some of the young ladies slept on sofas in the sitting-rooms, she did not see how all were to be accommodated ; she also spoke of beds on the floor.   Madame seemed annoyed, and said she must go and inspect the rooms ; at the same time, she gave us all leave to go out on to the shore, which we did in high glee, and I have a vivid recollection now of that walk, though, for a while, I almost forgot it in the exciting recollection of the events that followed it.

CHAPTER VIII.

THE TREASURE IN DANGER.

IN consequence of the crowded state of the house, our boxes had all been taken for the night into a small parlor on the ground-floor, and here we assembled to dress for the shore, while Massey, after the manner of confidential servants, grumbled about the crowd in the house, and at the notion that any of *her* young ladies should *come to this.*

" Coming to this " meant, sleeping for that night on beds made up on the floors of dressing-rooms ; beds having no curtains, and not being decked with the blue or pink rósettes that so lavishly adorned our pretty couches at the Willows. I must do us the justice to say, that we were very indifferent to the matter, and were glad to get out on the shore ; Madame having given the little girls into the care of the elder ones, and sent us alone, to that safest of safe places, a level sea-shore on a calm and fine day.

How delightfully fresh was the feeling of that evening ! The water was within a few feet of the steps of the house ; a very high tide, we were told, for it was the full of the moon. We walked on the broad sand-bank, watching the gambols of the rabbits, and picking up shells. The children were in the highest possible spirits. As usual, little May had been enticed away from Frances, with whom she was walking, by Caroline, and I accordingly took her place ; Frances and I walking on before the others, for their somewhat boisterous merriment destroyed to our minds the delightful peacefulness of the scene.

The girls descended the bank, and began to collect a little heap of shells on the sand. Frances and I sat down on the bank, through which a few bluish heads of grasses thrust themselves up. The sun, now about to set, gave a ruddy edge to the tiny waves, and to the sails of one solitary vessel, whose slow progress we were watching. Frances was evidently pleased with this singular prospect, for the level country on the landward side lay stretched before us, and all the splendor of sea-thrift, salt lavender, broom, heath, and rest-harrow pressing up the bank to our feet.

We were silently enjoying the scene, when little May's voice, in its naughtiest tone, arrested our attention. "Let me alone, Miss Baker; I won't, — I won't."

Frances turned quickly. Caroline had hold of May's arm, and was trying to hold her back; May was fighting, struggling, and crying in the most passionate manner. When Caroline saw that we were observing her, she let go of May, who, darting to Frances, flung herself on to her lap, sobbing, and sullenly exclaiming, "That she wanted to come to her Miss Chris-tiana Frances."

"And who wants to prevent you, you tiresome child?" said Caroline, coming up. "I am sure it is no sinecure to have to watch you: it is quite impossible to keep you out of mischief."

"You are not good," said Frances to May; "how came you to be so troublesome?"

"She will not keep away from the water's edge," said Caroline; "and the consequence is a wave came over her feet. I told her several times that it would be the case."

"You should not have let go her hand," said Frances, in French, "if you have no control over her."

May sobbed and pouted her pretty little sulky mouth, making an impatient gesture, as if resenting Caroline's anger.

"You often said on other days that you would n't tell,"

she exclaimed to Caroline ; "you said if I was naughty, my Miss Chris-tiana Frances should n't know."

Caroline was very anxious to stop this communication, but was not in time. Lest any more should be said, she now began to make friends again with little May, and produced some sugar-plums that seemed to be favorably received.

"We must go home," said Frances ; "the child's feet are so wet."

" I don't want to go home," replied the little girl ; " I want to get some more shells."

" O ! sea-water never gives cold," replied Caroline ; and while Frances continued to advocate a return to the house, Caroline kept coaxing little May towards herself with many sweet looks and loving gestures, till at last the child slipped from Frances, and Caroline ran off with her, and left us alone once more.

" Now what must we think of Caroline ? " said Frances to me. " Is it not wrong of her to do all she can to make that child naughty ? She has stolen May away from me, not that she may possess her, but that I may not. I do love that little creature ; it is very painful to me to be deprived of her, and to see her deteriorate so greatly under Caroline's rule."

" If you ask what I think," I answered, with some heat, " I think Caroline is a thief, and I have said so to her more than once."

"Well," sighed Frances, " I could part with my little treasure with less pain, if it was for her own good that she was enticed away."

And now even Caroline said it was time to go in, and we set off for the house, reaching it just after sunset. I do not remember the arrangements made about the sleeping apartments further than this, that either Frances or Caroline was to sleep in a farm-house about half a mile inland ; Massey being also accommodated there.

"Very well, then," said Caroline; "I will keep May to-night, and Frances shall go to the farm-house; Madame, it appears, has left this open to us." Madame was then up stairs with her own little girls.

Upon this a civil dispute took place between Caroline and Frances, both wishing to have May, and the former also wishing to escape the farm-house.

Massey observed that Miss May ought, of course, to remain behind, and she would take the liberty of putting her to bed at once. This could not be gainsaid; so the matter rested between the two disputants only. At last Caroline, as usual, triumphed. She asked little May, already sleepy and laid on her pillow, which of them should sleep with her; and she, overcome by the coaxing voice, and dazzled by the prospect of a change, said, "Caroline."

Poor little May, and poor Caroline!

So Frances set off to the farm-house with Massey, and very shortly we all went to bed.

Now I have before mentioned a little parlor on the ground-floor where all our boxes were standing. That was the bedroom appointed for Miss l'Estrange and me; a press-bed had been introduced, and Madame, having seen us both comfortably ensconced therein, left the room; but presently opened the door again, and desired me to get out of bed, lock the door inside, and take out the key. I did so, laying the key on the dressing-table, and peeping out for a moment at the beautiful calm sea, lying still under the broad moon. Her beams had made a wide, gleaming, silvery path across the sea, and in it nothing was visible but the vessel that we had seen during our walk: she had cast anchor, and her spars and rigging were all lighted up by the moon.

I got into bed again. I noticed that the curtain did not quite hang straight, for we could see the water as we lay ·

awake ; but we did not trouble ourselves about that, for we were both sleepy, and in a very little time we were in the land of dreams.

I do not know how long I had been asleep, when I dreamt that a very small black snake was sitting on the bed, and that every now and then she opened her mouth and hissed. It was a soft noise : *His—s—s—his—s—s ;* but it was so much more distinct than most noises heard in dreams, that at last I woke, and was quite relieved to find that the little black snake was not there.

I felt frightened still, and feverish, and in order to reassure myself after this disturbing dream, I sat up in bed, and, drawing the curtain still more aside, looked out upon the quiet sea. But such a sight met my astonished gaze, that I at once forgot the hissing snake, and all my soul was in my eyes. The moon was gone down ; but across the water lay a long path of light, precisely, as it seemed to me, such a path as she had made, only that this path was not silver, but of a rosy hue. Beautiful, beautiful sight ! I lay looking at it like one enchanted : every moment, as it seemed to me, that rosy path became wider and ruddier. What could it be ? There were no northern lights in the sky to cast that vivid reflection, and the vessel that lay in its midst at anchor could have nothing to do with it : it seemed to come from behind the house. Certainly it was behind me ; and as its fitful splendor widened and quickened on the edges of the breaking waves, I was just about to wake Miss L'Estrange to look at it, when, louder, clearer, and more terrific by far than the noise that had awoke me from my dream, I heard the little black snake again : *His—s—s—his—s—s—his—s—s,* and at the same instant, a light puff of white smoke came warm against my cheek, and I sprang from the bed screaming, " Wake up, Miss L'Estrange, wake, wake ; the house is on fire."

She presently woke, and for a few bewildering seconds we

ran helplessly about the room, then tried the lock, which, thanks to Madame's care, which perhaps saved our lives, we could not open. We then rushed to the window, to find the key; but air was indispensable, for the smoke sifted in fast. We flung open the French window, and ran out across the narrow pavement on to the sand, that we might breathe freely, and then we fell on our knees, and looked up at the house, crying aloud, to think of those that were within it. There we saw the cause of the great reflection on the water; a high chimney at the back of the house was on fire; it had, doubtless, already set fire to the beams. The roaring of the wind that fed it was like thunder, and the dancing, joyous, exultant shoots of flame that it sent up, reached so high that they seemed as if they would scorch the very stars. It was hot even at that distance; so hot, that we wondered what it must be inside; and like the troubled remembrance of a fever dream, I remember our rushing about, flinging stones at the doors and windows, and crying to Madame and to our schoolfellows by their names.

It could not have been many seconds that we did this. A shout came from the water behind us, and turning, we beheld a boat full of sailors; they were rowing straight along that fearful but splendid pathway; they had come from the vessel, and were within an oar's length of the beach. They pushed the boat ashore, the sea was almost as calm as a lake, and forming two abreast, six resolute-looking men, they marched up to the burning house. During the moment that this was passing, how much that house was changed! Every window was open: men, women, and children, awake and frantic, were rushing up and down in the verandas, to find some means of descending, and were crying and stretching out their arms, imploring help, and declaring that the staircase was on fire.

It was a very high building, and the two upper stories

were constructed of wood; each had a long veranda, but the upper one had no communication with the lower, and neither with the ground. I remember that these sailors had each a coil of rope on his arm, and that as they walked up to the house they cheered.

I remained, as if frozen with terror, to see what would follow; and Miss l'Estrange sat down on the sand, covered her face with her hands, and sobbed out her sister's name. A long low wing ran out from one side of the house; two of the sailors were on its roof in a very little time, and they were trying to fling up a rope to the people above. I saw this rope fall down five times, and I heard the fire roaring at the back, and the sparks crackling down in cataracts. At length it was caught by a child, securely tied to the verandah, and then, O frightful sight! I saw a sailor climbing up it.

Up that giddy height, sometimes touching a projection with his foot, sometimes swinging in mid air, from the length of the rope and the impossibility of its being held stretched by his comrades, but at last he was up and climbing over the wooden railings. Another sailor was upon the rope; the first had dashed into the house, which was all illuminated from within, and so hot that the papers were shrinking and peeling off the walls, and the noise and the smoke, and the showers of burning papers, woven fabrics, and other light materials, were covering us and the whole shore, and hissing in the water behind.

I saw that first sailor come out, and in his arms a large basket; it seemed to be a clothes-basket; he and another sailor were tying ropes to this basket, while the unfortunate people were clinging to one another, moaning and lamenting. Then I saw a sailor seize upon a little child, and begin to tie it into this basket; and I thought the frightful sight of all my schoolfellows, and the other people, sent from such a height in such a manner, I could scarcely look

at and live.   I turned sick with fear ; there was a dreadful
impossibility of standing still, or of looking.   Where could
I hide ?. Nowhere but in the room that we had left, and
rather than see that terrific sight I rushed into it.

It was glowing hot, but there were no flames, and the
smoke of the burning part of the house seemed drawn up
by the draught of the great flames, so. that this story was
quite clear.   It was the great chimney that had set the
place on fire above, and all the upper rooms were now
burning, having been set alight by the cataracts of sparks
that had poured down the chimneys.

I stood there an instant, relieved of my terror, and then
my eyes fell on the boxes.   Any kind of action at such a
moment would be a great relief; I thought I would push
them out of the room, and tumble them on to the sand ;
for I remembered that the sufferers above were only
clothed in their night garments.   So I began with frantic
eagerness to move out the lightest of these boxes, and my
recollection is very confused of what followed, though I
have an impression that a sailor and a woman came and
helped me ; also, that more sailors had landed from the
vessel, and that children with bare feet were running about
on the sand.   I can then remember being again on the
shore, possessed with a frantic terror of seeing that basket, but always occupied ; sometimes tearing the clothing
and the shoes from these boxes, and tumbling them farther
from the house ; sometimes catching a screaming child as
it ran past me, and forcibly clothing it, fitting shoes on to
all sorts of feet, and dealing out shawls, gowns, and railway wrappers to the ladies.   Many things passed before
me like changes in some frightful vision, lighted up by a
fire so bright that it seemed to shine not only upon us, but
through us ; Caroline was by me, cut and bleeding about
the face, while some people were going to carry her away ;
a great log was burning at my feet ; some sailors were by

me; and while I was tying shawls on many shoulders, they were wildly cheering that every living soul was saved. Madame was by me, frantic about her numerous charge, madly beating her breast, and crying after her children; and as for me, I had become cold as a stone, and a strange persuasion began to get the better of me, — that the whole scene was unreal.

Upon this I said to myself that I would venture to look at the house again; and what a sight it was when I did! The whole upper stories were burning away, blowing away, and melting away. Rafters white as snow were breaking off, and noiselessly falling in flakes all among us and over us. The sea, the sand, and the air were filled and covered with light morsels of charred wood, paper, chintz, and canvas; burning brands were jerked out to the water's edge; some, still alight, were floating out to sea; and though not a breath of air stirred, excepting round the house, the draft of the flames was so great that the light sand blew along towards it as it does in a high wind.

Presently there was a cry that the front would shortly fall, and all the people but our own party rushed away towards a boat-house that lay some roods to the left.

Two or three sailors were persuading Madame to follow, but she would not; she still cried that her children were not all found. I was uneasy, for I had not seen little May; but when I asked about her, Madame herself assured me that she was safe.

I do not know what was the matter with the girls; but their excitement was so great that they could not remain quiet; one or two were almost always missing among other groups, and some remained wildly running up and down without any apparent object.

I heard the sailors saying, that if they could not get the children counted over, they could not be sure that all were there; and then I heard them state, that they would put us into their boat and push off, so that we could not get away.

I was, no less than my companions, in a curious state of mind, and I remember laughing aloud, as I saw the sailors running after them, catching them one after the other, and putting them into the said boat, which they had left under the charge of one of their number, who kept it, with its gradually increasing freight, a few yards from the shore; it approached to receive the passengers. When we were all in, it became evident to Madame that none were missing, excepting poor Caroline, who was hurt, and had been taken to the farm-house inland. So she thankfully followed, and we sat staring at the burning house, not now more than half its former height.

We were partly distracted from watching it by a strange circumstance in the boat: it was that the great light attracted innumerable shrimps, and all kinds of small fish, and they kept leaping into the boat, and covering us with showers of salt water. We were engaged in throwing these unwelcome companions back into the water, when a great crash arrested us: the front walls fell flat on to the sand, and a long burning beam came crashing down upon the roof of the wing before-mentioned, and which had hitherto escaped the fire. At the same instant, a female figure was seen flying towards us, rushing over glowing brands, and leaping across blazing rafters; the figure never stopped but to ask some question of the sailors, and, guided by them, she sped towards us, fleet as the wind. Several voices cried out that it was Frances; and Frances, indeed, it was. She was breathless and faint with running, and she dropped upon her knees, stretching out her arms toward the boat, and crying out with the energy of despair: " I want my child; where's my child? give me my child, my child ! "

The horror, the confusion that followed, it is hopeless to

attempt describing. All the girls and Madame had thought that May, as usual, was with Frances : she was not. She was still, then, under the burning beam in the wing ; and when I recovered my scattered senses, after hearing this, I saw Frances stand with her arms held out, and her hands clenched, and I heard her say, " Oh ! oh ! " and then she turned round, and fled with a fleetness that nothing but desperation could have given her, straight over the sand towards the burning and tottering house.

13   S

CHAPTER IX.

THE TREASURE IS SAVED.

THE remark is common, that there are some moments which gather into themselves the feelings and the consequences that in ordinary times are scattered over weeks and years; such were the moments that followed, while the burning house sent up its volumes of smoke and flame; while the still water, just then at its lowest, washed softly against the brink of that now broad reach of sand, and yet glowed with that superb but terrible pathway; while we sat mute with terror and amaze; and while Frances fled fleetly away from us among the smouldering brands.

It had cost our sailor but little effort hitherto to keep his boat almost stationary; for there was no air, and no sea oh. He now, as well as ourselves, sat gazing with stunned and helpless wonder while Frances rushed away on her perilous errand; but suddenly starting, when, as I suppose, he found the tide had turned, and that we were drifting in, he gave a few vigorous strokes with his oars as he began to feel the pebbles grating under us. "Now, ladies," he said, in an excited tone, "I see what the poor young thing is going to do. Mind yourselves; for run after I must and will." And so saying, he sprang ashore, and flew after Frances with a vehemence and vigor that, far as he was behind, almost made me hope that he would catch her.

But now came again that "confusion worse confounded." The boat-load was once more loose on the sand, and I alone was still sitting in it; the French girls were all running about wringing their hands; the English girls were helplessly crying, and clinging about Madame, now calling on her to get Frances back, and now to save May; Madame herself was bewildered under this great misfortune, not doing and not attempting to do anything; for what, indeed, could she do but lift up her trembling hands to heaven and pray, and think, with distracted brain and agonized heart, of the great danger of one pupil and the almost hopeless danger of the other?

And I, as I sat alone in the boat, which was gently rocked against the beach with every return of the wave, saw the sailor's deep footmarks on the sand, and that every footmark was full of sea-water, and every drop of that water roseate with the bloom of fire-light, either from the ruin or from the sky. In accounts of all events that greatly excite people, we find that their own feelings and impressions are mixed with the narrative: mine must be also, for they seemed more real to me than external things; and, in spite of my despair, I did look down into those tiny pools, and I did observe the rosy tinges of the breaking waves and the rosy drops that fell from the now drifting oars, and I did say to myself, how very beautiful they were! But there is also in my mind a vivid picture of the scene. I was ordered by Madame to get out of the boat, and I managed to obey her. I see her still standing passive and stunned, — the girls rushing, and hysterically crying around her, — the sailors and people about the burning house, flinging water as well as they could on the low roof of the wing, which was rapidly catching fire, and every moment forcing them back and back, — and Frances, unnoticed by any of them, flying on to almost certain death, and, if possible, urged to still greater swiftness by the sound of the sailor's footsteps behind her.

She was near — she was nearer; I cried out, as if my

one childish voice could be heard so far away, beseeching the people to see her, to know what she was about to do, and to arrest her reckless steps. My heart sank,—I shut my eyes for a moment,—then I opened them, and saw her at the end of the wing, running up an outer staircase that connected its veranda with the sands.

A great wreath of smoke came down over her and hid her. The sailor was close at her heels. She emerged from the smoke, and still pressed on ; she reached a window, and such was the vividness of the light, that even at that distance I distinctly saw her fling her shawl over her hand, and then dash it through the glass. That was the last thing I did see : another great volume of steam from the water that they were sending up from below spread swiftly over her, and, when it melted away into the glowing air, she and the sailor had disappeared.

Next I saw a great confusion among the people below, and there was fast shouting, screaming, and rushing up and down. Several more people were upon the veranda, and, owing to a momentary stoppage in casting water up, the flames were covering the roof, and sweeping and swooping down almost to the ground. The place was, in short, enveloped in the flames, and the people were forced back. The wind caused by the fire tossed up the blue and red spires with a dancing, exulting motion ; the very walls seemed to be shaken, and to rock as the fiery serpents hissed and sang. There was a noise again of rending and splitting ; the wind tossed and whirled out the blazing curtains and the burning papers, and flung on to the sands rafters that scattered millions of sparks as they fell, and covered the sands like a nation of fireflies. And now we all, as by one impulse, began to run nearer ; and my mind, as I remember, was so completely overwrought, and so much off its balance, that I was unable to think what might be going on within that burning ruin ; but was only occupied with watching and following the footprints that Frances had left in the sand, and with observing the streaks of yellow that began to appear in the east. That Frances and little May were both dead I did not doubt; and in my bewildered thoughts I wondered whether their souls were then *going up* across the ridges of those clouds in the golden dawn.

But we also had drawn near, and the flush of that great heat was on our faces, shining in our eyes, and the wind of it was wafting our garments, and the thunder of it was stunning our ears, and shaking the ground under our feet. I cannot say that I remember it all, though I have impressions of some things which followed, — impressions which detach themselves by reflection from the terror, and the shouting, and storming, and warning cries, and heavy footsteps, and frantic flinging up of water by the men about the flames.

First, I remember that I strained my eyes; but smoke and flame so obscured the wooden wing, that I distinguished but little; the fire was fringing the edges of every overlapping board; but, after helplessly gazing (as it seemed) a long time, I had a momentary vision of a roof, and it was breaking in, and tiles were falling thick and fast upon a bed inside; for some of the walls were gone, and there was a black gap behind, and the bed for an instant seemed to be seized and shaken by the fire, and in less than a minute it was burnt and shrivelled up with all its ample curtains, and the floor had given way, and the bed had gone down. That bed had been decked with curtains covered with drooping poppies. Little May had been coaxed to sleep in it, partly on the plea that they were so pretty. Where was she now?

I did not move, but kept staring up at the devouring flames, as they flung themselves at the cool pale sky, with a wild, mad kind of frolic.

Ages and ages seemed to follow, then the people said that all was over; but at length a shout rose from the crowd, — there was a rushing to the old black ruin of the centre; then came sudden silence, followed by a long audible groan. I turned my face from the red fire, and found myself left behind, and I dragged my unwilling limbs onward, talking all the time aloud to myself, till I came in front of the central ruin, and there, climbing down the outside of a stack of chimneys by a few projecting spars, I saw the sailor, and he was alone.

I say the sailor, because we knew that it could be none other than he : but he was so completely blackened by smoke as to be quite undistinguishable by dress or feature. I said to myself that I had known, when he came out, he must be alone, and though I stood in the throng I cannot . recollect the actions of those about me during the wretched quarter of an hour while he slowly clambered down. I have only an impression that now and then the people cheered in order to encourage him, and I suppose all were too much excited to remember what followed, for I have never been able to get an account of it from any one.

But the next thing that I do remember distinctly is, that it was quite light, and the sailor was standing among us, and the flames had suddenly died down. I also noticed that many of the men, whose figures had been seen about all night, were countrymen, who had come, doubtless, from the villages round. These all had gathered about the sailor, who, faint, weak, and panting, was moistening his burnt lips with something in a cup. " Now, then, speak to the Madame, speak to the Madame," I heard one of the sailors saying ; and instead of eagerly wondering what the man would reply, a forlorn reflection strayed into my mind, that I had heard them address her as " the Madame " before.

But the man's speech, when he found breath to reply,

cleared away the cloud that obscured my brain, and I awoke at once to life and consciousness.

"I tell'e marm," he said hoarsely and faintly, "the young lady bè alive now, and I expect the little one may come to her senses again ; but how they are to be got down alive from the place where they are, God only knows."

"Then whère were they?" cried the crowd.

The sailor looked up to where a solitary pile of chimneys reared its blackened outline. There was an immediate and simultaneous rush round the ruins of the house ; and far up on a projecting platform, only a few feet wide, and apparently forty feet high, sat Frances, with something in her arms. This little platform seemed to be the remains of some floor, which had been burnt not quite up to the chimneys ; but how long it would stand was the question, and how long it would be before those crumbling chimneys came down.

It was now probably about two hours since the fire had first broken out, and it might be somewhat past four o'clock. No engines had arrived, which was not wonderful, as the nearest were twelve miles off; but the sailors (who had been hitherto the saving of every person in the house), though their exertions had manifestly tired them greatly, and some were bruised and scorched, no sooner perceived Frances sitting on the projecting height, than they gathered together, and gave a deep hearty cheer by way of reassuring her, and then ran here and there in search of ropes and beams, intending to attempt a rescue. As I was eagerly watching their efforts at making a scaffold, somebody cried out that "the Madame had fainted," and the attention of the unoccupied persons being thus attracted to her and to us, they carried Madame into an outhouse, which had been used as an extra carriage-house. There they obliged us all to follow, and then shut us in, bringing us wine and bread, and positively keeping sentry at the door. I cannot wonder that they did this, for the whole precincts of the house were highly dangerous ; red-hot tiles strewed the neighborhood of the wing; and though the fire had burnt itself out, the sand and the remaining walls flung fierce heat against us, and the water lying in pools as it had come down after being tossed in buckets on the fire, was quite hot, and still steamed. ·The sun was just rising as we were shut into the carriage-house, and we were very miserable through suspense ; but we had not long to wait for tidings of our schoolfellows. Madame had not recovered many minutes from her fainting fit, and began to sit up and collect her thoughts, when we heard tremendous and repeated cheers, then a rushing of many feet towards our asylum ; and at last the door was violently flung open, and in ran Frances with May in her arms.

CHAPTER X.

CONCLUSION.

WE all started up at sight of the rescued ones, and rushed round Frances ; a sort of silent rapture held our lips sealed ; for a while we could not believe she was uninjured, and we pressed closely about her, touching her singed and tinderlike gown, her disordered hair, her flushed hot feverish cheeks, and her delicate hands, that grasped May so closely. As for her, she said not a word, but held out the child ; and a long, low laugh of rapturous relief burst from her lips, but she neither shed tears nor stirred till Madame took May from her, and kissed her, exclaiming, in her native language, " O my God, I do thank thee." Here Frances laughed again, and cried a little, but still she did not speak.

Poor little May, how piteously she was crying, and how her tiny limbs trembled and shivered ! Her small hands were a little scorched, and her night-dress in some places burnt brown ; she did not seem to be seriously injured, but her terror was still extreme.

In spite of the anguish and anxiety that we had suffered about Frances, our demonstrations of joy at sight of her were, after the first moment of her entrance, by no means violent or noisy. We were all beginning to feel the peevish exhaustion of excessive fatigue. Some of the young girls crept into the empty carriages that stood in this asylum of ours, and dozed upon the seats ; others lay down upon a heap of clean shavings ; a carpet was brought in for May and Frances, — one of the few things that had

13 *

been saved ; and those noble, kind-hearted sailors went about from one of us to the other, giving us wine (almost like mulled wine, it was so hot) from black bottles, and serving it in a little tin cup. After this acceptable refreshment, Madame herself very soon fell asleep, and most of her pupils with her. I could not sleep at first, as the sound of the crackling fire still sung in my ears.

It was now broad daylight, and the watery, white sky was distinctly visible through a small, dirty window, excepting when a sailor, leaning his weary arms upon the sill, would indulge in a contemplation of the people whom he had helped to save. Many sailors appeared in this way, one after the other, and seemed specially to derive satisfaction from staring at Frances and her tiny charge ; and it sometimes pains me, even to this day, to think that we never had an opportunity of thanking them ; for when we awoke at last, and inquired about them, the vessel was gone. The sailors, we were told, had said they could not stay, for a breeze had sprung up, and "The Lively Sall" must proceed on her voyage.

"The Lively Sall!" What a name! Some of the girls were quite shocked, and in writing to their friends called the vessel "The Lively Sarah." A very handsome present was made to these brave men by the parents of those whom they had rescued; but I am often sorry to think that they had not our thanks also.

This, however, is anticipating.

About nine o'clock in the morning we all awoke, very much refreshed ; some water was brought us ; and from the contents of the trunks, which still strewed the sand, we were all made, with Massey's aid, exceedingly neat and clean. Frances seemed scarcely more fatigued than ourselves ; but if any question was asked her about the rescue, would answer with a shudder, "O! don't speak to me about that; it makes my head swim to think of it."

We now issued from the carriage-house. The fire was nearly out, — only smouldering. The hotel was almost level with the ground, and none but its disconsolate owners lingered about it. Engines had arrived, and had deluged the place when the flames were already dying down. But we did not stay to look about us. Madame was naturally anxious to see Caroline, who had been taken to the farm-house, where Frances had, earlier in the evening, been sent to sleep.

We hoped also to find breakfast there, and were told that all the other people, who had been sleeping at the hotel when it took fire, had left the hospitable farm already, in different conveyances, having been received there in the night, and treated with the greatest kindness and consideration.

We walked across the fields to this place ; and the smiling mistress met us at her door, all fresh, and clean, and cheerful, though she had been up nearly all night. She had set out breakfast for us in her large kitchen; and she now invited us in, at the same time assuring us that the young lady up stairs was not very much hurt. Of course, Madame went up instantly to the chamber, and there her own maid was waiting on Caroline.

Her injury was a long, severe cut across the brow, reaching from the parting of the hair to the corner of the right eyebrow. It was by no means dangerous ; but, alas ! it was most evident that it must leave a mark for life.

Several of us — I among them — crept up the stairs after Madame ; and though forbidden to enter the room, listened to what might be going on inside.

Caroline was in a highly excited state ; a surgeon had been sent for to attend her, and had ordered her to lie quietly in bed. The moment Madame entered, she at once declared that she was sure her face would be marked.

Madame had all the sweetly compassionate manner of an amiable Frenchwoman, and she soothed Caroline with hopes to the contrary, asked if she would like one of her schoolfellows to come and sit with her, and told her that we were all safe ; in fact, the great blessings of life and safety for all her large party did somewhat make it impossible, for the present, that she could feel much for Caroline's misfortunes. Not a question had been asked, and so little interest shown by Caroline, that we all thought, judging by this, and by the tone of her voice, that she was probably a little delirious.

"Yes," she said, when Madame again asked if she would like one of her schoolfellows to sit beside her. "Yes ; she should like one of them, but not Sophia, — Sophia would say she deserved it."

"No," said Madame, soothingly, "they are all extremely sorry, my child, — very much grieved indeed, my dear," — and Madame showed a good deal of alarm at the speech, for, in fact, not understanding it, she thought Caroline quite light-headed.

"Not Sophia," repeated Caroline, tossing on her pillow ; "I know I DID steal little May ; I know I am branded for a thief, and she will think so."

On hearing this I fled down the stairs, wringing my hands and crying with a sort of hysterical violence, no doubt partly owing to my late excitement : it was some time before I recovered my senses : when I did so I found that the woman of the house was holding me on her knees, in a pleasant arbor out of doors, and that an old gentleman, with a most pleasant face, was standing before her.

"Why, here's the Vicar, little Miss," said my good nurse.

"Ay, ay," said the old gentleman, "don't cry, my pretty little bird,—here are some nice gillyflowers to smell, and here is some cold water to drink. What! not one hurt in the fire ! what a good God is ours ; and how thankful you should be for such a merciful preservation ! "

He looked so very old, and so venerable, that I gazed at him with pleasure and curiosity, sobbing out, " I do feel thankful, sir, — indeed I do." His house was about four miles from the sea, close to the church, for it was a very large, thinly-populated parish, partly warren, and partly salt marshes.

" Please to sit down, sir," said the woman, wiping the seat of the arbor with my handkerchief, and still holding me in her arms ; " and I hope you 'll have some breakfast afore you go."

" Ay, ay," the old clergyman replied, sitting down beside us. " I 'm a great age now, Mrs. Peel, — almost past my work, — my Master's work."

" O no, sir ! not yet," replied the woman.

" Not quite yet. I must talk with these dear children before I go ; and I shall hope to pray with them and the French lady."

" Yes, sir ; that 's what they want ; you 'll make 'em feel quieter like ; for now they are all of a tremble."

I felt better, and we went into the house ; but I was not allowed to stay down stairs, and hear the delightful conversation and devout prayers of the aged clergyman. I was taken up stairs and put to bed. Some breakfast was given me while there, and I soon fell into a deep, dreamless sleep, from which I did not awake for hours.

When at last I did open my eyes, they fell upon a bed, for there were two in the room. Frances and May were lying asleep in this bed, and beside it stood a tall and most elegant lady, — a lady in a rich, rustling silk dress, and with a long Indian chain round her neck, which rested on the quilt as she bent over little May. She stood with her back to me ; but a round, old-fashioned mirror hung on the whitewashed wall before her, and in it I saw her face, and recognized it, though now it was changed, and illuminated by a kind of unbelieving joy, and though her eyes were overflowing with happy tears.

It was little May's mamma.

Every now and then she would venture to lift up the child's hand and touch it with her lips, but she seemed very much afraid of waking her and Frances ; and, but for this little action, stood motionless beside them for some time.

I knew that for several days she had been constantly expected, and that she possessed Madame's intended address at the seaside, and I thought what a happy thing it was she had not arrived a few hours sooner.

At last the mother's kisses becoming unconsciously more fervent, little May awoke ; upon which, forgetting her caution, she threw her arms upon the bed, and stooping over the child, exclaimed, with a laugh of exulting joy, " Who am I, May? tell me."

" Mamma ! " exclaimed the child, after a momentary pause, and continued to gaze at her with a sort of ecstasy, softly repeating to herself, " Mamma, mamma ! " But when her mother tried to take her up, she said, in a confidential tone, " Mamma, you must n't wake my Miss Chris-tiana Frances."

On hearing the little silvery voice repeating this already beloved name, and bringing so vividly to her recollection the peril that her child had just encountered, the mother burst into a sudden passion of tears, which woke Frances, who started up in a fright, uttering some confused words about the smoke, and the sea, and little May.

Finding herself kissed, blessed, and wept over by this beautiful stranger, was not likely to reassure her, and she did not recover from her bewilderment, till May cried out, " Mamma, mamma, you don't know what a great hole was burnt in my bed last night ! "

On hearing this, Frances instantly perceived who it was that was embracing her with such fervent expressions of gratitude and love, and she gave May to her mother, for on first awakening she had snatched her up in her arms.

May, who before being laid in the bed had evidently been carefully washed, and dressed in a clean embroidered frock, looked particularly pretty, though her tiny hands were still very red from the heat of the flames. Frances herself was also seen under favorable circumstances ; she was dressed in a delicate lilac muslin gown, and her fair hair was nicely braided. I was glad that Lady Merton had not seen them during their former sleep in the carriage-house, for then they had looked like two sweeps. I was also glad that I was neatly dressed myself, for in a very few minutes May's tall stately father stalked in, snatched the child, and bestowed on her a storm of kisses that resounded through the room. He then turned to Frances, who, with his wife's arm still round her, was sitting up on the bed, as on a dais. She had thrown back the quilt, and was gazing at him, half pleased and half surprised. Lady Merton took her hand, and putting it into her husband's, he kissed it, and straightway began to make a vehement incoherent speech about his gratitude, his thankfulness, what he should have done if coming home he had found his little one burnt to death, what his wife would have felt, etc., etc. But at a certain point in it, appearing to feel rather a choking sensation, he marched to the window, and then having sobbed two or three times, and called himself a fool quite audibly, he blew his nose violently, and came back as well as ever.

After this, to my relief, they all left the room.

And now I must go back in my narrative, and explain some circumstances, which did not come to my knowledge for some time afterwards.

It appears that some minutes before I awoke, and saw

that strange light on the sea, Caroline was also startled by a peculiar noise, and being frightened, jumped out of bed, put on her dressing-gown and slippers, and looked out into the passage. As I have before said, she was in the wing of the house with little May; but May, it appears, in her hurry and confusion, she did not think of.

According to her own account, she saw nothing, but thinks that she returned to her own room, and then beheld that ruby light gleaming between the curtains on the water; and ran out of the room, wishing to find Madame, for she was sure something was the matter. She ran to the great staircase of the house, and saw lights glowing under the boards; puffs of smoke seemed to pursue her; and being frightened, she fled before them up to the very top of the house, trying the locked doors, and crying, "Madame, madame!" Then, too much alarmed to know what she did, she tried to run down again; but fire was now visible below. She set her foot upon a board in her rapid descent; it gave way; flames spurted up, and the end of the board struck her on the brow, and she fell down a short flight of stairs. Recovering almost instantly, she sprang down stairs, and found herself among a crowd of people, all rushing to the great front drawing-room, and in her fright, confusion, danger, and pain, she never thought of the child.

She was saved like the other people, and did not know how much she was hurt, till she found herself safe on the sands. She was taken to the farm, and there Frances, already roused and dressed, met her, frantic to know what had become of May, and she said she did not know.

Little May's account was, that she woke in the night, and found the room full of smoke that almost choked her; that Miss Baker was not there, and then she cried as loudly as she could, and called her Miss Chris-tiana Frances a great many times; and she heard "some wicked men shouting outside ; " so she got up and crept under the bed to hide herself, — a thing she was in the habit of doing when it thundered, or she was otherwise frightened. This providential habit saved her life. She was almost suffocated when Frances rescued her, finding out her hiding-place by the gasping noise she made.

Frances and the sailor, dragging May between them, crept on their hands and knees along the passage to the house, for the flames pursued them, and prevented their return to the now burning veranda. Then they attained a room which had a servant's ladder-stair in it, and were compelled still to ascend, the fire seeming to force them up, and closing behind. They got up on a higher floor, of which little was left but the platform before mentioned, and they had not stood there long, recovering strength and breath, when the stairs and the room they had come through fell in, and in that dim light of gray morning, though now sitting in the open air, they were not observed from below, the noises being still so great, that they vainly tried to make themselves heard.

The sailor then finding that in that distraction of fear, that confusion of voices, and crackling of flames, his signals and shouting were of no avail, and seeing that they were not likely to be looked for in the right place, resolved to attempt a descent. How he accomplished it we never heard. I suppose it must have been dreadful to see him doing it, for Frances never could be induced to describe it but once, and then she burst into tears, and turned so faint and sick that Madame desired she never might be questioned about it again.

A bewildering day or two followed in the old farm-house. Caroline was still poorly ; but her cut was healing satisfactorily, and I, of course, after hearing what she had said of me in her half delirium, was particularly anxious to be attentive and kind to her. Accordingly, I was generally in

T

her room, and she was better pleased to have me than any one else, partly because I was nearest of all the pupils to her own age, partly because she perceived how truly sorry I was for her, and did not know its cause.

Poor Caroline! she was told that May was going away with her parents and with Frances, and she nerved herself to see May. The little girl was led in by me, and clung to me. I could feel her little heart beat.

"May, you are not afraid of me?" said Caroline, in a regretful tone.

The little girl stammered out, "No!"

"Kiss me, then, my dear little May; I am glad you are safe, though it is through no care of mine."

I do not know what baby fancies were working in the breast of May, but she appeared to think that by this kiss she should express some kind of reproach of her best friend. She turned away her little face as I lifted her up, burst into tears, and sobbed out, "I *do* love my Miss Chris-tiana Frances."

Caroline, on hearing this, lay down on her couch again and wept. She did not say a word; but as May still sobbed, I said to her, "Caroline wishes you always to love your Miss Frances."

Upon this the little creature rubbed away her tears with her pretty hands, and pursing up her rosy lips, gave Caroline the kiss. Then Caroline said, "Take her away!" but I had scarcely turned to do so, when the door was opened, and Frances came in. She was in her travelling dress, and evidently, though she had sought this meeting, she was in a great fright, while she affected to feel at her ease.

"O, it is you, Frances!" said Caroline.

Frances could not say a word.

"You are going away very soon, I hear," proceeded Caroline.

Still Frances stood mute, and had turned quite pale with agitation.

I wondered at Caroline's calmness. "I dare say," she said, "you are sorry to see me so disfigured, — though — though — "

"What will she say next?" I thought, in terror; and I dashed into the conversation, by informing Caroline that the travelling party was to start in half an hour. May, in the meantime, had gone down stairs, and Frances, with her cold hand, was holding me to prevent my following her.

"Frances," said Caroline, still the only speaker, "I did think I would not see you before you went; but now I am not sorry I did, for I see how much you pity me."

Frances burst into tears.

"It is very evident though," added Caroline bitterly, "that you think this, — this bruise a punishment on me. Your distress shows it"; and she went on; "but I suppose you have forgiven me for stealing your child, since she is yours again now, and bound to you for ever?"

There was something so regretful and so painfully calm in Caroline's way of speaking, that it only made Frances cry more and more bitterly, till at last I said, in desperation, "Frances, if you do not say something, I shall drag you out of the room; you are making Caroline worse."

This seemed to rouse her, and she rose up quite pale with emotion, and knelt beside Caroline's couch, taking her in her arms, and kissing her many times.

Her passion of tears and excessive emotion, so far from distressing Caroline, seemed to soothe her. She returned the embrace of Frances, and when the latter, still utterly unable to command her voice, rose up and hurriedly fled out of the chamber, she really seemed comforted, and lying back on her couch, said to me, with tears, "O, Frances is far better, — far more generous, and more forgiving than I am!"

So May's parents, and Frances, and her little treasure drove away. Caroline got rapidly better, and we all returned to the Willows; but the fair face was always marked with a long narrow scar, which disfigured the brow, and altered the expression of those beautiful eyes; but whether it proved a permanent memento to her, and whether the providential lesson it should have conveyed was duly learned, I cannot now tell to you, my reader, though at some future period I may take up the thread of Caroline's history again.

We returned, as I said, to the Willows, and I believe the scenes we had passed through had solemnized our minds, and been made instrumental in leading our thoughts to deeper and more serious subjects.

More than one of us felt desirous to dedicate to the service of our merciful God those lives which he had so graciously preserved; and though our short-comings have been many, both in remaining childhood and in giddy youth, I still believe that for more than one the perils and terrors of that night of awe had a salutary message, and were not suffered in vain.

EMILY'S AMBITION.

CHAPTER I.

EMILY WELLAND was an orphan, the child of poor
but very respectable parents, who had died when she
was too young to feel their loss, and had left her to the
care of her grandmother.

Few young people of her age and rank in life are better
instructed than Emily was, for she had been educated at
Aylsham School, under a certificated mistress, who was a
superior woman and respected by all. She was appren-
ticed as a "pupil teacher," at fourteen years of age,
and seemed to have a more than ordinary chance of doing well and getting on, for she was clever, and what
is called "sprack" in the part of the country where she
lived.

Emily lived with her grandmother in a cottage just outside the small town. It was a comfortable cottage, with a
garden in front, where the old woman grew a few potatoes
and cabbages. The thatch was green with lumps of moss
as soft as velvet, and there was a flower-bed in front which
all the summer was gay with stocks, and wallflowers, and
flowering myrtles, besides low-growing plants, such as
double primroses and red daisies. .

On pleasant evenings Emily would often spend an hour,
in weeding and watering the flower-beds; and very contented and cheerful she generally seemed at her work; no
one, to look at her pretty face, would have guessed how

little contentment she really felt, and how many things there were in her lot that she wished she could alter.

There was a Mechanic's Institute at the little town; — the subscription was five shillings a year, and for that sum subscribers might take out more books than it was easy to read, and some of them were not very well suited for the reading of the industrious classes.

Emily subscribed to the Institute, and used to bring the books home to read; stories, travels, poetry, history, nothing seemed to come amiss to her; but she liked the stories best, though she sometimes said she had a great mind to read no more of them, for they were all about ladies and gentlemen, and made keeping school and keeping shop, and that kind of thing, seem common and vulgar work.

Emily had a friend who served in a fancy shop in the little town, and the two girls would often meet at dusk, sit on the bench just outside the cottage, talk about their favorite characters in books, and describe to each other the sort of people they should like to be if they could change their station. Sometimes they would say they wished they had been born ladies, for they were sure they were more fit for ladies' work than for their own. Indeed they wished they could become ladies at once, nothing but money being wanted to make them such; but if the old grandmother was present, she would laugh at them in rather a mortifying way, and say in her broad Dorset dialect: —

"Go along, Mary Best! don't talk to I. If thou was dressed up as fine as the Queen, thou could n't play the lady without being found out."

When things of this kind were said, Mary Best generally took her leave, not without a toss of the head that in a lady would have been highly unbecoming, and that was vulgar and uncivil in a shop-girl.

Though Emily liked to talk nonsense with Mary Best, and wish herself in a higher station, she did not neglect to prepare herself for what was likely to be her own; she expected to be a schoolmistress, and she worked hard to qualify herself to be a good one. A certificate is not an easy thing to be got in these days, for the examinations are very strict: but Emily was bent on having one of the first class, and being both industrious and clever, it seemed likely she would succeed.

She was within six months of being out of her apprenticeship, and was hard at work preparing to go up to Salisbury to the Diocesan examination there, when one evening a neighbor came in and brought the news that a certain Mrs. Smalley had arrived in the town, and was stopping at the "White Hart."

"Your own niece, Mrs. Welland," observed the neighbor; "and they do say that she drove up in a fly, with a Leghorn bonnet and feathers, quite the lady."

"My own niece," repeated Emily's grandmother; "I wonder whether she will come and see her old aunt?"

"She can easy find your place if she wants to see you," observed the neighbor; "for you are not like a many, always changing it."

"I've kept myself respectable," said the old woman, "and never come upon the parish; so be she lady, or be she not, she may come and see I."

"They do say she is very good to the poor," remarked her friend.

"We are not poor," interrupted Emily, as red as a rose, "at least not poor enough to want anything from Mrs. Smalley."

"Poor child," replied the neighbor, "I can tell you what you are poor enough to want of her! I wish I was as near to her as you are, and I would speak up at once for my Mary Anne."

"So they do say she looked quite the lady," said the grandmother. "What changes there be in this world!
14

Letty a lady, money in her pocket, and drives up to the best inn in the town."

" Yes, you may well be proud," replied the neighbor; "but I suppose you won't call her Letty now. A first-rate London milliner, and has ladies of title in her show-rooms, and makes hundreds of pounds; but what do you think she is come here for, Mrs. Welland ? "

" Not to see her own folk, I 'll be bound," replied the grandmother, with a shrewd smile.

" Why, no; but it is to show a respect to the family, too. I was waiting at the Vicarage door to know whether they wanted any fowls ; I had sold all but my last pair, and while the boy was gone into the parlor to ask whether Madam had a mind to them, who should come up but Tom Trott, that is ostler at the White Hart : he had brought a parcel that had just come by the coach, so I asked him if he knew what Mrs. Smalley had come to the town for. ' No less,' says he, 'as I hear, than to have a headstone put up to the memory of old Letty Welland.' "

" Bless us ! " cried the grandmother ; " well, she might have done more for her mother while the poor soul was living ; but this is a mighty respect for all that."

" So I say," observed the neighbor. " It shows she is no ways ashamed of your poor sister. Does n't it, Emily ? "

" I don't know," said Emily ; " perhaps she does it out of respect to herself."

" That was, all I heard," added the neighbor. " They bought the fowls, and paid two-and-ninepence for them. Well, good-night, Mrs. Welland, and Emily. I must go home ; I am late already."

Emily went to bed that night full of thought. This relative, whom she had never expected to see, had often been talked of by her grandmother as having acquired money enough to live in luxury, and wear clothes as fine as any she made. " And what will my calling do for me ?" thought the pupil teacher ; "perhaps if I get a first-class certificate, and prove as good a mistress as Miss Cooper, I may get in the end a house to live in, and eighty pounds a year in all. That is too much to expect, but still it is not impossible. For that I shall have to work very hard, and what shall I be ? why, nothing but a teacher of poor folk's children, and what a common vulgar sort of trade that seems ! How hard it is that I should have to learn so much to gain so little, while Mrs. Smalley can make her hundreds by just fitting a bonnet well, and snipping up silk into becoming trimmings."

It so happened, fortunately as Emily thought, because it gave her a chance of seeing Mrs. Smalley, — it so happened that the next day was a whole holiday at the school, and when Emily came out at the cottage door, and stood in the shade at seven o'clock the next morning, and knew that she had nothing to do all day but to rest and enjoy herself, she felt what a pleasure it was to be free.

Emily had dressed herself in a clean lilac and white print gown, and had fastened up her hair more neatly than usual, half hoping that her cousin might come and see her and her grandmother. It was the middle of July, and the heat of the night had caused many of the flowers to shed their leaves. The little path was strewed with red and white rose-leaves. Emily picked them up, and then got a duster and polished the little casement-window and made everything about the cottage look tidy and respectable. Then she went in and had her breakfast with her grandmother, after which the old woman went out upon her usual market-day expedition, which was to sell cream cheeses for the wife of a neighboring farmer.

Emily being now left alone took up her plain work and sat close to the pleasant little casement, enjoying the scent of the rosemary and the sweet-brier: she half hoped that Mrs. Smalley would call, and yet, when about ten o'clock she heard the sound of a step on the path, she felt so shy that she could not look up.

However, she need not have minded, — the gown that now brushed against the lilies in the narrow path was not a silk one, and the voice that spoke in the open door-way was not a strange one.

" Ellie, is Ellie at home ? " asked Miss Cooper, the mistress.

" O yes, Miss Cooper, I am here, ma'am," said Emily ; " pray come in."

" How pleasant and quiet it seems here," replied the schoolmistress. " Child, you are highly favored to have such a peaceable home. — Well, I thought I would come and have a chat with you, Ellie, on my way to see poor Sally Eaton."

" Is her little girl dead ? " asked Emily.

" Yes, the mother sent me word of her death last night, and asked me to come and see her."

" She was a good little thing," said Emily, "and improved wonderfully when she had been at school a little while. She was not like the same child."

" So her mother said yesterday."

" She is a grateful woman," replied Emily, " not like Polly Gay's mother, for when you sent me to ask her to be more particular to send the child in good time, and I said it was a shame she should be so careless about the child's learning, when you took such pains with it, she answered, that there was nothing to be thankful for, seeing you were paid for teaching the child."

" Yes, to be sure," said the mistress ; " money will make us work, but money will not make us give our hearts to the work, — nothing but love for the work, or real good principle, can make us do that. So there was something for her to be thankful for, poor soul, if she had but known it."

" I can't bear to hear them say we teach because we are paid," said Emily, vehemently.

" Why, child," answered the mistress, smiling, "you would not teach, would you, if you were *not* paid ? "

" No, ma'am, of course not. I could not afford to teach for nothing."

" Well, but if you could afford it — "

" O," interrupted Emily, "if I could afford it, ma'am, I should be a lady, and then of course I should not teach in the way I do now. I should not drudge *myself*, in a school, but I dare say I should be just as charitable as Lady S. and Lady G., and the great ladies that one hears of. I should pay somebody to teach for me."

" Bless you, child," exclaimed the mistress ; "surely you don't think that would be the same thing."

" It would do as much good to the children as if I taught them myself," said Emily, "and it would be a vast deal pleasanter. I should get a great deal of praise, too, instead of being told that I was only doing my duty because folks paid me."

"Well, but Ellie, we can do all our duties in a selfish or in a self-denying way."

" Yes," replied Emily, "but it does not count for self-denial, ma'am; I mean, it does not count in the opinion of other folks. Nobody would say that you spent your life in doing good, because, you see, you are paid."

"Well, child, and is it not the will of God that we should earn our bread, — and have n't we a right to be paid ? "

"Yes," said Emily, sighing, "though, rather than be a poor teacher in a school, I should like to have been a lady, and then the good I did would have been in such a far pleasanter way, and no trouble worth mentioning. What are you laughing at. ma'am ? "

" Well," said the worthy mistress, "I ought to be ashamed of myself to laugh ; for to fret at the decree of

God that we shall not be ladies but working-women, is not
a light fault, and, Ellie, you should try to get grace to be
contented. But, child, I laughed at your notion of doing
good. Do you think I would change with such ladies as
you speak of? Have n't I kept school twenty-five years
and taught twelve hundred children to read right well, and
write pretty well, and know their duty to God and to other
folks? *Not but what it was my duty;* of course it was
my duty, and I have earned my bread by it. But child,
only think what an honor and an advantage it is to us, and
such as us, that we can't earn our bread without scattering
blessings wherever we go. Why, it might have been the
will of Providence that we should live by making artificial
flowers, or beads to trim dresses with, or sugar-plums for
little spoiled pets of children to make their pretty teeth
ache with. We should earn our money just the same then;
but what should we give for it, compared with what we
have the blessing of giving now? Why, nothing at all.
Six months after death a few faded cambric roses would be
what was left of our work in this world; our work, I mean,
that we got our bread by; but your work and mine, Ellie?
— I don't expect that to perish altogether."

"I never thought of that," said Emily, thoughtfully.

"Child," replied the mistress, "do not think that I am
boastful of my calling, just because I follow it. I am grateful certainly that I have such a good one; but the greater
the work the more the shortcomings show."

"It was very good of you to come and see me, ma'am,"
said Emily, for her guest had risen and showed signs of
intending to leave.

"Will you give me a sprig of rosemary, and a handful of
roses to put in the little one's coffin?" said the mistress.

"Surely, ma'am," Emily answered, and she came out
and gathered some of her sweetest flowers. After following Miss Cooper with her eyes till she disappeared, she

returned to her work with a sensation of greater respect for her than she had ever felt before. " I am glad," she thought, " that I did not tell her what a mind I had to see if Mrs. Smalley would teach me dressmaking ; and how I disliked the notion of teaching, because it seemed so *low !* Why, she would only have said as she did to Amy Price, '*Low,* child ! — wait a year or two before you presume to give an opinion ; it is too high above you to judge of it at present.' However," thought Ellie, " I am not at all sure that I shall keep to teaching, if I have a chance of finding some better employment."

At one o'clock Emily had some dinner, and sat quietly at work till half past four, when the grandmother came in hot and tired and ready for her tea ; so Emily set out the little deal table with the tea-things, the loaf and butter, and a small piece of cold bacon. Her grandmother put her basket on a chair, took off her bonnet, and they sat down to enjoy their meal. Another step on the narrow path, and a great deal of rustling, and then a tap on the open door, and when they turned, a stout lady, all silks and gauzes and laces and feathers stood there, and asked, " Is this Mrs. Welland's house ? "

" Yes, ma'am," said Emily, walking to the door, "will you come in ? "

Her grandmother had, in the mean time, brushed the crumbs from her lap with her hard honest hands, and turning half round in her chair was looking at her gayly dressed visitor.

" I suppose you don't remember me," said the grand lady, in rather a condescending manner. " My name is Mrs. Smalley."

" Yes, ma'am," said Emily's grandmother, " so I suppose, and I take it kind — "

" And this is your granddaughter, I see," observed the lady, sinking into a chair. " Well, I'm sure ! a very pretty young person she is too. Your garden smells very sweet after London, aunt."

The fine lady said this word in rather a low voice, but it gave satisfaction; and when in a tone of great condescension she said she would take a cup of tea with them, the grandmother felt more at her ease, and began to answer her questions and take her meal with tolerable comfort.

"She is a very genteel-looking, pretty young person," repeated Mrs. Smalley, staring at Emily, and talking of her as composedly as if she had not been present, "and she would look very well in my show-room."

Emily blushed deeply at this remark, but Mrs. Smalley did not continue the subject, presently saying, that she had come to the town partly with a view of putting up a monument to the memory of her mother; and that she had called on the Vicar, and asked to be shown her mother's grave, but that he did not remember which it was.

"My aunt was not buried in Aylsham churchyard," said Emily.

"So I found," replied the milliner; "I got the Rev. Mr. Ward to look into the book, and my poor mother's name was not in it."

"She was buried in D— churchyard," proceeded Emily, "and I remember the place quite well, for grandmother and I followed her to the grave. If you remember D— church, ma'am, you will know that it is but a short walk from this. You can see the spire peeping over the wood at the back of our cottage."

"I should wish to see the grave," replied Mrs. Smalley. "My feelings would be gratified by knowing the place where my poor mother lies, and my notion is, that a child ought to honor a parent, in death as well as in life, though, —ahem,— though the parent may have been in an inferior station."

" Surely," replied Emily, a little shocked.

" Therefore," proceeded Mrs. Smalley, " I shall go myself to see the grave, for as I said to the Vicar this morning, ' Sir !' I said, ' there is no disgrace in being connected
with the lower orders, provided the individuals know how
to conduct themselves respectably, for in the sight of our
Maker they and I are all equal.' I shall be glad of your
services to show me the way to D— church, Emily Welland."

" Yes, ma'am," replied Emily, but the respect with which
she had at first regarded their richly dressed and self-suffi-
cient visitor was rapidly melting away, and it vexed her to
observe that her grandmother sat perfectly silent, and
seemed unable to look Mrs. Smalley in the face. The
good old woman was in fact in a perplexed and troubled
state of mind, for·it naturally seemed to her curious that
her poor sister should have been allowed during her life to
receive parish pay, and should now be honored with a
monument. However, she had not much time for these
speculations, for Emily at Mrs. Smalley's request put on
her bonnet to walk with her to D— church. The niece
took an affable leave of her worthy aunt, who gave her a
sovereign which she desired her to spend in buying a new
shawl as a remembrance of this visit.

Mrs. Smalley had begun life as a lady's-maid. Her
mistress being a great invalid had interested herself, and
employed some of her leisure in teaching her, and making
her read aloud to her. After some years the butler and
maid married, and then the same good friend had helped
her favorite to set up business as a dressmaker, by which
she had now become rich and prosperous.

The young pupil teacher walked across the fields with
her, listening to her discourse, every sentence of which
showed that she had money and lived in luxury. At last
Emily ventured to ask her whether she wanted a young

person as an upper assistant in her business ; — she mentioned that she understood book-keeping, and was also
handy at her needle, and should like much to learn dress-
making.

To her delight Mrs. Smalley replied that if she wished
to learn she might enter her house on the same footing as
the other young persons, provided she did not mention her
relationship to herself, nor presume upon it. " As to anything higher," continued Mrs. Smalley, " that might possibly be in time, if you gave satisfaction, Emily Welland."

" I could not come till next January or February, ma'am,"
said Emily, " but if I can manage it then, will you receive
me ? "

" Certainly," was the reply. " I am pleased with your
appearance, and with what I heard of you this morning
from the Vicar ; and I have no objection to say that I will
befriend you so far."

" If grandmother has no objection," Emily now put in,
but she inwardly resolved that she would not tell her grandmother of the plan till her apprenticeship was over.

The grave of the old mother was found. It was a green
mound lying in the evening sunshine near a fine yew-tree ;
and Emily having pointed it out, made her curtsey and
took her leave, going home to her grandmother's cottage
full of thoughts about London and of " bettering herself "
and rising in the world, but not quite sure that she had
done right, "though, to be sure," she thought, " I need not
go to Mrs. Smalley in January unless I please ; if everybody
is against it, I have made no promise, I can keep school
after all. I wonder what John Mills would think if he knew
that I was thinking of going to London."

CHAPTER II.

I N a cottage very near Emily, John Mills lived with his
father and mother and three little sisters. His father
was a stone-cutter, and John had been brought up to the
same trade, but he had taught himself also to cut in wood,
and had carved a beautiful little model of a monument,
which he had given to the Vicar of A., who had befriended
him.

The consequence was that when Mrs. Smalley consulted
the Vicar as to who she should employ to make her sister's
monument, he named John Mills, saying that he was a
very young man, but one who had great talent, and would
take more than common pains. At the same time he
showed her the model, together with some drawings which
had been made by Mills, and Mrs. Smalley admired them
so much that she resolved to employ him.   •

Now John Mills had not had so many advantages of
education as Emily, but she had without knowing it been
of great use to him, for from his earliest youth he had
wished for nothing so much as to obtain her for a wife.
And though she did not seem at present to return his regard, and he felt that he had little reasonable hope of succeeding, he yet continued to make the best use of every
opportunity for improving himself, in order that he might,
as he thought, be more worthy of her. But John, modest
as he was, and humble in his thoughts of himself, was
actuated by higher principle than that which governed
Emily. Emily thought first of advancing herself, and
secondly of her duty; John thought first of his duty, and

did it, and secondly, he strove to advance himself, both in knowledge and in his calling.

John had early shown such a taste for carving, that a gentleman in the neighborhood who had seen his work proposed to place him with a sculptor in London, and also to have him taught to draw. But when the boy, who at first was delighted at the prospect, found that for a long time he should be maintained at his benefactor's expense and earn nothing, he shrank back and decided to stay with his parents, whom he could help by his weekly earnings. His father, though a clever workman, was often laid up with rheumatic gout in the hands, and could earn nothing during the winter months, and John rightly thought he ought not to go away even for the sake of improving himself, if he should thereby put it out of his power to help to maintain his parents, and put his little sisters to school.

"It would only be for five years," said his patron, "and at the end of that time, John, you would doubtless be able to earn very excellent wages indeed."

"Only you see, sir," replied the boy respectfully, "I might not live to the end of the five years, and then what would father and mother do?"

"Well, well," said the patron, "I have offered to help you, and in the end no doubt it would be to the advantage of your parents; but if they cannot spare you, I have no more to say."

"I shall be very thankful to go," replied the boy, with tears in his eyes, "please God my father's hands get better."

But his father's hands did not get better, and John worked on from year to year. Yet though he could not have the advantage of good instruction, he did not, as many would have done, content himself with entire ignorance; on the contrary, he studied all the books which threw any light on his art that he could procure from the Mechanic's Institute, or borrow from those who befriended him. He also read, and did all he could to improve his mind; but he had very little time; and he sometimes felt that if it had not been for the fear lest Emily Welland should think him an ignorant fellow, he must have given up striving, for it was dry work, with no one to direct him, or share in his labor.

The Vicar was his kindest friend, and when he had spoken to Mrs. Smalley, and induced her to employ him, he walked out to the cottage where John Mills lived to tell him of it.

The young man was at his wood-carving in a small workshop or shed that he had made for himself at the side of his father's cottage. It was a pleasant place overhung by two apple-trees, into one of which a clematis plant had climbed, and a white passion-flower.

"Ah, John," said the clergyman, "I see where you got the copy for that screen that you carved for Lady G—; here are the very leaves hanging down before your shed that you have wreathed round it."

"Yes, sir," said John, "and the lilies came out of Mrs. Welland's garden.

The business that the Vicar had come about was then mentioned, and very glad was the industrious young man to undertake it; but his friend noticed that he seemed tired and looked overworked, and he said to him before taking his leave, " I am afraid you work too long at a time, John, and your father tells me you sit up at night to cipher and read."

"Ah," said John, "but a young fellow had need work hard with his learning, sir, if he wants to marry a school-mistress."

"O that 's it, is it?" replied the Vicar, kindly.

"But she," proceeded John, "she keeps so far ahead of me, that I reckon I have very little chance; as fast as I learn one thing, I find she knows another."

"And yet you do contrive to improve yourself, John; and there are your wood-carvings, too; you should show them to Emily Welland, man: if she excels in one thing, you do in another."

The young man smiled. "I have shown 'em to her, sometimes, sir," he replied; "but she calls carving 'whittling.'"

"Well, well," answered the clergyman, smiling in his turn, "but that is for want of knowing better, John, and the best wives are often not easily obtained; Emily Welland is a very superior young woman."

"Superior, sir!" replied John, warmly. "Ah, you may well say that; there's nobody like her."

That same afternoon, as Emily and her grandmother were sitting at their tea about half past four o'clock, the latter told her granddaughter that she had heard a report in the town respecting the monument which Mrs. Smalley meant to put up to her mother's memory. "It is to be a grand thing, not in the churchyard, but in the church, as I hear," said the old woman, "and they do say that John Mills is to make it."

Great was Emily's surprise, and so great her curiosity to know what sort of work John Mills could bestow on the monument, — that when her grandmother proposed that she should step into the cottage where Mills lived, and ask the particulars about this matter, she made no objection, but put on her bonnet and took her grandmother's message.

Passing through his mother's garden she reached the sunny little shed where John Mills worked, and found him with a sharp tool in his hand carving a leaf on the lid of a small box. John wiped a little bench for her to sit on, but Emily preferred to stand, leaning against the side-post of the shed looking about her. She had not entered the place for some time; and though she did not understand much about the work he was engaged in, she observed at once that some of it was very different from the common articles which she had seen produced by workmen, or even those which she had seen John Mills's father carve when she was a little child, and loved to watch him when he was cutting the angel faces for the church.

John soon told Emily what she wished to know, and added, " I was to wait on Mrs. Smalley at the White Hart before she left the town, and hear what her notions were about the stone. She wished to have an urn on it — I said I could carve that very easy, but I should like better to do a wreath of leaves."

"And why not the urn ? " said Emily.

" Why, because that is only an imitation sort of thing, that we should never have thought of putting up, only that there were nations who used to burn their dead, and they collected the ashes in urns, and when they carved a marble urn, it was a natural way of reminding them of the dead."

" I like to see folks represented on their tombs, lying with their hands up praying," said Emily.

" Yes, but that would be too expensive, too grand for what I am to do: this is to be what they call a mural tablet, and very small, just the name and age, and one text. So I proposed to carve a garland of leaves, and twist them with a ribbon, on which I could cut the words ' We all do fade as a leaf.' "

" Poor old Aunt," said Emily; "and when folks see it, they will think she was a lady, and no one will doubt that she had plenty of good clothes and lay warm and comfortable at night, and yet, John, it seems very respectable to have a monument, does n't it ? I think I should like one myself."

" Mr. Ward said once in his sermon," observed John, " ' Why should we regret that the remembrance of us

should perish from the earth, if our names are written
in heaven?'"

"How you remember the sermons, John," said Emily;
"it must be that you think of them more than I do; but
when I hear that sort of thing said, I cannot help wishing
that I was great enough to be remembered here, or good
enough, or wise enough."

"We all wish, you see, to be the upper and not the under," observed John; "now for my part, I always keep
wishing that I could carve stone as well as carving can
possibly be done, even as well as *Gibbons* carved wood; if
I could but carve like him, I think I should be happy."

John rose as he spoke, and waded among the delicate
wood-shavings to a rough table. "Look," said he. "Mr.
Clements, the gentleman that was so kind as to wish to
put me to school, came here six weeks ago, and said if I
could carve him a figure, he would take it to London and
have it valued, and whatever it was said to be worth he
would give me for it." John lifted up some coarse wet
cloths as he spoke, and exposed to view a kneeling figure
moulded in clay.

"An angel!" exclaimed Emily.

"No," said John; "I mean it for a figure of Hope.
You see it looks up, and has wings to fly upwards with;
but I have made it kneeling, to show that it is a humble
Hope. It keeps looking on and upwards; but though its
wings are spread ready for flying, you are to think that it
does not see the way yet to what it wishes to reach, and
indeed expects to reach when the time comes."

"You should have put an anchor beside her," said Emily, "and then everybody would have seen what she was;
however, she has a beautiful face, John, and she makes me
see what a different sort of thing your hope is to mine.
Do you know, I believe if you had been sent to school as
you wished, you would never have made the figure waiting
to fly because she does not see the way."

"I did not mean to put anything about myself in the figure," said John, coloring.

"But," continued Emily, "you say this Hope expects to reach whatever it is looking for, when the time comes."

"She would not be Hope if she did not," said John.

"And yet if I had made this face, I should not have let it look so calm," said Emily. "Folks are only calm when they expect and wish for nothing better than they have got. Now, I wish and expect and hope for a great deal that I have not got; and the more I do so, the less quiet I am, and the more restless I grow. John, I think if I had been you, I must have gone to learn drawing and all those fine things that Mr. Clements offered to have you taught. I can see that it was *your* duty to stay; but if I had *been you*, I am sure I could not have seen it."

"They must have gone into the workhouse if I had left them," said John.

"But then you would have come back quite a different person," proceeded Emily; "and by this time it would have all been over, and you would have taken them to live with you, and you would have been quite a grand man! — we should all have been looking up to you."

John started on hearing this thoughtless speech, and said, "Should *you* have looked up to me? — should you have liked me better then?"

Emily blushed; but she was too conscientious to let her careless words do harm, and she forced herself to say: "I should not have respected you so much as I do now; and as for liking, I like you very well as you are, — we are very good friends. And, John," she added frankly, "if you think I do not care more for you than I do, just because you are not better off, and not getting on, you are mistaken; for, to tell you the truth, I really expect that you will get on far better than I shall in the end."

John looked up surprised; but he shook his head and

laughed at her remark, and said she must be making sport of him. Still he was pleased, and ventured to ask her if she would let him copy her hands as models for his figure. " I have only pictures to copy from," he observed, "and they will not do. Mother's hand has got rough with hard work, so I have been obliged to leave the hands till I could get some to copy; and if you would hold up yours in this way, it would be such a help to me."

Emily said she would, and promised to come and sit to him the next half-holiday; and then she went home feeling far more respect than she had ever done before for poor John, and wishing she could follow his good example; for she had sense enough to perceive his simplicity, his strong feeling of duty, and his industry, while at the same time she felt and acknowledged to herself that she could not make up her mind to be so straightforward in the pursuit of what was right at all risks. " I am sure I could not do it," she thought; "and what a good thing it is that I have no call to give up an advantage for the sake of relations and parents ! "

On the appointed evening Emily took her work and went to John's cottage to have her hands copied for the figure. She knocked at his mother's door about five o'clock in the afternoon, but John, whom she had expected to find waiting for her, was not at home ; he had gone to the town to fetch some medicine for his father, who was suffering much from pain in his lame hand.

Emily found that she was in the way, for the sick man was very fretful and restless; she therefore withdrew to the shed, and sat down on a bench just within its wide door, taking out her knitting to occupy the time. There were strange things in this shed; grim old stone heads with features broken and defaced, quaint carvings which had been brought from a neighboring church to be copied ; and, standing on a settle, several large jugs full of field-flowers, apple boughs with fruit on them, delicate trailing tendrils of ivy and hedge creepers which John had collected to copy his carvings from.

The floor was strewed thickly with dust, yet the shed looked comfortable, and even neat; and the kneeling figure, which John had set ready for Emily's visit, seemed to her to have grown more beautiful since she had seen it last.

"It is all very fine," thought Emily, "to be able to make such beautiful things, but poor John will not earn much by this, I should think; — let me see, I should say that, if I was kneeling down in that position, my foot could not be seen by any one standing facing me, — I'll just try."

Emily accordingly knelt down, arranged herself and her dress as nearly as she could in the attitude of the figure, put up her hands, and found that it was as she had thought, — the foot, unless a little twisted, could not be seen. Before she rose, a sudden diminution of light made her look up to a hole in the back of the shed which was roughly fitted with one pane of glass. She saw a face looking in. It was not John's face, and she started up, and hastily took her work and sat down again on a stool, while the owner of the face walked round the shed and presented himself at the door.

Emily looked up and saw an elderly gentleman with a pleasant countenance : in fact he was smiling.

"Good evening," said the gentleman, "are you John Mills's sister?"

"No, sir," replied Emily, "only a neighbor."

"I am come to see the figure he is to model for me. Ah! very good; did the boy do this entirely himself, I wonder? Very good, very good indeed, poor fellow."

"Yes, sir," said Emily, who supposed that she was expected to say something.

"You take an interest in it, I see," said the gentleman, still smiling.

"I promised John that I would sit to him for the hands," said Emily, a little vexed ; "but I knelt down just now to see whether the foot was right, sir, for I thought it was not."

"How should it be, poor fellow, when he has had no education?" replied the elderly gentleman. "No, I will do what I can for him ; but his is a case of genius wasted, talent obscured for want of knowledge. The foot is wrong decidedly, as you say, but the face is exquisite." .

"Yes, sir," repeated Emily.

"I am sorry the poor fellow is such a fool," continued the gentleman, to Emily's surprise ; "talk of duty! a man's first duty is to himself. Charity begins at home ; that is to say, with number one. Don't you think so, young woman?"

"No, sir," replied Emily.

"Well, well," said the gentleman, "no more do I ; but really it is such a shame to think of genius like this lost and wasted for want of training, that it makes one talk at random, and puts one out of temper. He'll never be anything but a superior sort of cabinet-maker all his life ; he does not understand the first principles of art."

Emily had no answer to make to this : she went on with her work, and was considering whether she could withdraw, when the gentleman who had been scanning John's model with great attention, turned to her and said : —

"Have you got a gown made of any kind of heavy woollen material that is not stiff?"

"Yes, sir," said Emily, very much surprised.

"Well," he answered, "if you would do me the favor to put it on and come here, I would show John how to make these folds more simple."

Emily was very good-natured, and therefore, though she would rather some one else had been found to perform the kind office for John, she did not hesitate to go home and take out her winter gown, which, though neither bright-colored nor new, certainly was just what the gentleman had required : it was very heavy, and had no stiffness in it. She put it on, and came back to the shed, where she found John as well as his patron.

"Thank you, I am much obliged to you," said the gentleman, "that is exactly what I wanted ; now will you be good enough to place yourself in the attitude of the figure ?"

Emily did so, and the heavy clothing fell about her, as she could herself see, in larger and more simple folds than those which John had chosen ; she continued to kneel while John stood at a distance with his patron, who pointed out to him very openly the defects in his drapery, and desired that he would remark the effect of the evening sunlight upon it. "But this," said he, "is such a little place that you really cannot retire far enough, either from your model or your work, to see how they look : yours is indeed the pursuit of art under difficulties ; however, if your young neighbor will sit to you frequently, and if you study what books you can get, it is just possible you may do something worth mentioning, — just possible. Well, I am pleased with the figure on the whole, John. If your young neighbor will allow you to sketch these folds before she rises, she will confer a favor."

So saying, he nodded to John, made a little bow to Emily, and went away.

"Now, John," said Emily, "if you wish to draw my gown, — the worst and ugliest gown I have got, — please to be quick, and begin."

John did not look like himself ; he was very grave and serious ; even Emily's presence did not seem to cheer him, for he heaved a deep sigh as he went to fetch a coarse sheet of paper and a carpenter's red pencil.

"John," said Emily, "what are you thinking of —"

John repeated Mr. Clements's words: "'It is just possible you may do something worth mentioning, — just possible,' that was what I was thinking of," he said.

"He did not say so because he thought you wanted wits," said Emily, "but only because you had not had schooling to teach you how to do this sort of thing. So you need not be so desponding; you may be able to get good instruction after all."

"I don't expect it," replied John; "father's hand has been very bad all day and very full of pain, and I went to the doctor for his medicine, and asked what he thought of the case. Says he, 'I am afraid he will never be any better; indeed I see nothing else for him but being crippled in his hands altogether.'"

"I am sure I am heartily sorry," said Emily.

"Mr. Clements is very good in ordering things of me," observed John; "but I hardly know how it is; he makes me feel miserable after he is gone, at least till I have had time to come to myself: he has a way of putting things that makes the things I wish for most seem to be a duty, when I know that they would be sins. He said to-day: 'Well, young man, sometimes I think I must give you up, for you have neither the real good of your family nor your own good at heart. You won't be at the trouble of learning.'"

"What did you say to that?" asked Emily.

"I said I could not see that it would be for the real good of my family to go to the workhouse. 'Yes,' says Mr. Clements, 'it would, if you could raise yourself in the mean time, so that in a few years you could take them out and make them a handsome allowance.'"

"There seems something in that, John," said Emily; "it does not sound so unkind when he puts it in that way."

"He said to-night, 'You have no ambition,'" observed John. "'O yes, I have, sir,' says I; and I thought to myself, though I would not say it to a gentleman that does not seem to think much about religion, — I thought that perhaps he would give me up altogether if he knew how many times a day I said over to myself the prayer in the Litany:—

"'From all blindness of heart, from pride, vain-glory, and hypocrisy, Good Lord, deliver us.'"

Emily did not answer. John went on diligently drawing the folds of her gown, and presently added: "That prayer seems to me sometimes as if it was made on purpose for me. Blindness of heart is just the thing that comes over me when I want to go to that school; everything seems to change, and I can't see that it's my duty to maintain father and mother, nor to stop and finish father's work that he has promised and cannot do; it all seems as if it really was my duty to go, till I pray that I may be delivered from the blindness; and then I can see that, if any other young fellow was in my place, I should think his duty was plain enough; but I did not mean to preach to you, Emily."

The evening sun was now going down, and its rays lighted up the shed and the jugs of flowers, and the figure and face of Emily Welland, as she knelt quietly with her hands folded while John sketched the folds of her gown. She was very silent, and her face became serious and thoughtful; indeed she was thinking much, and those thoughts were important to her and to John.

She had felt, while he last spoke, how far more upright and earnest was his mind than her own; she had also felt that, while she was with him, her worldly and ambitious views and wishes for herself often faded into the background. She always felt herself to be his superior as far as knowledge went, she had received such a good education; but in good principle and a desire to do her duty, she was so sensible that he was her superior, that she

could not be with him for an hour without seeing fresh
proofs of it. "I do not know such a good young man,"
she thought; "and as for liking him, I really think I shall
never find another that will come up to him. Did n't he
say the other day that he had never wished in his life to
marry any other woman, but that he could not believe
there was such a happy lot in this world as his would be
if he could win me? Well, I like him very much, and if
I did marry him I feel sure he would make me better; but
then, — there would be an end to all my hopes of rising. I
could not go to London; I should be a poor working-man's
wife. No, I must not do it: I will not come here often,
or he will make me respect him and like him so much that
it will end in my promising to marry him. I am sorry he
is only a working man; really I am very sorry for him,
poor John!"

"Emily," said John, with a sigh, "it is finished now; I
am very much obliged to you. I never had such a pleasant half-hour before; it quite made me forget Mr. Clements
and all my troubles; but the drawing is finished. What
have you been thinking of this long while, Emily? I wish
I knew."

"I have not been thinking of anything that would please
you," replied Emily, rising and gently shaking the saw-
dust and shavings from her gown. "Well, as you have
done, John, I must go, for grandmother will be waiting for
her supper."

The sun was now getting low, and just as the last sunbeam disappeared from her face, and ceased to light up
the shed, his mother came to the open door, and told him
his father's hand was so painful that he must go again to
the doctor and see if he would come and try to relieve it.

So John went away: and as Emily stepped out into the
quiet evening air, talking with John's poor care-worn
mother, she felt that it was a hard thing to be a poor man's

wife, and see him disabled and not capable of doing anything for her and his children, while at the same time so much of her time was occupied in nursing him that she could not go out herself to work and earn something towards their support.

The next day poor Mills was very ill, and from that time for five weeks he lay in bed suffering with rheumatic fever, and unable to feed himself or turn his feeble head on the pillow. His wife and his son spared no pains to nurse him, and denied themselves many comforts in order to pay for his medicines and medical attendance. At first all looked as neat and comfortable as usual about them, but as time wore on and he got no better, the garden became full of weeds, and the vegetables were left to run to seed; the little girls, instead of going to school so clean and tidy, began to look ragged and forlorn; John's mother became haggard and pale with watching and fatigue, and John himself grew thin, his cheeks hollow, and his eyes dim.

CHAPTER III.

EMILY did not see Mrs. Smalley any more before
she left the town; and as she had to teach in the
daytime, and very often to go to Miss Cooper also in the
evening to receive lessons from her, she had not very
much time to spend in thinking about leaving her present
occupation and taking to dress-making; but the more
she did think, the less she liked that a situation such as
Miss Cooper filled was to be her ultimate position in life,
when her relation lived in luxury, and had so many advantages and pleasures.

Poor Emily! she did not know, or she forgot, that
while one dress-maker rises to riches and lives in luxury,
five hundred struggle with poverty, and barely earn a
maintenance.

She forgot that health as well as skill, and patrons as
well as industry, were wanted, and she constantly said
to herself, "Let me only get to London to Mrs. Smalley,
who has no child to leave her business to, and I will
engage to be a good workwoman; and then, if I make
myself useful to her, she may get fond of me, and I
may be her successor, and live in that fine house of hers,
— who knows?"

By frequently thinking thus, she brought herself to believe at last that, let her only find her way to Mrs. Smalley,
and her fortune was made; and she began to dislike the
work that she now had to do, and to think that, as she had
made up her mind not to be a schoolmistress, there was
no need for her to prepare so industriously for the examination.

She was teaching a class one afternoon, and it seemed to her that they did not read so well as usual. The little ones spelled the words and lingered over them till she became quite tired of their sounds. It was part of her duty, to question the children on the texts they read. When the one, — " And having food and raiment, let us be therewith content," had been finished, she proceeded as usual to ascertain whether they understood it; while, at the same time, her own thoughts continually strayed to the subject that now so constantly occupied them.

"What does food mean, children ? "

" What we eat, ma'am."

"What does raiment mean ? "

" What we have to wear, — Sunday clothes and work-a-day clothes."

" What does content mean ? "

Silence in the class.

" Come, you know very well; you had it explained to you in the gallery this morning."

" It 's what we all ought to be," said one.

" It 's very wicked not to be contented," remarked another.

"Very true," thought Emily ; but she added aloud, " Tell ·me the texts that you were taught ; perhaps they may help you to explain what it is to be content."

" ' Be content with such things as ye have : for He hath said, I will never leave thee, nor forsake thee.' It means that they were to be satisfied, ma'am."

" To be sure ; I knew you could tell me if you would give your mind to it. Now tell me the other text."

" ' For I have learned, in whatsoever state I am, therewith to be content.' "

" Who said that ? "

" St. Paul did, ma'am."

" Ought we to be contented, then, as he was ? " — " Dear

me," thought Emily, "how strange that I should have to
teach them this, when I feel so differently!"—"Ought we
to be contented, children?"

"Yes, ma'am."

"Why should we be? Who is it that orders how much
money and how much food we shall have, and whether we
shall be laboring folks or gentle-folks?"

"God does. Everything belongs to God."

"Then God could easily give us a great deal more than
we have if he chose, and if it was good for us?"

"Yes, sure."

"And does God love us?"

"Yes, ma'am."

"How do we know that?"

"Because he gave his Son to die for us."

"Then, if it was good for us, we may be quite sure that
he would give us more; and so we ought to be content,
because God knows best, and he has only given us a little."

Emily sighed as she finished her lesson, for the reason-
ing did not content her. She had spoken to her grandmother respecting her wish to go to London, and had told
her what Mrs. Smalley had said. Rather to her surprise,
the promise given that she should be received and taught
dress-making had delighted her grandmother, who had
sajd at once that she should like it to be accepted as soon
as she was out of her apprenticeship.

Emily therefore walked to the Vicarage when school
was over, to tell the Vicar her determination; and as she
went she thought of her own lesson, specially of the last
words, "because God knows best, and he has only given
us *a little.*" "I am not so sure of that," thought Emily;
"I do not believe one of those children ever wanted a
meal, or a decent suit of clothes; they are at school, too,
and have tolerably comfortable homes; so, while they are
children, they are almost as well off as children can be. *I*

have only a little, for I know of so much more ; but that has nothing to do with the duty of being contented ; for St. Paul was contented even when he suffered want, which I have never done."

Emily reached the Vicarage, and asked if she might see Mr. Ward. Her heart beat a little when she was shown into his study ; but she managed to explain her errand, and added that she had thought it her duty to speak thus early, that there might be time to select a person to fill her place.

Mr. Ward looked very much vexed, but he said not a word ; and Emily, feeling more doubtful as to whether she was doing rightly than she had ever felt before, went on explaining her reasons, till she began to see that they were not very satisfactory, nor very creditable to herself. At last Mr. Ward spoke : —

" You have quite made up your mind to this, Emily Welland ? "

" Yes, sir."

" Because," he added, " this dress-making affair seems to me to be a sad descent in life for you, — what people would call a come-down."

" Sir ! " exclaimed Emily, astonished at this view of the case.

" It may be your duty to go," continued the Vicar ; " and I suppose you consider that it is, as you are so decided about it. If so, I could not conscientiously oppose it ; but if not, it really seems to me to be throwing away all your present advantages, and lowering yourself for nothing."

" I never thought it was a duty, sir ; nothing of the sort," exclaimed Emily.

" What do you think it, then ? " replied the Vicar.

" An advantage, sir," said Emily.

" What ! to be a needlewoman ? "

"O no, sir; not a common needlewoman. I should be with Mrs. Smalley."

"But you would have to begin at the beginning, would you not?"

"Of course I should have to learn the business, sir." ·

"And, as you have already learned one business, to begin another would be throwing yourself back, especially if the second business was inferior to the first."

"But, sir," said Emily, "if the second did not suit, I could return to the first."

"I do not understand much about feminine occupations," replied Mr. Ward, "and therefore I cannot tell whether dress-making would unfit you for teaching; but it seems strange that you should wish to try."

"I might rise to be like Mrs. Smalley," replied Emily.

"The person who called on me about a gravestone?"

Mr. Ward did not intend to speak slightingly, but his unintentional mention of her as the "person" vexed Emily, for it made her see that he had not been deceived for a moment into supposing that she was a lady.

"Yes, sir," said Emily; "she is my cousin, and has made a good property by dress-making."

"I suppose she has made you some promise of taking you into partnership, or leaving you her business, as you seem so anxious to throw up a certainty for the sake of joining her."

"O no, sir; she only said she would teach me the business."

"Well, Emily Welland, you must do as you please."

"Then you do not approve, sir? I thought, as it seemed a rise in life for me, you would think it my duty to close with it."

"We differ as to whether it is a rise; and if it was, that would by no means make me think it your *duty* to accept it. It is, as you know, a duty to fit ourselves for the station in which it has pleased God to place us. It may be natural, it may be allowable, it may be advantageous, to try to rise from it; but in this case I cannot see the duty. You are placed where you are by Providence, that is to say, your present position has arisen out of circumstances which took place without your will or ordering. As a little child you were put to school; you were quick, and rose to be a monitor; then, as you were not strong enough for hard work, and showed an aptitude for learning, you were made a pupil-teacher; then, as you proved apt at teaching, you became a teacher, and looked forward to being a schoolmistress. You now wish to break away from your place and station, and step into a different sphere. I will not say anything about rising or sinking, for that has really nothing to do with the matter. You wish to change your occupation; then you should first have reason to think that you are not throwing aside work which Providence has assigned to you, and are not rashly making work for yourself which it was never intended you should do."

Emily sat silent a few moments, and then answered rather despondingly : —

" I do not see how any one is ever to rise, or to change, sir, if it is not right to do it without being sure beforehand that he is not leaving work assigned to him by Providence."

" I will show you what I mean. If teaching had not suited your health; if you had found that you had no natural power to manage children, and could not acquire it; moreover, if you had felt that you had not aptitude for learning the things required of you, and I, feeling it too, had asked you to look out for another situation: then, if Mrs. Smalley, coming here, had said, ' Emily Welland, I will teach you dress-making,' I should have said, ' By all means go with her; here is a provision offered to you in the course of Providence.' "

Again Emily pondered; but teaching had become distasteful to her now that she had some definite prospect in view to take its place, and she therefore replied that she would think of what Mr. Ward had said, and took her leave.

She walked home in no very pleasant frame of mind, and felt especially vexed at Mr. Ward's remark as to dress-making being no rise for her. "Does he mean to compare Mrs. Smalley," she thought, "who dresses in the handsomest silks and lace, has a handsome house and a footman, and such plenty of money that she even talks of retiring and living on her means, — does he mean to compare her with Miss Cooper, who has but one silk gown, has scarcely saved a hundred pounds, and works as hard as a servant? Surely, Mr. Ward must be joking, or, perhaps, as he has taken a good deal of pains with me, he does not like me to leave the school just as I am beginning to be useful, and so said what he could to make me dislike dress-making."

She walked up to her grandmother's cottage-door, and was met by the old woman, who asked her whether she had been to inquire how their poor neighbor was. "I hear he was worse yesterday," she observed, "and Mr. Ward came to read with him."

Emily turned and walked up her neighbor's garden to the cottage: the onion-beds were overgrown with weeds, and the cabbage-leaves reduced to mere skeletons by the multitudes of green caterpillars that now fed on them undisturbed; everything told of neglect and poverty, and the dirty blinds and uncleaned windows, added to the desolate appearance of the place. "Poor folks!" thought Emily, "it is not their fault. John has hardly time to get his work done and run errands for the things his poor father wants, and in the evenings he has other things to do than to weed the garden. As to Mrs. Mills, I wonder how she contrives to sit up night after night. It is plain that this long illness is a terrible misfortune to them."

Emily tapped at the door, and John's mother answered it, and coming out and shutting it behind her, stood outside a few minutes to talk to her young neighbor. She said John had been up all the previous night, and was now asleep ; and her forlorn appearance and weary air touched Emily's heart, but at the same time she thought, "Should I look like this in the course of years if I married John ?" for, strange to say, though she had made up her mind not to marry him, she constantly reasoned with herself as to the propriety of thus rejecting him· in a manner which showed how much she really respected and liked him. His mother, without intending it, strengthened Emily's resolution that evening by remarking that her son had been obliged to pawn his best clothes, and sell some of their furniture, in order to pay the rent and the doctor.

Emily was sincerely sorry for them, and as she went home again, and saw the three little girls bickering together under the walnut-tree, and one of them fretting and crying, she turned aside to ask what was the matter.

" Sally would make her hands all black with pricking the green walnuts," observed the elder child, " and mother had said she was not to do it," so they had taken them from her.

Sally, a stout ruddy little girl of seven years old, was very sulky, and sat shaking her shoulders and crying ; her hair was all tangled, her frock torn, and her pinafore dirty.

" If I were you, instead of quarrelling out here," said Emily to the children, " I should ask mother to lend the little tub, and I should wash out these dirty pinafores."

" Father won't let us be in the house," said the elder child ; " he can't abide any noise."

" You might set the tub out of doors," replied Emily.

15 *

" Mother has no soap," was the quick answer; " she used up the last bit washing out a shirt for John."

" Well, at any rate, you might mend Sally's frock; look what a state it is in ; a great girl nearly eleven years old ought to be able to mend all the younger children's clothes."

" Mother said she would see to them herself one day," drawled out the little girl ; and a squabble beginning again about the walnuts, Emily withdrew, for she found she could not make any impression, and was shocked to see what a change a few weeks' neglect had made in these once orderly and cleanly children.

The next day was Sunday, and John when he got up dressed himself for the first time in his life in his threadbare working clothes ; his father, when he came into the living-room, was asleep in his settle-bed. His mother, who had been up all night, was also sleeping with her weary head resting on her arms. John sat down and looked about him ; he felt wretched, and so low in his spirits that when the eight o'clock chime began to ring he could hardly refrain from tears, and he wished it was not Sunday. " I got on pretty well through the week," he thought, " but to wear these old fustian clothes to-day is very hard. What shall I do all day ? Go to church I cannot of course ; and as to books, I've none — that I have not read over and over again, now that I have left off subscribing to the Institute." So saying he got up, and went softly out of the room to his shed, where he sat wearily, looking about him for half an hour, when his three little sisters came in, one with part of a loaf under her arm, and a second with a teapot in her hand.

" Mother said they must have their breakfast in the shed," they told him, " for father was then asleep." John cut some bread for them, and reached down a mug in which were some branches that he had been drawing from, washed it, and gave each child a mug of the cold tea from the teapot ; he then took some himself; and there was something so desolate and sad in his appearance, that the children were made silent by it, and sat quietly before him waiting till he should speak. At last John looked up, and his face cleared. " I have been a long time thinking, but I have made up my mind now, children," said he. " It is too late for the Sunday school, but Polly do you go up stairs and get your Sunday bonnets, and bring a comb to make your hair smooth, and I shall take you all to church."

Great was the surprise of the children. John go to church in his working clothes? they could not have thought it ! — but they could easily go, for mother had not pawned their best tippets, and there was one clean pinafore yet for each of them at the bottom of the box ; so they went to the pump in the garden and washed their hands and faces, that their father might not be disturbed by any noise in the house ; and then their clean pinafores and tippets and their decent little bonnets were brought, and they were ready.

When John saw them, he thought they looked better than could have been expected ; but all the brushing that . he could give to his clothes did not make him look like anything different to a working man in a very shabby suit of working clothes.

" Giving up the clothes I pawned, seemed nothing," thought poor John ; " that was a duty to father, and I did not grudge it; but to go to church and show myself to everybody just as I am now, seems the hardest duty that ever I had to perform. Come, children," said John aloud. " It 's time we were off; but there 's no harm in our going the back way."

" Lass," exclaimed old Mrs. Welland, as she was taking off her neat black bonnet and her new shawl, after the morning service; "Emily lass, come here, there's John coming up the garden with his work-day suit on."

"Yes, grandmother," said Emily, "he has been to church."

"Church! go to church like a pauper?"

"I suppose it was his duty to go, grandmother, and his mother told me they had made away with their best clothes."

"Duty, duty!" repeated her grandmother; "don't talk to I, Ellie. If folks can't go respectable and decent, they'd better not go at all."

"No, grandmother, you don't think that; if you had to pawn your best things, you might feel that you would not go to church; but surely you respect them that will."

"The girl talks like a good book," replied Mrs. Welland, shaking out her shawl, and folding it carefully; "she always does; but wait till thy Sunday things be at pawnshop, and —"

"And see what I shall do," interrupted Emily. "Why, grandmother, I don't think my pride would let me go and show myself as John did this morning; but for all that, I know he did right."

John did not know that as he walked up the little garden his neighbors had observed him through their casement. The fact was, John was much more comfortable than he had felt for some time; he had gone to church as a painful duty, and in its performance his obedience to the demand of conscience had been rewarded by a feeling of peace and comfort, that made him wonder he had been so much cast down. There was no change in his circumstances; his father was still very ill, his mother weary, his house and garden going to wrack, and poverty creeping upon those whom he had long worked for; but his heart was lightened, and as the prayers went on, often texts came into his mind which soothed and quieted it, and specially one which was

still consoling him as he walked up to his cottage home, —
" Casting all your care upon Him, for He careth for you."

His father, when he entered, was rather more free from
pain than usual, and was pleased when his dutiful son gave
him an account of the sermon, and read a chapter to him
while his wife prepared their dinner.

This, though not what they had been accustomed to in
their better days, was more ample than they could afford
on ordinary occasions ; and when the sick man saw it,
and saw his little girls neat and clean as of old, it revived
his spirits, and he said he would sit up, and try if he could
eat a little with them.

In the afternoon John sent the children to the Sunday
school, and sat with his father, while his mother went and
lay down to sleep on the children's bed.

It was well that John had that quiet Sunday, and that
he made up his mind early to go to church in spite of his
shabby clothes, or in spite of his fear lest Emily and her
grandmother should look upon him as sinking in life and
losing his respectability. If he had yielded to temptation
on that first Sunday, the same reason would have existed
for his absence the next, and the next, and he would have
lost his peace of mind, and all the comfort that he derived
from worshipping God in the clothes that it was now his
duty to wear.

For the next two months no contrast could be greater
than that between the circumstances of these two families.
Comfort, cleanliness, order, and competence in that of the
Wellands's. Misery and sickness, poverty and disorder, in
that of the Mills's.

The poor suffering father became fretful and hard to
please ; he knew that his illness was wearing out his wife's
health, and he saw his son grow thinner and paler every
day, while he was often disturbed by the noise made in the
garden by his neglected children, whom he could no longer

afford to keep at school, and who became daily more fretful and unruly for want of something to do, and some one to look after them.

Emily all this time went daily to the school, and came back in the evening fresh and cheerful, very often with a parcel in her hand; for she had saved a few pounds, and was now spending them in buying for herself a handsome assortment of new clothes, such as she thought would do her credit with Mrs. Smalley.

Often and often, as Emily sat at work in the now short evenings, John Mills saw her from his shed. He used to work there with a common lamp, and its light shining through the one pane of glass before mentioned, served to remind Emily of how hard he worked, and how late, for she often went to bed long before this light was withdrawn. He was still busy on his figure of Hope. But it was Emily whose heart was full of hope; his heart sank lower daily at the prospect before him and his parents, and he often worked far into the night with a trembling hand and a stomach faint from want of food.

One night in November, after dark, some one rapped at Mrs. Welland's door, and John entered, his eyes sparkling, his cheeks flushed, and his whole appearance excited and eager. Emily was standing up holding a pretty pink muslin dress, almost too light and gay to be serviceable to one in her rank of life. She had just finished it, and as John came in she was saying to her grandmother, "That is a good thing done : I am so glad I have finished all these flounces." John thought he had never seen Emily look so pretty before, for she too was flushed, and her eyes sparkled with pleasure as she looked at the dress.

" She will look just like a lady in it," he thought, and he glanced down at his own threadbare garments and shabby shoes.

"You are quite a stranger, John," said the grandmother kindly.

John could not answer; he had not wished Emily to
see him with unmended shoes and patched coat, and had
therefore absented himself from her lately; but now a
sudden feeling of triumph had made him forget his shyness for the time, and it was not till he opened the door
and saw the comfort that reigned within, — the cosy fire,
the pretty Emily with her new dress, and the grandmother
frying bacon for supper, — that a sense of his inferior
circumstances and the poverty and distress of his home
made him feel more strongly than he had ever done before, how much his wished-for wife was out of his reach.
"I have finished my figure," he at length stammered out,
"and though she is not as pretty a thing to look at as
your pink dress, I thought perhaps, — I wished you would
come and look at her, Emily."

"I will to-morrow, John," replied Emily.

"Not to-night?" asked John, "do come to-night; I
have stuck up two candles to light the shed, and she
looks much better by candlelight than by daylight."

"Go, Emmy," said the grandmother, "and John, lad,
do thou come back to supper with us."

In the days when John was more prosperous and Emily
less ambitious, she would not have been so willing to
comply with his wishes; but there was something so sad
in his gaunt face and so humble in his manner, that she
had not the heart to refuse, and she laid aside her delicate muslin gown, and put a shawl over her head.

It was a very mild, calm night, and Emily stepped
through the little garden over a carpet of poplar leaves
with which the paths were covered, greatly to their advantage, as she thought, for they served to hide the
weeds. John had borrowed a lantern of old Mrs. Welland, and he held it low as Emily walked that she might
not tread on the borders.

· John had gone without his dinner that day, and spent the twopence that it would have cost him in buying four candles to light up the shed, for he had a great wish to see how his figure would look by candle-light. Two of these candles were set in rude blocks of wood, and the others were held by two of his little sisters, who, when Emily entered, were standing solemnly just where he had placed them, throwing the light full on to the figure of Hope, which was set in its usual place on the rough wooden table.

Emily had intended to say something kind and sympathizing to John about his work that had cost him so much trouble and care ; but when she saw it, everything she had thought of went out of her head, and she stood gazing at it as silent and motionless as the children with the lights.

What a wonderful circumstance, that out of all his misery, poverty, and care, should have come that snowy white thing with a rapturous face, hands so devoutly folded, a smile so calm and holy, and wings that seemed to Emily so buoyant and ready to fly, that every time the children's stirring altered the shadows on them, they seemed to waver and move, as if ready to spread themselves and bear John's beautiful Hope away !

While Emily stood fixed in surprise and admiration, John's mother came in and said, "If Mr. Clements does not give him two pounds for that, I shall say it is a · shame."

"O, at the very least it ought to be two pounds," echoed Emily ; and she looked at John, who smiled.

Emily caught the meaning of the look, and said, "You expect more ? "

"I would take less," answered John ; "but I am sure it is worth more."

"That's the first conceited thing ever I heard thee say, lad," observed his mother, with a sigh.

" I did not say I *expected* more than two pounds, mother," replied John, "so you need not be uneasy. I shall let Mr. Clements have it if he only gives me five-and-twenty shillings, for whatever I get for it will be extra. I have not spent one regular working-hour upon it yet, when I had work to do."

" When is Mr. Clements coming to see it?" asked Emily.

" He has seen it," said the mother; "he came this afternoon just afore dark, when John was out."

" And what did he say?"

" Said nothing good nor bad, but sat on the block staring at it and whistling to himself, till my poor legs ached with standing behind him."

" Strange man," said Emily; "did n't he even say he liked it?"

" Not he, but sat till it got so dusk he could n't see it well; then got up and walked out. ' The lad has done it,' says he, 'and I 'm no prophet. Good evening, good woman,' and off he goes."

" Then it is better than he expected," said Emily, " I am sure of it."

" He did not expect that he would be so quick in the carving of it," continued the mother; "he has only had the alabaster three months."

" I should have been a vast deal longer upon it, you know, mother," said John, " if I had not been unfortunately out of work the last five weeks."

" That," thought Emily, "is no doubt the reason why they have been obliged to pawn so many of their things," but she did not say anything.

John continued. " It has been in hand for six months, and I may say it has been in my mind for two years, and I have drawn something like it over and over again, but could not get it to my fancy; at last I took to modelling it, and

w

then I was ignorant enough to be pretty well pleased, till Mr. Clements showed me so many faults."

" And after all this thinking and toiling you will let it go for two pounds," interrupted Emily ; "why, John, that is little more than two weeks' wages."

" Two pounds would pay our bread bill," said John, " and Mr. Clements will show the figure, and try to get me orders for more ; of course I would not do another for the same sum of money, but while this first one stops here nobody sees it, and no good comes of it."

" To be sure," said the mother, "whatever Mr. Clements will give, that John should take, say I ; for he has now got the promise of some common work, and that 's regular wages, much better than toiling and wearing out his strength with making fine things for gentle-folks ; but now he has had his way, and a very handsome thing he has made, I will say, poor boy, though I was always against his meddling with those fiddle-faddle things ; I would a deal better see him cutting common mouldings as his father did before him."

" But you see, mother," remarked John, " I am very ambitious ; I am not content to do common work ; I want to do the best kind of work that there is to be done in my calling, and I want to do it in the best kind of way."

" Well, lad," retorted the mother, " I wish thou was n't ambitious ; as far as I can see, ambition after this fine work makes thee often go with a hungry stomach."

As John had never neglected any common work for the sake of the finer sort, and had walked many a weary mile lately in search of it, he felt the injustice of his mother's speech ; and when his little sister said, " I know John's clemmed * to-night, for he had no dinner, and that 's all along of the figure," he felt extremely angry, and would perhaps have answered sharply, if his mother had not add-

---

* " Clemmed " — pinched with hunger.

ed, " I must go to the father, he will be wanting me ; and
John, lad, don't keep the candles lighted long, they will last
us a week in the house."

John put out three of the candles as she spoke, and took
the fourth in his hand to the door.

" Good-by, Mrs. Mills," said Emily ; " John, good-night,
and thank you for a sight of the figure. O, I forgot, you
are coming in to supper with us."

" No, thank you," said John ; and he colored and looked
so thoroughly vexed and ashamed, that Emily could not
press him ; she knew he was too proud to come and satisfy
his hunger at their table, now that his little sister had said
he was clemmed.

" Poor lad ! " thought Emily, as she reached her comfortable bower, and turning her head, saw John still standing in the open doorway of the shed, with the candle in his
hand ; " poor lad ! he looks very thin and pale. What is
he doing now, I wonder ? "

The night was so perfectly calm that the candle burned
in John's hand quite steadily, and its light enabled Emily
to see him distinctly, though he could not see her ; and
she watched him going with rather an eager face along
the little path that was strewed with poplar leaves, and
picking up leaf after leaf till he had collected a handful.

" What does he want with them ? " she thought ; " he
cannot make a supper of them ; I wish he could ; going to
carve them, I reckon. As the candle shines on them they
look as yellow as gold." She went in and ate her supper ;
then, before going to bed, went out of doors again to shut
the cottage-shutters, and then saw John in the shed with
the candle, and the door wide open ; he had a large sheet
of paper stretched before him on his rough easel, and she
saw that he was intently drawing upon it, and that he still
held the leaves in his left hand.

As long as the candle afforded him light, and till it was

burned down into the socket, and his hands were chilled with the night air, John went on with his drawing, and when he at length crept into the cottage he felt glad and elated, though very hungry; and he fell asleep pleased to think that one thing he had worked at was finished as well as he knew how to do it, and that another was begun which promised to be better.

"I quite forgot to ask how John was getting on with poor old aunt's monument," said Emily the next morning to her grandmother. "Not getting on at all," was the reply. And then Emily heard, to her surprise, that John, having told Mrs. Smalley he could not afford to buy the stone for the work, she had said that when he was ready to begin carving she would advance the money for it. Accordingly John had written some time before this to say that he was ready to begin, and that a letter had, after a long delay, been sent back, written by one of the assistants in the business, and that it declared Mrs. Smalley to be far too much engaged to attend to the matter at present, but that she would write when she was at liberty.

"His mother told me so yesterday," observed Mrs. Welland. "It shows what a power of business she has."

"Yes; but it shows that she forgets what consequence it is to poor folks to be paid at the proper time," said Emily. "Now, all the time that John has been out of work he might have been finishing the monument." As Emily was soon about to place herself with Mrs. Smalley, she was particularly sorry to find that she was careless and inconsiderate in fulfilling her promises, and she several times made inquiries as to whether the money had arrived, but always with the same result.

There is no need for me to describe all that took place in these two families till Christmas-time; it is enough to say that Emily worked hard, both at her examination papers and her clothes ; and when the Christmas holidays began, she was spoken of by Miss Cooper as the most promising and clever, as well as the best-informed pupil-teacher that she had ever had under her care. "She would be sure of a first-class certificate if she would keep to her present employment," said Miss Cooper ; "indeed, she is quite fit to take my place even now."

But no ; Emily had done her duty by her scholars, and had completed the course of instruction appointed for her. She did not intend to do anything further, and when the examiner commended her, and paid over to her what she had earned, she thanked him, and went home resolved never to enter the school-room any more.

It cost her some pain to take leave of Miss Cooper, and of those children whom she had brought on in their learning ; but she did it, shut the school-house door after her, came home with the money in her pocket, and began with her grandmother to calculate what it would cost her to go up to London.

The same night a letter was written to Mrs. Smalley, who had said that she could receive Emily at any time, but should require two days' notice ; and now all seemed to smile on the industrious girl. All her new clothes were ready; her books were in excellent order ; "And no doubt," thought Emily, "I shall have time for reading and improving myself; all I have to do is to buy myself two boxes, pack up my things, and take leave of my friends."

. But it so happened that the next day, when old Mrs. Welland went to the farmer's wife for whom she sold butter, she sat down in the kitchen, and related Emily's intention of leaving the town for London ; and the farmer's wife observed that it was a long, long journey for a young girl to take alone.

"O, she is a steady girl," said the farmer. "But it is a

mighty long way, and she will get in just at night, and London is full of sharpers and thieves, as we all know. I would not let her go all alone if she was mine ; she may be robbed at the station, she may get her pocket picked, and nobody knows what mischief."

"What you do say, sir, be terrible true," replied the grandmother.

"There's Mr. Glover the ironmonger going up the day after to-morrow," observed the wife ; "why should n't she go with him ? I'll engage to say he would see her into a cab with her boxes."

"Is it so far that she cannot walk to Mrs. Smalley's ?" asked old Mrs. Welland.

"Bless you," said the farmer, "she can't walk five or six miles in London as she might do hereabouts ; and what is to be done with her luggage, if she did ? No, no ; depend on it she ought to go with somebody that knows London ; do you speak to Mr. Glover, and it will be all right."

So the grandmother did speak to Mr. Glover, who seemed to think it was highly necessary that a young country girl like Emily should have somebody to look after and protect her, and, though he made a great favor of it, he said he would see her safe to London, and put her and her boxes into a cab, if requested.

When Emily heard of this she was very sorry, for she wished to have an answer from Mrs. Smalley before she set off, and she did not like to start from home in such a hurry ; however, her grandmother drew such a picture of the terrors of London, as represented both by the farmer and the ironmonger, that she consented to go with the latter, and began to pack up her things in haste, and not without a little sinking at heart.

Old Mrs. Welland could not read, and as she was too proud to ask her neighbors to read letters to her, she desired Emily every fortnight to send her an old newspaper, or a little tract, or anything of the sort that she had by her that would come for a penny, and as Mr. Glover was only going to remain in London a week, she calculated on hearing of Emily's safe arrival from him.

If Emily could have stayed till nine o'clock on the third day after she had written to Mrs. Smalley, she might have had an answer ; but unfortunately the cheap train by which she and Mr. Glover were going started at seven. It was quite dark when she came out of the cottage door, after giving her good old grandmother a hearty hug, and ran down the cottage garden to wait for the omnibus. John Mills was standing there ; he had carried her boxes down for her, and was now waiting to help in putting them on the omnibus when it should arrive. A third box was standing beside them, and that, John told her, contained his figure. It was going up to London, by Mr. Clements's orders, by that morning's train.

Emily, in her large comfortable shawl, her neat merino dress, and nice bonnet with its little net veil, looked the picture of health and youthful beauty as she stood out there in the early daylight ; but John, in his threadbare clothes, and with his thin face, looked hardly fit to be her companion. Notwithstanding this, he could not help saying to her : "Would there be any chance of your liking me, Emily, if I got on, and we got over these troubles ?" But Emily shook hands with him and said : "John, I hope you won't talk in that way ; I do like you, but I shall never be anything but a friend to you." As she said this the omnibus drove up, the boxes were put on the roof, Emily set off for London, and John went back to his shed.

CHAPTER IV.

IT was a wet Christmas that year, and during her long journey Emily saw little of the scenery that she passed through. The winter day closed early, and it had been dark three hours when they at length arrived at the station, and Emily found herself in London.

The noise and confusion at first bewildered her, and she was glad she had no harder task to perform than to stand by her boxes while Mr. Glover got a cab for her. In spite of the pushing and jostling of passengers, who were distracted because a box or a bundle was not yet forthcoming, and in spite of the civil " By your leave " of the porters, as they pushed past their luggage-barrows, she contrived to stand quietly till her good friend came to her, got the boxes put on the cab, handed her in, gave directions to the driver, and shook hands with her.

She was now alone, and the cab began to move through London streets ; the brilliant lights, the splendid shops, the crowding passengers, dazzled and delighted her ; but she felt very anxious as to her reception by Mrs. Smalley ; and moreover, she feared her boxes would be wet before they reached their destination. Almost every street they turned into Emily said : " I wonder whether this is it ? I wonder whether this is where Mrs. Smalley lives ? " but no ; on they went, till all the shops were gone, and rows of private houses succeeded. These were very handsome, but looked cold and inhospitable, with all their windows shut and curtains drawn against the world without ; but the longest street, even in London, has its last house, and at the last of these, in a particularly long street, the driver stopped at length, and thundered at a remarkably imposing-looking door.

"Dear me!" thought Emily, "I wish he would not make such a noise. I hope Mrs. Smalley won't be angry."

Emily looked up at the large blank house, and then at the pavement, on which rain in such quantities had been splashing all day, that it was washed quite clean from the dirt and blacks of London, and shone with broken and uncertain reflections of the street lamp.

The driver knocked again, and Emily noticed that this house differed from most that she had passed, in having no lamp in the hall : at last a dim light was visible inside, and the door was half-opened by a particularly dirty-looking servant, with a black cap on, and curl-papers beneath it.

"Dear me!" thought Emily : "I suppose the footman only answers the door to Mrs. Smalley's grand customers. What a dirty servant for such a grand house! However, she had not much time for reflection, she paid the driver, and ran up the steps, asking humbly : —

"Do you know whether Mrs. Smalley expects me?"

The woman looked confused, and as the driver was already setting Emily's boxes within the door, she said : —

"What's these for? I reckon you've mistook the house?"

Emily now found that she was a little hard of hearing, and repeated her question : —

"Does Mrs. Smalley expect me? Is she at home?"

"Mrs. Smalley?" repeated the woman ; "why, miss, she has left this two months."

"Left!" repeated Emily, shocked and frightened. "I did not know that ; please tell the cabman to wait. I must go on to her. Do you know where she has moved to?"

" No, nor nobody else," replied the woman, coolly.

" Then I can't go to her to-night," said Emily, frightened, and feeling all the desolateness of her situation. " Oh ! what shall I do ? Please let me come inside for a moment ; I shall be quite wet."

" If you want the cabman, you'd better say so at once," observed the woman, " for he's just a driving off. There, you're too late ; that gentleman has called him."

" Please let me stand inside," pleaded Emily, " till I can consider what to do ; the lady will not object to that, will she ? "

" Lady, there's no lady. The house is empty, and I am put in to take care of it. You may stand in the 'all, if you like, for a few minutes."

Emily came in and stood, the picture of perplexity and distress. The woman stood beside her, with her greasy tin candlestick in her hand, which she tapped every few moments impatiently with the door-key ; Emily looked up the desolate uncarpeted staircase, still strewed with shaving-like lengths of paper and wisps of hay, in which the furniture had been packed, and said : —

" Surely you can remember, or find out for me, where Mrs. Smalley has moved to ; it must be somewhere at this end of London, on account of her business."

" It's nothing of the sort," replied the woman, impatiently. " Mrs. Smalley is not to be found anyhow ; she has run away from her creditors."

" Run away ! " repeated Emily, aghast.

" I said run away plain enough, young woman," repeated the dirty warder of the house. " You need not stare like that. She could not pay her debts. They say she spec-'lated in railways ; however, one fine day Madame was off, and the bailiffs came in ; and there has been a sale, and that's all I know about it."

The rain spattered and splashed outside, and the dirty

candle guttered inside. Emily was wet, weary, hungry, and altogether cast down, and she said to the woman, —

"Would you be so kind as to let me sit by your fire, and give me something to eat? I could pay for it, and for a bed, if you would."

Perhaps the rough housekeeper found Emily's voice persuasive; perhaps she pitied her distress and admired her youth and beauty; for she certainly softened her voice a little, and said, less gruffly, —

"Well, I've been a-washing to-day, and the place ain't to say comfortable, but you may come and sit by the fire, if you like. O yes, you may come."

How different was everything she saw and heard from what her fancy had so frequently pictured! Here was a London underground kitchen hung with wet clothes, a huge range screwed up to its narrowest proportions, and those not half filled with a smouldering fire. All the light was afforded by the one candle, which had shown her the empty hall and the desolation up stairs. Emily sat and shivered and pondered. Tired, hungry, and dispirited, what could she do? She earnestly hoped that she should not be turned out that night, and when her entertainer agreed to let her share a very uncomfortable and by no means clean-looking bed that stood in one corner of the ample floor, she felt truly thankful, and asked for something to eat, which was set before her on consideration of her paying for it.

Emily ate and drank, then sat with her feet on the fender, and pondered again till the woman was ready for bed; but, tired as she was, she could not rest during this her first night in London. The dull noise of distant vehicles, the rattle of those that passed the house, her own self-reproaches and regrets that she had been over-persuaded to come up to London before an answer had been received from Mrs. Smalley : all these things together kept her

waking till morning should have appeared, but it dawns
very late in a~London kitchen in December; and when,
after one hour's sleep, she awoke, roused by her companion, who was dressed, she heard to her astonishment that
it was eight o'clock, and saw that the darkness was then
sufficient to make them dependent on the well-known dip
candle.

The woman casually remarked, that it was rather a foggy
morning; and Emily, looking out, had her first experience
of a London fog, which to her surprise changed from
amber to brown, and from brown to a greenish grey, more
than once before their cheerless breakfast was over.

After breakfast, Emily said she would go and endeavor
to obtain a situation with some other milliner, as Mrs.
Smalley had failed her. But as hour after hour wore on,
and she could hardly discern the opposite houses, her companion declared that it would be highly dangerous to go
out, for she would infallibly lose herself; and Emily,
though sorely against her will, felt that her present asylum,
dismal as it was, was better than having her last night's
experience over again. So she sat lamenting her haste in
coming up to London, till, the fog becoming more white,
she had light enough to see to read, and got out a book,
with which she beguiled the time till dinner was ready,
and after that, as some bread was wanted, she insisted on
accompanying her hostess to fetch it from the baker's. So
dismal a walk she had never taken; the fog hemmed them
in, and she felt as if her country lungs could hardly breathe
in it; but at least it was new and strange, and when they
turned out of their own street into one which was crowded
with people and full of shops, she was bewildered and yet
pleased with all she saw; with the grand windows lighted
up as if it was night, and even with the people who pressed
past her showing their shrewd pale faces, and then vanish-
ing in the fog. She did not walk a quarter of a mile, but

could not help being glad that her companion had not suffered her to go out by herself, and when they reached the empty house again, she was really thankful for the shelter it afforded.

Emily was to pay half of what the various articles for their meals had cost. There was a piece of beefsteak, some tea, some bread, a cabbage, and some potatoes. Emily set these items down on a slate, and put her hand in her pocket to draw out her purse. It was not there, and she looked towards her work-box, saying : —

" I must have left it behind me."

" No, you did n't," said the woman ; " for I remember particularly saying to you, ' take a shilling or two in your pocket, but don't take all your money if you have much ' ; and says you, ' No ; I may want more than that,' and you put the purse in your pocket."

Emily searched again ; it was certainly gone.

" Surely," said the woman, " you never walked·about in that fog without minding your pocket ? "

" I never thought of my pocket," said Emily, " and I don't believe in such a dark day anybody could find the pocket-hole."

" Why, what 's this ? " asked her companion. " Dear, dear, I never gave it a thought to tell you to mind your- self ; I thought you 'd sense to watch over your own earn- ings. Look here, they 've been and cut a hole in your gown, and got a hand through it, and carried the purse clean off, as I 'm a Christian woman ! "

At first Emily could hardly believe that so great a mis- fortune had happened to her. She started up, declaring that the purse might have been left in her work-bag ; it might have been dropped on the floor ; but after several fruitless searches, it became too evident that she had been robbed, and she sank down on her chair quite pale with agitation, and sat motionless, till her companion at last roused her by asking the color of the purse.

"Was it purple leather or green?" she said.

"What does that matter now?" muttered Emily.

"Matters a great deal," was the reply; "because I 'm going off to the police-court about it."

Emily roused herself, and seeing her companion already dressed in her shawl, and pinning her bonnet-strings, thanked her, gave the required description, and added: —

"But it 's no use telling the police, Mrs. Smart. I feel sure, now that I come to think about it, that the purse was stolen while we were pressing up to the pastry-cook's window to look at those cakes; and there was nothing in it but money; no note or post-office order that might be known again. O dear me! O dear!"

"Well, well, child, don't cry and take on; pickpockets are taken up sometimes with the things they stole upon them; so don't give way."

So saying, Mrs. Smart walked off, and Emily wept at her leisure. She was naturally hopeful, and even when she found that Mrs. Smalley had failed her, she consoled herself by thinking that she could get a situation with another milliner, or she could, if that proved impossible, come home again when the Christmas holidays were over, take her papers to the diocesan examination at Salisbury, and give up her dream of making a fortune as a London milliner. But now she had no money wherewith to return, and her pride was deeply wounded at the notion that she could not return to Dorsetshire without selling those handsome clothes which she had bought in order to fit herself, as she supposed, for her new sphere. No; she felt that she could not and would not do that. She must stay in London, at least till she had earned enough to go home with; but in the mean time she must live. She owed Mrs. Smart two shillings and fourpence; she must get her to take payment in the shape of some article of clothing, and she must get work at once, — to-morrow, whether the day was foggy or fine.

Mrs. Smart soon came back; she was kinder to Emily than could be expected, considering that she was quite a stranger to her. She told her that till she got work she might have her bed free of charge, provided she could pay for her food: coals, candles, and house-room, she received for her trouble, as well as a small weekly sum.

"So you are welcome to stop, young woman," she observed, with condescending kindness, "for I find it lonesome being here by myself, specially o' nights."

Emily was grateful for this kindness, but felt how much she had already come down in the world, when a dirty and ignorant woman, such as Mrs. Smart, could lay her under an obligation, and treat her with patronizing pity.

That night, weariness made her sleep in spite of sorrow, and the next morning was tolerably fine, and the buoyant spirits of youth in part returned to her, and she dressed herself neatly and went out early to seek for a situation. Mrs. Smart had counselled her to ask her way only of the policemen whom she would see from time to time, and by no means to remain out till it became dusk. She also told her that there were no less than three milliners in a street very near at hand, and having given her ample directions as to how she should find it, she shut the door after her, and poor Emily went forth alone to seek her fortunes. She could not well be robbed now, for she had nothing in her pocket, and she thought she could not well fail in finding work in a place which contained such multitudes of employers.

The winter day wore on, and though Mrs. Smart had charged Emily not to be late, the lamplighter was in the street when she answered the door and let her in. Wet, pale, and weary, she came in without a word, closed her dripping umbrella, and sat down in the dim kitchen, as she had not spirit or strength enough left to divest herself of her out-of-door dress.

"Had aught to eat, child?" asked Mrs. Smart.

Emily's shivering figure drew itself up, and she seemed to shrink from being questioned, but when asked again, she answered, "No."

"Well, the tea will be ready in a minute. Got a situation yet?"

"No," repeated Emily.

"I did not expect you would, child, in such a hurry. Dear me, some folks expect situations to come in crowds the minute they wants 'em, just as black beetles come when it gets dusk like."

Emily knew to her sorrow that the illustration of the black beetles was not drawn from the good woman's imagination, but from her familiar daily life; indeed, while she spoke a large one peeped from a crack, and came on briskly towards Emily's foot.

She started up with more alacrity than even the prospect of a home could make her, in order to get out of the way of her black fellow-lodger, and as she wearily walked to her box, and took off and deposited therein her bonnet and cloak, she listened with languid patience to Mrs. Smart's moral sentiments, which went to prove that she, Mrs. Smart, thought that young people ought not to expect too much, seeing that, as far as it appeared, they never got more than a little; however, they ought to think themselves well off when they had a good house over their heads that never was built for them, nor such as them. "A house," continued Mrs. Smart, wandering from the point, "that has five bed-rooms and two dressing-rooms, let alone parlors and pantries, and what not, and which is now empty entirely, along of them railways, which is the greatest conveniency that ever was for them that want to travel, and I wish there was more of them. Now, child, come to your tea."

Emily drew her chair to the table, and as she drank the

steaming tea, and ate the bread and butter, her fainting spirits revived a little, and the color returned to her cheeks.

"It's a little strange, too," observed Mrs. Smart, "that you could not meet with any work, child, for this is a busy time, and most of the houses very full of work."

"I could have got work if I had been willing to do it for almost nothing," said Emily. "I've been sent away for all sorts of reasons. One said she never took young girls to teach, — they were more trouble than they were worth; and one said she should expect a premium, and pay me nothing for the first six months; and another said I did not *look* as if I should suit; and the last offered such a little for a day's work, that I could not pay you for my food with it; and I saw a good many who would have nothing to say to me."

"You're too high, child, too high by half. You don't look like a prentice girl; and you speak so fine, and dress so smart, that they don't know what to make of you," replied Mrs. Smart. "Now, if I was you, I would rather work for sixpence a day than sit idle here like a fine lady."

Emily sighed bitterly, and felt with keen shame that, though this advice was most distasteful to her, Mrs. Smart had a full right to offer it, for she was giving her that tea, and allowing her to run in debt for her food.

She sat silent, however, and could not assent to the remark that it was better to work for sixpence a day than be idle like a fine lady. Fine lady, indeed, in a dirty kitchen, and about to sleep in a dingy bed; fine lady, without a penny in her pocket, or a friend within two hundred miles of her, or any prospect but hard work, or any hope but to return speedily to the very occupation she had considered so much beneath her!

The downward path in life is always easy; when once descent begins, it is not only hard to rise, but hard to pre-

vent the further decline. Poor Emily found this to her
cost; she went out several days in search of work, but
did not succeed in getting any that she thought it worth
her while to take. She had no money, and by degrees
the contents of her boxes had been disposed of, — some
to Mrs. Smart; some to the pawnbrokers in the neighborhood, — till, by the time she had been a month in London,
she had not enough of her good outfit left to bring in
money for a journey home ; and the chance work she had
done from time to time had only served to show her how
hard was the work of a London seamstresss. It had not
occurred to her, when first she took a shawl to the pawn-
shop, that it would be difficult to get it out ; and this way
of raising a little money seemed so easy, — moreover, she
did not particularly want the shawl, — so it went ; and she
got taken on as an "extra hand" at a very grand millinery
establishment, where the wages were not very bad ; and
when by the day that she had saved enough to take her
things out of pawn, she determined to leave that part of
London, and go and apply for a situation at the office of
the Home and Colonial Schools Society.

Emily did not know what she should have to undergo
as an "extra hand" ; she found it hard to sit up night
after night till two or three o'clock, finishing the endless
wedding orders, or mourning orders, or ball-dresses, which
poured in upon the fashionable milliners, and had been
positively promised for so early a day that it seemed
impossible that the promise could be kept.

Day after day, as the over-dressed and pompous head
of the house sailed into the workroom, Emily heard,
with a sinking heart, "I would n't disappoint Lady W.
on any account ; that blue silk dress must go home punctually at six o'clock. Let the cerise tarlatan be put in
hand immediately, as well as the white and amber ; Lady
Georgiana was positively promised that she should have

them both to-night, in time for Mrs. A.'s reception, that she may choose which she likes best. That mourning order ought to be in a greater state of forwardness ; the young people cannot go home till it is finished."

Being only an extra hand, Emily had to return to her home at whatever hour of the night the work was finished ; and as the heated workroom, with its unwholesome atmosphere, made her feverish and weak, the sudden change to night air, rain, snow, or fog, had a very bad effect on her constitution : she became pale and thin, and her eyelids heavy and red with overwork and bad light, and her gait stooping, from constantly bending over her task.

"There's a letter for you," said Mrs. Smart, as she opened the door to her one evening in March.

Emily took it with great pleasure ; it was the first letter from home. She saw that it was in John Mills's handwriting, and addressed to her at Mrs. Smalley's.

"He does not know of my present circumstances," she thought ; and she took the letter down and read it with avidity : — .

"DEAR MISS WELLAND, — Your grandmother has felt very unwell this past week, and last night had the doctor ; but he does not seem to think there is very much the matter with her, — at least he said he saw no reason why she should not recover. She does not think so herself, for she told my mother she was sure she was taken for death, and she wished she could see you ; so I said I would write, and I was to say that if Mrs. Smalley could spare you she would take it very kind.

"I feel that you may think it odd I cannot call you Emily, but I know there is a great difference of station between us now, and you are living in luxury while I am only a workman, so I began this without taking the liberty to write your Christian name, and now, for fear you should misunderstand, I must tell you why.

"You have such a kind heart that I know you will be glad to hear of father being better, so that now he can sit up all day and amuse himself with netting; and as for me, I sent up the figure that you know of, and Mr. Clements wrote me word that a gentleman he knew had valued it at fourteen pounds, 'which,' said he, 'is more than I expected, and it is not convenient to me to give such a sum for it, therefore I have sent it to be disposed of at that price.' Would you believe that I should be so well off, Miss Welland? A great lady saw it and bought it, and Mr. Clements has forwarded me the money, so now all our debts are paid, and what is better, I have got an order for another figure from the same cast.

"I have not heard anything from Mrs. Smalley respecting the monument; and if you should find an opportunity to mention it to her, I should be very much obliged to you.

"Perhaps I may be in London before long, for as soon as I have carved this new order I shall have money in hand to last the family for seven weeks, and therefore I think I shall have a right to leave them for that time ; and I think of walking up to London to see whether I can improve myself or get higher wages than I now earn. I shall not take the liberty to call on you unless I hear that it would be agreeable, for I know I have no chance with you, and I would not wish that you should think me troublesome, though I shall always be, as long as I breathe, your faithful lover, JOHN MILLS."

Emily read this letter over and over again. She was made very uneasy by the account of her grandmother, who would scarcely have asked to see her unless she had firmly believed herself to be dying. But to go to her was out of the question. Her work did not quite pay for her board, and her clothes were slowly diminishing. She had been nine weeks in London ; nine weeks divided between hard work and the scarcely less hard work of seeking for it. She knew that return, for the present, was impossible, and she went to her task the next. morning with a heavy heart, intending to write to John by the next day's post, — not to tell him how gladly and thankfully she would return if she had the means, but to beg him to send her further particulars, and to give her love and duty to her grandmother.

She left work, however, so late on Saturday night, that it was Sunday morning before she reached home. Another letter from John awaited her, — a long, considerate, and most kind letter ; and she thought so herself as soon as she could see to read it for her tears. Her grandmother had died quietly very soon after the first letter had been posted, and her son and daughter had been sent for from the village in the neighborhood where they lived ; they had taken possession of what the good woman had left, and had accepted John's offer to write and give Emily an account of her death. Moreover, they had sent word that Emily had better stop where she was, and not think of spending money in coming home, as there was nothing for her to do. A very fulsome message to Mrs. Smalley was also conveyed by John from the said son and daughter, and a humble request that she would permit their mother's name to appear also on the much-talked-of monument.·

It was well for Emily that the next day was Sunday ; it gave her time to shed her natural tears over her kind old grandmother, and to write to John.

She now felt that she had no tie to Dorsetshire, no object in returning, that she was thrown entirely on her own resources, must work for her bread, and strive earnestly to rectify the mistake she had made, and rise again into the position she had lost.

As a proof, however, that adversity had not been without its use, she hesitated long between pride and a desire
to be sincere; and at last sincerity so far triumphed, that
she told John she felt sure he would never hear from Mrs.
Smalley respecting the monument, for that Mrs. Smalley
was not able to pay her just debts, but she added, — partly
to save John from anxiety respecting her, partly from a desire to keep her altered circumstances from her little world
in Dorsetshire, — " I am with quite as grand a milliner as
Mrs. Smalley ever was, and one who employs more work-
people."

So much she could say with truth ; the rest of her experience she left unsaid, but she added several expressions
of friendship for John, which that kind-hearted fellow
prized highly, and which, if he could have known how Emily's mind was turning to him in her trouble, and how
much more highly she thought of him than she had done
in her prosperity, he would have prized still more.

And so John was getting on, and rising slowly out of
that poverty and distress in which she had seen him ;
John, whose conscientious scruples had prevented him
from taking one doubtful step, and who had suffered so
patiently, not only poverty, but the want of that teaching
which alone as it had seemed could enable him to
rise ; John was likely to have it at last, and could have
it lawfully.

Emily thought much of this ; she repented of that craving ambition which had made her formerly so discontented
with her lot, and she now felt that needlework was but a
poor exchange for the pleasure of teaching, and the comfort of being able to make some use of that love of order
and talent for governing children, which all who possess
invariably wish to exercise, especially when they have once
had the opportunity of doing so.

" Let me only get my things out of pawn," was her

thought, "and I will apply for a situation at one of the schools in London, or I will even venture to set up a day-school of my own." But week after week wore on, and instead of taking her goods out of pawn, more and more had got into the hands of the pawnbroker, for the simple reason that she never got enough regular work to enable her to pay for her board. At last, in despair of ever earning wages to pay for her food, she resolved to bring her food down to the level of her wages : a natural resolution, but not wise, for poor Emily was not accustomed to the London air and the late hours, and the close application that she now had to submit to, and when to these she added a meagre diet, she soon found, not that denying her appetite made her hungry, but that she could not eat even what she provided, and left at every meal some of her bread and of the two or three radishes which she had substituted for butter, meat, or cheese.

· She was getting out of debt to Mrs. Smart ; but this did not give her the pleasure she expected, and a degree of sleepiness was creeping over her which made her often sit at work in a half doze. A kind-hearted companion, who sat next to her, took pains to keep her awake, at least when any of the superiors of the house came in ; but Emily dozed again as fast as she was awakened, and one evening, happening to be dismissed early, she was conscious of a degree of drowsiness, even in the street, which it required all her little strength to resist.

O how welcome was the shade of the desolate hall, and the repose of the dingy bed, after the light and noise of the street! Emily felt that, come what would, now she must rest ; and the next day, though conscious of repeated assurances from Mrs. Smart that she would be late for the workroom, she fell away from one doze to another, and wished for nothing but to lie quiet, and drink, whenever she woke, a long draught of water.

At last, late in the afternoon, a sharp, distinct voice decidedly woke her.

" Sleep, sir ? she does nothing but sleep, and for the last ten days she has eaten, as one may say, a mere nothing. "

It was Mrs. Smart who spoke, and Emily felt that some one took hold of her hand. She opened her eyes, and met a quiet, steady gaze fixed upon her. Mrs. Smart had evidently fetched a doctor.

" I am not ill, sir," said Emily.

The doctor smiled compassionately, and continued to feel her pulse, but Emily could not attend to what he said sufficiently to answer his questions. She heard him say, "The girl has a great deal of low fever hanging about her," and then the old faint drowsiness came over her again. She felt pleased shortly after to have a cup of tea given to her, but after that, night and day began to be confused in her mind, and though she was never absolutely delirious, she could not govern her thoughts or speak connectedly.

Every day the doctor came to see her, and she felt a kind of satisfaction in seeing his calm, attentive face, and in hearing his quiet questions ; " And how do you feel to-day, Emily Welland ?   No pain ? that's well."

" She never complains of anything, sir," Mrs. Smart would remark. Mrs. Smart had become very kind and good to her now. " She is as patient as a lamb," was her frequent observation ; "and if I ask her how she does, she always says she 's better."

A long time passed in this way. At last, one afternoon, Emily opened her eyes and observed that it was Sunday. She was led to make this observation because she saw that Mrs. Smart had cleaned herself, taken off her curl-papers, and put on the green mousseline-de-laine gown that she never wore but on Sunday afternoon. After lying still a while, looking about her, she observed that her own two boxes were gone from their usual places, and this made her still more wakeful. She was aware that whatever illness she had suffered from was passing away, and she found strength to repeat in a faint tone, " Mrs. Smart! Mrs. Smart!"

Mrs. Smart was toasting bread, and when she came at Emily's call she brought a piece with her, and some tea, telling her that the doctor had said she was much better, and when she awoke might eat and drink a little.

"I know you have been very good to me," said Emily, looking at her; "you have nursed me and I was nothing to you."

Mrs. Smart was evidently not sorry to hear Emily speak sensibly ; and perhaps, after the trouble and pains she had been at, she was also glad to find that her patient was grateful.

" I have done according to orders," she replied, "and the doctor knows I have n't sold more of your clothes than I could help ; it was all done with his knowledge."

" Have I anything left ? " asked Emily, humbly.

" Yes, child, your best pink muslin gown, and your best pair of boots, and your prize-books, besides the clothes you went to work in."

At another time this news would have shocked Emily ; but now she was returning from the dreary delusive world of fever to sense, life, and reality, and thankfulness was her prevailing feeling, and she took the toast and tea with such relish as those who have never been in her circumstances cannot possibly understand.

It was a chilly day in the middle of April when Emily had left her work ; it was a hot morning early in June when she crept languidly forth again in her working clothes. The pink muslin dress and the best boots had followed her other possessions, and, in the expressive language of the poor, she had nothing now but what she stood upright in.

The kind-hearted doctor had told her to call at his house in the neighboring square, of which he had promised to lend her the key, that she might go in and sit down under the trees and enjoy the quiet and the comparatively fresh air.

Emily entered the square, and sat down under the shade of some young lime-trees. The air revived her, and the quiet and freshness of the place did her good; but she was recovering her strength slowly, and was aware that her natural anxiety about the future was keeping her back. She sat long, with her pale cheek leaning on her hand, meditating as to what course she should pursue. She possessed but one sixpence now, and was not strong enough to work; moreover, her friend Mrs. Smart would not long be able to afford her a shelter, for the house was let, and in less than a fortnight the new tenants would dispense with her services.

CHAPTER V.

THE last six months seemed to Emily like a dream. She felt deeply that she had made a great mistake ; but as she had long regretted it, and wished to repair it, she thought it rather hard that she had been unable to do so. The one false step of leaving her own line in life in which she had grown up, and which she was so well fitted for, she did not now see how to rectify; first, for want of money to reach the different places at any one of which she could have been examined for her certificate ; and secondly, for want of clothes, for London had made sad havoc with the one gown and bonnet that she had left. She was not strong enough to take a teacher's situation now, and though she thought it very likely that her old friend and mistress, Miss Cooper, would be very glad to recommend her in case she came back, and might have influence enough to induce the Vicar to overlook her withdrawal, she felt with a pang of pride that she could not bear to go back dressed almost like a beggar ; and moreover the journey would be expensive, and there was no one from whom she could borrow the money, so that must be given up.

What then should be done ? She pondered long, and at last decided to apply personally at a place in London which she knew well by reputation, a training-school, where she could go in, as she thought, on a humble footing, and work her way till she had earned what would buy her some decent clothes, and then go in for her examination, and try to obtain a situation in which she could maintain herself.

She felt that her present delicate appearance was against her, but that she thought would improve every day. What she most objected to was her very shabby dress, and her short hair (for her long dark locks had been cut off); and she was sure the other young teachers with whom she would have to associate would look so nicely, dressed with their well-made gowns, neat bonnets, and glossy hair, that she should suffer heavily from a sense of inferiority. .

"But at all hazards," thought Emily, "no more dress-making and shop-working for me. I have seen something of that, and I may just as well expect to be made queen as to be taken into partnership with one of my employers, or even to earn enough to maintain myself comfortably."

It was something to have decided what course to pursue, and this made her feel better and easier in her mind, though painful visions haunted her of haughty looks from the young girls in the training-school, and contemptuous withdrawings from her and her dingy and threadbare gown.

The next day early she set off on her errand, making herself as scrupulously neat as she could with what clothes she possessed, and creeping slowly along, that she might feel tolerably fresh for presenting herself before the committee whom she expected to see.

Mrs. Smart, who, dirty and slatternly still, had taken a great liking to the friendless girl, walked with her for a mile, and then, with many directions and encouragements, and a present of a new penny roll, which she was to eat when she felt faint, left her to pursue her way full of hope, though still weak and white-faced from illness.

"It will be the old story over again," said the good woman, "but she shall have a rare tea this day, even if I pay for it." So she stopped at a shop and bought two mackerel, and then a Yorkshire cake for toasting; and home she went to the black beetles, in whose lively company she did not miss Emily, though, to do her justice, she sincerely wished her all success.

Emily would not be home before four o'clock, she felt sure, so she ate some bread and cheese at twelve o'clock, and spread what seemed to be a sumptuous board in the afternoon, — broiled mackerel, bread and butter, and cake, and a lettuce.

Just as everything was ready, she saw Emily coming languidly down the area-steps, and let her in, but said nothing to her. Success was certainly not written on the poor pale face, and though faint with hunger, she scarcely showed any pleasure at the sight of those appetizing viands. Not a word she said, but threw off her bonnet, and sunk into a chair with a heavy sigh.

"Well, well, child," said Mrs. Smart, taking failure for granted, "this is only the first day; you can try again to-morrow."

But the only answer was : —

"O, Mrs. Smart, I wish I had never seen this wretched place ! "

"Well, I'm sure !" replied Mrs. Smart, rather tartly, "that's mighty civil to me. You wish you'd never seen me, then; and I've been the best of friends to you. There, come along, and get some tea, and don't be down-hearted. I hate to see folks down-hearted; it makes me think o' my own troubles, and I've had a many on 'em."

Emily, thus admonished, drew her chair to the table, and though Mrs. Smart seemed not to be in the best of humors, she heaped her plate with substantial food till the poor girl felt her strength revive, and her weary spirits begin to rise a little.

"So they won't have nothing to say to you, eh, child?" asked the good woman.

"No; the gentleman at the first place I went to said, 'Have you been ill, young woman?' 'Yes, sir,' I said.

'What 's been the matter — a fever?' 'Yes, sir.' 'What sort of fever? nothing infectious, I hope.' So I said, 'I believe it was low typhus.' 'Bless me,' says he, 'and only just getting better! How could you think of coming among all these candidates, and expect to teach in the school? It was exceeding wrong of you, young woman, to come here;' and I assure you they were in such a hurry to shut me out, that they would not allow me time even to inquire how long it would be before I might come again. Well, it was nearly the same thing at the next place I went to, and at the last I do believe they took me for an impostor; they looked me up and down, and then said they were sure I was not strong enough for any sort of exertion; but one of the gentlemen said he would give me a recommendation to the Consumption Hospital; and when I said I was not at all consumptive, he says, 'Well, well, in two or three months, if you are better, you may come again.'"

Emily made this long speech almost in a breath, as if she knew she must give some account of herself, and wished to get it done as soon as possible, and alluded no more to the painful subject.

She went out the next day with the same result, and sat drooping in the evening in a way that made the dirty housekeeper's heart ache. Not a word was said to her, and after a restless night she went and brought home some shop-work, and began to stitch as fast as her then trembling hand would let her.

"What, child, going to try shop-work again?" said Mrs. Smart.

"I must live," replied Emily. "I am getting into debt to you for my board already, and I 've no chance of getting a teacher's situation till I look more healthy, and my hair is longer. Seeing it only an inch long, everybody that I apply to asks if I have had a fever."

Mrs. Smart replied, in a liberal spirit, that the next time Emily went out after a situation she would give a friend of hers, who was a barber, a sixpence to lend her a wig with long ringlets. And Emily thanked her, but inwardly resolved not to accept her kindness.

So the days wore on till the new tenant came in, and Mrs. Smart hired a little room to live in, Emily going with her. And now that she dwelt among the poor, Emily found herself not so much cut off from sympathy as she had been hitherto, for a lady, who was district visitor there, called on her, and when she found how beautifully Emily could work, she got her some children's dresses to make, for which she received very much better pay than she had earned hitherto.

But Emily's recovery was very slow, and so much sedentary occupation did not suit her, so that she was often ailing, and therefore frequently received a visit from this new friend, who, when Mrs. Smart was out at work, would sit and talk kindly to her, and give her the best advice she could, considering how little she knew of Emily's circumstances.

Like other persons who had been compelled to pawn good clothing, Emily felt that the small sum she had received upon it was nothing compared with its real value to herself, and she worked very hard to get the interest paid on some of her most useful articles, and, if possible, to get them once again before the year was over.

She felt that a tolerable appearance of health and some decent clothes were absolutely needful, if she wished to be a teacher, and with unremitting industry she worked, seldom having more than enough time to fulfil what she undertook, partly owing to the kindness of the lady visitor, and partly to her obliging and civil manner and neat work.

At last Christmas came round again, and Emily had been able to get some of her possessions into her own keeping; she looked stronger, and her hair was growing as quickly as could be expected; moreover, she was beginning to talk more openly to her friend, the district visitor; and when this lady found that she was denying herself many little comforts, and every moment of leisure, for the sake of taking the remainder of her clothing out of pawn, she one day offered to lend her two sovereigns, saying that this would save her from having any further interest to pay, and that she might take everything out of pawn, and pay back this sum at her convenience.

Emily was very grateful for this kindness, and agreed to pay two shillings a week to her kind friend till she had restored all. The mere circumstance of being so trusted did her good, and revived her spirits; and when she got back her comfortable clothes into her own keeping, she could take more pleasure in her needle, for she had now a character to maintain with her visitor; she had been trusted as well as employed, and she resolved not to spend one day even in looking after a teacher's situation, till she had paid back every farthing.

In all her distress and loss of health, Emily had never so far forgotten her bringing up, and the excellent instruction she had received, as to neglect attendance at church, or a due observance of the Lord's day. She had, like John Mills, been tried as to whether she would and could present herself in her working dress; and perhaps at first it was the recollection that, even in his native town and among those who knew him, he had not shrunk from this plain duty, which nerved up Emily to do likewise. Like him, she ventured forth shamefaced and forlorn; but like him, she often came home refreshed and strengthened for her week-day task, and she found a blessing where she had only gone as a duty. In the days of her prosperity she had often been a careless worshipper, and a little thing would make her attention wander; but now she needed this weekly refreshment, this reminding of holy things, to make her hard work easier, and lead her to think amid the turmoil of the great city, that often seemed as if it would sweep her away and swallow her up, of that heavenly city which hath foundations, whose builder and maker is God.

From her childhood she had been accustomed to read a chapter in the Bible before she retired to bed; but during her sojourn with Mrs. Smart in the empty house, she had often reached home so late, that her weary eyes were not fit for any further occupation, and if she had gone through the task mechanically, it would have made no impression on her mind.

Now, however, that she shared a little room with her old friend, and did her work at home, she resumed her former habit, and often read the chapter aloud to Mrs. Smart, after a return from the day's charing, that kind creature listening with due attention, and evidently supposing that it was more Emily's duty than her own to be religious and devout; because, as she observed, —

"The girl has learning, and is to be a school-missis."

But Mrs. Smart derived much benefit from Emily besides this nightly reading; for Emily kept the room so clean and comfortable, cooked her such a cosey little supper by the time she returned from her charing or washing, and was so pleasant and good-tempered, that Mrs. Smart thought she could do no less than yield to her persuasion that she would come with her to church; so she put on her best things one fine Sunday morning, and set off in good time to the free seats, remarking that it was a highly *respectable* thing to go to church, but not apparently aware that it was a necessary thing, which could not be neglected with impunity by any who had opportunity to attend.

CHAPTER VI.

WE must now leave Emily Welland for a time, to follow the fortunes of her old friend John Mills, whose prospects began to brighten at the same time that hers became clouded.

John came up to London about the time that he mentioned in his letter to Emily, and several times in the evening he came and walked before the house where Mrs. Smalley had lived. He observed that it was not tenanted. As Emily had told him that she worked for a milliner who was quite as rich as her aunt had ever been, the poor fellow had foolish visions of her present manner of life that were very far indeed from the truth. He supposed that all success had attended her, for she had not told him that it was otherwise. He fancied her prettily dressed, and looking handsomer than ever, engaged in the light and pleasant occupation of trying on shawls and bonnets for beautiful ladies, and sometimes getting a drive in the milliner's carriage.

"I only hope her head will not be turned," thought honest John, "for what with the riches one sees on all hands, and what with the succeeding so well as everybody seems to do, it is very difficult not to grow covetous, and forget the world to come in the prosperity and happiness of this."

By that speech it will easily be seen that John was a successful man, for as the unfortunate often learn to look at the side which harmonizes most with their own circumstances, and observe poverty, loss, and descent, so the successful see most the riches and prosperity around them, and if they are rising in life they can think of many who ' are doing the same.

John, as we have said, walked several times past the house formerly occupied by Mrs. Smalley; because it was the only place in London where he knew that she had been. She had not told him the name of the milliner for whom she worked, but had allowed him to address to her · to the care of Mrs. Smart. He therefore had no clew to her abode, and when the house was let he ceased to pass it, and utterly lost sight of her, for she did not correspond with any one in Dorsetshire, and he sometimes thought with pain that this might be because she now felt ashamed of her old friends.

John stayed in London for a year, for the money he earned by his carvings was enough to maintain his family, though he bestowed so little time on them as to leave him abundant leisure for improvement. He came back, as his mother phrased it, "quite the gentleman"; but by this the good woman did not mean that he held himself high, for she distinctly declared to a neighbor that such was not the case; but that his manners were improved by intercourse with his superiors, and his language cleared from provincial expressions, for John had not forgotten his old feeling, that a man "who wanted to marry a schoolmistress" had need to take pains with his learning; and though he had quite lost sight of Emily, and could scarcely hope to see her again, much less obtain her for a wife, she was still a spur to him, and having long wished to feel, he could now begin to feel, that he was not unworthy of her.

Mr. Clements had been very kind to John; had given him introductions to several artists, and had procured for him first-rate instruction. The pupil proved more apt than the master could have hoped, and was soon so much the fashion in the circle of his patron, as to become independent of any help, and to have more orders than he could execute.

But John had excellent sense : he had come to London to improve himself, and improvement he would have even at the expense of present profit : he therefore executed no more carving work than sufficed to earn for his mother the customary weekly sum, and to provide for himself a bare maintenance.

The time passed quickly with him, and might have passed happily, but that he could not forget Emily, nor cease to long for her society; but he supposed she was well off, and that this ought to content him, and he came to his family cheerful and full of hope: he had obtained what he wanted, and more ; he had satisfied his craving for instruction ; he had seen some of the finest wood-carvings in existence ; he had decided that carving in wood and not in stone was to be his art, and he had a reasonable expectation that he should be able to earn an abundant and even handsome maintenance.

And now there was no need to work in a chill shed and eat coarse food ; John hired a pretty house in a good garden, and removed his parents to it. It was such a short distance from the old cottage that he could see distinctly from his pleasant workroom the gable end and the windows of Emily's former home, the little casement where he had often seen her sitting at work, and the tall white lilies which had been his models years before.

It was the time of the midsummer holidays when he returned and placed his mother in her new abode, which the good woman declared to be " quite a paradise, — in fact, it had a parlor within and a little orchard without, and if that did not constitute her a proud and happy woman she wondered what would. So she bustled about with a little servant whom her dutiful son had hired for her; and considering the place to be far too good to be lived in,

she was for sitting in the parlor only on Sunday after-
noons, lest some harm should happen to the little square of
Scotch carpet, and the six cane chairs which stood by the
walls.

John, however, made a decree that his father should sit
in the parlor every night during the warm weather, in his
own particular easy-chair, and play a game at chess with
him, for that was almost the only amusement the poor crip-
ple could enjoy. " After which," said John, " you·will sit
there, mother, and work, for it looks comfortable, and is
far cooler than the kitchen."

To this the mother consented with secret pleasure, but
stipulated that the family should return to the kitchen to
eat their supper, and that the children should sit there to
learn their tasks. " If they want to look at their father
and me sitting like gentlefolks," said the good woman,
" they may come outside and see us through the window."

Of this permission the Misses Mills frequently availed
themselves while there was any novelty in the sight ; but
people soon grow accustomed to comfort, and Mrs. Mills
learned before the cold weather set in not only to see a fire
in the grate, but even to drink tea in the parlor and see her
children sit there.

But nobody enjoyed the parlor so little as John did, —
John, who had provided the small square of carpet which
was reckoned such a luxury, and the six cane chairs which
looked so glossy and yellow. John was sometimes in low
spirits now ; for though he strove to be thankful and glad
of the great change and happy ease of his present life, a
conversation that he had had with Miss Cooper soon after
his return weighed on his mind, and cost him many a restless hour.

Miss Cooper had called to see him, and had asked what
he knew about Emily.

" Nothing," said John.

" I was afraid so," answered Miss Cooper, sighing;
"poor girl ! "

"Why poor ? " asked John. " I never doubted that she
was quite as well off as I am ; she can hardly be better
off."

" No, no, Mr. Mills," replied the schoolmistress ; " I
know Emily well, and I am quite sure that, if she was in
good circumstances, she would have written. Why should
she not write to me that am her old friend ? You may be
sure she would have done so and given us an address — "

" Surely you don't think she is dead ? " exclaimed John,
turning cold and sick at heart.

" O, no ; I have no ground for such a thought," said
the schoolmistress : " but I say, unless there was some
reason for it, she would write."

" She said in her letter that she worked for a rich milliner," observed John.

" And what is that ? No more than working for a poor
one, as far as earnings are concerned, and I know that
those must be small. Unknown girls from the country do
not get taken into partnership or made confidential assistants, as Emily expected her aunt to do for her. No, John,
depend on it she has made the best of matters to you, but
I feel sure that if she was really comfortable, she would
have written to me and told me so, and asked me to come
and see her, for she knows that I have a sister there, and
that I have been talking of going up to stay with her, for
a long time."

But John, though this conversation made him uneasy,
struggled against the feeling, for it seemed to him unrea-
sonable ; he argued with himself that Emily was very
clever, and was therefore sure to get on ; she had excellent principles and would not do wrong ; the only real
danger for him, he considered, was, lest she should marry
some other man before he had a chance of showing her

what a comfortable home and what a well-informed husband he could now give her, if she would but change her
mind and like him well enough to be his wife.

"John, I expect you 'll soon be thinking of settling,"
said his mother, one day when he came home with a new
American clock for the best kitchen, "but don't marry a
dawdle, lad ; take a good sprack lass, whoever she be."

"I shall never marry any but a Dorsetshire girl, mother," said John, who well knew that his mother was thinking
of the gaily dressed daughters of one of the drapers in the
town, — girls who would never have thought of him in his
former circumstances, but who now were particularly civil
to him, and to his mother, and to his young sisters.

"Well, lad," said she, "though I be not Dorsetshire myself, I have no objections to thy having a liking to it and to
a good Dorset lass, only providing it be not Emily Welland thou sets thy heart upon."

"And why not Emily Welland ?" exclaimed John.

"Why not? because she will never like thee. John, it
vexes me to see that face in the carving shed ; I know
very well whose face it is."

"I carved that figure for my own pleasure," replied
John, "and it has been a comfort to me. Why would you
have me give up my hope and my ambition, mother ? "

"Ambition ! why, lad, sure Emily Welland cannot hold
her head higher than thine now. Ambition indeed ! "

"It has always been my ambition to be worthy of her,"
said John, calmly, "and if I cannot forget her, what is the
use of talking about my settling, mother ? Are you so very
anxious that I should settle ? "

"No, lad ; we 've struggled through a good deal together ; I 've been used to be the first, and I don't want to see
another woman set over my head, — that 's the truth."

"I knew that before you told me," said John, smiling.
"Look here, mother ; we shall know what time of day it is

now to a minute, and I 've bought father a new waistcoat,
and you a tea-caddy."

"He does not look as if things went well with him," ·
thought the mother, as her son retired to his workshop.
"I 've seen him look cheerfuller when he had but a crust."

John went to his workshop and there worked hard, having bravely resolved to look on the bright side of his circumstances. He had everything in this life that he cared
for, and more than he could reasonably have hoped ; but
one thing was denied him, — the knowledge of Emily's wel-
fare. This he was not to have ; and, like a wise man, instead of indulging melancholy, and relaxing his efforts to
improve himself in consequence of this anxiety, he resolved rather to redouble his exertions, not to allow himself one idle moment, and to take for his special motto the
text, "Whatsoever thy hand findeth to do, do it with thy
might."

With his might he carved, with his might he read and
attended lectures, during the week ; with his might on
Sunday he taught in the Sunday school, attended divine
service, listened to the sermon, and strove to make a good
use of the hours spent at home. So passed a year fruitful
in exertions, full of improvement and success, and on the
whole a very happy year, though still the memory of that
face to which his mother had alluded was dear to John,
and he did not wish to forget it.

He had carved a figure, as he said, for his own pleasure ;
and in his workshop he had made a small recess, with a
little door to shut it in. Sometimes he would open the
door and look at his work ; it was the best and finest he
had ever done, and represented a young girl stepping over
fallen leaves ; loose and light as feathers they looked, owing to the carver's skill ; and a shawl was drawn over the
head, which fell in simple folds down the youthful figure ;
the face was Emily Welland's ; but it was more as she

looked when seated at her work in the London garret than as John had known her in the earlier days of her prosper-ity, for it had a gentle and thoughtful expression that it then very seldom, though now it habitually wore.

It was drawing towards autumn; London was emptied of nearly all who were rich enough to go out and enjoy the air and freshness of the country; the parks were dusty and hot, the grass scorched, the streets close, and the passers through them frequently looked tired and languid. Even strong workmen wielded their tools less actively than usual, and street-beggars plied their trade with less alacrity and ready impertinence. The weather was too much for them. Work was very slack with the needlewomen, — the ladies were out of town; the dress-makers, no less gaily attired, had followed in their wake, and there was nothing stirring. In a quiet little square, however, the committee of a society for promoting emigration was sitting; that is to say, three members were sitting, the remaining nine be-ing out of town.

To the committee-room of this society a well-dressed young man was shown just as a young woman left it by another door.

"Mr. Mills, I believe?" said the chairman, and then, looking at the new-comer, "You come for information, I presume, not for help from the society?"

"O, no," said John Mills, for he it was; "but I am taking my family out to Sydney, and some men whom I now employ wish to go with me; it is on their account that I want to make some inquiries, sir, concerning this society."

"You could give them regular employment there?" asked the chairman.

"Yes; I have taken a contract to supply all the carving required for one of the new public buildings there. I want workmen, but they cannot go without their families."

17 *

Upon this followed an account from the chairman of the amount of assistance given by the committee to deserving families, and the care taken of their members, — especially of them during the somewhat wearisome voyage. John listened with interest, but he had not much time to spare, and was about to say that he thanked the chairman, and would retire, as he had received the requisite information, when one of the committee said in a careless tone to the other, " By the by, that young woman might do for a teacher, though too young to superintend the women. Did you tell her to apply again ? "

Some doubtful answer was made which did not reach John's uninterested ears, and then a book was referred to for a name.

" Let me see," said the chairman, turning over the leaves of a book, "applications accepted, Clara Hope, Ellen Smith ; applications declined, Emily Welland —"

John had already risen to make his parting bow, the bell was rung, and the door was opened, a person had already appeared to show him out, when the name of the rejected applicant struck upon his ear, and he stopped with a sudden start. Emily Welland.! It was not a common name, and John immediately asked to have it repeated, and to be allowed to copy the address. These were soon given to him, and as he stood soon after leaning against the rails of a dusty square, and looking upon the scorched grass and dingy trees within, his heart beat high with hope and wonder, for this Emily Welland was the young woman whom he had seen leaving the room as he had entered ; her face had been turned from him, but, excepting that Emily was the same height as she had appeared in the cursory glance he had cast towards her, there was nothing in this girl's appearance that even reminded him of her.

Neat, trim, fresh, and well dressed, with a light elastic step, an erect figure, the real Emily rose before his imagination. This young woman was certainly neat, but to his country eyes there was a dingy look about the very plain bonnet, and an appearance of poverty in the common black print gown and shabby shawl, which few young maid-servants would have presented even in their every-day costume. Yet the name was Emily Welland. It was worth inquiring into, he thought, so he strolled out of the square and called a cab, reading the address to the driver from the paper in his hand, for John had plenty of money in his pocket, no need, and indeed not time to spare, for walking now ; the distance was four miles, and he had some purchases to make on his way.

So he·stopped at several shops, asking for things that no one buys but emigrants, — sun-bonnets for his mother and sisters, pegged chessmen to be used at sea, and other things which took some time to choose, but which did not divert his mind from the possibility that he might after all be on his way to see the long-lost Emily.

At last the cab threaded several narrow and dingy streets, with rags stuffed into broken panes, dirty Irish children lying on the pavement in the shade, and dirty mothers squatted beside them with backs to the wall.

John now laughed outright in the cab, and called himself a foolish fellow for coming on such a wild-goose chase, as if the delicate Emily lived in such a hole, he thought.·

"She never went down a place like this in her life, I 'll engage," he said to himself ; " however, on I 'll go, and see for myself that it is some other person of her name. There is nothing like seeing, to drive foolish thoughts away."

Presently the cab stopped. John found himself an object of interest. A cab did not often visit the alley ; and two pale-faced children were looking in at the open windows and making their remarks to each other respecting his dress and appearance.

" That' s the court you want, sir," said the cabman, pointing down a still narrower alley.

John told him to wait, and not without some trepidation went down it, and looked for the number upon his address. There stood the house; it was three stories high, and the room he was to find Emily Welland in was the three-pair back.

He mounted the stairs, and knocked at the door in question, then tried it, and found it locked; but a young woman with work in her hand looked out from the front room, and said her neighbor was out.

· "What is your neighbor's name?" asked John.

"Welland," was the reply. "There was an old lady named Smart that used to live with her, but she's just dead."

"I wanted to see Emily Welland," said John.

The woman took a key, opened the locked door, and John walked in eagerly, and began to look about him with an attention which appeared to surprise her. Not a trace could he find; not a book, nor a box, nor even an article of any kind, which he remembered as having belonged to the pupil-teacher, was to be seen. The little room was clean, but bare in the extreme: a bed, two or three chairs, a table with work upon it, and a box, were all it contained, excepting the smallest of corner-cupboards, the door of which stood open. John walked up to it, and looked in at the few cups and plates, the morsel of butter, the small piece of bread, and the tiny tea-caddy.

This scrutiny seemed to alarm the woman. Perhaps she thought he was a policeman in plain clothes, for she colored, and remarked nervously, that all the people in the house were very respectable, and that Emily Welland had never been in trouble. ·

"What is Emily Welland's occupation?" asked John.

"She takes in needlework," said the neighbor. "What did you please to want with her, sir?"

John felt that this was a natural question, but he hardly

knew how to answer it, especially as a decent-looking woman, evidently fresh from the wash-tub, stood wiping her arms just outside the open door, and two girls were peeping at him from the staircase.

" I merely wished to speak to her."

" Gentleman says he merely wished to speak to Emily," shouted the neighbor in the ear of the washerwoman, who was deaf.

The washerwoman, in that peculiarly internal voice often used by the deaf, replied that if the gentleman had any work for her, he had better leave a message ; and this reply was repeated to him by the other neighbor, who told him at the same time that Mrs. Brian was a very respectable woman, and washed for Mrs. Green in the Square.

" I have no doubt she is very respectable," replied John, repeating their favorite word, and as he spoke he was conscious of a gentle step coming softly up stairs.

He heard it even while the neighbor shouted this complimentary sentence into the deaf washerwoman's ear, and he felt that it was close to the door.

" There 's a gentleman wants to speak to you," said one of the girls.

John's eyes were on the ground ; he felt so ashamed of having tracked out one who might have had great reason for wishing to remain unknown, that for an instant, though he saw the skirts of the shabby black gown, he could not raise them to see the person who stood before him.

" John," said Emily, in a quiet voice.

" Yes, Emily," replied John, with his old humility, " I beg your pardon if I intrude."

" No, you don't intrude, John," said Emily ; but after glancing at him, she looked round the bare room and at the poverty-stricken neighbors, and reddened as she had hardly done since she left Dorsetshire.

She then took the door-handle in her hand, and the

neighbor somewhat reluctantly withdrawing, she closed the door, and she and John looked each other in the face for the first time.

Emily saw a well-dressed young man, strong, healthful, and with an intelligent expression; prosperity appeared in his independent bearing, his manners were improved, his appearance even justified the epithet that those women had bestowed on him of "the gentleman."

And John saw a quiet, gentle-looking creature, with a pale cheek and a thin hand, privation written on every line of the subdued and somewhat sickly face, which was still pretty, though in all but mere features greatly changed.

"I have had a great many troubles since I saw you last," said Emily, quietly.

John shook back his curly hair, and felt as if the words he wanted to say were choking him, but at length he muttered, that for his part he had had many blessings, and no trouble at all worth mentioning, excepting the not having been able to find out anything about her.

"I had got nearly clear of my difficulties," said Emily, "and was hoping to get a teacher's situation, when my good friend that I lived with fell ill, and wanted so much nursing and doctoring, that I had to part with almost all I had on her account, and give up my thought of teaching."

Emily began this speech very bravely, but when she got so far, she shed a few tears, and stopped to wipe them away before she went on.

"There is nothing now to prevent my taking up teaching again. I have been to look after a situation to-day, and I hope I shall get one in time."

John had not a word to say; it was evident that Emily did not intend to allow him to condole with her; but he was determined not to go, so he boldly sat down, and Emily set her bread and butter on the table, and remarking that a neighbor of hers would lend her some boiling water, took away her teapot, and left him for a minute or two alone.

When she came back, she cut up the bread; they drank some tea; and Emily was drawn on gradually to tell of her past troubles, and the three years she had lost out of her life, and John to tell of his intended voyage, the growth of his sisters, and his father's notion that the voyage would be the making of him, and be the means, most likely, of restoring his crippled hand. At last, when tea was over, Emily remarked that she had some work to do, and irresistible curiosity bringing in the deaf neighbor, John felt compelled to go, but he had told her that he should come again and see her, and to bring her a book that had been her grandmother's, which he had bought of her uncle, because he had seen her read in it when he was a child.

And now Emily was left alone, and as she sat at work silent tears stole down her face. The contrast between herself and John was painful to her in the extreme; but she was not the same Emily in mind and thought who had been so ambitious and self-seeking as she sat in her grandmother's pleasant cottage. Sorrow and privation had, with the blessing of God, made her see not only her mistake, her too great desire for ease and for a higher station, but had opened her eyes to the state of mind under which she had cherished ambitious hopes and present discontent.

The race is not always to the swift, nor the battle to the strong; this she felt had been proved in her case. She had received swiftness for the race of life, but she had been vain-glorious, had stumbled, and now the person in whose way had been placed so many impediments had outstripped her, and shown her that all her advantages, all her favorable circumstances, all her intelligence, could not weigh against the blessing of Providence upon the simple performance of humble every-day duties.

Nearly three years of her young life, as she thought, had been lost utterly, — lost as far as advancement and usefulness went; for with the help of her kind friend, the district-visitor, she had scarcely got back her clothes from the pawn-shop, when Mrs. Smart fell ill, and she felt that she could do no less than return the kindness this good woman had shown to herself. It was not a case for a hospital, nor could she leave her for the day to teach, and after a few bitter struggles with herself, principle got the upper hand, and she resolved, whatever might be the disadvantage to herself, to remain with her first friend in the dreary waste of London, and return her the good will and kindness she had shown to her in her trouble. It was no easy task that she had taken on herself. The illness was soon declared incurable, and, one by one, almost everything the poor woman possessed went to the old resort; there was no other means of procuring her food or medicine. Emily's possessions, so lately redeemed, followed once more, for her needlework done at home was not sufficient to maintain them, even with the help of parish relief and charity.

By slow degrees the lamp of life burnt low, and now Emily derived a blessing in her turn from the poor woman whom she had by gentle urgency and kindness persuaded to attend to those things which belonged to her peace. Now she saw a patience under suffering which made her own task in waiting and working easy to her; now she received such gratitude and affection as made her mind turn gratefully to that Redeemer who had done so much more for her than she could hope to do for her fellow-mortal. At last the sufferer died, blessing and thanking her; and Emily, when she returned from the funeral to her empty room, thanked God that she had been enabled to be of use, and turned her thoughts again to her first calling. She was now free to teach, if she could meet with a situation ; and being told of the society where John had heard her name, she applied for a free voyage to Australia, on condition of teaching the young female emigrants, and keeping order amongst them on board ship. She was thought too young, but hope was given her of a passage, not as a teacher, but as taught ; she might go as one of the young people, if she liked ; but she must be under the matron, and conform to the regulations in all respects.

Emily blushed deeply on hearing this, and asked for time to consider ; but, as she walked home, her quiet and now truly humble mind revolved the matter. There was a situation as teacher to a ragged-school that she believed she could have at once, if she applied for it ; but if it should fail her, she thought she would go to Australia under the discipline of the matron spoken of. And thus she began life under fairer auspices, and with every reasonable hope of success.

She looked about her little bare room and thought to herself, with keen annoyance, that she could have wished her old friend had not seen her in her poverty and degradation ; this one painful circumstance had hitherto been spared her, for none of her former acquaintances had found her out, but to-day the one whose good opinion she most cared for, and, as she thought, looked on her as being now far more below him than he had ever been, in her opinion, beneath her.

Perhaps, if she could have heard John's own account of the matter, she would have been consoled, for when his mother remarked to him the next day that he seemed to be in very good spirits, he gave her as a reason that he had met with Emily Welland's address, and had been to see her. His mother, who was packing a box, looked very

z

grave on hearing this, and said, "Lad, don't deceive thyself with any false hopes."

John made no reply, and his mother added, "She was
always proud. And how did she receive thee, my lad?
How did she look?"

"She looked pretty," said John. "I don't know that
she is quite as blooming as she was, but for all that she is
very much improved, — wonderfully improved."

"Ah," cried the mother, shaking her head, "improved,
— that's to be expected ; London ways improve thee, and
they would her. But she's out of thy reach, lad, with her
silks and her flowers. Thou must not be so ambitious.
Improved, is she? Well, is she in partnership with the
grand lady she worked with?"

"No, mother, I am sure she is not," answered John ;
"and when I said she was improved, I did not mean in
such things as her dress or her manners. I meant that
she looked so gentle, — so, — just what a woman should
look. I am sure, if you could see her now, you would not
say that she was proud."

The mother shook her head and went on with her packing, which absorbed her attention, and she soon began to
talk of the "Black Ball" line of packets in which they
were all to sail, of the comfortable new outfits, and of her
husband's joy in the prospect of the sea voyage.

John would have liked to tell her of Emily Welland's
circumstances ; but seeing her so much interested in
other matters, he stood by her silently reflecting on those
words of Holy Writ : " He putteth down one and setteth
up another."

" I hope, mother, we shall not forget in our prosperity
the good God who helped us in our distress," he said at
last.

" No, lad," replied the mother, and presently said, " I'm
not proud, I'm only thankful."

"Mother, have you forgotten Emily?" asked John.

"No, lad," she answered. "Art going to see her again?"

"Yes," said John; "and I shall ask her to marry me. Wish me success, mother."

Upon this the good woman looked up, and rose from her box.

"Wish thee success, lad! — ay, to be sure; but I don't expect she will marry thee. I thought as thou had sold the figure, — thou had forgotten her."

"No, mother; but when I came to reflect that I had been offered thirty pounds for that figure, and that there was no fear of my forgetting the form of Emily, I felt that it was a sin to keep it by me, for that thirty pounds would enable three families to come out to us, for the society I told you of only asks ten pounds, and will provide all the rest. What had I done, mother, to help others in token that I was grateful to God who has helped me? — Why, nothing, and I had no money to spare, when all we required was bought, — indeed, I had nothing but that; so I just touched the face a little to take away the likeness, and parted with it."

John's mother on hearing this wished him success again, and off he went, leaving her to the occupation that she thought so delightful, — that of folding, sorting, and packing an abundance of good neat clothing for herself, her husband, and her children. Sometimes during the afternoon she thought of John, but oftener of the outfits, though she did heartily wish him success, for Emily Welland was the wife whom she had always wished he might have.

At last, when it had become quite dusk, and she had had her supper, and retired again to the little bedroom of the lodging, and was wondering whether she could pack any longer without a candle, she heard her son's step as he came slowly up the stairs, and when he entered, without saying a word, she felt sure that he had been disappointed, and said to him with motherly affection, —

" Well, lad, there's more than one good lass in the world, thank God."

" Yes, thank God for that, mother," replied John ; " but I 'll thank Him first for giving me the one I asked for."

" What ! " exclaimed the mother, really surprised and pleased, " did she take thee, after all, and not say, as I thought she would, that thou was too ambitious, lad ? "

" No, mother," said John ; " but we have been talking about being ambitious, and Emily says she is sure there must be two kinds, and that hers was the wrong one, so she sent her love to you, mother, and I was to tell you that she knew you had often thought her ambitious, and so she has been : she has been always wishing, she says, to rise and do a higher kind of work, instead of doing her own work in the highest and best way."

" Ah," said the mother, " that last is thy kind, lad."

" I wish it to be," said John ; " so, mother, I must try to take that ambition with me, as Emily will to leave her ambition behind."

THE END.